ENCLAVE

ENCLAVE

KIT REED

ENCLAVE

A Tom Doherty Associates Book

New York

ENCLAVE

Copyright © 2009 by Kit Reed

A Tor Book
Published by Tom Doherty Associates, LLC
175 Fifth Avenue
New York, NY 10010

www.tor-forge.com

Tor® is a registered trademark of Tom Doherty Associates, LLC.

The Library of Congress has catalogued the hardcover edition as follows:

Reed, Kit.
    Enclave / Kit Reed.—1st ed.
        p. cm.
    "A Tom Doherty Associates book."
    ISBN 978-0-7653-2161-9
    1. Private schools—Fiction. I. Title.
PS3568.E367E53   2009
813'.54—dc22

                                                    2008046433

ISBN 978-0-7653-2162-6 (trade paperback)

First Edition: February 2009
First Trade Paperback Edition: August 2010

Printed in the United States of America

0   9   8   7   6   5   4   3   2   1

For the other geeks in the family
—Mack Reed and Ko Maruyama
with love

ONE

SARGENT

Departure Day. It's almost time. Gangplank up, repel all boarders. Destination: the last safe place.

See them come streaming down the hill, running ahead of end times. At the dock, my boat bobs up and down in rough waters as adults on rafts and in launches try to make it through the steel nets protecting the harbor— anything to get their children aboard. The world behind them is going to hell and there's only one boat leaving for Mount Clothos. Mine.

I do what I have to. Correction: I do what I want. I was stalled on the road to nowhere when the whirlwind struck and something spoke to me. It blew in out of nowhere and knocked me flat. Truth sat on my chest and made me listen. When I got up, I knew.

The world is diseased, and the carrier? Society.

How do you fight a deadly plague?

You try.

Isolate the patients. Protect the young. Your kids are infected;

you know it and you came to me. Think of the Academy as protective quarantine. Face it, you'd pay anything to get them off the scene. You want them in a place where nothing can touch them, no coke dealers and no paparazzi, no suicide bombers, police raids, no freak attacks of nature, no wars.

Correction: you want them stashed someplace where they can't hurt you and they won't embarrass you. On Mount Clothos, behind dense stone walls.

Why not? You can afford it. Here at the top of the world they are protected, far from bad influences, opportunists, skeezy friends. When the seas turn red and the sky goes black they will be protected.

Like the installation, your children have been secured.

You bitched about the cost when you delivered them but I know what you were thinking when you handed them off. *Cheap at the price,* and if you don't understand it, good riddance and fuck you.

They, not you, are the issue here. Your failures are my children now. I have my marching orders.

They come from a higher power. When the voice in the whirlwind spoke I was **in country,** which our troops have been in a few too many of lately— pointless wars in barren terrain. Where I was, the fighting never ends. Yeah, they told us going in that the war would last about ten minutes. Sure it would. They have to tell you *something*.

Things happened that you don't need to know about. I did things. People died, but that's not the worst of what we did.

Yes I'm ashamed. It was not pretty. Unlike the others, I survived. As I walked out of the firestorm it came to me— OK, like a shout from something huge, and tremendously pissed off. Marching orders for the rest of my life.

You will make up for what you did here.

WHAM.

When I got up I was spitting tears and shrapnel and everything was different. I heard it loud and clear:

You will create a place where no evil comes.

Welcome to the Academy. I love this life, I hate it and sometimes I'm afraid of it but I do it. Don't ask. There's no way I can explain. I do it because I do it because I do it, so whatever you paid to make this happen, whatever your misgivings, know this:

I keep the children safe.

Nothing that drops from the skies or shoots out of the earth can touch us on Mount Clothos. We are impregnable. The air space has been secured; if I tell you how, I'll have to kill you. I have military training, your guarantee that I know exactly what to do and how to do it. Whatever goes on outside, whatever comes out of the skies, they are protected.

I will preserve them and in the process I will improve them, so you can rest your heart. Think of us as your last line of defense. The line in the sand between your out-of-control children and the horrors and corruption outside.

We know society is hell, but kids don't see it. How could they, they're only kids! Look at them— beautiful and brainless, unwitting victims of things as they are. For your progeny, rolling into the Academy like loose cannons, the sealed environment is the perfect solution. No way on. No way off. Only one way up the mountain, egress secured. You can relax; your problems are my problem now.

Safe inside my citadel. Worth every million you pay.

God knows you've already spent billions, paying their way out of the drug busts, buying back blurred screen shots of crystal meth infusions and split beavers, greasing palms to diffuse the fallout from all those DWIs and public meltdowns, the in-and-out-of-rehab videos. Then there are those things you can't buy your way out of: tabloid speculation about exactly how far along your treasure is on the road to paparazzi-rehab-reckless-endangerment hell.

To say nothing of blogs in which they revile you and the evil spawn of hidden Webcams streaming video of your heirs' excesses live, 24/7. Other aberrations that we won't mention here, compounded by the pressure of multimedia exposure, worldwide.

It isn't just terrorism or war or global warming that scares you. Your kids are out of control and face it, younger and younger kids are melting down. Whether or not the world ends tomorrow, admit it. You want your little psychic train wrecks taken care of. Well, lay down your burden. Think of your problems as contained.

Nobody gets into the compound without my OK. Nothing does. Our walls are impenetrable. The monks built their cloister on a crag so high that nothing could get in and nobody would bother them in those dark, Dark Ages. The stone walls and lead window-frames deflect even the strongest signal— all built in the fifth century. It's as if their God put a finger on the future and found it rotten to the core.

Perfect. Cell phones are useless here. Stand at the top of the bell tower and you still can't get a signal.

Better: the Academy computers are networked but not connected, thus protecting the integrity of my server. Clever, right? Think of it as a security measure; we wouldn't allow typhoid carriers in here. Why let the sick world inside? There are viruses out there fierce enough to bring down a rhinoceros. Leave it to some fool kid to click on the wrong thing and infect us all.

This also protects them from social contagion. They can forget their iChat and IM and online computer shooter games that waste time and eat the mind. Their MySpace and Facebook pages are gathering dust. They won't be browsing porn sites or hooking up in online sex rooms, either. There will be no seductive messages kited in from outside to infect their hearts, no filthy porn slideshow/videos/Internet propositions for you, kid, and no shopping online— like, what genius can deliver a package to the top of a mountain nobody can find? No sleazy downloads, we'll ream that junk right out of your heads.

Zero access eases the transition and, frankly, it prevents collusion. If they want to communicate they can damn well talk.

Think of your late-adolescent problems as cadets in the corps of life, scrubbed and neatly uniformed, pristine. Clean slates for the Academy to write on.

In addition to meeting life unplugged they live without TV, but we do show weekend movies in the common room; by the time we run through the thousand DVDs in my collection, I'll be done here. The news our charges get from the outside world is the news I give them. We show footage nightly in the Refectory to keep them on their toes. They need to see how bad it is out there, so they'll thank whatever gods they have that they are safe, so trust me.

Inside these walls even the craziest of your kids will shape up, cut off from the infected world. My hand-picked staff is here to see to that, special thanks to Steve Joannides, my tech guy, who made all this possible, and my registered physician's assistant, Cassie Rivard, who took a leap of faith to join us because more than anybody here, she believes in the enterprise. OK, she believes in me, and I . . .

She's everything. I just haven't told her yet.

With the world outside going to fuck and conflagration, I have this to do. I protect the kids. *I will make them who they ought to be.*

Never mind who I was before. Now I am this.

Someone named me after the famous painter, but the kids call me Sarge. That works. In fact, it is appropriate. I was a Marine. I came up through the ranks and the Corps was good to me. I enlisted, like any other boot. Rose to drill sergeant. NCO. I served in a couple of our shitty wars— who didn't. Led a platoon **in country** on my first tour, got selected for OCS.

When I shipped out on my second tour I was a line officer, a lieutenant, that's LT Sargent Whitemore, USMC. We landed on the Fertile Crescent like the first Ping-Pong ball in a grade-school nuclear reactor simulation; wars popped up everywhere, flying every whichway, out of control. I came home from that one a Major. I hate war but I loved the Corps.

It saved me. It taught me the protective power of control.

I started out wild, like the kids you're jonesing to get rid of. The military schools you in the uses of discipline. That's what keeps Marines going through fire and destruction, *Semper Fi.* Do things by the numbers and you can walk through shitstorms without blinking, fight hand-to-hand with tigers and come out smelling like a rose.

When it comes to discipline, I am a master.

It's what brought you begging.

That and security. In matters of personal safety, location is everything. Mount Clothos has defeated climbers for so many centuries that after a while, even pilgrims gave up and society forgot.

Nobody comes, and . . .

In case you were worried about runaways, nobody goes.

This old ark warded off outsiders for two thousand years before I found it, and no wonder. It sits in bedrock on a peak so high that nothing grows. Unreachable, except by us. There are no beaches at the bottom of this mountain to draw tourists, no cutesy villages, just a mess of crags like a miniskirt on a giant dick.

There is only the peak.

You won't find us on any map. For reasons my IT guy Steve Joannides and I are not at liberty to explain, the coordinates dropped out of every known database. They will stay lost, thanks to Steve. It won't matter who comes looking or what applications they use to run the search. They'll never find us. And if push comes to shove and someone does show up, we are well fortified.

If anything or anybody living makes it, I have automated shoreline batteries up and running 24/7, heavy artillery sufficient to repel all boarders.

Nothing touches us.

It's central to what we're doing here.

Let the world blow itself to perdition if that's what that asshole in Washington wants, women and children first, no problem. Mine are safe. If something goes wrong in the sky or on the plateau we can always go deeper— the abbey on Clothos is a honeycomb. There are caverns below the ones we've occupied; only Benny knows how many or how far down they go. I could house hundreds in the undercroft alone, and that's exclusive of storage space. My Security people are quartered below, so your kids can go on thinking this is just another school.

The crypts are packed with supplies to keep us into the fourth millennium, and fresh water runs in underground springs. Old Brother Benedictus has every known fruit and vegetable growing year-round in the dome I built over his garden, and he ranches mushrooms in subcaverns, but he won't tell us where.

Never mind how he ended up on board— that's another story. Let's just say that in terms of service on Clothos, the old monk makes me look like a jarhead whose boot-camp buzz cut is still fuzz. Abandoned baby, brought up by monks. The old man is wise the way old souls are wise. He knows every crypt and chamber in the cloister and every subterranean cave, and if he wants to pray in his room instead of coming to our movie nights or showing up at morning assemblies? Fine.

Benny showed me things I didn't know about and told me things I had to know. Like how the monks melded safety and freedom, or the illusion of freedom. Tactics for a guy with a hundred kids to contain. And keep happy.

OK, not happy. Contented.

Contained.

They have no choice.

The mountain is high, the water troubled. Some days the skies are black and on other days, water boils up red as blood in the ocean thousands of yards below. Nobody has to tell these kids that we are besieged by signs and wonders or that the old, decaying world is doomed. They can see it hanging in the air outside. Even the hardest cases must know.

Inside the Academy, they are safe.

TWO

BROTHER BENEDICTUS ISN'T REALLY A MONK, WHICH THAT nice Mr. Sargent doesn't need to know. Although Benny isn't really a monk, he looks like one. Slight, ascetic, with his remaining hair neatly shaped into a tonsure. He follows the Rule. He observes the Liturgy of the Hours. He does his job in the greenhouse, tending vegetables and picking leafy greens for Chef Pete's salads. He harvests mushrooms in the crypt for Pete's special lasagna, but it's understood that he will go to the former chapel at certain times even though there's nothing happening there.

It seems right to him.

His new boss is a stickler for order, so Mr. Sargent and the Hours are a good fit, which is just as well, Benny thinks, although what this means exactly, he is not certain.

Actually, Benny needs routine just as much as Sarge does, but for different reasons. It holds him up. Meanwhile the monastic progress of daily Lauds and Matins, Vespers and Compline fits nicely with

Mr. Sargent's bells announcing class and mealtimes and the Order of
the Day he posts on the bulletin board. Then there's the trumpet. At
dawn and at bedtime the old halls ring so convincingly that Benny
doesn't know to this day whether it's a real person out there playing,
or Mr. Sargent's Victrola. Military airs, he supposes, but they don't
sound warlike.

Mr. Sargent keeps Benedictus around like a sacred object. As if
he's some kind of talisman, although he doesn't say that. He says
having a monk on board adds the right measure of gravity to the
Academy.

Benny doesn't have the heart to tell the boss that he isn't really
a monk. He happened into the cloister by accident and inertia kept
him here. He was abandoned— marooned on this earth— when
disease picked off the monks one by one and Brother Sixtus, the
last of the order on Clothos, blessed him and died. It was like losing his father. The Benedictines were the only family Benny ever
knew.

By the time the Academy helicopter landed on Mount Clothos,
the old man was wearing the habit Brother Sixtus left behind when
his spirit flew off and left his body here. Benny put it on because by
that time all his shirts had been scrubbed to tatters and both pairs
of his old pants were out at the knees and the seat. Sarge doesn't
have to know. The head of the Academy holds Brother Benedictus
up as a shining example of the way things ought to be, and a hundred young people stand with heads bent and shoulders hunched
resentfully, listening.

They don't have much choice.

"Guys," Sarge says before he reads off the Order of the Day after Roll Call but before breakfast, "If an old monk like Brother
Benedictus here can keep to the schedule and do it without complaining, so can you." Then in case they don't get it, he adds, "It's
the least you can do."

In fact, Benny is a civilian, which would disappoint Mr. Sargent if he knew.

It might compromise the old man's situation here, and this is the only situation he knows. Unlike the generations of monks who came before him, he didn't arrive as a prayerful youth begging to be admitted to the cloister. He's here because he had no choice.

He was two months old, give or take. Nobody's quite sure. He grew up here and he's just too old to start over, which is why he stays. Well, that and the impossibility of departure without a partner to man the basket relay the monks used to go up and down the mountain. To operate the basket relay he needs at least two men, and Brother Benedictus is the last.

The basket used to be the only way people came and went, but that's all changed. Benny's scared of the shiny new transit capsule hovering at the top of its chute. He can't leave in the capsule. If he tries, Mr. Sargent will find out before Benny can figure out how to enter the chute and get the thing open. The machinery terrifies him. Technology always has.

No surprise, given the boundaries of monastic life and the fact that it's the only life he's ever known.

Unlike postulants, grown men who forsake earthly things to enter monastic communities like this one, Benny got found.

On that particular day a young man lingered at the bottom of Mount Clothos because he had doubts. He thought he wanted to enter the order, but at the last minute he panicked, which Benny didn't find out until Brother Sixtus died. As he paid off the captain who ferried postulants here, the surf came up. He should have tugged on the rope to signal the monks, but at the last minute Sixtus thought about solitude in the cloister, the finality of the rock. There were women back home. There were other possible lives.

Just then a monster surge of water broke on the rocks and

belched up an oil drum. It hit the shore with a hollow **BOOM**, exploding his doubts. Sixtus barely glanced at it. *This*. He tugged the rope. *I want this.*

For men petitioning to join the Benedictines at the top of Mount Clothos, the basket was the only way up. The mountain was high. The ride was perilous, and could only be undertaken in high summer, when the ice ledges had melted and the intricate relay system would work. Sixtus had been waiting months for this day. There was a signal from above. A stone dropped at his feet. There was a message attached. He read the note.

When the basket landed he had five minutes to get in and tug on the rope. Otherwise the launch would come back for him and he'd never see the island again.

Then he heard cries rattling around the inside of the steel drum. There was something alive in there. It sounded like a baby. It couldn't be a baby. He went closer.

Amplified by the container, the bawling was tremendous.

"I should have taken you to the mainland," Sixtus told Benny, a long lifetime later. He was on his deathbed and they didn't have much time. "But the basket landed, and it was either or. Oh Benny, I am so sorry."

"No need." Benny did not ask either or *what*. He would do anything to keep Sixtus alive. He stroked the old man's hand. "No need!"

Five minutes. Sixtus had five minutes to divest everything he had and say goodbye to the world. There were no electronics permitted in the abbey, no reminders of the life going on outside. At the first relay station he would be searched and if he didn't pass inspection he would be sent back down. He had been fairly warned. On ledges at a dozen relay stations high above him, monks were posted in pairs, waiting to haul him up hand over hand; like many things in religious communities, it was a collaborative effort. The monks set a time limit. In its own way, this was their first test too.

"You were crying, I didn't think. There wasn't time!"

"Shhh, Father," Benny said. "The Rule. I understand."

"But I had to save you." Sixtus groaned. "Either way."

The order had its reasons. Too many boys imagined they wanted the order, the Grand Silence, but that was before they saw the place. Faced with the terrible reality of the mountain, too many young men of good faith lost heart at the last minute, so this was a test. If the aspirant failed to tug on the rope within five minutes, the monks above would declare him unfit or unwilling, and pull the empty basket up.

On the horizon, the launch lingered. If Sixtus turned back, he would not be the first. He had to move fast. A baby's life, his future in the order depended on it. If the monks waited for him to save the child, fine. If the monks didn't wait for him to do this, then the hell with them. He wasn't about to give the future to a bunch of religious who were blind to human need.

He ran for the oil drum, wondering how in God's name he would open it. If he made it in time to save the child and get back to the basket, he made it. If not, he would hail the launch and they would both leave.

"It was either or, Benny," the old monk said, all those years later. "Either or."

The lid to the drum flew open. The baby inside blinked at the light. Then it smiled at him. Whether or not his five minutes were up, and Sixtus never knew, the basket waited. It was like a message from God.

At the top he put the baby into the arms of the abbot, who promised the order would take care of both of them, for life. The monks named the baby Benedictus, after the saint who founded the order. They took him on as a gift from God.

By the time Benny was big enough to know the difference, his rescuer wasn't a postulant any more. He was Brother Sixtus. When he was old enough, Brother Sixtus let him help in the monastery garden, where he cultivated the few vegetables that grew in the greenhouse, the only fresh food the monks had. Now, of course, Mr. Sargent has erected this beautiful temperature-controlled dome in which Benny tends so many crops that he is forever scurrying, scurrying, desperate to keep them alive. He's never seen this much green in his life. He loves these growing things. He loves them so much!

He wonders what Brother Sixtus would make of this, but it's been years since Sixtus blessed him and turned his face to the wall. He has been alone for longer than he knows.

Working together in the greenhouse all those years ago, neither of them knew that in time Brother Sixtus would become abbot. God knows that neither of them knew he'd be the last. There are times when disaster moves so stealthily that nobody hears it coming until too late.

Then a monk fell ill. Another fell ill. One by one, the others fell. Brother Sixtus was the last; he didn't tell Benedictus the story of his abandonment and discovery until the Final Days.

While disease tiptoed through the cloister and the ruined choir looking for new victims, the old abbot and his last confrère retreated to the chapel because until the end, Sixtus observed the Liturgy of the Hours. When he could no longer stand or kneel, he prayed sitting. When he became too weak to sit, Benny made a bed for him in the nave, where he prayed facing the altar, fixed on the crucifix. Behind it, sun came crashing in through the stained glass representation of the risen Christ. The old abbot was on his deathbed, although until the last day, both he and Benny pretended he was not. When the last abbot's breath began to fail him he beckoned.

Benny knelt at his side.

"Closer."

It was time.

"Bless me, Father."

The last thing Benny expected to do was hear a confession. "Oh, please. I'm not a priest!"

"Shut up and let me tell you." With an effort, Sixtus went on. "It's my fault you ended up here." Then he told the story. All of it. He finished with a phlegmy rattle. "My son, I am so sorry."

"But I love it here!"

"No." The abbot put his hand on Benny's head. It was more than a benediction. He sighed. "It's the only place you know."

"Father, this is my life."

"I'm afraid it is." Then Sixtus finished, with regret. "I could have called the captain and waited with you until he picked us up. I could have lost my vocation and saved you but I was greedy, I wanted both."

A sigh like a groan came out of him. "To save you and join the order, I had to bring you here."

Benny's whole life in the world flashed before his eyes at that moment along with all the lives he might have had, but brought up in the cloister as he was, with no contact with the outside world and no information about it allowed except what filtered in with . . . never mind who. Without it, all the images were blurred. He had no idea what it would have been like.

Sixtus said, "God forgive me, I was so selfish. The monks gave me five minutes."

"No, Father. You must forgive me."

But whether or not Benny liked it, the old man confessed. "I was afraid if I waited, I'd lose my nerve!"

"Oh!" Benny said, diverted by the abbot's guilt. Dear God, he almost told him. He still can. He still can!

Then the last abbot said, "Take care of them, Benny," although Benedictus was the only person left.

"Wait," Benny cried. "Take care of me! Bless me Father . . ."

But Sixtus was caught in the great wind that would blow his soul away, saying with all the love left in him, "Take care of them all."

"For I have sinned." *Confess,* he prayed, *please let me confess!*

But Sixtus died.

Benny used herbs to preserve the mortal body of the late abbot, Brother Sixtus, and incense to cover the smell. He exposed the body in front of the altar in the chapel where so many other abbots had lain in state, which is what you did. For three days he kept vigil, saying the prayers for the dead. Early on the third day three bats flew down from the high arches and circled the coffin like messengers from nowhere. Benny is not easily spooked, so he finished the third day and said the appropriate prayers over the coffin. Then he wrapped the body in linen and closed the lid on his mentor. It was awful. He laid Sixtus down with the others, far below the undercroft. The brothers, the abbot, every member of his earthly family is gone. They are all sleeping in the crypt.

He forgets how long ago that was.

Before Sarge and his people came, Benny almost died of loneliness. For a long time, he thought the situation was temporary. That the disease that took all the others would take him and he would be free, but it didn't. He looked at his tongue in the mirror, hoping for signs. He felt his armpits, but to no avail. He wished he would go crazy and escape the solitude. Then he prayed for new monks to come, that they'd bring the priest he could confess to and thus be forgiven for the One Bad Thing he had done in his life, the sin so grave that he never told even Sixtus, but he was stupendously alone.

For all he knew they were down there right now, with no way up the mountainside. New monks could be waiting on the rocky skirt with no idea that Benedictus was pining up here. With nobody to help him with the relays, how could he get down the mountain, how could he tell them? How could he bring them up?

Alone, Benny prayed. He followed the Liturgy of the Hours just as he had done every day of his life. Although he could not say Mass he said all the prayers. He observed the Great Silence, no feat in the deserted cloister. He didn't yell, although he could have. He didn't rage against fate and he never cried.

The routine kept him in place. It is his armature.

Benny doesn't know how long he tended his plants and kept the Hours before the helicopter landed like a giant dragonfly outside the Victorian greenhouse where he worked before Mr. Sargent built the dome. Without access to worldly things and with limited information, Benny looked at the glinting fuselage and came to his own conclusions. He didn't mistake Mr. Sargent and his men for angels or space aliens, a concept he'd picked up from a postulant when he was a boy, and he didn't for a minute think they were sent by God. He thought of them as astronauts landing on the moon as described by Brother Edward, the very last postulant, who'd seen them on TV when he was a child.

Benny wasn't afraid. He was excited.

He never told Mr. Sargent or his men about the disease, or about all his brethren sleeping far below the chapel, wrapped in linen and lying in the deepest crypt. He was afraid to tell them anything that might scare them, because he didn't want them to leave. More than anything, he wanted them to stay.

In the year since then— miracles!

Soon they were landing heavy equipment by helicopter. Life as Benedictus knew it was changing fast. Helicopters landed supplies from the mainland and a chef for the Academy, and the food . . . the food was glorious! Exotic. Rich with fats and spices. It was unlike everything Benny had ever tasted.

He felt unworthy. He couldn't explain. It wasn't only the secrets he kept— the holy dead, the mortal sin on his immortal soul. The new people were so quick and complicated. He was so plain.

"Don't worry about your position here," Mr. Sargent said. With strong, unbroken sunshine highlighting that white-blond hair, he looked like God. Like a god he said, "We'll need an expert gardener in place long before we open the Academy."

"A school." A school! Benny's heart leapt up. He imagined small children in cassocks, marching in orderly lines. The Hours. The abbey restored again. Fealty to the Rule. "God be praised." *New souls,* he thought with joy. *New souls.*

"Don't thank God, thank me."

If only he'd known!

He told Sarge everything, except what happened to Brother Sixtus and the others. It's as though the plague was no freak of nature, it was something he did. His dirty secret. An outward and physical sign of his guilt.

Benny showed the Director all the secret places— well, almost all of them. He grieved to see the stained glass go when Sarge renovated the chapel, along with the altar and the sacramentals. He wrestled the giant crucifix into the alcove outside the chapel and down a flight of stairs into his cell before construction began.

It stands there now like an eschatological symbol, towering over his narrow bed. Even though he didn't have the authority, he begged Mr. Sargent to allow him to deconsecrate the place. He prayed for forgiveness and did what he could.

The drilling equipment frightened Benny but he understood that to make the Academy functional, the staff needed something more regular than helicopters and better than the basket relay to bring up people and supplies. By that time the relay stations had stood unused for so long that there was no telling what time and weather conditions had done to the pulleys, to say nothing of the ropes.

Mr. Sargent was so proud! "This is it, Father Benedictus."

"I'm not a priest."

"Brother Benedictus," Mr. Sargent said.

"I'm not a . . ."

"Brother." Mr. Sargent slapped him on the shoulder.

". . . monk." Overwhelmed, Benny mumbled in a voice so low that not even he could hear. The Director slapped a button and a door slid open, revealing the new shaft and a metal capsule with a circular bench seat.

He opened the hatch. "I'm taking the hovercraft to the mainland to pick up a few things. How would you like to be the first passenger to go down with me?"

Doors to the world he didn't know flew wide open, a great black sucking hole. Benny backed away from the void. "Oh," he cried.

"How long has it been since you went to town?"

"Oh . . ." He was backing away so fast that he alarmed Mr. Sargent, who has never been anything but kind to him.

"What's the matter?"

"Oh," Benny cried, terrified and grateful and deeply, greedily excited but still backing. His voice came out in a thin, wavering stream that he could not cut off. "Oh. Oh. Oh, no!"

"No matter," the big man said. "Another time." He slipped into the capsule with an easy grin. Others followed. The door to the tube closed. *Whish.* They were gone.

Safe. Benny collapsed, gasping. Safe! At least that's what he thought at the time.

Mr. Sargent made many trips after that first one, organizing, setting things up, bringing in equipment and supplies. Refurbishing the monks' cells so that where for centuries the brothers slept on narrow pallets in cells ornamented only by the small cross at the head of the bed, his students would find neat, insulated cubicles with comfortable beds and brightly colored plasterboard covering the cold stone. There are hooks for posters. Gaudy bedspreads. Rugs!

For Benedictus, who grew up with burlap and stone walls and

only the formality of altar cloths and stained glass to catch his eye, it was like looking at a million flowers. Out of deference, Mr. Sargent let him keep his cell pristine.

He was filled with waiting. Excited, in his own way.

THREE

SARGE

Dictators and billionaires, geek geniuses and movie stars and crime lords broke the bank to hand over their kids to me, same as you, and you were thrilled.

Not everybody was thrilled. On Departure Day some of your children came screaming, e.g. the neo–Brat Packers, separated from their makeup kits and blow dryers, whatever they smoked, shot, snorted or otherwise ingested to float their sexy little boats. The fat Birch kid lit into his dad with bunched fists and bared teeth, frothing and howling. Before I could stop it, Cassie and I saw Harold R. Birch, top-rung climber in the Fortune 500, shake the crap out of his bawling twelve-year-old.

Birch Senior was shouting, "Do you want to stay back and die? Do you want to burn up when the earth explodes? Do you?"

"You know what I want." The sole heir to Birch Aerospace let it all out, yowling like a werewolf in heat, "I want boobs!"

Think about it. Master of the universe, and your boy wants to be a girl. Poor Birch, poor kid! Cassie and I were running to break it up when Harold R. Birch, aerospace magnate and snotty, tight-assed Harvard man, dropped to his knees in his Hugo Boss suit. Master of the universe, reduced to begging. "Son, the world is ending. I'm only trying to save you!"

Zander slashed his father's cheek with his stick-on fingernails. "If things are so fucking bad, you go!"

Birch smacked the kid into the metal detector. Zander hit so hard that tears flew while his dad spat, "Selfish, thoughtless little asshole, look what you've done to me!"

"So *that's* what we're doing here." Cassie ran to stop them.

Exactly. *Protecting the kids.*

Birch stood over the sobbing kid, bellowing, "You'll thank me later." Next he told the lie that is making me rich. "I'm doing this for you!"

"It's OK, Zander. It's OK." Cassie shoved Birch aside, shielding Zander while he recovered. I love that girl; she always knows how to make people feel better. "It's OK, sweetie; I'll look for an estrogen substitute for you."

He got up and followed her like a lamb.

By that time the parents were in a panic, like the boat might shove off before they got their troublemakers on board. I saw grown women herding their young into the hangar like Noah loading the Ark when the first drops fell: "Hurry, the world is ending!"

At some level, they all believed.

You had to, or this would never play.

Everybody has to believe in something.

On Departure Day your children howled, "I don't care," but the wild white rings around the irises, the flash of naked teeth told us that they were scared enough to lay back and let us take them. Yeah, they care.

They'd damn well better.

If they don't, they will. They are my children now.

Meanwhile, we maintain order.

It's our business.

Brother Benedictus says the cloister was set up to do something similar. Benedictines came across the sea from England so we speak the same language. They brought the discipline. Daily office. Call to prayer at regular times, which they called the Liturgy of the Hours. The penance.

Our regimen is somewhat different. If this used to be a religious establishment, the buildings have forgotten. The young can sock-skate along stone floors worn smooth by generations of monks so long ago that there is no trace of them. In a few of the cells we found initials, dates in Roman numerals, cryptic carvings of crosses and Greek lettering: the chi and the rho. Fish symbols with the Greek characters; ICHTHUS.

ΙΧθΨΣ

Gives me the creeps to remember, but it's not a problem now. It would have freaked the kids, especially the smalls. We laid in layers of insulation covered with Sheetrock painted in sunny colors. I replaced dreary stained glass with beveled glass windows reinforced with steel wire, so no power on earth can break them.

Instead of staring at dismal scourgings and crucifixions in five colors our kids can look out at our crazy skies and remember every day of their lives here that we are protecting them from disaster. It's fitting.

The Gothic chapel where we hold assemblies is the only reminder that people used to worship here. I removed the altar and the cross before we began the renovation, but I left the carved legend above the archway leading into the new Assembly Hall because it fits the enterprise:

LUX ET SERENITAS

Serenity. After everything. No. Before anything, I want serenity. And, God, outside. Outside!

When lakes incinerate and the waterways turn to rivers of fire, when the earth is belching flames, where will your children be? When your beautiful, flawed sons and daughters are running wild in the landscape, shaming and reviling you, what would you give to remove them to a quiet place where they will be contained and protected? What would you give up to send them here? How much would you pay?

Plenty.

FOUR

CASSIE RIVARD IS A GREAT PA— INFORMED, INTUITIVE, BETTER than most doctors, but she is by no means the sturdy rock Sarge thinks she is. As a matter of fact, she's a little shaky right now. Nor is she all that dedicated to the enterprise. Sarge is all about saving the kids. Cassie isn't, although she likes them well enough.

She is dedicated to Sarge.

She signed on as physician's assistant on this Godforsaken crag because of this, and she did it without question. When she first came to Clothos Sarge offered her one more chance to reconsider. It was the last. He took her face in his hands, studying the landscape reflected in her eyes: the ascent, sharp enough to defy a mountain goat. The lack of vegetation. He said, "It's a lot to ask. You want to turn back?"

"Nono," she told him, even though the mountain was bleak and forbidding. The launch approached through roiling surf. She saw blood and bits of *something* floating in the water.

"When we get to the top, don't look down," he warned. "At least not until you're used to it."

He was right. Their fortress sits so far above the toxic sea that no birds fly. The drop is stupendous.

Cassie didn't look down and she never looked back, either, although she did have that bad moment on Crete the day they processed the inmates. No, Cass. Do not ever speak of them as inmates. What did Sarge tell you? *What we do here is less important than what they think we're doing.*

Don't look down, girl. Don't look back and don't ask questions. Do your job and maybe he will love you.

She set up the Gothic Infirmary during the week before term began, dutifully scanning the kids' charts into the system. The details were disturbing. There's nothing they haven't done to their bodies, and it is appalling. Sure, she'll serve here as long as she is needed, although the terms of her contract, the chill that pervades the ancient stone walls of Academy and— face it— the events of the past few days have left her with misgivings.

To begin with, now that everybody's on board they are officially sealed inside an ex-convent or monkery or some damn thing at the top of a totally isolated mountain, as in, there's no way off. There are no *people* down below. No town, no other buildings. Nobody comes, nobody goes. The personnel here inside the Academy will be her only company for the duration and frankly, she is not very impressed with them.

Well, except for Sarge.

Now, isolation is not a problem for her, at least not right now. Cassie left a world of grief behind when she got off that plane in Athens and jumped onto a rusty biplane headed for her interview on Crete, which is where Sarge did his hiring.

There are problems at home, and she's damn glad to be shut of them.

She does, however, have reservations about the Academy doctor. Among other things. The old fop showed up a tottering hop, skip and jump ahead of the official deadline, took to his quarters and hasn't been seen since, except for that medical fiasco on Departure Day, when the old fool's needles kept snapping off in the arms of sobbing kids.

Then there was the chaos on Departure Day, which shook her more than she cares to admit.

Any sane woman would have taken one look at the scene and headed for high ground. Any sane woman would have refused to work with Dr. Mel Dratch, with his shaking hands and his greasy lab coat splotched with spilled serum.

She had her bad moment at the intake hangar, but she shook it off. She's here. God knows it isn't the job, although it's all she can get right now. It isn't even the money, although it's good money. Or the location. If she wanted religion, she could have joined a convent. Convents, you can always leap over the wall if things get tough. Here it's a four-thousand-foot drop into the ocean.

In spite of which, Cassie has signed on for the duration.

Given all the givens, probably she's crazy.

Maybe she just needs to be in a place where she can see Sarge every day.

She's been in love with Sargent Whitemore ever since they were kids in Beaufort, when because of certain things that came down in high school, he joined the Marines. When the bus took him away to boot camp at Parris Island she cried because she realized she was in love with him. At night she used to park on the mainland and count the lights on the base, wishing herself there; did he even know how much she missed him? She was in love with Sarge when he came home on that first leave, even though they only saw each other that one time, between boot camp and that special school at Quantico— she thinks it was Command and Control; God, how appropriate. She went up to Virginia to see him before he shipped out; they both had complicated feelings. That war. But she loved him.

She loved him even more when he came back changed, although it's been hard. She saw the afterglare of too many explosions in those pale eyes, as though the irises had blown.

Cassie will always be in love with him, even though he doesn't know it. Sarge is so bent on his mission that he doesn't see her, not really, he only sees the shape of his hopes. He has no idea that her face changes color and her throat tightens when she's getting cranked up to talk to him.

Sarge always was great looking— square jaw, strong profile, white-blond hair. War has aged him, unless it took the boy she loved and forged him into something different. Now that he's lost the military buzz cut he's ruggedly handsome, like the profile on a medal struck in the image of God. Sarge doesn't so much believe in God; he wants to be a god, which is one of the problems with men, as Cassie sees it. In high school he was captain of everything. They traveled in different worlds. She used to lie in wait just so she could bump into him in the halls. They both knew it was no accident but he was sweet with her; he let her pretend that it was. Nice smile. No wonder she gets all shy around him.

These days, she usually sees Sarge in profile. He is fixed on something that she can't see, some ideal that floats like a feather in the middle distance. In a way it's like approaching Captain Ahab, who keeps his spyglass fixed on the white whale regardless, or trying to get Lord Nelson's attention in the middle of some major sea battle.

Her boss marches through the days like a good soldier— correction, Marine— and because she loves him, Cassie follows.

She knows the man believes in what he's doing, but at the moment, Cassie isn't exactly sure what he's trying to do. *Save the children,* she thinks, because that's what he told her.

"You've seen their charts."

She has, and God knows these kids need saving. She just isn't sure what Sarge is saving them *from*. Bad parents? Themselves, or the end of the world?

So this is the rock-bottom detail that bothers Cassie most. The end of the world. If there really is a predictable end of the world, that he is saving everybody from. They are totally sealed off here, isolated from outside sources of information, so she doesn't know.

The end of the world? Here inside the Academy, its timing and placement are an open question.

FIVE

SARGE

When he staffed the Ark, Noah had to advertise, for all the good it did. Not me. These days even a blind hermit could see the problems are endemic.

I sent the brochure to the precious few. Word got around. The bidding opened a week later. Within twenty-four hours, every place in the Academy was filled.

We notified the highest bidders.

The staff and I took the hovercraft to Crete before dawn on the designated Departure Day. The chosen hundred and their parents and guardians were waiting outside the intake hangar. They were there for hours before we arrived— some of them for days. In spite of the lack of amenities in that isolated nick in the Cretan coastline, some had pitched tents a week ahead just to be first in line. They were that anxious to finalize the arrangement and hand their children off to us.

By the time we entered the harbor the rich and the mighty

were standing like so many sheep, massed inside the enclosure that protected the intake hangar from their hysteria. My on-site people had checked thumbprints and moved the eligibles inside our electrified fence and activated it before the sun came up and believe me, it was for their own protection.

My Cretan support staff don't know what we're doing on Clothos, but they do know a mob when they see one.

Cassie and I watched from the bridge of the hovercraft as we entered the harbor. On that part of the coast everything stood crank-sided on the craggy hillside, like cutouts slotted into a raked stage for us to admire. From the highest point on our boat we could see everything: the dock, the hangar perched on the hill and behind it the Taser fence crackling and sparking as the crowd outside the enclosure surged against it.

They were still coming.

Cassie saw them before I did. "Look!"

The hillside was black with people, like army ants massed for the attack. The ridge was crowded with parents arriving too late. Tycoons and A-list celebrities jumped like monkeys, scrambling downhill over the backs of the fallen as if lives depended on their being first. In a way, they did, but it was far too late for threats or bribery; it was too late to do anything but join the frantic mass howl of frustration that came roaring downhill on the wind, echoing in the harbor.

Cassie grabbed my arm and then let go as if she'd just burned herself. "Oh," she said. "This is bad. Very bad."

"Don't worry," I told her, "We'll handle it."

"But there are so many!"

This pissed me off more than it should have. "Why are they here? They got their rejections last week!"

She grimaced. "Like anybody ever believes NO means them."

They came even though the bidding closed at midnight on the first of the month and my entering students' places were allocated accordingly. The rejection letters went out by FedEx weeks before, signature requested, but they came anyway.

People even richer than you came to me in the final days; they came at me with bribes. They made threats. Nothing they said or did could move me. Sealed inside the cloister on Clothos, I was impervious, and no parent alive dared hurt me before Departure Day. They held back on the outside chance that I might fit in one more— theirs. And as for you who said, each in your own way, "Would money make any difference?" I wouldn't have minded owning that diamond mine outside Pretoria or the entire state of Utah, but I could only take a hundred.

The air was thick with their pleading, nothing you could make out, but painful to hear.

They covered the hillside above the hangar. A living reproach.

I could only take a hundred.

And then my old girlfriend from Beaufort, loyal woman that I thought was *so strong* grabbed my arm again, and I saw that she was shaking. "Look at them."

"Come on," I said to steady her. "Let's go inside and get started."

The shouting was terrible. Her face was a mess of conflicting emotions. "Look at them all."

"Don't look. Try not to listen." I gripped her hand and led her down the ladder and to the rail, where the rest of the staff was waiting for orders. Once I got her off the boat and into the shadow of the hangar, she wouldn't have to see them any more.

Cassie hung back, wailing, "There'll never be enough places. Who will take care of them?"

This is not a question I can answer. I did what you do. I took command. "OK then," I said to the assembled staff. "Let's get this operation going!"

Good old Steve. He saluted smartly. "Yes sir!"

I moved Cass down the gangplank and onto the dock with my voice, never mind what I had to tell her, that's classified. It was hard, but I gave my only friend everything I had to give her that day. To get her moving, I told her things she wasn't supposed to know. Never mind what, you don't need to know. Then I said, "In times like this, you do what you have to."

"OK." She lifted her chin. Brave girl. "OK."

Steve went. Cassie fell in behind him and the others followed. I stood back while she and Steve led them up the ramp from the dock into the hangar. I was the last inside.

Outside in the holding area, our paying guests were getting edgy. Not the kids, the parents. There was ranting. These are powerful people, remember. Not accustomed to waiting. The wealthy rejects swarming down the hill toward my hundred chosen and their parents in the enclosure, the zap and crackle followed by screams as intruders collided with the Taser fence, put my paying customers on edge. It made them pushy. I heard threats. Every phone in the place was ringing.

At the far end of the hangar, designated dorm parent Dave Bogardus stood with his hand on the switch to the giant Rolo that opened on the hillside. "Now?"

"Now."

My staff hurried to their stations, anxious to begin so we could get on with it and get this over with and get out, which is what you do in tight situations.

Even the skies threatened. Nobody wanted to stay on Crete any longer than it took to do this. Once we had the last of our people inside and the intake door rolled down for good, the mob outside would give up and go.

Unless they didn't. I didn't know. The pressure was horrendous. I nodded to Dave, who's also our guidance counselor. He opened the intake door and we let them in.

Parents milled in the reception area, restive and imperious. Their young were angry, uncertain. Conflicted.

Some of our charter students came willingly and some came in restraints, but scared and willing or spitting and furious, they all came, rushed along by parents who would give anything to hand off their uncontrollable, inconvenient children. They already had. They did it when they made the necessary wire transfer. Now all they had to do was sign off on them and go.

They had *goodbye and good riddance* written all over their faces.

Poor kids. What choice did they have?

I looked at their paperwork and ticked them off one by one, all the ones that passed muster. A few, I had to turn away. Dave and his people took care of the dismissals, with Dr. Dratch nearby to administer the necessary tranquilizers and my Security people in charge of removal— in civvies, to keep from alarming anyone. The successful parents were— how to put this?— giddy with relief. Every time the door opened and another pair of parents left the hangar, laughing because they had finally put down their burden, the mob outside raised another howl. They were like refugees begging for standing room on *Il Fugitivo* for the last flight off a doomed planet.

Which in a way is what they were.

Inside the hangar, families exchanged looks. Parents said what parents say: "I guess this is it." They meant to sound sorry, when everybody knew they were glad. And the kids?

You don't want to know what they were doing. It was pitiful, watching them milling around in the intake area, waiting to be processed.

The hell of it is that most of the students I protect and defend here never wanted to come to Clothos, not even with parents warning them that raging hellfire was about to boil over and destroy them. In spite of the instructional videos we supplied to every client. In spite of the apocalyptic images on every screen when you loaded it.

Ruin would be raining down on the planet in sheets, their parents told them. Hell on earth, they said. You don't know what hell is until you feel the fire. Scripted, yes, with every word crafted to strike terror. They warned their struggling young that their very hides and hair were at risk and when they had them sobbing with fear they explained that we at the Academy and we alone could save them, parents everywhere saying: *Trust us.*

Fool kids, they knew something was up, you could see it in their faces. *If it's that bad, why aren't you coming?* Some of my kids may be hellacious little bastards, but they are honest.

Don't you see, they can only take a hundred, their parents told them. *We're risking our lives,* they claimed. *We're doing it for you!*

Yeah, right.

It was the parents who lied or begged and threatened and bribed to get their toxic treasures admitted, handing their bad seed off with groans of delight as the last one moved into the processing booth wailing, and the door marked PRIVATE closed on him.

Some fought bitterly after they were handed off, but Dave Bogardus took care of that with a little help from Askew, the assistant coach. In addition to an advanced degree in psychology and highly developed people skills, Dave is a black belt, and back in Beaufort High School, Coach Askew made it to the semifinals in the Golden Gloves.

Control demands a combination of discipline and muscle. Askew and Bogardus saw to the muscle part. I did the rest.

Some kids said a civil goodbye to their parents; some punched them in the belly and swore vengeance or, in a few cases, refused to speak even though weeping mothers fell on their knees and hugged them, sobbing as they begged for forgiveness. It wouldn't matter what passed between these parents and their young. It didn't matter whether my clients were truly sad or only pretending to be sad to leave their flailing, self-destructing, out-of-control progeny with us.

Once they'd steered that kid into the processing booth, the parents never looked back, not a single one. They ran for the side exit. All-terrain vehicles came spidering out of the rocks to whisk them away and I can tell you, they went gladly. Relieved of the terrible burden of responsibility, they went back to their lives.

Meanwhile, my faculty processed the students according to placement— the smalls, twelve and under, including Zander Birch, who was so close to turning thirteen that he barely made the cut; the nubiles, the ones teetering on the brink of adulthood, some a sexy danger to themselves— Marla Parsons the hotel heiress and Sylvie D'Estart the oil princess being the most prominent— and some druggy or so dangerous that when we shook them down knives fell out, garrotes and hidden firearms.

Cassie isn't only the Academy person I am closest to, although that's the most important thing about her; she's a nurse. Sorry. Physician's Assistant. She's also an empath, so I had her do the intake interviews while Steven entered the particulars in his laptop and scanned passports into the system before Dirk Fedders tossed the originals into the lockbox along with credit cards, driver's licenses and library cards, anything that would let them reenter society before I broke my vow and turned them loose, which I will do only under extreme circumstances, since I am engaged to keep them inside the Academy for as long as it takes.

How long will it take? Not clear.

To do what? Don't even think of asking.

Listen, it's for their own good.

By noon my hundred had all been registered and processed, checked for parasites and STDs, even the youngest, because given who they were and what gnarly situations their frantic parents had pulled them out of to bring them here, anything was possible. They'd had their regulation haircuts, they'd had unsightly tattoos lasered off, all studs removed and piercings surgically closed; Dr. Dratch is as skillful at removing disfigurements as he is good at disease control. Electronics, we confiscated for the common good. In exchange for reduced wages, my men on Crete are having a hell of a yard sale. Jewelry and civilian clothes were stashed in footlockers against the day; the young were all in school uniforms, although with some of the upperclassmen, it had been a struggle. Now they were milling and grumbling inside the hangar as my intake staff went through their luggage, separating what personal items they could take to Clothos from items the Academy does not allow, as I made clear when I posted admissions requirements.

Books are OK, clothes and a few personal items, but for the good of the enterprise, no hair gels and no makeup, and, more important: no cell phones, MP3 players, DVD players, video games, Game Boys or PlayStations, no laptops or PCs, if you want to know the truth, we don't want the contents of those hard drives. There will be computers in every room, don't worry, the Academy will take care of you. We shook down the kids. Hidden iPods and flash drives fell out of them; some people cried. Maybe it was the tension.

It was time to begin boarding.

SIX

KILLER STADE

What are you, you motherfuckers, pushing us around like the all-powerful almighty Whatever? Like, you have some kind of divine fucking right to shoot us up with busted needles and shake us down, so you end up with all our cool shit?

Yeah well not every asshole on this boat is an asshole. Just so you know.

When I saw the way things were going back there in the hangar, first crack out of the barrel I offered up my MP3 player, which is no big deal, for I have better toys.

Here, asshole. You want it? Take it, enjoy. Which they did. Go ahead, fucking strip me to fucking half past naked and shove me into this scratchy, retarded uniform when what you're really doing is making sure you get everything— the laptop, Game Boy, PDA, which I handed off before we even got to the metal detector.

I did it to keep their minds off . . .

Never mind what special item I kept, if I tell you, I'll have to kill myself.

Any asshole with a brain in his crack and a flashlight strong enough to see up there would know my Xbox was a decoy, but this Sarge guy's people fucking snapped at it. I cussed them to perdition and back so they wouldn't guess the truth.

See, I don't fucking give a fucking ratfuck if I lose that or my PlayStation or that sleep-in-front-of-Wal-Mart-for-days-just-to-be-first-to-get-one next generation Wii any more than I care about the top-of-the-line Treo that Mom paid too much for, although I did feel bad about my Spy brand pen that's really a digicorder *with* video capability, there's shit going on here that Mom needs to know about.

My stuff? Factories made it, not me.

So take what you want. The real deal is pretty much locked up inside my skull. Well, there and inside that leather looks-like-a-farewell-notebook that a dumb father would give, that you are supposed to write your thoughts in. You passed it through the turnbuckle without a second look while I cleared the metal detector so fuck you all, you musclebound tards.

I don't give a fuck what you do to me, do you get that, assholes? Do you?

So go ahead. You can take and sell my electronics, you can do what you want with them and you can burn my cool outfit and stick me in this shitass zombie jail uniform, but you can't touch me. You can laser off my tats and turn my hair back to dirt brown if you want to, fuck you very much. No, you are fucking welcome, so go ahead. Roll me for cash and stick me with needles and let the big kids beat the shit out of me and you will never, ever get to the bottom of Killer Stade.

They got me but they can't get at me, if you know what I mean. Do you know who I am? Fuck no. Shit, you're all fucking ignorant and clueless meatheads, except maybe that stacked nurse-whatever down there working over electrified spazzboy. Shit, he just fell down frothing again.

He scares me, but I love it. With him self-destructing, nobody notices me. On line back there in the hangar, waiting to go through the metal detector? They let my treasure come in along with my copy of *Advanced Calculus* from the university library with the exercises in the back filled in, and in ballpoint. I do them when I'm not logged on to *WoW,* where I rape and pillage under another name. They've taken away the good stuff and are checking what little I have left against their list: **Personal Items Allowed.** They've got my best toys and inside I am going *shit yourselves and die* and they're going, "He certainly has a lot of books." Then they see *Advanced Calculus* and eyebrows go up.

Captain Brainstorm, *come on down.* The motherfuckers are impressed. They'd be toast on *WoW* where I am at a level where few players dare to go. Plus me being charged with murder, what with everything. And the notebook is loaded but you assholes never gave it a fucking second look because you didn't have a clue.

Find a seventh-grader doing calculus and even Nazis will fall down creaming in their pants, to say nothing of the assholes checking us into this fucking jail, 235 IQ, they are sosooooo impressed.

So hey, the screws— excuse me, the guidance counselor and the assistant coach— just pushed that and the notebook containing important pieces of my brain through the turnbuckle and they were going hmmm, well, if the boy's *that* smart. And I cleared the metal detector without hearing a single *ping.* My hidden item went through right along with the other books the assholes let me keep because on paper, I'm so fucking smart.

I said what I said. "Goodbye cruel world."

Then. Holy fuck.

I heard something hit the cement with this terrible, sickening WHAP! It was this kid's skull. He just fell over. It hit so hard that I don't know why there wasn't any blood.

It turned out to be Teddy Regan, who was on line in front of me. Out of nowhere, this blond-haired nobody, this innocent who-me type crashed like a tree in a high wind. In two seconds this flyweight turned into a great big fucking infernal machine.

I guess he was having a fit.

Thank you, dude!

Spit everywhere. I picked up what remained of my shit and moved in for a closer look.

It turned him into something else. He was down there on the cement arching and spinning on his butt like a lunatic Frisbee or a break-dancer that the mad professor had ripped off from a wax museum and hot-wired. Like *that* this kid turned into a buzz saw with hands and feet whirling, yow!

This guy I hadn't exactly said hello to flew apart like an old-fashioned spring-wound toy, revolving faster and faster and he was kicking, lashing, fuck!

He almost fucking got me and I was crazy by that time, backing and going, "Help!" I guess I was squalling, at least I think that awful noise was coming out of me.

I was too wired to be embarrassed and too scared to know. I was, like, *Oh God oh God oh God get him away from me.*

So here's a thing about this place where they're taking us which for all I know is my mom's Death Row substitute, not too far out there, considering what I did. Even serial killers get their Last Request.

OK then. I have this, like. Last request?

When we get there, could you please lock this Teddy up somewhere safe? Like, far away from me. You could pad the walls and then he can flail to his heart's content and not get hurt? It's not like I want anything bad to happen to him, but wherever you put him would you please, please soundproof the place so next time it happens, I won't have to know?

The frothing part is scary, but that's not the scariest part. It was two seconds later when this boy my age turned into a chunk of white marble and lay there staring, like the *Evil Dead*. He was so totally not moving that flies could light on his eyeballs and skate around.

I don't care where they put this kid Teddy Regan as long as they don't put him in with me.

He might be an OK person when he's standing up which hasn't been lately but I'm here to tell you, what just happened wasn't only fucking gross and egregious and scary. It was like *The Texas Chain Saw Massacre*, and in a couple of places where he was flailing down there on the floor in the midst of all these great big strong assholes that were trying to subdue him, unconscious or out of his mind or what, the little fucker drew blood.

It isn't the getting hit that I'm scared of. It probably isn't the frothing or the out-of-body part. It's the you-never-know-when-or-what that comes with living with a kid who self-destructs without notice and either jets out of his body or stops being a person long enough to scare you shit.

Yeah I mouthed off when they lined us up in the hangar, but I don't think that was what set him off, so back off. You can fucking well forget what I said and if you can't forget it, at least forgive me, OK? Give me forty lashes, make an example, do what you want. Look. If you want me to, I'll apologize or whatever.

I mean, look at us lined up in this fucking hangar with the sky outside all maroon and us with zero idea of what was coming, which none of you fuckholes cared enough to tell us. What was I, hanging tough or being brave when I said what I said and freaked everybody out?

Goodbye cruel world.

I take it back!

Look. I don't care what you do to me once we get to this end-of-the-world lifeboat or reform school lockdown jail place you're taking us— which is what it is, no matter what Mom says. If you're putting me on Death Row for what I did, just kill me now, and if not? Listen. When you're assigning roommates? I don't care who it is.

As long as it isn't him.

He scares the crap out of me.

SEVEN

SARGE

"Goodbye cruel world."

Weird. A silence fell like an asbestos blanket dropped on the place from a great height. Then that reedy voice cut into it, sharper than a box-cutter. It was a kid, this weedy little smart-ass kid.

Killer Stade, who is shaping up to become a problem. Never should have taken him, although the terms are good. He does, after all, have a history. Lots of our clients have been to court for crimes and misdemeanors but as far as I know, he's the only murderer. He doesn't look like a risk, he looks like a snotty twelve-year-old, which is what he is. The little shit ruined Departure Day.

Where does a kid that size learn to project like a third-rate actor playing to an empty house? He filled the room:

"Goodbye cruel world."

It was like ripping a hole in a thunderhead. Smalls and nubiles and near-adults alike, my people began to cry.

The air in the hangar was thick with emotion.

A boy who had slipped through a loophole during the required pre-Admissions physical fell down in a seizure. It was quiet, skinny Frederick Regan, Dratch tells me we never should have let him in but I'm not sorry we took him. Hohenzollerns back there in the family tree, the parents rule a small but distinguished European country, they just didn't tell me what his problem was. Royal blood and he was frothing and howling like a little wolf. My heart went out. Kids around him began to cry. Soon all but the toughest were crying.

Even the staff was shaken.

It took several tries but Dr. Dratch injected heavy tranquilizers and my poor sick boy was still at last, shivering but quiet. He must have known that I would take care of him, after all, it's what we're here for. Besides, the royal family is paying plenty. He's doing fine now, in case you were worried. I put him in with Stade. He's a tough little bastard and not afraid of anything.

When Regan seized, the kids surrounding backed off as though they'd bumped into a corpse. You'd think death was contagious and they might catch it if they touched him.

At a nod from me, Chef Pete started handing out lunches in plastic clamshells as a distraction, even though it was late afternoon. His double chocolate cake is spectacular. The hangar fell quiet, but in a better way. The young sat on the floor with their heads bent, muttering thickly through chocolate.

Mine, I thought. It was exciting. *They are mine to form and watch over and take care of.* Whatever their lives were before they came here, I will make them better.

"Sarge." Cassie's voice was coming from a place I didn't know. "Why are you smiling?"

This is not a question I could answer. Not in the little time we had. "We're done here. Time to shove off."

Cass said, "It can't be."

Wardwell, my language teacher said, "Thank God that's over." You don't have to like kids to be an effective teacher.

"Well," Dave said in a cheery, let's-begin voice. Before Clothos, he was a motivational speaker. I need him, which doesn't mean I like him.

I put up my hand. "Soon."

Five more minutes for the lunches. Ten for hand wipes and trash disposal. There were toilets on the boat. It was almost time to begin boarding.

My heart leapt up. I turned to Cassie, full of joy. "It's beginning." I reached for her hand but she wasn't glad, she was upset. She jerked away. I saw her face crack open.

"I can't be here." She bolted up the ladder to the observation booth.

There was no stopping her. I followed. Outside the glass booth, streaks of orange chased each other across the sunset sky. It was maroon. "Cass!"

"Air!" Before I could stop her she smashed open the door and scrambled out onto the catwalk that ran along the tin roof.

I followed her out. The woman has been in this project from the beginning. She wasn't the first person to answer my ad, but she's the first person I hired, although her trip to the island came later. It isn't exactly love, but I'd die if anything happened to her. "Wait!"

"I just need some air!"

Outside, there was chaos. When you're as busy as we were you don't always hear signs of trouble. No, you don't want to hear it. Until we came up on the roof, Cassie and I had no idea how many there were, how angry they were, or how desperate. There were thousands.

How can people not understand what I mean when I tell them there is no wait list? Shipping magnates and studio chiefs were piled up out there, frantic to make me take just one more.

Instead of dispersing, they were still coming.

You can imagine what it was like. The sky above Crete was the color of blood— perfect background for the departure photograph. Our hovercraft waited at the dock just outside the hangar while on the hillside above us, the mobs swarmed over the crest and surged down, overflowing the narrow road and running over rocks, falling and getting up bleeding from the stony surface of the slanting hills that embraced the harbor. My books were closed. The chosen few were inside the hangar. Signed. Sealed. Delivered.

But still they came. And would not stop coming.

"Sarge." I thought Cassie would choke on her own grief. "We can't just leave them here."

"Shhh," I said. "We took everyone we could. In fact, I took a dozen extras. Can't that be enough for you?"

Her look told me it wasn't.

"I'm sorry, it has to be." What could I do? Let down an inch and you invite the deluge. They'd swamp the launch, ruin Clothos.

The Cretan police converged on the mob, marching downhill in full riot gear. They used Tasers, teargas, everything in their arsenal against this terrifying gang of rich, angry rejects, and dispersed them. Shore batteries would keep them from trying an attack by water; we had heavy wire netting jiggered to explode on contact; it would stay that way until the net parted and we left the harbor.

My hovercraft floated like a crouton in a soup bowl, waiting.

The boat whistle blew. We were close to departure.

I touched Cassie's arm. "We'd better go."

She pulled away.

"Are you OK?"

She couldn't answer.

I looked at Cassie. Tears sheeted her face. I gripped her wrist. "Do you not want to do this?"

"It's just so sad."

Below us, the hangar shook as the dockside Rolos went up. We heard the rush of feet as our student body surged forward. Rails shot into place and met the mesh overhead, securing dock and gangplank against escapes and intrusions. My hundred enrolled students would be filing out in another minute, clean and shorn and neat in their new uniforms— the chosen hundred along with the extra handful I'd taken for certain reasons. Some I took because I couldn't afford to send the parents away unsatisfied. There were the special others. It wouldn't take long to board them. I said, "No it isn't. It's business."

"Shit," Cassie said. She's only gets tough when her emotions threaten her. "Just, shit."

"Don't. We're only trying to help them." I pulled her along the catwalk to the harborside so we could watch the boarding. I thought seeing life march in order would reassure her. Bad timing.

At the top of the plank a boy broke loose and hurled himself through the narrow gap between the protective rail and the deck. A wave smacked the boat just as he plunged into the mess of foam that surrounded the hovercraft. Instead of hitting the water and escaping, he got fouled in the moorings as the boat pitched, trapping him between the chains. I pulled her away before the colliding links tore him to pieces.

"Oh God," she said, "this is so awful."

"Shhh. Shhh."

"That poor kid!"

"If they can help him, Cassie, I know they'll help him." We both knew nobody could.

Her voice went weird. "All the kids."

"Shhh, Cassie. Don't."

"But we're leaving."

"Don't," I said. I was a little *verklempt* myself. It was a very big step we were taking. "It isn't the end of the world."

Her voice dropped. She shot me a loaded look. "Or is it."

This is not a point I was prepared to address.

She sobbed. "It's just so final."

I grabbed my friend Cassie's arms and held her close so she

wouldn't see the bloody chunks in the spume. I murmured into her ear so she wouldn't hear the roar as our new students broke ranks and crowded the rails, screaming at the carnage. I sealed her ear with my mouth, filling it with sound. "Depends on what you need to think."

Like a snake she lashed back at me. "Or what you think you're doing!"

My look laid her open to the bone. "You know what we're doing."

"No," she said.

"You know it just as well as I do."

She sobbed. "I only know what you told me." Another sob; she couldn't help it. "It's just so final."

I hugged her close, shutting out her doubts along with a couple of my own. "Don't worry," I said for both of us. "Nothing's final."

Unless it is.

At the end some of them prayed, as though prayers would make room for one more when the boat was filled and the gangplank had gone up, when they were waiting for me to board so we could shove off and every dormitory bed on Mount Clothos was already committed. Never mind.

"One more," they cried. Screamed. Threatened. "Just one more!"

As if I alone could help them. In a way, that's true. Given the world the way it is, maybe I alone can help them.

You do what you have to do. We took off without looking back.

Everybody knows that when the boat sails, it is gone for good.

On Clothos, we are safe.

Secure. And thanks to good old Brother Benedictus, days in the Academy march in order. According to the rule. Now, what we do is not what the monks used to do, but my people are learning. Like the monks, we do things by the numbers: for Lauds, read Reveille. Think Taps instead of Compline. Daily repetition of the Hours, sweet and reassuring. Meals, classes, sports, all go by the clock, including time for reflection immediately following the last study hall of the night. Sweet old Benny's not too bright but he's my prop and my mainstay. He knows the discipline better than any. Look at him! Quiet, comfortable in the habit. At peace. He walks the halls like the outward and visible sign of what I'm trying to prove here.

Serenity comes with knowing what to do and when to do it. Monks know. So do Marines. We live according to the rule. Fortified by the numbers. The Order of the Day.

EIGHT

THE DAY THE ACADEMY HOVERCRAFT WENT OUT AND MR. Sargent and his staff came back with the promised students, Benny was frightened and excited. What would it be like with the cloister where he had lived for so long filled with outsiders?

With the basket relay, it would have taken days to board them all, but Sargent used his new hydraulic chute. The young people came up in groups. At first Benny was delighted. New postulants! Then they burst out of the capsule angry and frightened, punching and squabbling, and the real trouble began. There were too many. They were too loud. Who could observe the Grand Silence among children crowded, many of them, two to a room? This is not what he expected, he thinks, fretting. It's not what he expected at all.

Although he's much too shy to talk to the children, Benny sees the truth in their bewildered, angry faces.

It's not what they expected either.

Now the monks' renovated cells are filled with surly, silent teenagers and pushy smaller children all giggling and tumbling, running wild in the halls without caring what old man or which object they bump into and career off of, willy-nilly. They don't apologize, they just keep running. It's hard for Benny after a lifetime of the Grand Silence followed by more than a decade of solitude. It's just so hard.

Tonight he can hear every one of them breathing, a hundred alien souls rustling and turning, filling the night with wild, secular dreams that disrupt the Grand Silence. He should welcome them, after all, they are lost children that this man Sargent presumes to save, but from what, Benny wonders, and how? The Director goes on in that big voice about the end of the world, but at the end of the world, Benny knows, there will be only one Savior.

Then what are they doing here?

Why are the children so unhappy?

Benny can feel them, cluttering the air with the sound of their breathing. He knows in his bones which ones are still awake tonight, complaining and conspiring, and he knows which are laid out cold in their beds, flailing and cursing in their sleep. Although it's the dead of night and an outsider would assume that everything is quiet, Benedictus hears the clamor of a hundred restless souls trapped here on his mountain, struggling to be released.

The abbey at Clothos is his home, but the young intruders abuse the silence in ways that break his heart. Instead of listening for the silence and absorbing it, they lash out angrily, kicking the walls as though they think the cloister is a jail. Some have stolen forks and knives from the Refectory and gone to work on centuries-old doors; some are gouging away at the stone around unbreakable windows in an attempt to get out.

How could they get down the mountain if they did escape? He imagines the young intruders bunched on the narrow skirts of stone at the bottom of the mountain, staring out at waters where no boats come. What if they did make it down to the ocean?

What would happen to them then?

Benny shudders.

He wants them gone. He doesn't want them gone. For whatever reasons he feels sick all the time, now that they are here. These loud, reckless young people threaten his soul. They blunder around the cloister in groups, heedless and redolent of the outside world. They bump up against each other like animals, changing the quality of the air. They compromise the space the order kept pristine for so many hundreds of years.

He prays for the small ones. At night they cluster like puppies bunched together for warmth. There are others, like the frightened, angry near-women with their tightly packed, burnished bodies, that Benedictus fears, and there are the rude and defiant adolescent boys, the liars and the bullies, that he dislikes, but he prays for them.

He prays for them all.

The more he sees of Mr. Sargent's chosen students, the less Brother Benedictus likes them, but he prays for them anyway. Every night he goes into the vaulted assembly hall that used to be the chapel and says a prayer. First he asks the Holy Ghost to enlighten them so they can be happy here, for Sarge's sake.

Then he gets down on his knees and prays to God the Father to keep them safe.

NINE

KILLER STADE

So, Mr. Bogardus comes in steaming, "Do you know what time it is?" He flips on the light and glares at me. I am in the top bunk, which means we are pretty much eye to eye. The bed is rocking like a raft in a tsunami but up here I'm safe. All that and Mr. Bogardus is going, "I said, *do you know what time it is?*"

What does he think, I am ignorant? Fuck yes I know. This kid Regan is down there in the bottom bunk flailing like a broken BattleBot, and it's 4 A.M. in the morning. Teddy has been frothing and all since, in the dark it seemed like forever, and I want Mr. Bogardus to make it stop. I want not to *be* here, but all I can find to say is, "Help him."

Instead he goes, "Well, *do you?*"

It's the stupidest question he could ask so I go, "Like I give a fuck."

"Language!"

"He's spazzing." By this time Teddy has trashed the bottom

bunk and the whole bed is rocking like we are in *Exorcist I*. With the lights on it's even worse because if I hang my head over to check, I'll have to see him doing it. I am pretty much screaming. "Fucking do something!"

Mr. Bogardus goes, "That's enough!" He is trying not to look at Teddy.

"You have to do something!" I hate this place. I fucking hate this fucking place and don't you fucking tell me, "language" because I don't give a fuck what the fucking regulations are, and don't give me that look like you are wounded and, like, all disappointed in me. "And if you go 'language' one more time, I will fucking kill you."

"I didn't say, 'language.' I said, THAT'S ENOUGH."

"Fuck you, Mr. Bogardus . . ."

"Language!"

". . . just make it stop!" Then I snarl, but in no words Mr. Bogardus can make out. Below us I can hear Teddy, like, ratcheting up his guts. It sounds like they are coming out in long, pink snakes, it's enough to raise the dead and I can tell you, they will be screaming, SHUT UP!

And fucking Mr. Bogardus? He's all, "Cool it, Stade."

You'd think it was me causing the trouble here. Teddy Regan is fucking seizing down there, breaking up into a million little pieces like it's his very first time, and Mr. Bogardus isn't even thinking about putting a sock in his mouth so he doesn't bite his tongue off, or giving him a shot. The kid's a raving disaster and here is Mr. Bogardus looking at his fucking watch and hissing, "Do you know what time it is?"

His fake gold wristwatch is big as a Frisbee, no way he doesn't know the time. It's four-oh-five, asshole, but I'm not about to say it. He knows what time it is, I know what time it is. Time is not the issue here, it's Ted. "Why do you keep asking what time it is?"

He is getting all tired, which jazzes me. "I'm trying to make a point."

"Look at your fucking watch!"

"Oh, Killer. Language. You know Sarge doesn't like . . ."

"Fuck Sarge." I don't mean it! Unless I do. It's hard to know how to feel about a guy who comes on like a preacher or a world-class rock star. Like he could step up and save you from Whatever in a pinch. He has a face like one of those big stone idols in our art book, like, you can't tell if the guys in loincloths thought they were carving gods or devils or both. "And fuck you."

"Lang . . ."

"Don't."

I am defeating Mr. Bogardus. He tries, "Go back to bed."

"I'm *in* bed."

"Then settle down."

"I can't!"

"Good night, Stade. Don't bother me again."

Below me, Teddy sounds like he's winding down, but, really!

I like the kid when he's not falling down spazzing, but when he gets like this it scares me shit, OK, there. I said it. Plus, you never know when he'll do it again or how bad it will be. I am freaking to break the heart of a loving God, we've been in this hole three weeks and this is like, the fourth fucking time he's had a fit. I go, "What about Teddy?"

Mr. Bogardus bends over the bed like he's feeling Teddy's forehead and taking his pulse. Oh, yes he is pretending. Like Teddy can hold still long enough for anybody to lay a hand on him. Like I could hold still, with a fist punching my brain so far out of my body that I might never get it back. Real Teddy is out there somewhere, way far away from his head, which I don't even want to think about how it looks right now. His head, I mean, without Teddy in it. Like a dead person. I've seen it and I know.

Mr. Bogardus straightens up so we are eye to eye. He looks at me dead-on and lies in my face. "It's OK, Stade. He's OK. He's done. Now settle down."

I go a notch louder. "Fucking liar!"

At least he does not go, "Language." Instead he gives me a firm, "Night night," and although he can not bear to touch him, thwaps Teddy on the butt. "Night night."

"Wait!"

"Bedtime. Night night." He heads for the door.

*Don't go, Mr. Bogardus. Don't go. I **told you not to put me in here.** Stick me in Solitary if that's the only bed you've got, Mr. Bogardus. Throw me in the brig or push me off the edge of the fucking mountain, just get me out of here!* "Wait for me!"

"Bedtime!"

"I can't stay here!"

"But you will." He pushes me back into my bunk and goes out the door.

"Don't turn out the light!"

He turns out the light and leaves, like he can hardly wait to get out. Bastard, bastard. I am alone with, like, a dead person. No, worse. I can hear Teddy in the bottom bunk, he is banging around down there foaming like the dogs of *Doom* and Bogardus, bastard, bastard, he didn't do shit to help the kid, I hate this place.

I hate my life. Come back, damn you, just help him shut up and I'll do anything you want. I'll be good and I promise I'll be quiet, OK? I will get A's in every class. I promise I will never make any trouble for the whole rest of my life. Just shut him up or nail him down, OK? Put a rock on his head if you have to, and get me the fuck out of here.

"OK, don't come back. Be like that." In another minute I'll be foaming at the mouth and spazzing worse than Teddy. Then an idea comes to me. I go, "You'll pay." I don't know how yet, but I will do it. I will make him pay. I yell, "And I mean it!"

Like Mr. Bogardus can hear. By that time he is back in bed and I am right back where I started.

Alone with a sick kid and half a plan. Dunno how I'm gonna do this, but before this is over I'm going to get out and get even. Mr. Bogardus has to pay. He does. I'll get back at him for leaving us and I won't just be doing it for me, I'll be doing it for Teddy too. I hate the Academy. I hate Mr. Bogardus. I hate you all, I hate everybody in this fucking place except possibly Nurse Cassie, who is nice to kids and sweet to poor old Ted there even when he's spazzing, and I especially hate fucking Mr. Bogardus for putting me in with fucking Teddy Regan in the first place when I told them and I *told* them, he turns out to be the one who gave the order for us to double up.

Instead of giving me my very own room to my own self as promised in the brochure Mom showed me to get me to go along with this, Bogardus matched us up on Departure Day. She made certain promises. The rest happened fast.

Shit, I only went along because of the brochure. Well, that and that the police investigation hadn't closed and their only suspect was me. INTEGRITY OF PERSONAL SPACE it said right there, with a picture of this cool room like you would want if you were going to college. Bookshelves. Places for all your action figures. Lockers for your personal things.

"I don't want to go to boarding school."

Mom said, "Think, sweetie. It's a lot better than jail."

She had a point.

Single room, guaranteed. In a place so far away from home that they'll never catch up with me. A place for all my stuff— that is, all the stuff they let me bring, which wasn't much. My books. Pens. There are laptops in the room, but, shit. No Internet, which I didn't know at the time. I never would have come. I would have jumped off that fucking boat and fucking drowned like that other kid.

Crete was kind of pretty, in an ugly way. The rest, not so much. When we finally got inside the hangar they took my stuff. They did it before Mom signed the final agreement. Then they, like, handed me a tag that said I would be in a double room.

I was like, "Mom. Mo-ooo-m, this is a gyp!"

But she just smiled like fucking Judas, going, "Sweetie, this is for your own good." So you've gotta wonder, did she know about the double room when she paid the money and signed off on me, did she already know how shitty it would be?

Well, fuck you, Mom, and don't go telling me about how you sold the penthouse and all your jewels especially to save me from Armageddon, that probably isn't even true. If I can't skateboard or run free in the mall or hang out where I want when I want with whoever I want, if I can't meet my friends on *World of Warcraft*, who the fuck cares if the world blows up and you paid a bundle to keep me alive?

Trust me, death by firestorm looks better than this creepy, weird, *weird place*. Truth now. If you'd known it sucked, would you have signed anyway?

Don't answer that!

Fuck, I'm only in here because of what happened.

Mom, it was an accident!

When this really bad thing went down with Mr. Berringer that day after school, when they finally caught me and brought me in, Mom came down to the police station and boy, she was pissed. She never asked me what really went down or how it came down. I tried to tell her but the bitch didn't give me two seconds to explain. She just paid off the Director and bought off the cops and turned me over to Sarge.

Like that. On Crete.

We were coming down to the wire. By that time there were overflow people coming down on the fence outside, begging Sarge to let their kids ship out with the rest of us, like cows floating off to get turned into steaks.

It was the next-to-last minute and Mom still wouldn't let me tell her what really came down that bad day after school. *It was an accident!* We were down to the wire. She was about to go. It was embarrassing, I was sort of crying. "Just let me come home, I promise, I'll never do it again."

"Honey, don't look at me like that." She smoothed her hair and pulled on her gloves. "I just know you're going to love it there."

I shouted, "You can't leave me here. You can't fucking leave me here!" I begged, but she was in high departure mode. I was, like, dying, so who gives a fuck, really? Who gives a fuck about me but me? "Mom. Mo-om!"

Mom, I didn't mean to do it.

Too late for that, right? My mouth was still going, but she squished me to her squashy front so she wouldn't have to hear. I pounded on her until she let me go. Then I totally lost it. I don't remember what I said.

She left me anyway. Shit, if you want to know the truth I was desperate but she backed out fast so she wouldn't have to deal. There were, believe me, a lot of parents leaving fast. I yelled some things. She kept on backing. Then it was too late. She was so, soooo out of there.

Mr. Bogardus mooshed me and Teddy together right there on the deck. The truth was they didn't have enough rooms for the kids they took because Sarge overbooked, but Mr. Bogardus was all sanctimonious. He went, "Don't fight it, Stade. This is for your personal development."

They stuck me in with Teddy, and that was AFTER he had the fit.

I fucking hate this fucking place. It's nothing like Sarge promised when he lined us up on deck for his welcome speech. When the big guy gets going, its like one of the gods stepped down off his throne to talk to you.

You'd follow him anywhere. Well, fuck Sarge. I don't give a rat-fuck what he had to do to get us off Crete in one piece that day, like, they were after us and the skipper had to boogie to get shut of them, whoever they were. It's not like I wanted to go, I'd have jumped off the boat and gotten chopped into shark bait like that other kid, if it hadn't been for the razor wire and the guys with rifles lining the rails, plus there were so many rows of us jammed in side by side by side by side that it was hard to breathe and I couldn't move. I don't care about the reasons, there is no way in hell that I can live like this.

I mean, Teddy's OK and all, but when his eyes roll back in his head and his teeth get all pointy and weird, you know sure as shit that he'll be whipping around like a live wire in another minute and one of us is going to get hurt.

It isn't the fit that's so awful, it's waiting for it.

Plus, just now, after Mr. Bogardus left? It got quiet. Like they used to say in the movies, too quiet.

Then he says, "I was sick as fuck."

And I say, "Language."

And we both start laughing.

I hang my head over the edge and shine my flashlight into the bottom bunk, where Teddy is looking a lot like a store dummy or a stone Ken doll. Interesting, since the last time I looked, he was twisted around like a broken Slinky in a car wreck. "That fuckhead Bogardus," I say. "He was supposed to . . ."

". . . give me a shot. He's afraid to touch me," Teddy says.

Ugh! "Sorry about that."

At the same time he is saying, "Sorry about that." Then he goes, "I hate when that happens."

So I go, "Me too."

We are, OK, bonding.

Now, I know what I'm doing in stir, but this kid Teddy is, like, your chronic good boy, looks like an ad for a school for gifted kids, smiles, mostly, always knows the answers in class but is too cool to tell. He's the kind who always does his homework, makes his bed, washes up and combs his hair before dinner, gets places on time. I know why I'm here, but, why did they send Teddy Regan here?

I check him out. Now that he isn't spazzing he looks a lot more normal than me. As for the fit, he's over it but he isn't quite over it. He has to lose the shakes or he'll never sleep.

I'm way too pissed off to sleep so I decide to talk him through. "So. What are you in for?"

"Do you mind not shining that thing in my face?"

"Sorry." I turn it off.

He tells me, "That's better," but that isn't what he means. It turns out there are things you can only talk about in the dark. Finally he says, "I'm here because my family doesn't want the people to see."

"See what?"

"'Member what I just looked like? 'Member that?"

"Yeah."

"Scary, right?"

I don't want to talk about it, so I don't.

"They're afraid the people will find out we have bad blood."

"What?"

He chokes it out. "They think if I have a fit in public, the people will use it to depose us and overthrow the crown."

I ask him, "What people?" when I really mean, *What crown?*

"*The* people, stupid. They watch us. It's like being on the big screen all the time. Like, when we have to line up on the balcony and wave at them on holidays, at Christmas they come with field glasses so they can see us sitting in the open carriage for the parade. They're, like, watching us all the time."

Doh! "Oh, you're the prince guy."

"Pretty much."

Mom told me there would be royalty on Clothos, like that

would make me want to come. It was right there in the brochure. It went, CHOICE OF THE ROYAL FAMILY, it just didn't say which one. Mom is, OK, a social climber, so I ask, "Um, did somebody *pay* them to stick me in with you?"

"Probably."

"Stupid Mom, like she thinks I'll marry your sister and turn into a king."

"It wasn't her." Now he is all embarrassed. The words are really hard for him to spit out. "They're scared to let me sleep alone."

I'm sorry, it just pops out. "Well I'm scared to sleep with you!"

"I'm sorry."

"Oh shit, I didn't mean it."

"It's OK," Teddy says, "When I get like that nobody wants me around. I have *grand mal*. That's French. So they stuck me in here." His voice goes into the dark shadows. "It wasn't my tutor's idea, like they told me. It was them. Not Mom, maybe, but my dad, I'm certain. He can do anything he wants because he's king."

"But he told you this is for your personal development." I groan because I know.

"Right. See, if they don't have to watch it happen, they can go along la la la, pretending that there never was a me."

"That sucks."

"Totally." Then he says, "That isn't the real reason."

"What?"

"Sometimes when I get like that— like, when I fall out?" It's like watching a spooky horse: all teeth and white rings around the eyes. "I see things before they happen."

"No shit!"

"I saw somebody shoot my grandfather, and then they did. I think they're afraid of me."

"Awesome!" Teddy is waiting for me to freak so I go, "I didn't mean it about the being scared to sleep here," although it is a lie. As he doesn't answer I guess he knows it, so I go, "It's fine. Really."

He doesn't say anything.

"You're an OK roommate."

"When I'm not . . ."

"Yeah." We are both sadder than fuck. To make at least one of us feel better I say, "Wanna know how I got my name?"

"You're gonna tell me even if I don't."

"OK then." Like Teddy, I am glad we are talking in the dark. For me this is like hauling a bucket out of a deep, deep well.

He goes, "OK what?"

"It turns out I killed a guy."

"Holy fuck."

"Yeah. I didn't, like, murder him, I more kind of, like, exploded him?" Teddy's gonna know this is not really a question. It's just the way we talk.

"Cool!"

"Not really. It was an accident. My fault for taking stuff out of the lab after science class. Two things that if you mixed them, stuff blew up. I was gonna explode something at home, you know, in the back yard. Except on the way home this guy came along? And offered me a ride?"

"Dude, you hadda know better." For a prince guy, Teddy is extremely cool. "The guy must have seen you coming and . . ."

"That isn't it."

"You mean, you didn't see him coming."

"No. I did. The thing is. The thing is . . ." It takes me a while to tell him the worst part because it was so obvious and I was so fucking stupid. "It was somebody I knew."

"Fuck."

"Language!"

We laugh, but it is a nervous laugh.

"It was a *teacher*. This Mr. Berringer, that taught Latin at our school? Clean shirt, nice car, nice smile. So I got in the car and yeah, you should of been there. You'd have known what was coming, but stupid me, he was my teacher so I trusted him. He was driving me the long way, no problem, he was my teacher after all, we were having this discussion about Latin verbs. So I just went along and went along until we didn't turn at my corner and I was like, 'Mr. Berringer, where are we going?' And he was all, 'I just want to show you my *special place.*'"

We don't need to go on with this part. I cut to the chase.

"So I mooshed the one plastic bag into the other plastic bag inside my backpack and jammed it on his dork and jumped out of the car. Bottom line, I blew the bastard up."

"That's awesome!"

"That's not what everybody said." Then I stop talking and Teddy doesn't say anything and we both lie there in the dark, thinking. Then I ask him, "What did they tell you to get you to come to this fucking place?"

Teddy says, "They said the world is ending soon, and this is my only chance to make it into the future. Like, they had bought me into the last safe place, the Academy is the second Ark."

"Right," I say, and I am getting bitter, "and all about how they gave up everything to send us here."

We are falling into a rhythm. Teddy parrots, "And they weren't sending us away, they were saving us."

Why does this sound so familiar? "Right."

"I told them I'd rather burn up or whatever with them."

"And my Mom was like . . ." As I say this it occurs to me that these things were scripted. "I am her gift to the future."

Teddy sighs. "Right. Plus, they were doing it for our sake."

We chorus, "For our own good."

"About our parents . . ." For a long time we listen to Teddy thinking. It doesn't make much noise. He just drums his fingers on the bedcovers, *tappa tap tap. Tappa tap.* Then he says, "If it's all that fucking dangerous out there, wouldn't they be shoving us overboard so they could climb onto the raft?"

"Oh fuck," I say.

Teddy says, "Oh, fuck."

TEN

SARGE

The intake interviews are almost finished. So am I. Four an hour all day every day, since I have to classify every one of these kids before making any major decisions on policy.

We all know nobody came willingly. Getting them to stay is another matter. To a kid, they claim they'd rather take their chances out there in the universal earthquake or tsunami or atomic holocaust or whatever triggers the end, but when it comes down to the tough rock bottom of it, they're pretty much committed to saving their hides. After I lay it out for them— we are the last safe place, I follow with a question period.

Bogardus helped me craft all-purpose answers that settle them down for the short term, at least. With the D'Estart girl I finish ten minutes of careful explanation with the usual, "Any questions?"

On the body language meter, Sylvie D'Estart is scoring zero. She gives me a glassy stare.

"You understand, you're here for your own protection."

This is when they're supposed to thank me.

Some of them do, but not Sylvie D'Estart, who arrived on Clothos in a rage, along with her posse. These teenaged celebrity hags sans sexy outfits and minus the tats and cascading diamond studs that pass for personality are harder. Uniformed and deglamorized, they are still bitches. I wait.

Finally I prod. "This will be good for you."

She has to sit here until I end the interview. To speed things along, she performs an eye-rolling "Sheesh" straight out of *A Child's Garden of Expressions*. You've seen it on the covers of all those checkout counter magazines. Gets up as if that passes for an answer.

"Not so fast. You know why you're here, right?"

She yawns. "The 'rents are getting rid of me?" *Take that.*

"They're saving you." *Back atcha.* I don't know if I'm pissed at her for arguing or pissed at myself for arguing back.

"Yeah, right." Not a very big deal, batting your eyes when your false eyelashes are back on Crete along with the rest of the you-go-girl crap you brought, providing 'tude for a whole new owner. "Like this isn't a great big Dumpster."

Shit. She knows the truth. "Look," I say. "It's better than jail."

"This *is* jail."

"Right. OK then. You'll do your service hours on bathroom detail."

"Toilets!" She sticks out that arrogant jaw, product of generations of WASP inbreeding. "Do you know who I am?"

"I know exactly who you are. Toilets. Showers. Floors."

"And you're doing this to me . . . why?" It's clear that she's forgotten how she looks. Dirt rings hang around her famous neck and that trademark hair is lank and greasy.

I dismiss her with, "Training in personal hygiene."

Zander Birch is another matter. Keeps himself immaculate, which is not the problem here, just don't say *he* in his presence. Nice kid. Tries to do the right thing. Bright, alert, eager to please, no problem, really, except that he's my biggest problem. Multiple shrinks failed to change his mind, and. What's on his mind? He wants to change.

Starts sobbing before I can open his folder. I don't need the file. We both know the story.

Kid thinks he's a girl, when what I see is the product of the drunk on the assembly line who dropped this engine inside the wrong body. In short, he feels pretty. He just doesn't look it. Why is it always the hulking louts who want to transgender? Thirteen, and he showed up for Departure Day in high drag, either to prove something or to spite his father. Either way, he came out of intake without the mini and the fishnet pantyhose and the silver earrings that looked like jointed fish. In the uniform, he could be any guy. Six months of illegal hormones, according to his file, electrolysis, and with the regulation haircut, he looks like a fullback on steroids. The only thing missing is the stubble. The kid is miserable.

Like all the others, he is fighting this. End of the world hell, he wants his freedom.

This makes me groan. Anything I say about the advantages the Academy offers will be wasted but I have to try. "He's doing this for your own good, Zander."

His voice goes somewhere else. He must have been practicing. "Alexandra." Shit, it convinces me.

"Alexandra. See, the world is . . ."

"He doesn't care what the world is. He wants me to die."

This raises a question I am not prepared to beg, so I tell the kid, "I'm sorry about the no hormones."

Another sob. "He threw them out of the car."

"OK," I say. *If you will just stop crying!* I don't usually do this but I ask, "Is there anything we can do here to help you?"

"Let me go."

"Not an option."

"Let me die."

"Neither is that. We have to figure out how to get you through your time here."

"How long is that?"

"I can't say." To forestall the obvious questions I create a diversion. "So, OK. Hormones are not an option here. Neither are the outfits. What are we going to do about you?"

"You're not going to let me bunk with the girls, are you." It is not a question.

"No."

He's getting cranked up to tell me why he came in here sobbing. "I don't belong with the boys."

"I put you next to a dorm parent so they wouldn't beat the crap out of you."

"Mr. Bogardus doesn't like me."

"What do you want? I gave you a single."

"I want to eat at the girls' table."

"Like that's gonna work."

"I need people who *get* me." He's pushing hard. "Back home I had girl friends. I mean, friends that were girls."

"That's not an option, Birch."

"Alexandra." His eyes are filling up again. "Girls, like, girls *get me* instead of trying to beat the crap out of me. At home they used to help me with my hair and now look." With the regulation haircut, he is a living reproach. "And you won't even let me wear lipstick."

"I'll do what I can with what I've got here, um, Alexandra. Bogardus will help you. He's a clinical psychologist."

"He picks his nose and flips it at me."

"For crap's sake, don't cry!" I am thinking fast. "Tell you what. I'll get you an hour with Ms. Rivard. Woman to. Ah. Woman, OK?"

He does not brighten. I can see the whites of his eyes.

"Look, in a lot of ways she's better at getting inside people's heads than Bogardus."

But the kid is too quick for me. "I don't need a shrink, I need a surgeon. You know what kind."

Crap this is hard. "Uh. I thought maybe talking to another woman would help." Bingo. When I said "another woman" just then, I saw him blush.

Still, he is wary. "Aren't you going to tell me this girl thing is all in my mind?"

As far as I know, it pretty much is. Unless it isn't. I don't have enough imagination to get inside this kid's head. "I don't know what to tell you, except hang in and I'll see what I can do."

What this means, I can't begin to guess.

This boy is smarter about life than his father thinks. "You have a very good attitude."

"I'm not famous for it."

"You didn't tell me to shape up or ship out."

"OK then, Alexandra." Shit, I didn't. Look at the kid, staring at me with those big, confusing eyes. Am I growing soft in the job? I cough, but she doesn't leave. I try, "Yeah, well." To end this, I have to lie. "It's. Ah. It's almost time for my next inter-view."

Unlike everybody else I've seen today, Alexandra leaves the of-fice smiling. Unlike the other kids she says, "Thanks, Sarge."

Next up is Teddy Regan. There is no sales pitch needed here, no list of explanations, no discussion about the nature, timing or placement of the end of the world. Whether it ends or not, it's all the same to him. I cut to the chase. "You know you're in here for the long haul, right?"

"It's as good a place as any," Regan says on a note that tells me he's sad and that he's been sad ever since the first time he fell down in public years ago and far away from this place. He understands better than any of these ignorant kids what he's doing here. Unlike the sex maniacs and borderline detoxers in the upper forms, unlike the major felons and the chronic car thieves among the celebrity kids, this boy never did anything bad to anybody, I see that in his record.

The only bad thing he ever did was embarrass the royal family. The seizures are getting more public and more frequent. Not the kind of thing the rulers want their subjects to know. God damn them all for making a perfectly nice boy look at me the way he does.

Too much time sitting in my office with the door closed, too much time looking into too many sad, sad eyes has leached the living blood right out of me. There is no yes, aye or no here, there is only me feeling guilty for doing what I'm doing and taking the top off the royal treasury in exchange for doing it.

Now, I don't care what happens with the royal family of a third-rate casino country, but I'm feeling like shit about the citizens and I feel bad for this kid whose only transgression is having a brain that electrifies him like an industrial-strength Taser. I want to give him everything I have but all I can come up with is, "I'm sorry."

Then the youngest son of a family that's been ruling since the Huns and Vandals stopped kicking each other around gives me the second smile I've gotten out of a long day of interviews and he says, "Don't worry, it's nothing you did. And it's not anything I did."

Dammit to fuck, kid. Stop *smiling*. I have to get rid of him. "One, if there's nothing more that I can do for you . . ."

Then he says out of nowhere, "Well, there is one thing."

"Extra desserts, Prozac for Killer," I tell him. "You name it."

Before I can get it out, he starts shaking his head.

I say, "Lecture on the meaning of life and the truth about the universe?"

"No thanks. Just. Who's that weird guy I see bopping around in the halls every night?"

"What?"

"Every night since we got here. He's just *around*."

"Beats me. Must be staff." Shit, I think. Security in the living quarters? Dratch on a bender? Is Wardwell slipping his moorings?

"I don't think so. He's too weird."

"Describe him."

"Tall," he says, "long without being skinny. Hair down his back," he says.

I am flipping through the Rolodex in my head. "What else?"

"Black hair, blacker than anything you see in the movies and this white, white skin."

"Nobody on the roster like that." My mind is racing. Coach Askew in drag? Some mad monk that Benny never told me about?

"In the dark he looked like he was glowing."

"You're sure."

"I never saw skin like that, not even in the hospital."

There is no way to ask nicely. "Does your, um, disorder ever make you, ah. Hallucinate?"

"Trust me, I can tell the difference."

By this time I am desperate to change the subject. "Could be a ghost. This heap is plenty old enough."

"I know what I saw."

I am embarrassed by his scorn. "Regan, I'm sure you do. OK then." The bell rings for evening mess. I've been sitting here that long. I get up. "Well, that's it for today."

"Aren't you going to . . ." He is sitting there looking bilked.

"Follow up? Sure, and that's a promise. Tell you what." No time for this, I am thinking. Not the time to let this kid and his imaginary friend drop a wrench into the gears, not now that we are up and running. I throw it back into his lap. "Start a log. Note the times and circumstances of each sighting. We'll get to the bottom of this."

I see him weighing it. My promise, measured against the way things are. "But sir."

I like the guy. I don't want to embarrass either of us by letting

him know I've assessed the situation and drawn my own conclusions. Before I turn smartly and exit the office I drop his wild card
back in his lap. "You're in charge. Come back when you can give
me enough to go on."

ELEVEN

CASSIE IS ON HALL DUTY, A JOB SHE CAN DO FROM HER DESK. The glassed-in cubicle sits at the junction, where the four wings of the abbey meet. From here she can see everything that goes on in the halls. Until the lunch hour is over and Sarge's students are back in their classrooms, she's in charge.

It's her job to keep order and if necessary, to break up fights, but nothing happens here. In the three weeks she's been working this shift, nothing has. If only somebody would cut loose and holler. If only they'd fight! Where lunch hour in any normal school is a madhouse, these kids go past like little sleepwalkers, wandering from here to there.

It's as though the Academy has broken their spirit, and it worries her. These kids' well-being is her responsibility now. With Mel Dratch drunk half the time and barely functional, it's her responsibility.

Here at the crossroads of the cloister, Cassie watches, and she waits for at least one child to ask for help. If they don't need help, could they at least speak to her? They don't make eye contact as they shuffle by the booth. It's not kids freezing in front of adults, either; they're the same wherever they are now. Cassie knows.

From where she sits, she can see everything.

The monks built their abbey on a cruciform plan, with the chapel at the head. Massive carved wooden doors protect the Benedictines' place of worship; now it is the Assembly Hall. She can barely make out the paler patches of wood where religious devices were planed off.

To her right is the Academy's classroom wing, to her left the hallway that opens on public rooms: lounges, Refectory, kitchen and, at the end, Sarge's office. At her back is the dormitory wing, with its swinging doors to the Infirmary marking the far end. Behind those doors she has everything ready: meds, instruments and dressings locked in steel cases, neat white coverlets tight on two dozen beds. In case.

Something stirs in the dusky hallway and her head comes up. She sees Brother Benedictus dart out of the shadows, heading for the massive wooden doors to the Assembly Hall. One opens a crack and the old monk slips inside. Sweet guy, he probably forgets it isn't a chapel any more. She wonders what he makes of the red banner above the lectern, with its Marine Corps emblem embroidered in gold. Sarge's renovations changed a lot, she thinks. Just not the nature of this place. The silence never really went away. Look at the kids gliding along these halls. They go along with their heads down like little monks. As though something is weighing them down.

Sometimes in the night she thinks she hears chanting, but that's not what's bothering Cassie today.

It's the kids. She is especially worried about the girls. The lively, overtly sexy teenagers she first saw on Departure Day are doing badly here. Not because they are making trouble, really. Because they aren't.

The school's dozen divas pass the nurse's cubicle several times a day, with the infamous Marla Parsons and Sylvie D'Estart in the lead. Famed, really, for starring in lurid YouTube videos and thoroughly reported busts for various offenses, all dutifully reenacted on reality TV, the skanky little wildcats. What are they, fifteen? From here she sees Marla and Sylvie and their posse, a dozen girls shambling back and forth to class like so many rag dolls, boneless and devoid of energy. It's troublesome. Three weeks in this place and they've lost the flashy glamour that made them who they used to be.

On Departure Day Marla and Sylvie and their posse of glossy heiresses and Hollywood brats stormed into the hangar like late-model Brat Packers, doomed to celebrity. Brash in spangles and heavy makeup, with spangled pantyhose covering the distance between their stilettos and their microskirts, these girls were amazing. They were sassy and brassy, fresh from magazine cover shoots and personal reality shows on E!, haughty and bright and gaudy, switching along like floats in the Rose Bowl parade.

What's happened to them?

All the showy, embarrassing baby celebs who made headlines and humiliated their fathers or shamed their moms with their drug habits and celebrated brawls, minis that barely covered those smoothly waxed pussies, chandelier earrings and overstated hair, all those YouTube starlets with their operatic breakups and rush trips to rehab are bland as oatmeal now.

As mild as milk.

Famous for being infamous, these girls have fallen into line so smoothly and quietly— so fast!— that it's as though they've always lived here in the Academy.

Cassie has to wonder. Is it the Academy mystique that did this to them, or something Sarge whispered in their ears? Is it the hush in the abbey that made them lose touch with who they are? It's hard to know. Cassie has no idea what the monks were like, chanting in the chapel, walking in orderly lines. She can't begin to guess what secrets are buried here. It's as though the vaulted roof of the converted monastery closed on these kids like the lid of a jewel box, muffling all sound. They move like marbles on velvet here, gliding along silently, without touching. Separate. Hushed.

Remodeling, Sarge moved heaven and earth to erase every reminder of the building's past. There's nothing left to tell his students that monks used to live and worship here. The last incense fumes blew out of the place years ago. What makes these kids go along in a hush, too timid to talk in church? Why are they so subdued?

For more than one reason, Cassie is concerned. Sarge is going to great lengths to help them, but they aren't doing very well. If they hate the place, why aren't they acting out? She knows enough about people to know that rebellion doesn't go away overnight. There are stages. Kids fight it. They argue. They have to grapple with authority until they come out the other side. They have to go through all the stages on the way to reconciliation and understanding.

Then they can look back at the idiots they used to be.

After which, she thinks sadly, *they just might change.*

These kids don't argue. They don't fight. They're indifferent. They shamble along like little zombies, neither here nor there.

Their bizarre inability to care is disturbing, but Cassie has a worse problem. What if it's an early symptom of some condition she doesn't know about? What if they're in the early stages of disease? God knows what bacilli thrive in the bats in the undercroft, or what's in the water and what colonies of bacteria lurk in the crevices of this old place. In case of illness, she is the last line of defense.

It wasn't supposed to be this way.

She came here because Sarge said there would be a doctor on staff. Getting a qualified GP was his first priority, but it turned out to be the last position he filled. Dr. Dratch looked good on paper. MD from Johns Hopkins, residency at the Mayo Clinic. His resume was flawless but they should have known.

Only a desperate person or a damaged one would sign an open-ended contract to work on an isolated peak with no escape clause and no set finish date. Everybody on this staff has a story. If they didn't, they wouldn't be here. Either they're running away from something or they have something to hide. Most, like Cassie, are here to get past some private grief, but it stands to reason that the situation would dish up at least one disaster.

Theirs is Mel Dratch, MD, PC. Instead of turning up when the staff first came on board the Academy's boozy doctor arrived with his stash the night before Departure Day, too late for Sarge to hire a replacement.

Sarge confiscated the booze but next morning the good doctor staggered onto the hovercraft cackling, he'd figured out how to get drunk anyway. He was so hammered that Cassie took over after the first few inoculations went wrong. When the Regan kid had his seizure in the hangar, Dratch ripped the boy's arm in several places before he got the needle in. Sarge has turned out Dr. Dratch's quarters several times and come up empty, but Mel lurches into meals and assemblies smelling of rum. The old fool has figured out how to compound the stuff— a miracle of compression, she thinks. With no raw materials and no equipment that they can find, the man can make bona fide 90 proof hooch. He ought to patent the process and get rich, but how? Communications are limited to interoffice business. Nothing goes out from the island and no messages come in.

Nobody leaves until Sarge declares the mission completed and releases them. It's in the contract they all signed. They are here for the duration, whatever that means. If push comes to shove and one of these kids comes down with something, they are stuck with Cassie and Dr. Hand Tremor here, whose brain hung up an OUT TO LUNCH sign years before he arrived.

In the start-up phase Sarge went to great lengths to make the island safe. He's told them about the shore batteries. He says there's a shield— ions, something. She doesn't know. He had nice Steve Joannides put up an impregnable firewall to defend the Academy computer system from viruses, worms, anything out there that might compromise the network. "With this firewall, all our computers are bulletproof. Nothing gets in and nothing can take us down," he told her, and like a dumb broad watching her football hero make a Statue of Liberty play, which she used to do when they were kids back in Beaufort, Cassie sat in the bleachers going, clap clap clap.

What was she thinking?

The electronics may be virus-protected but where physical health is concerned. . .

Cassandra Rivard, thirty-four and still counting, Cassie, who stands five-four and weighs 120 soaking wet, is the firewall.

Disease travels fast in closed communities. If anything happens, she's in charge.

Sarge had everybody on Clothos immunized against every conceivable evil, but you never know. There are diseases out there that even doctors don't know about. Diseases they know about but can't cure. If the unforeseen strikes even one of these people, if even one kid comes down with anything that might be remotely contagious, it's up to Cassie to isolate the patient before it spreads, and Dr. Dratch?

Drunk in his room.

Cassie may be a lot of things, but she is not careless. She doesn't go out looking for trouble, but the possibility makes her vigilant. It keeps her alert.

This is what bothers her about the older girls.

Something is not right.

Maybe they're depressed. They damn well should be. Those uniforms. This place.

She isn't sure.

Hell's divas are, quite simply, not themselves. Three weeks in this place, and look how it's changed them. On Departure Day they stalked into that hangar like supermodels, switching their butts like upscale hookers cruising Times Square. Now they drift through the halls with their heads bent.

As though they aren't using their bodies, just inhabiting them.

It's sad. She watches them for symptoms, but there are none that she can see: no coughing, no runny noses, nobody turning green at the sight of food. Passing the famously raunchy Marla Parsons in the hall, Cassie trailed her hand across the girl's cheek, checking for fever. Marla's face is cool. So is Sylvie D'Estart's. These adolescent glamour queens came in looking like thirty-somethings, but the passports Sarge collected set the median age as fifteen— God what were they doing driving drunk? With their skins scrubbed clean and eyes devoid of makeup, they look twelve. Raucous, feisty and aggressively sexy when they first came, they were beautiful in their own way. Now look.

They are different people here.

Sylvie and Marla and their posse come out of the Refectory with their heads down, shuffling like old women in their regulation crepe-soled shoes, a cruel 360 from the spiky Manolos and Jimmy Choos they tottered in on, flaunting their beautiful legs. Sarge says he ordered rubber shoes to protect the ancient stone floors and staircases, but Cassie is not so sure.

If you take away a peacock's plumage, do you break its spirit? She doesn't know. She does know that when Sarge laid out his designs for school uniforms, he was proud. Frowning, she squinted at sketches of neat jumpers, boxy sweaters, neat shirts that needed no ironing, shapeless blazers with epaulets.

He saw her expression. "What's wrong?"

"I don't know."

"It's part of my incentive program. If they do well, they get gold stripes on their shoulder boards."

She couldn't help it: her voice sank. "Oh."

To cheer her, Sarge handed her a swatch of gray flannel. "A man in Edinburgh is making them to order. What do you think?"

He seemed so proud. She was more than half in love with him. "Do they have to be gray?"

"It's a nice, neutral color," Sarge said. "Fits in with what I'm trying to do."

"You never explained."

"You'll see it happening," he said with a visionary grin. "It's like watching the Creation at ground zero on Day One."

"But, uniforms!"

He gave her a look. "It's part of the plan. To form a person, first you have to break them down."

"You're scaring me."

"It's hard to explain."

"You're taking away their freedom. Isn't that enough?"

"It's for their own good."

"You're taking away their identity!"

Sarge grinned that infrequent thousand-watt grin. "My point. Doesn't matter where they come from or what they used to have. They are all equals here."

"But uniforms, Sarge. They're not prisoners."

"The uniform is the great equalizer," Sarge said. He never lets her forget that he used to be a Marine. "Take it from me. In the Academy, we earn our stripes."

She didn't mean to grimace; she couldn't help it. "It's just so . . ."

"Don't." He gripped her hand and that old electric shock went through her. She loves him but he was trying too hard to explain.

"I'm looking for the real people under makeup. No more trading on their looks."

"Girls don't travel on their looks, Sarge. They care about how they look." Cassie summed it up: "Their *look*. You know."

Snapshot of Sarge, not getting it.

"It's about self-respect." She wasn't sure he caught the distinction. "They want to prove they're individuals."

But Sarge was fixed on something Cassie couldn't see. True visionary, the bastard. With that resolute glare, he looked like a statue of himself. After some thought he said, "First, they have to find out who they are. Trust me."

She does but she doesn't. He doesn't understand women, that's clear. Cassie developed her own look years before she hit junior high. It's something girls do. They have to do it to set themselves apart— or prove that they belong. Both, she supposes. She defeated the high school dress code with costume jewelry hidden in her hair, regulation necktie worn with a flip, superhero buttons pinned to the underside of her collar. She defied them by rolling her waistband to shorten her pleated uniform skirt. There was no explaining this to Sarge. As far as he was concerned, the discussion was over. She sighed. "OK, if you want uniforms, then, fine. Uniforms."

"Agreed."

"Whatever you put on these girls," she warned, "it's all about the look. They'll find a way."

When he shook his head, she didn't argue. She just thought: *he'll see.*

She was wrong. Three weeks, and these girls have nothing going on. Partly, she supposes, it really is the uniforms. Heavy gray wool can weigh a person down, but that isn't really what's going on. Cassie has been in the world long enough to know that a sexy girl in a croker sack can still flirt.

Not here. The older boys and girls pass in the halls without missing a beat. They don't speak; they don't bother to look up. Marla and her posse file past as though they no longer care. Those brilliant flirts with glittering eyes are passive and expressionless now. They show no interest in the boys shuttling back and forth on their way to class and— this is troublesome— the boys have little or no interest in them.

In ordinary circumstances they'd be yearning and leering whether the girls noticed them or not. Here, they pass *this close* without looking up to see who just went by. Boys and girls alike have lost all interest in the bodies inside the uniforms. It's as if gender is not an issue here.

It's like watching part of something die.

These kids don't look sick to her and they don't act sick, but there is definitely something wrong with them. She ought to tell Sarge; she doesn't know what to tell Sarge. It sounds so nebulous. It's too true.

I'm sorry, they don't look well.

She wonders if it's pheromonal— something Sarge had added to the water or the food. No, he's not that person. Schooled in the military, he puts his trust in discipline. Maybe the altitude changes them. Is the air on the mountaintop so thin that it neutralizes pheromones? She doesn't think so. She's been working here for weeks and she is— yes— strongly attracted to Sarge. He's deep in his work, but she thinks he feels it too. When they are together she gets, what. Feedback. But the girls . . . Those lifeless boys. It has to be pheromonal. They don't seem to have any emanations going any more. Whatever spark these wild girls had blazing in them before the Academy is gone.

When they stepped out of the capsule and into the abbey at Clothos, something died, and she doesn't know why.

Now, for Cassie Rivard, being a-hormonal, or dyshormonal, if that's what it is, would not be such a bad thing. It would be a relief. She hasn't told Sarge what she was running away from when she applied for the job and flew to Crete for the interview, and he doesn't press her. Everybody on the staff is running away from something. Even Sarge has a story.

Yes it was a man, but Cassie thinks bad backstory is what it is: backstory. Past. In a way, which past event or trauma turns people into who they are is irrelevant. It may be an explanation, but it's never a solution. If she learned from what went wrong with her lost love— *relationship* is a tacky word for whatever consumed them; *breakup* is a cheap word for the way it fell apart— if she learned anything from losing him, fine. She can autopsy the past when she's an old, old woman with nothing better to do. The issue is what she is doing now. Going forward. Playing the hand she's been dealt.

Bad analogy. Playing the letters she picked out of the Scrabble bag.

"Ms. Rivard?"

"What!" The voice startles her because as far as she knows, she's alone. Oh, it's one of the smalls, a six-year-old whose head barely clears the top of the desk. "What is it, Delia?"

The child's pink face bulges like a party balloon— not mumps, Cassie notes with relief. She's just upset. The little girl strains until words pop out. "Daisy Ferris is haunted."

Automatically, she feels Delia's forehead. "What makes you think that?"

"I saw it in the night."

"What, honey?" She pops a thermometer in the child's ear, just to be sure. "Hold still while I do this." She looks at the readout: normal. "Let me look down your throat. Go aaah."

"Aaaaaah."

Normal. "Now, what did you see?"

"You know how you can see your breath when it's cold out?"

"Watch my finger, Delia. Follow it with your eyes." Eyes are tracking, pupils responsive to light. "Yes, I know what that's like. What about it?"

The child says in thunderstruck tones, "I saw this thing coming out of Daisy in the night . . ."

"You must have been dreaming."

". . . and it was green."

"Or it was your imagination."

"It was not. I saw it bending over her bed!"

"Well, we can't have that. Tell you what, Delia." She reaches in her pocket for a box of Tic Tacs.

"Then it saw me looking and it disappeared."

"If you see it again, take one of these."

Delia goes on, determined to finish. "I think it went back inside her."

"These pills will make it go away."

"Can I take one now?"

"If it'll make you feel better, sure."

Delia pops it in her mouth and for the first time ever, smiles.

"One now and one before you go to sleep tonight, and first thing in the morning, I'll come in and check on you." Then Cassie says carefully, "Did this ghost look like a person or just like frozen breath?"

"It didn't look like breath, it was a person. It was all greeny yellowy, and I got scared." For a second there the whites of Delia's eyes look chartreuse. "It had . . ." Then the bell rings and she bolts.

Hallucinations, Cassie thinks. Oh, fine. Unless it really was a dream. At least it isn't a symptom, it's just a fluke. She picks up her bag and heads for the Infirmary. She is locking the monitor's station when the massive wooden doors to the ex-chapel crack open just wide enough for Brother Benedictus to slip out. The old man catches her looking and backs into an alcove where he clings like a spider, trying to pretend he isn't there.

She gives him a loud, "Hello, Brother Benedictus. Hi!"

His face shoots out of control.

"Can I help you?"

The old man's mouth makes a crazy zigzag, as if he's terrified or secretly in love with her. It's impossible to know.

"If you need anything, I'll be in the Infirmary." To ease his heart she smiles, adding, "Just so you know."

With an anxious, beatific grin, he flees.

TWELVE

SHEELA

I hate the girls. In my guts I hate Marla and I especially hate Sylvie, and I hate all their wannabe friends with identical coat hanger hipbones and inflatable lips, talking the talk in their Prada underwear with Gucci-sized bags under their eyes. They tramped into our fancy stone jailhouse in lockstep like they are the best and greatest, only people in the universe and we are mere rugs for them to walk on, plus, in the world outside I knew these people personally? It wasn't only they despised me, they couldn't see me for dirt.

Well, heh!

Those coat hangers are well padded now, halfway to overstuffed. The eye makeup and lip gloss are gone; the kiss-me lips have shriveled up.

Everything is different now.

Now they're my new best friends.

These idiot girls crowding into my room every night used to be famous for being famous, and not only in 90210 and Bel Air, Malibu and certain private clubs off Sunset. They were famous worldwide. The bitches were always in the news. I suppose it didn't hurt that they were born gorgeous, unlike me, although I am here to tell you that being ugly is not such a bad thing. People like me learn the hard way how to live by their wits.

But, skinny, slick multimedia bitches! When we coexisted in greater Los Angeles their hair was perfect and anything the matter with them, plastic surgery could fix. They got bit parts in movies and mug shots on magazine covers, not all of them nice, because they were also famous for being infamous when they were running wild out in the world. Loathsome Sylvie got in love with three different guys in Vegas and married them all one weekend in spite of that she's barely fifteen. Tiffy Dix and her boyfriend dangled over Rockefeller Center in a Plexiglas cube for a calendar month and Marla, Marla starred eighty weeks running in her own reality show on E! Like, Marla vomits. Woo!

Look at them now.

The second they hit Clothos they lost their shine, like spelling trophies that you threw in the closet and forgot. Our runway-perfect classmates started packing on pounds the night we got here and they scarfed up that first plate of boarding school food. Frankly, they've let themselves go. These days they don't care enough to put on lipstick, which is the only makeup allowed. It's like after the studs and earrings came out they gave up on everything else.

Half the bitches have stopped washing their hair.

Now, that's extremely weird.

In Brentwood and Cannes and Tijuana they were all about the shoes, the makeup, the outfits, they could do *whatever* and Daddy would pay. When they self-destructed, rich moms swooped down in Learjets to take them away to some posh rehab with a gold-plated revolving door. Now, my mom makes more money than all their dads put together and they know it, but it made zero difference in my popularity at the corner of Wilshire and Rodeo Drive.

The thing is, I was too ugly to hang out with. At least that's what they said. I know Mom paid her people extra to get me into parties, but I went alone and I stayed alone. When I walked into a club she owned, I walked in alone. That's just the way it was. It didn't matter what I spent on the outfit or how nice I tried to be, I was pretty much shunned. I could see these same girls snorting giggles behind sequined fingernails and hiding behind their guys, and if I pretended not to notice and went up to them smiling and all, "Hi," they fell all over themselves escaping, like, *eeeewww, get away!* Like a plum nose and a big butt are catching and acne can rub off on you.

Being spurned and all makes you brave. Plus, it made me re-sourceful, which is coming in handy around now.

"So what's the big problem," I asked Sylvie now that we are friends.

"What do you mean problem, I don't see any problems," she said because although we're friends, she's not all that good of a friend.

"Your hair looks like crap, for one," I said. "You used to look amazing, and now you look like you don't give a shit."

"Why should the moon bother shining when there's nobody around to see?" she said enigmatically, and she walked away like everything was fine and nothing was different, proving that our friendship is all about the candy, that's as good as it gets.

I'm all, "Wait a minute," but she doesn't. They never do, not even now, when we are trapped here.

There's something hinky about this place and like me or not, we need to talk. Walking in here blind, a pig could figure out that something is terribly wrong, but of course pigs are smart, and the posse? Lazy, ignorant skanks.

What do they think, that the hovercraft let us off at a new kind of rehab? Instead of asking questions, they're all laying back like we are all at a spa with French food and tea dances included, pool guys will come and the party will start any minute now. Like we can leave any time. As if the Academy is getting fixed to hand out sarongs and orchid leis for us to wear on the gangplank whenever we want to go ashore, with all the teachers lined up singing *Aloha*. You'd think we could go home whenever we want.

As if!

I have to get their attention. Whatever it takes, and I'm here to tell you, it takes a lot.

Look at them crowding into my room, grinning and making all nice, like we've been girlfriends ever since the sandbox where, frankly, they used to kick sand in my face and fall out laughing because I cried. In assembly Mr. Sargent says you have to love a person for themselves, but how could anybody love Sheela Mortimer, with this face like a cross between a tree toad and the part where a baboon sits down?

Even I don't know if I love me for myself.

It's more like: I love me for what I can do.

Right now what I'm trying to do is get these girls to pay attention. There's something wrong here, and I can't crack this place all by myself.

I'm using chocolate. Marla and Sylvie and their posse went from shitty to smarmy and despicable the minute I flashed the first Godiva box. Never mind how I get candy, I just do. Wads and tons of it, which means after Lights Out, after Miss LeClair, who is dorm parent for our pod, goes, *"bon soir"* and blinks the hall lights as a reminder, all those Beverly Hills and Vegas and Manhattan skanks sneak out of their poufy beds and come creeping down the hall to my room, which is at the tippy end.

"Heeey Sheela, what a nice room!" I haven't seen them like this since the last batch of truffles, which was last night.

"Oh, Sheela, your bedspread's sooo soft."

"Sheela, those posters are extremely cool."

There are so many of them in here that there's noplace left for me to sit. So, do I push even the stupidest one off my bed so I can sit instead of standing here smiling like an asshole? Do I grin apologetically and squeeze myself onto the bed, knowing the least they could do is scrunch over, considering?

Hell no. I just smile for the audience and hand out the chocolates, and while they eat I stand here with my face wide open, nodding like a gigantic bobblehead and hating myself for letting them use me, and this is the craven, rock-bottom truth. Even though I am smarter than they are and my mother could buy and sell these airheads and I know they are shallow and despicable, the weakest, sickest part of me wants to be liked.

Shit, it's just nice to have kids in my room.

And they think I don't know why they're here. Like I don't see their mouths watering. You wouldn't think candy would make that big of a difference, but when you're, like, sensually deprived, as we are on Clothos where everything is gray, it does. For the first time in my life I am surrounded by friends. Ostensible friends, but friends. Is it a sign of weakness that I'm all, *what a rush?*

Look at them, crowding around in their crap flannel nighties with the Academy seal, they don't even care that they look awful in regulation pink. They have totally let themselves go. Zits and no makeup, stringy hair like they never had back when there were paparazzi and YouTube. Plus they really are putting on the weight.

So this is Question A. Don't they notice, and if not why not?

Unless this is Question A. What exactly is causing this?

Am I the only person who thinks something about our situation is not right?

The rest of them are going around all happy, or something like it, in spite of that we are basically imprisoned here. Coming on to me, all charming and energized and polite. Cooing, actually. It's enough to make you yack. "Ohhhh Sheela," they go, "You are the best." They are, like, on automatic. "Isn't she the best, everybody?" And, "You really have the prettiest laugh!"

And then Sylvie— Sylvie!— is all pointing to my regulation nightie and squealing, "Pink is a really good color on you."

Pink is awful on me. I look like a boiled shrimp. "Thanks." Nice going, girls. Before we got here you wouldn't give me the time of day.

Do they think I don't know it's about the food? Unless maybe they think the eminent Daphne Mortimer, aka my mom, has enough money to make the world not end and furthermore pay their parents to forgive them, so we can leave. Like that would ever happen. Little do they know, the woman was thrilled to slough me off. The cool thing is, these girls are too dopey and self-absorbed to wonder why I, who they've never been anything but shitty to, am being nice to them. They're too full of themselves to imagine that I might have reasons. They think it is their due, chocolate truffles On Demand in my primo extra-large room. I'm not about to tell them the real reason they're wallowing in Godivas, why should I? What do I owe them?

"Have some more," I say, and the whole time I am sweeter than the Belgian cream truffles they are eating, smiling at them like a circus clown.

Marla, the wicked queen, puts on her party voice to say, "Oh, thank you." Then she gives me her best celebrity smile and I see chocolate in her spit bubbles and chocolate smeared between those perfect capped teeth which, frankly, are turning green because she has stopped brushing.

When you stop caring about sex, what's the first thing you care about? Food. That's another thing.

Why am I the first one to notice that these notable bimbos who used to collect boyfriends like tattoos which, incidentally, have been lasered off, never talk about boys? Why am I the only one in the Academy to pick up on this bizarro change in them? You'd think packing down truffles was the only thing these girls ever cared about, when they are famous for manhandling cute guys for the videographers and staging sex-fueled meltdowns too hot for YouTube which, now that I mention it, we can no longer access. Do they care that we're cut off from the world?

They don't.

Inside, the clever part of me is going, *Don't you think this is weird?*

The question then, is why I don't take advantage of that they're off boys right now and no longer give a crap about how they look, and outshine them. A little makeup would do it. I could cut bangs. And unlike my new best friends, I'm keeping my figure, such as it is. But I shuffle along like the rest of them because I'm thrilled to look like part of the gang, any gang. Excuse me. Posse.

Look, I've been ugly for so long that I'm used to it. Boys don't give a crap about me, so why should I care that Marla and them no longer give a crap about boys? Serves the heartless bastards right. Besides, for the first time ever, I have friends. It's nice, not being alone all the time, never mind that it's the chocolate. So I keep the truffles coming and go with the flow.

I pull the divider out of the box and expose the second layer. "More?"

There is a tiny mob scene as they close in and I wonder if they hate themselves for gorging or if they're gorging because deep down, they've always hated themselves. I wonder whether they even notice what they are becoming, gobbling candy in my room. It's like the biggest rush left for them is the sharp taste of chocolate, that jolt of sugar spreading in their mouths. I love it. I hate it. I want those truffles just as much as they do, but I won't have any. Call it my little victory.

"So," I say when I think they are sated. "What's new?"

They knock themselves out trying to oblige me, but nobody has much to say.

"Um, ah. Sameold, sameold," Tiffany says.

"Pretty much sameold," everybody says.

Marla shrugs with that indifferent, chocolated smile. "You know."

"Yeah right, Marla," everybody says. "You know."

"Yeah right," I go, because it makes me feel like an insider. I have things to say but I don't want to spoil the moment. "I do."

For the first time in my life I am popular. For the first time ever, all the cool kids are hanging out in my room. So I reach into my drawer and bring out another box of truffles and hand them out like Queen Whoever, which in this circumstance is pretty much who I am. I have the candy, which means I have the power, and don't they crowd around and smile at me then!

But you don't change into a pretty person overnight. All those years of exile have an ugly by-product. I'm tickled to have them here but I don't necessarily wish them well. My girls are too zoned out to know it, but with every truffle they are filling out. The first place fat shows up is in the face. *Keep eating,* I think. *You don't know it, but you'll be sorry. Enjoy, you airheads.* The meanest part of me is thinking, *You have **no idea** how fat you're going to get.* To look at them you'd never guess they were walking eating disorders that looked like social X-rays when they came. Designers kill to hang clothes on racks like that. Now they are bigger than me.

I'm trying to keep my mind on the party on my bed but I have to wonder. Is Sarge trying to homogenize us? I sit there and watch, thinking: *Keep going, maybe you'll turn into the ugly ones, and I'll end up prettier than you.*

Then I think: *cool!*

Finally even Marla is stuffed and dizzy from the sugar rush.

Now maybe I can get them to forget about candy for five minutes and we can talk. To find out what the conversation is, I have to start the conversation.

"So," I say, "who do you think are the cute guys here?"

Somebody says, "Fuck the guys."

Sylvie stifles a yawn. "Who wants to do that?"

"Nobody," Marla says.

"No, really. Which guys?"

"None of them. Been there, done that," Marla says. "It's boring."

It's my room, which means I have the guts to tell her, "You should know." I do not have the guts to add, *You slut.*

Without batting an eye the girl who used to be famous for shuffling boyfriends and exes and wannabes and annulments like a three-card monte dealer goes, "I'm over that."

Now I ask the central question. "Why?"

Marla bites into a truffle and holds it up to see what it looks like inside. "Beats the shit out of me."

I push, but only a little bit. "Maybe when we get out . . ."

"If we get out." She throws away the uneaten half.

Sylvie yawns for real this time. "I'm sick of them."

They all knock themselves agreeing because she is still the leader, even though she doesn't give a shit.

This would be interesting, if the guys here weren't acting just as dead, which is pretty much the case. The upperclassmen slog along the halls with their backs hunched and their heads bent, like they're looking for something very important on the floor. They're so limp that even I, who am so starved for love that I would kiss anybody, have zero interest in them. I try, "What about men?" When nobody answers I say in the sexy voice, "I mean, real men."

Somebody says, "Same thing."

"What if you saw one that wasn't . . ." I decide not to tell them about the strange guy I think I saw outside the Assembly Hall last night, black hair, white, white face and long body, this unknown person slouching along in the shadows like a wolf.

Nobody picks up on it. We are sitting here in silence, pretty much. Since I have an agenda, this is not good. It means think fast or they'll pick up and go.

I try on an idea. It doesn't quite fit, but I'm still working with it. I say, "Don't you think Mr. Sargent is cute?" He is, but not that way.

"Nobody's cute," Sylvie says, and you know what? It's true. Not us, not them, at least not here.

I go, "So he's more, like. Charismatic."

Their faces light up, but only a little bit. So yeah, our rugged leader Mr. Sargent has this thing going that, when he talks, you would do anything he asks. It's a magnetism thing. When he smiles, which is not all that often, you would follow him anywhere, but where is he taking us? Another of those things I have to figure out. I don't know where to start so I just start.

"Like, he can get people to do whatever he wants?"

No answer. My new best friends are all about the truffles.

I clear my throat to get their attention. "Guys!" It's time to focus them on our situation here. With a little cooperation, maybe I can get us out. I turn to Marla, who, with Sylvie, is in charge. Correction. Was in charge. I stick it to her. "Don't you think it's kind of weird?"

Marla's always been a bitch, which is what made her and Sylvie leaders of the pack back when they were still prowling. She's half-asleep and it's clear that she's done with this topic. Yawn. "I think this is too boring to talk about."

Because we are not done with this, I say the unspeakable. "What if it's um, because they did something to us?"

Nobody looks up. Nobody bothers to ask, "Who?" Candy's gone. They don't care.

Damn Marla, damn her guts, she doesn't even pretend to care.

She just looks at her fingernails, which— please!— she has chewed down to bloody cuticles, and drawls, "So who here wants to start a pool on which day is the end of the world?"

Sylvie sneaks the candy box closer when she thinks nobody is watching. "It's gotta be soon, or we wouldn't be here. At least that's what Sarge says."

While everybody else is nodding and going, "Yeah," "Uh-huh," "Right," she pops the box into her lap.

The skank is rooting around for the absolutely last truffle but I grab the box away, making clear that she doesn't get it back until she gives me some kind of answer. "How do you know?"

"Well, to begin with, the war!"

She might be right: we see terrible, terrible things on TV.

Like it or not we watch the news every night before dinner, when Sarge turns on the big plasma screen in the Assembly Hall. Everybody but me would rather be watching music videos, but something about the nonstop montage of fires and explosions hypnotizes them. And me? Something about it gives me the creeps.

Like, is this real stuff that's really happening that Sarge is show- ing us, or is he running the same footage on a really long loop? Three weeks of this and all those suicide bombings and exploding ammunitions dumps start to look alike.

I can't prove any of it is repeating or that some of what we're seeing is CG but, still. I stick it to Sylvie. "What makes you think the world is really going to end? I mean, besides Sarge telling us."

"Well, um, the sky is a really funny color."

Jane Dexter has her hand up like she thinks we are in class. Ei- ther that or she thinks I am giving candy for right answers. "The panic on Crete. Blood in the water. If the world doesn't end, it probably ought to."

Naturally I press a little harder. "Was that, like, world-ending stuff we saw back there on the hovercraft, or just Crete on Departure Day?"

She gets all crestfallen and doesn't answer.

"Well?"

"Get over yourself, Sheel." Marla is all *fait accompli*. "Of course the world is going to end."

Sylvie knows which side her bed is buttered on. "Why else would our parents send us here?"

"You don't think that's, like, a pretext?"

Not my problem their vocabulary sucks. They are all sitting around not thinking and humming through chocolate, going, blink, blink, blink.

Words of one syllable, Sheela. I am as patient as I can manage which isn't very, the way things are. To get their attention, I have to snap the candy locker shut.

Every girl in the room goes, *"What!"*

"OK, listen up. What if it isn't? Ending, I mean. What if they only told us that to get us here?"

A fortune in truffles and they aren't giving me shit. Marla yawns. Sylvie stretches. Tiffany shrugs. "I dunno."

Now that the candy is off the scene I turn and face my new best friends head-on, and empty-handed. "What if they did it to get rid of us?"

Their faces go through bazillion changes.

Everybody says some version of: *Oh.*

"So," I ask them, "what are we going to do about it?"

You would think this would be the big moment, but no. Marla stands up and a dozen candy wrappers fall out of her lap. "OK then."

Sylvie stands up. Tiffany stands up. Jane Dexter stands up. They are all popping up like mushrooms, aggressively bland.

"Not so fast." Mom taught me the tone of command: I use the

great big boardroom voice, but it isn't working. "I *said*, not so fast!"

One by one they start leaving. I never beg and I know better than to shout after them. We are done for the night.

THIRTEEN

IT'S LATE. IN THE DORM WING, IT'S AFTER LIGHTS OUT, WHICH means that everything is working the way it should, Sarge's darlings are stashed for the night.

For Cassie, it's the end of a long hard day of which the hardest part, she decides, is saying good night to Sarge in the staff lounge and listening to her footsteps on the stone as she makes her way back to the same empty bed in the same empty room. When she was with Evan, years passed when she hardly thought of Sarge. Now she thinks about him all the time.

The breakup with Evan left a void in her life. There was ugliness that she won't talk about. She was backing away from the brink when she flew to Crete. Now she thinks it might have been better if she'd confronted it and gotten past the pain. It would have been liberating, she supposes.

Now where there was a void in her life, there is only Sarge.

Back in the empty Infirmary, Cassie checks the contents of the cabinets against the inventory; with a drunk on board, you never knew. Then she opens the doors. There's an hour blocked in for late sick call, but nobody ever comes. She supposes she could wake up Mel Dratch, whose job this is, but why bother?

In case of emergency she could probably rouse the old crock, but she has it covered. Frankly, she doesn't want to hear him puttering in the cabinets, jabbering excuses with that phlegmy, hungover cough. She has her book and she could use the silence. She is reading *The Magic Mountain*. It seems appropriate.

She is deep in the Berghof with Hans Castorp when a shadow scuttles into the room so abruptly that she jumps. "Who's there?"

"Don't freak. It's me."

Killer Stade. Not the first kid you want to find alone with you in an isolated place. Word is that the stringy little twelve-year-old with the raccoon eyes killed a man. No wonder he can't sleep. She sighs. "Please don't ask me for sleeping pills."

"What do you think I am?" Quick on the draw, he snaps, "If I want downers, I can go down to the fucking Science lab and make my own."

"I'm sorry. I was—"

"Judging a book by its cover."

She blushes. "Afraid so."

"Well, cut it out!"

"Sorry." Yes, she is studying him. His reputation walked into the room ahead of him and she'll admit it, her first thought was: *Don't hurt me.* Up close, Killer Stade isn't half as scary as the stories about him. He's a little boy. She thought he had smeared black makeup around his eyes, or paid for cosmetic tattoos. Instead the bruised-looking rings say that Killer can't sleep. Guilt? She doesn't know. "Is it true that you really . . ."

"Killed a guy?" Up close, he is nonthreatening and much too young to look this unhappy. Sweet-faced, troubled kid; he asks nicely, "Could we please not talk about that, please?"

Gently, Cassie offers, "If you need something to help you sleep better, maybe I can . . ."

"Not going there, thanks. No way." He lifts his head. "That's not the problem."

"Then what . . ."

"I need you to teach me how to give a shot."

"Tell me you're not . . ."

"Using? Shit no. It's Teddy. He keeps spazzing out in the middle of the night."

"Isn't Mr. Bogardus on top of that?"

Killer whips his head around. "What do you mean?"

"He's dorm parent. We prepared him for emergencies. Trained him. We also gave him enough meds to hold that boy for a month!"

"If you want to know the truth, Mr. Bogardus doesn't want to touch him."

Her back stiffens. "He isn't giving the shots?"

"Not so's you'd notice."

"But he's supposed to . . ."

Killer shakes his head.

"That's terrible."

"Yeah. It's like, nobody's getting any sleep. I'm up top freaking and Teddy's down below, spazzing out. The kid is gonna hurt himself."

She doesn't know how to phrase it gently but she tries. "When Teddy gets like this, how long does it go on?"

"Long. Longer every time."

"But Mr. Bogardus is supposed to . . ."

"Well, he doesn't," Killer says. "The first time it happened I called the motherfucker, like you said. He came in all pissed, like, don't bother him. So next couple of times I didn't, and Teddy got over it OK. Then last night, Teddy. Ah. Agh." In spite of himself, he shivers. "Last night it was pretty bad."

"Where was Bogardus?"

"Like, ignoring it? Until he came about the noise. He was all, shut up and fuck you, and then he was out the door."

"He's supposed to administer the meds!" When they go unchecked, seizures can do permanent damage. PA or not, every intelligent person knows, and Cassie can tell you right off that mulish Dave Bogardus knows. She explained the problem and the procedure in detail when she taught him how to slip the needle in.

"I told you, he's scared to touch him." This is not the kind of kid who cries, but Killer Stade is near tears. "I think he hopes Teddy will die."

"Oh, Killer." She picks up the house phone. "I'll get him down here and . . ."

"No nooo," Killer cries. "Whatever you do, don't call him! All I want . . ."

Cassie waits. One false move and Killer will implode. "Do you want me to come see him? Teddy, I mean."

"No way. He doesn't know I'm here!"

"OK then," she says, and waits for the rest to come out. It takes longer than it should.

"All I want . . ." The boy wants to tell her, he doesn't want to tell her. He has to tell her but he can't, quite. They are both dying by the time Killer blurts, "I want you to fix it so I can give the shots."

She studies him. She wants to force Bogardus to do his job, but that's not useful here. Her arms fly open; she can't help it. "I'm so sorry."

Killer backs away from the hug with a glare that says, *Nobody hugs Killer Stade.* If Cassie tries, he really will kill her. Instead she pulls out the orange she brought back from dinner. "OK then."

Killer almost grins.

Carefully, she explains the difference between subcutaneous, intradermal and intravenous injections. She shows him how to prepare the hypodermic. Apply the needle to the bottle thus. Push in the plunger and slowly draw it out. Get rid of the bubbles. Tap tap. She lists the steps he should take to keep Teddy from hurting himself. Then she picks up the orange and tells Killer how, once he has Teddy stabilized, to find the right spot and slip the needle in. Then she shows him. Next, she lets him try. One orange isn't enough. Together, they raid the kitchen, bringing back grapefruit. They keep at it until Killer finally gets it right. He puts the supplies she gives him into his book bag and turns to go.

She calls after him. "You know, I can get Bogardus fired."

With the back of his hand Killer sketches the mountain. The island, a dot in the sea. Their isolation. "No you can't. Thanks anyway."

"I didn't do much."

"This is all I need."

"If you run into any more trouble," she says weakly, "let me know."

"Don't worry." Standing there in the doorway the boy looks small and tough and very brave. "I'll be fine."

"Do you have another name besides Killer?"

"Yeah, but you wouldn't like it."

"Try me."

He gives her the grin of all grins. "It's Ralph."

"OK then. Ralph."

Too late. He's gone.

It's just as well. Mel Dratch lunges out of his private office with his face creased from sleep. He is wearing a shaggy blanket like a serape over the white coat. "Was somebody here?"

"I have to go."

"Wait," he rumbles. "Who came?"

"Later. I have work to do." Turning away, Cassie goes to her own quarters before he can make another of his boozy passes at her, and locks the door. OK, she thinks. Thank heaven her first patients came with problems that are self-contained. Specific to them. Hallucinations. Epilepsy. Nothing contagious. She could not say why this makes her shudder, but it does. Firmly, she reminds herself: nothing catching.

Yet.

FOURTEEN

SARGE

I love this place at night.

I love watching the kids with their heads bent over dinner in the Refectory, I love the changes I see in their faces as they watch the news. They came here struggling, spitting, screaming, engines of disorder. Now look at them. These are my people and this is my place.

After the last inspection I come in here to stand the midwatch. I begin here, inside the second of two locked doors. The first is to the superintendent's office, complete with photo mural of Mount Clothos, big desk with my PC and the nameplate on the leather-bound blotter.

The second is to the inner room. Its location is so secret that only Steve, my IT guy, has ever been in here.

I am alone in the dark with only the glow of the server to steer by: running lights to see me through whatever comes next. After eighteen hours of reassuring my scattered, unhappy staff with their needs, after a long day of carrying a hundred messed-up kids on my back, I love the solitude.

I love the silence. With everything stowed and everybody quiet for once, I listen. As if one of these nights I'll catch the echo of generations of dead monks chanting.

Look. Hundreds of more or less ordinary men like me gave up life in the world— light and color, love, sex and violence— to be here inside the citadel. What were they looking for? They left behind everything that makes people happy to come to this Godforsaken peak for no clear reason. Brother Benedictus says the monks believed that at the top of the mountain they could get closer to the thing they wanted most. Which he tells me is God, for whatever that's worth. Whatever it means. What does God mean?

I see it this way. They left the world to do what they had to do.

OK then, what does that make of me?

It's too soon to tell.

Whether or not this is a question of definition, I listen.

The walls give back silence and I grin. The monks are long gone. Whatever they had here is over. This is my place now.

But I listen.

One of these nights, after personnel and supplies have shaken down and our systems are all in place and up and running, I will hear the heartbeat of the Academy.

I don't know the name of the star I'm steering by or where it's taking us. No problem. It's enough to know where I'm coming from.

This.

When I shipped out for my last tour of duty in yet another third-world country where we weren't wanted, the captain walked the bridge of the attack personnel transport that carried us. His orders didn't call for it but he was on duty all night, every night. The ship carried a thousand men. Every night the skipper stalked back and forth on the bridge, one man pacing on a loop far above the heads of the thousand sleeping below— more than three hundred in the ship's complement, almost seven hundred Marines going off to die, most of them, although nobody said that.

What happened after the battalions landed was not the skipper's concern. He was responsible for their safety and well-being for as long as they were in his ship. Stalking back and forth on the bridge, the captain felt the vibration of the engines, the heave of the waves under the bulk and mass of the ship plowing through the night with attack troops on board.

Comprehending it.

He held the lives of a thousand men in his hands and he could not rest even though he knew everything was in order, everybody stowed.

I had night duty on that crossing, so I know.

I was the Marine MP on the bridge our first night at sea. I was there every night from the day we shoved off from the Brooklyn Navy Yard until we landed at Gwadar. When I came up to the bridge at midnight to relieve the man on the late watch, the skipper was still up and pacing.

I saluted and took up the midwatch. The skipper paced as though he was alone in the world so I kept silence: regulations. Except in case of emergency, speak to your commanding officer only when spoken to. I didn't have to ask.

He didn't tell me, but I knew exactly what was going on.

At my station on the bridge with a thousand men below decks and the engines churning, I understood the power and the pressure of command. What a rush!

One man, responsible for so many lives.

Now I am that person.

When the morning watch relieved me at 4 A.M. I went down the ladder to the main deck of the attack personnel transport— APA to you. Instead of going below I paced, circling the deck as if still on duty. If the skipper didn't sleep, why should I?

Now I have my own command.

Alone like this, I can feel the skies rushing past us as the Academy sails on through the night.

After Taps I always wait an hour, until everything is quiet. Then it's time for rounds. A good officer leaves everything shipshape, so before I leave my quarters I get my personnel folders and paperwork squared away. When everything is secured I go into my office and shut down every application on my desktop PC

Then I sever its connection with the server for the night. I don't want some fool wandering into my office and discovering that he can get a connection. I've told the staff it's impossible, and that's the way it's going to stay.

Then I lock the office door, in case.

I always begin and end my rounds in here, with the server. Nobody but Steve Joannides, IT wizard, knows that the carved mahogany panel behind my desk conceals the door to the inner compartment where the server lives.

Now that we have everything up and running only I speak to the server. I tell Steve it's for his own protection, which, in a way, it is. They can't catch him unless he shows himself on the Internet. As it is, he's happy enough masterminding the nightly newscasts we show on the monster plasma screen in the Refectory at 1830.

Before I leave the inner office I check the DVD locker. I have to make sure Steve secured the special DVDs after tonight's newscast. Keeping our news videos locked up is imperative. The kids need to believe they're watching fires and explosions streamed live into the Refectory every night at chow time.

We do what we have to, to obtain the objective.

My DVDs are part of the program. Safe as they are here, protected from outside influences, i.e. information that might stir them up, the kids have to believe. This operation depends on it. To keep them contained when they want to be out fucking and drinking and snorting and otherwise tearing up the universe, we have to convince them that what they see on the big screen in the Refectory every night is the truth.

They get their nightly doses of disaster with their dinners, invasions and fires and explosions blooming on the big screen in high-res full color as they eat. Sit back kids, no talking through your food and no passing notes, which is what you are reduced to now that text messages are over for you. See what it's like out there in the world and thank your stars that you are safe here with us in the Academy, safe in the heart of the mountain. Relax, and enjoy.

This is their only source of news, not that any of them watched the news when they were out in the world unless their smug faces were on it, although they sometimes picked up news accidentally, when a favorite show got preempted by an invasion or the destruction of some national landmark, and boy were they pissed. Or regular programming was blown away entirely by late-breaking news, when some formerly pretty country got blown off the map by one of the big guys that get off on starting new wars, laying waste and pillaging because they can't get enough.

"Shit," these kids used to say when that fat face came on with another sober announcement. "I want my MTV."

Now TV news is all they get. Not counting the news I keep up on in the secret compartment where the server lives, there is no television here. We show weekend movies in the Assembly Hall. That's good enough for them.

My people know what I choose to let them know, and by people I mean both students and personnel.

It's essential to the discipline.

It's healthier for the staff.

Knowing we were in for a long tour of duty here I brought plenty of vid on rising global chaos, mashups neatly edited to look like fresh news. Steve is the only staff person who knows. Great hacker, Steve. And he owes me. The boy's dodging a federal charge that would keep him locked up for the rest of his life— nothing dangerous, but Homeland Security, the oil dudes and a major munitions conglomerate are plenty pissed. The Feds were closing in on the shack in the Rockies where he had holed up.

I pulled him out before the Feds could make the arrest.

Let's say he needed to start a new life in a safe place. The hair, he can always dye. Dratch used to be an epidemiologist, but after the scandal, he did plastic surgery on the quiet to stay afloat. If he ever sobers up he can change Steve's face so even his girlfriend wouldn't know. Round the jaw a little, maybe. Add a bump to that noble Greek profile and nobody will guess who he used to be. A little miracle of reinvention and he'll be good as new.

I had the boy working on effects for months before Departure Day, compiling hour upon hour of frontline video and blurred screen shots of sinkholes and riots and tunnel collapses, plus low-resolution scenes of suicide bombings and assassinations that could be YouTube replications of monstrous events. He included tsunami shots and hurricane and earthquake damage and eruptions and made sure that some of them look like shaky disaster videos captured today by a witness who happened to have a phone. On top of that we have our own garish sky and the color of the water at the base of the mountain to convince everybody here that the world is indeed ending.

While the newscast runs, I watch their faces. When their jaws drop I know we've done this right.

As far as the staff and our charges are concerned, life as we know it is imploding. We need them to believe it, and we need them to believe it's happening soon. This is the story we told to get them here and this is the prediction we have to protect if we expect to keep them here.

Not bunker mentality, but close.

Ergo, the DVDs. We have enough to show them in rotation for

a year without repeating, if that's what it takes, and we'll keep showing them for as long as it takes.

Unless it takes too long.

I click tonight's DVD back into its slot and watch it rotate a notch before I close the locker and back out of the inner room. It takes an extra slap of the button to make the panel slide shut.

It's time to walk the sign of the cross.

Not that I'm religious. The pattern was laid out by the monks who built this place a thousand lifetimes ago. To walk the halls of the Academy I've created inside the protective stone shell of the cloister, I honor the design. I have no choice.

My office is at the end of the left arm. Proceeding toward the center I inspect the public rooms, looking into every door. I check them off one by one: lounge and library on my right, all quiet, with furniture lined up for inspection and books neatly shelved. Refectory on my left, everything shipshape, with the students' tables laid for morning chow, long benches just so, and at the captain's table where the staff sits, every chair is placed in exact relationship to all the other chairs, with mine at the head. In the galley, the shining stainless steel surfaces are bare, with cookware and utensils washed and stowed. Chef Pete oversees the cleanup with the care of a surgical orderly. No salmonella or E. coli here.

Along the way I keep an eye out for Regan's mystery man. Several nights of this convince me that there are no extra personnel, a fact of which I assured him yesterday. I even checked with Security, who are quartered below. If anybody untoward showed up, my man Chris Tackett would be the first to know. Everybody on board is accounted for.

Still, at the intersection I take a long look in every direction, alert to the possibility of shadows drifting across the corridors.

Then I cross the T and enter the classroom wing, where I check out the classrooms to my right and my left. If I find anything out of order it shows up in that teacher's fitness report and they all know it. Tonight the classrooms are in order: clean blackboards, desks lined up like jarheads on the last day of boot camp, even in that idiot French teacher's room. It's pretty clear Wardwell was one of my mistakes, but he's shaping up. Turns out that first warning was enough. I find everything shipshape in his classroom, so, fine.

Even the rankest civilians are beginning to learn.

By the time I reach the long dormitory hall that ends at the foot of the cross it's so late that every one of our charges is in the sack. Instead of opening doors to check on the sleepers I march to the end of the hall, hoping I'll see that crack of light that outlines the Infirmary door on nights when Cassie works late. I need to show support because she and I both know that my other staffing mistake is the doctor.

If she's up, I can always get coffee. Every night she offers and so far I've refused because I'm not sure of our relative positions here. Commanding officer and . . .

It would be nice to go in. Sit for a minute before I finish my rounds. Talk, because except for laid-back little Steve Joannides, she's the one person I can listen to for more than ten minutes without wanting to bang my head against the wall. So far our conversations have been about procedures, the kids, the Order of the Day, but I'm pretty sure we have other things to talk about. Once I get all my systems working here, maybe I can figure out what they are.

Tonight the Infirmary is dark. Disappointed? Yeah.

I make an about-face to prove I don't care and head back up the hall. At the intersection, I look into the glass booth. Cassie isn't there, either. Why should she be? It's almost midnight. Ten minutes to midnight, when the midwatch begins.

On these inspections I like to finish in the Assembly Hall, here at the head of the cross. I love to stand there with the building behind and below me, absorbing the space.

The captain, comprehending the scope of his power.

No matter what comes down in the world outside, this place is proof against it. My people are protected by the stone walls and stone arches, the lead-and-steel armature. By the discipline. When it all comes down, there will be the discipline. Everything by the numbers, everybody in position.

The responsibility is tremendous.

Standing here, feeling the building around me with its generators humming and the entrances and exits sealed, I can rest because the Academy is secured for the night. Centuries ago this building bonded with the mountain, stone on stone. Not even an earthquake can shake it loose. The monks didn't have much to work with but like the ancient Egyptians, they had nothing but time. Given the will and the vision and, OK, the continuity of personnel, they built for the ages.

The cloister sits on bedrock rooted so deep in the earth that when they moved in for the renovation, even my structural engineers couldn't tell me how far down it goes.

Whatever comes down outside, we are protected. The parents told their struggling wild cards what I told them. The walls are proof against disorder and danger. The children are contained. Nobody admits it but every parent knows and I know that the Academy is designed to keep them in. Until this experiment ends and I can tell them the mission is a success, nobody comes and nobody goes.

OK then. Back to my quarters. Open the panel and go into the inner compartment. Alone here with only the green dots of light from the server to steer by, I can rest. This is the heart of the place.

I love this room, I love the silence. I . . .

"Sir?"

"Joannides!" I do not say, *I told you never to bother me here.*

Steve says what he says every night. "Time to back up the server."

"No need." This is not the first time we've been over this. When push comes to shove, I don't want anybody messing with it now that he's run the diagnostics and seen to it that everything's installed, not even Steve. "Your job is done."

"In your dreams, Sarge. It's never done." That grin. "Geeks know."

"If anything comes up I'll take care of it."

"But you don't . . ." He does not finish, *know what I know.* We both know that if he does, I will deck him.

I have my pride. I have my pride and frankly, now that I've pried his hands off the keyboard, there's stuff stored in my server that not even Steve knows about. I tell him, "No."

"But Sarge, you don't know what's out there. A shitload of new viruses cropped up after you disconnected me, Trojan horses, worms, even you have to know there's something new every day. Bad stuff. Stuff even I can't cure."

"I'll be careful."

"Everybody needs a backup."

"I'll be *careful.*"

"Careful is never enough."

He is pissing me off. "Firewall's in place. I'm the only one in here and trust me, I will not do anything stupid. The system is secure."

"In case," Steve says. He of all people is alert to the world of accidents and surprises opened by that "in case."

I tell him what I always tell him. "I've got it covered. Now, stop second-guessing me and get some rest."

"But sir . . ."

"Sir?" That makes me laugh, which offends him more than me

blowing off his best intentions. "If anything comes up I promise. You're the first person I'll call."

I watch him out the door.

Enough.

Who needs sleep. I have the midwatch.

Downtime.

FIFTEEN

THE FIRST TIME BENNY SAW HIM HE WASN'T SURE HE'D SEEN anything at all. It was in the garden dome. Since the Academy opened he's been going up there at night to pray at Compline because except for the hum of the heaters and fine spray from the mister, the silence up here is profound. He can't get enough of it. Constant contact with others has left him twitchy and anxious. They mean well enough, but if one more of Mr. Sargent's teachers tries to start a conversation, Benny may just die.

Eighty years of the Grand Silence, and now this.

After Brother Sixtus died Benny thought he would die of loneliness. Now he thinks that might not be so bad. There is no peace on Mount Clothos. At least it's quiet here in the dome. Set down in the single flat place among the crags like a lid on a roasting pan, the garden dome is a place of shadows in spite of the artificial sunlight the system provides. Outside, rocks loom. In here, he thought he saw an angel move. The figure was long, graceful. It was so swift that he couldn't be sure it was there.

"What?" he cried, and at the sound of his own voice, he shuddered. *Too loud,* he thought. He wasn't exactly praying, unless he was. *Forgive me, I'm too loud.*

He still can't say whether it was only the garden's sprinklers entering mist mode, but a sound, or the hint of a sound brought his head up. He thought he heard something or somebody going, "Shhhh."

"Oh Lord," he said the second time. Half-praying, half-saluting, he put the back of his hand to his forehead and bent on one knee. "Oh, Lord!"

There was no response, but the shadow moved.

Weeping, he lowered his hand. By the time he got to his feet the shadow— vision or angel? Intruder? Product of the imagination? He didn't know— was gone.

He only knew that where there had been nobody but Brother Benedictus here in the dome tonight, alone in the garden, there was a Presence.

For the first time in his life on Mount Clothos, he felt threatened.

The voice he produced was pathetic. Creaky and sad. "Who's there?"

"Shhhh."

Astonishment punched all the breath out of him. "You called?" Again.

In the end he cried, "What do you want?"

Scrawny old Benedictus no-last-name, an ordinary man who has lived his whole life in the abbey, was laid wide open and trembling. Exposed on the mountaintop with only the transparent dome to protect him from the naked sky. For a simple man with only the Rule to steer by, it was terrifying.

He fled the garden.

The next night, he decided to complete the Hours in the chapel— *Forgive me, Mr. Sargent. The Assembly Hall.* It seemed safer.

Instead of being reassuring, the stripped chapel at night was daunting. All the vigil lights were gone. The arches met in shadow far above his head. Even with low-intensity lights burning above the lectern, it was too dark. Its emptiness taunted him. The old man missed the familiar, comforting figures of the Virgin, St. Joseph, St. Benedict. Dear Father, he missed them. He missed St. Francis and the Infant Jesus of Prague too, sweet-faced companions of his childhood. As a child growing up in a congregation of celibates, he used to look into all those painted faces and pretend he was surrounded by a loving family.

Now the voices of the statues removed by Sargent Whitemore's workmen whispered around his feet and rose to the vaulted ceiling. Kneeling on the stone, Benny whispered, "If only you'd come back."

Outside a bell rang, signaling the end of evening study hall. Even with the great doors closed he could hear all those restless souls outside the chapel, children bumping into each other, grumbling; he heard chairs screeching as people got up from their desks, rubber soles slapping stone as the stragglers went running down the hall. Someone cried out. Someone else groaned in complaint. In cells where Benedictines used to pray in silence, dozens of furtive conversations were going on; it made him sick.

Crossing himself, he ducked into the confessional. It had survived the renovation for reasons known only to Mr. Sargent. Showing off the Assembly Hall to Benny the day it was finished, he had made a little speech about it. "Educational tool," he said. "Look at the paneling. The curtains. The screens. Says it all about what used to go on in this place." Sarge growled as though he thought this was a bad thing, "No offense intended."

Benny didn't know that the modern response was supposed to be, "None taken." He said, "Did you used to be a Catholic?"

Mr. Sargent turned on him with a sharp, proud look. "I used to be a Marine." He patted the confessional. "Object lesson for the students here," he said, but did not explain.

Benny saw it as a place of refuge, the one spot in the abbey where he could pretend things were going on as they were before Mr. Sargent came. He knelt there wondering whether, if he'd thought to tell the new leader about the plague that took beloved Brother Sixtus and all the others, the superintendent would have left without desecrating the place. He was just so happy not to be alone. He didn't want to scare them off . . .

"Forgive me," he cried. *It is my fault they are here.*

He didn't really expect a response.

Someone said, "Bless me Father, for I have sinned."

Benny's hands flew up. "I'm not a priest!"

"I need your help," the other said. "I need food and bandages. Antiseptic to clean this thing out."

"What's the matter?" Benny said, "Who are you?"

Then the other asked the strangest question. It is one Benny mulls daily. Intensified by the enclosure, the unseen penitent's voice was low, compelling. As though Benny can answer if he tries.

"Do you know who I am?"

This struck Benny in such a deep, unfamiliar place that it made him tremble. "Who *are* you?"

"If you don't know, I can't tell you."

This is so sad! "Why not?"

"Just help me. I'm hurt."

Why me, O Lord. "Why me?"

"You're the only one here I can trust."

Flattened by the pressure of his expectations, Benny wailed, "What do you want me to do?"

"Food, please. Antibiotics. Something for the pain."

"I'll get the doctor."

"No! No, please. They can't know I'm here."

"Oh, son," the lonely old man cried and in a mad conflation of images imagined that part of his plaster family had come back for him. His plaster family was just that, and the knowledge hurt. It was so sad! There was something so particular, so intimate, about talking to this stranger in the dark that Benny repeated in a brighter voice, "Son?"

"Thank you." That's all he said.

Now Benny takes food and medicine to the confessional on a regular basis, picking times when the Assembly Hall is not in use. He has no idea what the stranger does during the long hours when the former chapel is empty. Is he reading by the dim light in the priest's portion of the booth, or does he stalk the halls? Does he plot? Does he spy? Does he pray? Benny doesn't know, any more than he knows whose face he sees behind the dense screen in the confessional, sitting where generations of priests had sat over thousands of years.

Young, he thinks; he can tell from the sound of the voice, which thanks to the antibiotics Nurse Cassandra gave Benny when he complained of a sore that wouldn't heal, is getting stronger. When she asked to see the place he slapped both hands over his groin with a desperate, "I can't." Now he has to limp whenever they pass in the halls. Every night at Compline he has to beg God's forgiveness for deceiving her.

Well-made, he thinks, from the shape of the head, an outline barely visible through the mesh. It's hard to judge a person you can't see, but Benny believes the outsider is handsome in the way of the absent statues of the saints he loved for so long.

Well-intentioned, he thinks, without knowing why. Something about the stranger's reticence is reassuring. That he asks no questions, except the one. That he asks for nothing but Benny's promise to keep his secret, which Benny does.

He would like to kneel here in the darkness and talk to the stranger at length, but they have developed a ritual that gets them through these encounters without putting either of them at risk.

If Benny starts talking he may begin to weep out of guilt over sins long past and from sheer loneliness, sobbing over the long-dead congregation and what's become of the abbey since he let the intruders in. He's afraid the stranger will ask him once again, *Do you know who I am?* Does he? Should he? It troubles him. If the stranger starts talking he may tell Benny something that obliges him to tell Sarge about the uninvited guest. These encounters would end.

It seems safer to keep conversation to a minimum. This is, after all, an abbey. Silence is appropriate.

Every night Benny puts the necessary objects on a tray and slides them under the curtain. The stranger says, "Thank you," in that light, sandy voice. Then Benny says, "Pray for me."

The stranger never says that he will. Instead he responds, "No, Brother . . ."

"I'm not a . . ."

"You pray for me."

Something in his dark tone makes Benny promise, "I will."

Each night when Benny comes with the new tray he finds yesterday's cup, the bowl and the spoon washed and ready to be returned to his monastic cell, which he keeps pristine because he does his best to live according to the Rule. He preserves them in memory of the old order, which he prays one day will be restored. Like his visits to the confessional, it makes him feel at one with his past.

With the outsider to take care of, which he does in silence, he feels improved. It's as though part of the old life has been restored.

Of course he has questions. Where does the stranger sleep? Does he come out of the confessional when nobody's around? Does he leave the chapel when the Academy is sleeping? Does he roam freely in the halls? What does he do in the hours when Benny is working in the dome, or asleep in his cell? The questions keep asking themselves inside his head until the racket is too loud to ignore.

They must be asked.

He'll do it tonight. He won't leave after the stranger thanks him. He'll let the silence grow until the pressure is too much for the mysterious outsider. Then they'll talk.

Shaking with excitement, he sets down the basket outside the door to the priest's side of the confessional. Then he knocks three times and slips behind the curtain on the penitent's side. He kneels where he has knelt so many times, to make his confession.

Cold as the stone walls are, it's hot inside the confessional. Benny wonders if the stranger brought in a pot of charcoal to warm himself. He kneels in silence while the stranger opens the narrow door on the chapel and pulls the basket inside. He is trembling with excitement. Benny says, "Peace be with you." It's what he always says.

The stranger says his usual thank you, but Benny hears: *Do you know who I am?* The question hangs in the air between them. Benny asks if there's anything he needs. The usual exchange. *I'll ask him,* Benny tells himself, and waits for an opening. It's hot in the booth. *I have to ask him.*

"Pray for me," the other says. It's the usual farewell.

Instead of saying his usual, "I will," Benny says, "And who will I be praying for?"

The stranger's voice goes deeper. It's almost a groan. "For someone who needs it."

This makes Benny bold. "Who are you? Where did you come from?"

For the second time since he dropped into Benny's life the other says, "If you don't know, I can't tell you. Pray for me."

Benny knows this is his cue to say "I will," and go. Instead he asks, "Are you still hurt? Are you sick right now? Just tell me if you need something for a fever."

"You'd better go."

Benny should go and he knows it, but now that he's started, the questions keep coming. They just go on pouring out. "How did you find us? Did you climb up the side of the mountain to get here, or did somebody drop you out of the sky? Is there a shield up there or not? We're locked in here, how did you get inside? Why are you here, and what do you want? Just tell me, what do you want from us?"

"Shhh," the stranger says. "You'll bring them."

At some level Benny knows this, but his voice gets louder and louder so that by the end he is shouting, "What are you doing here?"

Then a hand rips the curtain aside and light floods his cubicle. Her voice is as clear as an angel's. "Brother Benedict, who are you talking to?"

"Nobody," he cries. After so many long minutes kneeling in the dark, waiting for the stranger to fill the silence with answers, he is blinded by the light. He can't see who is speaking. Is she friend or avenging angel or another of his plaster saints come back to reproach him?

"What's going on?"

He isn't exactly lying when he says, "Nothing, I promise!" but he crosses himself as a little penance, rocking with fatigue and blinking into the strong light.

She holds out a hand to him. "Come on, Benny, don't be afraid."

"Oh, Miss Cassandra."

"Yes." She grabs his wrist with both hands and helps him up off his knees. "You shouldn't be kneeling in the dampness at your age, not with your arthritis." He won't have time to ask the girl how she knows he's arthritic because the nurse or whatever she is has turned him so they are facing. "What were you doing in the Infirmary last night?"

"I . . ." Pressed for an answer, Benny commits perhaps the first sin of his life. He lies. "I didn't. I wasn't."

"Benny, I saw you. And what about the night before?"

Like St. Peter in the Garden of Olives, he denies it. "I wasn't there!"

"Oh, Benny," she says, shaking her head. "Now, tell me what you've been doing with the stuff you steal."

"I have a disease."

"My antibiotics? The dressings? What kind of disease?"

Lies beget lies. *Father, forgive me.* "Nono, it was a hurt."

"Morphine?"

"It was an emergency."

"Every night?"

"It won't go away."

"I'd better take a look."

"Oh please, you can't. It's Down There." Foolishly he says, "I have a fever."

"I don't know," Cassie says. "You look all right to me."

"*Had* a fever." Benny tries, God forgive him, he tries. "We can go. I'm cured now."

"Sure you are." She silences him with a long, hard look. "Now tell me, what are you really doing here?"

"Compline. I pray."

"Not this way, I don't think. Not here. You don't pray out loud and you know it." She puts both hands on his shoulders and fixes him with her eyes. "Now, if you had an unhealable wound, I'd know it. Tell me who the real patient is."

SIXTEEN

"WHO ARE YOU?" WHILE POOR OLD BROTHER BENEDICTUS
frets at her elbow, Cassie is pounding on the confessional door.
Whoever's inside the priest's compartment just locked it tight. She
tries, "I know you're injured, now come out."

"Don't hurt him." Flailing in a frayed homespun habit much
too big for him, Brother Benny looks like a big brown chicken de-
fending her nest with threadbare wings.

"Does he speak English?"

"Yes."

"Dammit," she says, louder, "come out and talk to me."

"Don't yell, you'll bring them." The old man is terrified.

"Who?"

He doesn't answer.

She says to whoever's in the booth, "Don't be afraid, I'm here
to help." She puts her ear to the small cross cut in the door. The

person in the booth has stopped breathing. "Nobody's going to hurt you, now come on out."

Benny plucks at her arm. "Please don't. He's sick."

"Sick!" Disturbed by the possibilities she says urgently, "Come on out. I'm here to help you."

Only Benny responds. "Nurse Cassie, don't!"

"I'm not a nurse."

"He isn't hurting anything."

She says in a tone only Benny can hear, "Unless he's contagious." She's thinking fast. Get him out. Get him into quarantine, assess the situation.

"I'll take care of him, I promise."

"What makes you think you can?"

"Oh, don't," Benny cries. "Just let him be."

"Who's in there?"

Now the old man's wrinkled face flies into a million little pieces. "I don't know!"

Oh, this is bad. What are they doing here? She tries a softer tone. "Come on out," she says to the man hiding behind the priest's door. "I won't hurt you."

Nothing changes inside the confessional. Nobody answers.

"Really. It won't matter what you've done." When that doesn't work she tries tough love. "Come out or I'll get Sarge to come and crack you out." Pause. "He was trained in interrogation in the Marines."

There is nothing but the sound of time passing. Bats whizzing in circles under the Gothic arches high above.

"If you won't come out, I need to know your symptoms."

Benny clucks and flaps anxiously. If she persists, will he peck at her eyes?

She says to the closed door, "At least tell me, is there a rash? Are you running a fever?"

Benny tugs, "Nurse Cassie, Nurse Cassie . . ." If he doesn't come out soon the poor old man will have a coronary.

"Take a look at your arm, your leg, whatever's injured. Do you see purple streaks? Unlock that door and come out or you'll die."

He doesn't stir. He doesn't speak. There's the outside possibility that he's comatose. What if he's died in there? If only Benny would hush so she can listen for him!

"If you won't come out, will you cough for me?"

"Nurse Cassie, please."

"Benny, don't." With a gesture she learned from that Catholic kid in fifth grade, Cassie crosses herself and pulls back the curtain to the part where the person kneels to confess.

"Oh!" With a reverent nod, the old man backs off.

Cassie slips behind the curtain. She kneels where Benny was kneeling tonight when she found him and pulled him out.

As she does so, the little panel the priest slides over the grille to signal that confessions are over snaps shut. OK then. Not dead. She doesn't like the finality of the click. She touches the grille and recoils. It's hot. "I know you can hear me. Listen. I'm here to help you, no matter what you've done or why you're hiding."

The intruder shifts position, but only slightly.

"I know you can hear me."

The warm air inside the confessional is unnaturally still.

"Look," she says, "you don't have to come out right this minute. If you want to, we can just talk. I'm Cassandra Rivard, and in case Brother Benny didn't tell you, I'm a PA. That's a physician's assistant, we're trained to do most things doctors do and you don't want *this* doctor, trust me. You're better off with me."

Nothing.

"Really, you can tell me anything. Where does it hurt?"

She thinks she can hear him stop breathing.

If she finds the right thing to say, he'll start. "Benny says you speak English. Just so you know? I'm from the States."

He is either breathing or not.

After a long time she adds, "But I can't practice there."

In its way, the silence is seductive.

She confesses, "I guess I'm lucky I can practice at all." One more minute in this deep silence and she'll let go of all the gories on the last, bad boyfriend and the lengths she went to, just to keep the man happy; she may even tell what she did to keep him going on the days when he raged like a trapped wolverine, and how awful it was when he died and she got caught with the stolen Demerol. Details she tries to keep from herself. She staves it off with: "Now it's your turn."

Then she waits.

Cassie doesn't know whether it's genetic or the result of her training, but she has an intensely keen sense of smell; it's not necessarily pleasant, but even from a distance she can tell who is sick and who isn't, who's clean and who is not. She gets a *sense* of a person. Tonight, she gets nothing. She doesn't know how long the fugitive has been living in the priest's cubicle— Brother Benny came to her for meds and dressings for the injury days ago, so it's been at least a week— but the overheated air in the confessional smells of dust from the ancient velvet curtain, that's all. As if the stranger on the other side of the closed grille isn't really there.

She says into the silence, "They took my license."

Finally she says, "That's why I'm on Clothos. So I can work."

In an odd way, the silence is restful. For a while. Then it begins to get on her nerves.

She says foolishly, "I can see why Catholics get off on kneeling down inside these black boxes. You can dump all your baggage on somebody you don't have to see."

A long time goes by.

"You just drop it the priest's lap and walk away. Then he has to carry it." Now that she thinks about it, the possibility makes her angry. "And he's stone bound not to tell."

The silence is intolerable.

She says in a low voice, "So am I."

Finally she says, "So why don't you just dump your problem, whatever, on me?"

This can go one of two ways. Either the man hiding in the priest's hole cracks and spits out his story, or Cassie cracks and starts up pouring out her soul to him— her soul or what's left of it. This makes her angry. Gnawing her knuckles, she waits.

She hears only his breathing— measured, serene. No ordinary person stays that still.

"At least let me look at your wound! You are injured, right?"

The silence makes her even madder.

OK then. Bad cop. She shouts, "Do you want to die?"

Benny gasps.

"Answer me! You have two minutes," she shouts, louder. Then she begins to count.

When nothing happens she hammers on the divider with both fists. "OK then!" She almost topples the old monk on her way out of the booth. She rights him and says in a tone that the stranger locked inside the priest's hole can't mistake, "Sit there, asshole, I'll be back. You should have come out when you had the chance."

She slams the great doors to the Assembly Hall on her way out. Shit. Colossal mistake. Go ahead, idiot, broadcast your intentions. What's he going to do, sit there and wait for you?

Two minutes alone and Benny will have him on the run.

What was she thinking? She needs to find Sarge and get back before Benny disappears her prisoner. Sly old man, for all she knows he has the infected prisoner out and running; thank God he's too old to run fast. Pray God the intruder is too sick to move any faster than Benny does.

The mystery frightens her, but not as much as the risk of sudden violence, or the prospect of contagion. Who is he, and what in hell is he carrying? Flu, staph infection, gangrene? She doesn't know.

She breaks into a run, padding down the silent nighttime corridor toward the superintendent's office. There's light showing behind the frosted pane at the far end of the hall, so at least he's up, but she is frustrated by distance. She'll never get there in time. "Sarge!" Her voice sounds thin and plaintive. If she can call loud enough to penetrate closed doors, maybe he'll come out of the office and meet her halfway.

"Sarge!"

Hurry, Cass.

Damn the no cell phones. Damn this damnable prison. Damn living like a nun.

Hurry! No telling what they'll do or where they'll hide. "Sarge?" She calls, "Sarge, I need you."

For all she knows Benny and his mysterious friend are hightailing it for some secret passage only Benny knows. They'll be underground before she can stop them if she doesn't get help and get it soon. She has to grab him before they disappear into some rabbit hole that Sarge doesn't know about, winding down into the caverns far below. The man in the booth is sick and weird and he's hiding God knows what. Is he also dangerous? Terrorist or scout for unknown invaders? She doesn't know. If she can't stop them innocent old Benny will take his charge somewhere deep that Sarge can't follow. They'll disappear into the warren of crypts that honeycomb the mountain far below the level where Sarge's massed crates of food and fuel for the generators are shored up against the end of the world. Images of destruction pile up in the shadows behind her, rushing her along. What if he's here to pollute the mountain springs or destroy the food? What if he's here to . . .

"Sarge!"

Threatened, she runs faster.

"Sarge," she calls, hurling herself into the superintendent's office without knocking, "Sarge?"

Where is the man, off on his rounds? No, he's here somewhere, not at his desk, not shelving books on the shelves that line his office, either; she doesn't have to see him to know that he's nearby. She knows.

The ways Cassie Rivard knows Sargent Whitemore are intensely physical. Although they've never fallen down together she knows him to the bone. Coming into the space the man occupies daily is extremely intimate. There are elements. His scent in the books and the papers he handles. His impression in the desk chair. Air disturbed by Sarge, moving through it. Without seeing him she senses his presence: the mass of Sarge's body, the clean, specifically personal smell of him . . .

Oh shit, she thinks, fourteen years old when you first saw the boy, what kind of adolescent magnetism was that, how did he not notice, and how did he make you fall in love with him and not look back when he walked away? You grow up, you go out into the world and do things; you try to move on and when you come back you realize that whether or not you want it, you're his for life. What the fuck is your problem, lady, pheromones?

Rushing into the Director's office, she won't know to look for an open door in the spot where nobody knows there is a door— a slice of shadow that marks an aperture behind the desk. Spinning in place, she calls, "Sarge, Sarge! Where are you?"

It's disturbing. He's here but she doesn't see him.

"Sarge?"

Where is he anyway?

"Sarge!" She opens the door to the sleeping quarters, and rushed as she is, Cassie is daunted by the narrow, tautly made bunk. *Where are he and I going to* . . . Troubled, she calls, "Emergency!"

Like *that* he is behind her, filling the air. "Cass!"

She whirls, dumbfounded. *Where did you come from?* "Help. Assembly Hall, fast!"

"What are you doing here?"

"Hurry, before he gets away."

"What?"

"Intruder. Hurry."

"A minute."

"Now!

"I have to . . ."

"No time. He'll get away. Come on!"

"Cass, I need to secure the . . ."

Sarge turns away but she seizes his hand, assuming control. "Now. He's infected."

"Infected!"

"Possibly contagious." Cassie's next words unleash Sarge and send him thudding down the hall at a dead run. "We have to isolate him before it spreads!"

SEVENTEEN

KILLER STADE

I don't know if it's altitude or some kind of druggy spices that Chef puts in the food but I'm kind of getting used to this place. When Sarge stands up there in Assembly and talks about how he's saving us from the End of the World he makes you want to believe. There is this, like, *shine* in his eyes. Thanks to him, we're waiting out the Last Days in comfort and safety. Well, safety at least. According to Sarge, the Academy is the last safe place.

Then he goes on about how we're all here because we're special, although nobody looks very special to me. Not even that girl Sylvie, who was in movies, or Teddy, who really is a prince. Teddy doesn't *feel* very special, we both know that, but he is the real thing and so is Sylvie, or she used to be.

We are all different, now that we are here.

Sarge tells us that it's for our own good. When he gets up in Assembly, which is often, the big man says that when the wars end and the sky clears and things stop erupting, we, his little elite corps, will still be standing, ready to go out and rule the world, so, yay.

I guess, but I would soooo like to get the fuck out of here.

At these assemblies Sarge tells us it's too dangerous to go outside, he used to be a Marine, so he should know. He says we are sealed in for our own protection, hence the Plexi over the courtyard and the garden dome. Sarge says you wouldn't want to breathe the air out there, it would boil your lungs and fry your liver, and the sky is so red that half the time I believe. Besides, when he shows video of explosions and tsunamis and volcanoes barfing flaming lava, it pretty much makes his point. He says we are all lucky to be here, and I guess he's right. At the end of every Assembly he raises his right hand like Noah or freaking Moses and sort of intones, "I am here to keep you safe."

I'd feel better if he didn't have those lame-ass misfits lined up on the platform behind him, our faculty looks like a herd of rejects and rehab runaways and witness protection weasels that got stuck here because they're not fit to be walking around out there in the world.

At least the prince guy and I are getting along OK. We've been cool ever since Nurse Cassie taught me about the shots, which puts us both into positions of power.

Teddy knows he can punch me when his brain is fixing to fry and I will snap to and shoot him full of enough whatever-it-is to keep him from spazzing and falling out.

And I know for sure that I can get that needle in.

Like, we have taken control.

Plus, now that he's taking his pills that Mr. Bogardus flaked on, it hasn't actually happened. Nurse Cassie freaked when I said, "What pills?" and she found out Mr. Bogardus hadn't bothered to break the plastic bubble seal on the bottle. Then she said, "It's not your fault, wait here," and went roaring off to stick it to Mr. Bogardus. She came back with red knuckles from where she smacked him, and a bottle of Teddy's magic pills.

When I brought them back to the dorm, Teddy and I had words. He said in this, like, regal tone, "Flush those down the toilet. Now."

"No way. Cassie says you gotta take these."

He was all, "I hate them, they make me stupid."

"Dude, you can't do me like that, you see what I'm saying?"

"Not really."

I hate when he spazzes out. "Dude, one more fit and you and I are done."

"But my mouth dries up and my whole life turns gray."

The poor shit. Prince or not, I shook him by the collar. "You want to have a-fucking-nother fit?"

"I want not to be stupid!"

"The last one you had, you trashed your fucking laptop."

He did. When he got weird and started thrashing it went sailing into a wall. We threw it in the closet and now he's sharing mine.

"I don't care, I want to feel like a person."

"Then act like one!" I kind of had to yell, even though I saw his point. I cranked up and gave him the good old Killer glare.

He glared right back.

Then I grabbed him and shook hard. I yelled so loud that the words kind of sprayed in his face about which I am sorry, but not so much. I was, like, all pissed off and so totally in his face that he knew I meant it. "Take the fucking pills or I will fucking murder you."

Unlike Coach Askew, Teddy believes.

He knows I am called Killer for a reason. He pops one daily like he's supposed to, so we can stop going around scared all the time. Plus, he doesn't look stupid to me. The only dumb thing he's done so far is cry in the night when he thinks I can't hear him, because he's worried as shit about that royal rotten family that stuck him here, like, OUT OF SIGHT, OUT OF MIND, washing their hands of him. He talks about them all the time. He cares about them not caring about him, which is a stupid, sad thing for a really smart kid.

Here's how stupid it is: how can he give a fuck about a family that swept him under the rug like a dusty rat turd? Never mind, we're helping each other get through here, and when Mr. Warriner or *whoever* flakes and classes go south because their head is out to lunch, which is often, I can sit in the back next to Teddy and laugh.

Unlike Teddy, Coach Askew is bone stupid and butt-ignorant. He runs the middle school drill team, aka Fitness Class. Because this stone heap is way too old to have a gym, the beefy asshole gets off on marching us out into the freezing courtyard so he can yell at us. The Plexi ceiling keeps out the snow but they can't heat the place. *Mens sana in corpore sano*, Sarge says, so Coach stands out there in the cold blowing that fucking whistle like to split your fucking eardrums if you miss a step. He is interested in yelling, which he does a lot.

Coach is convinced that people like me and Teddy, who can't keep in step, are mentally disabled, except he isn't that polite. He hollers "Tard," like he thinks that will shape us up and then he sticks the whistle back in his mouth so he is, like, breathing *fweet fweet fweet*.

So Teddy starts off on the wrong foot grinning like a developmentally disabled poodle and I stick out a foot and trip whoever's next to me on the other side.

Then Coach goes, "Fuckups like you don't belong in this platoon, you're so stupid that you belong in jail." Guess nobody told him what I really ought to be in jail for, although Mr. Berringer brought it on himself. An hour alone in the Science lab and I could shut Coach Askew's blowhole forever, but right now Science is not the science that interests me. Mostly nothing interests me. Even Mrs. Earhard's English class doesn't interest me because she's just like all the others. They stand up in front and go through the motions in whatever you happen to be taking, they stand up there bone-stupid and going: drone, drone, drone.

The teachers are crap but I am deep into this class called Technical Arts, and for a reason. We take it with dweeby little Mr. Joannides, he seems like a nice guy but we are never going to be friends. In fact, he's afraid of me. I guess he's heard what I did.

But the Tech lab is full of chips, wires, all the good stuff. Me and Teddy have been staying after, so when Steve clears his throat for the last time and runs away for fear of being left alone with us, we can sneak stuff under our sweaters and take it back to the room. Me, I want to do a few more things to my special, secret, modified iPod that not even Teddy knows I have. I don't know why Mr. J. is afraid of Teddy, but I know why he's afraid of me.

I want to, like, grab him and go, "Oh, Mr. Joannides, don't worry, I need you more than you need me," for he is a sharp techie who could answer all my questions, if we could only get friends.

I could just up and ask him, like, "Internet much?" but that would be giving it away, which at present I can't afford to do. Here's the thing.

We are cut off from the outside world.

When I boot up in the morning all I can bring up is the Academy Web page and the only downloads are podcasts of the morning news, which look suspiciously like the nightly news that gets dished up along with Chef's noxious stews and whatever Sarge is making him put in the desserts that keeps everybody but Teddy and me a little bit too mellowed out.

No Internet, how am I supposed to chill? Everything I try gives back: SERVER NOT REACHABLE. I am going crazy here.

Another month off *World of Warcraft* and everything I've won and traded, to say nothing of the band of warlocks that I've worked for years to organize and played with for so long, will just slip away. I'll lose it all, including every weapon in my armory and all my rewards that I played all night most days, just to collect. Shit! My warlocks will fall apart without me around to buck them up and whip them into shape. Our arm of the Burning Crusade is probably burning down to nothing now that I am out of the game, one more month away from Azeroth and my reputation will be shot to hell.

Unless one of the other players— fucking Fayerweather!— has muscled in, in which case, double shit! There go all my talents, there goes my reputation in the game, there goes Scrunty, my combat pet and worse even, there go all the other greatest people that I've never met that I have marshaled around me, playing to win, especially Michiko, my online girlfriend, who lives in Yokohama, Japan.

If I don't log on soon, will I lose her to Fayerweather? It is, after all, an MMORPG; that's, Massively Multiplayer Online Roleplaying Game to you. God only knows who's out there flirting with my warrior girl, or what else is going on.

I am losing control in the only world I really care about, and it's driving me nuts. Plus I would like to check my e-mail to find out if anybody from *WoW*— Michiko!— has mailed to ask where am I, am I OK, since I haven't logged on since Departure Day, and I used to be there every night, Michi must be freaking by this time. I would like to mail Mom and tell her exactly what I think of her for sticking me in here and I would like to mail my old principal and tell him exactly why I blew Mr. Berringer up and incidentally I'd like to crawl the news and see if when they shoveled out his apartment they found Mr. Berringer's whips and leather shit to say nothing of his stash of kiddie porn.

I would also like to Google the real story on these wars. The stuff Sarge dishes out sounds a little hinky to me, which especially sucks when you can't get online and check anything out for yourself to find out the truth. Like, when you're living in a vacuum, people can tell you anything they want.

Anything, and how are you supposed to know?

Teddy, he has other reasons. Like finding out how this revolution in Whatever-ograd came out and whether his folks are alive or dead. For a kid who got sent up the river for something he never asked for and can't help, he is way too soft on them. At least I murdered a guy.

And, my mom?

She can go ahead and marry her fucking new boyfriend or drop into a crater in the next quake and burn to ash in a flaming pool of lava for all I care. But Teddy is better than me and probably too nice. He worries.

Fuck you, Mom.

Like I care.

What I do care about is getting back into the game. It's not like *Doom*, which I could play on my secret iPod daily, safe as it is inside its sweet little case mod. I could play *Doom* to break your heart if I cared which I don't so much right now, because my heart is broken by not being able to log on to *World of Warcraft*, which is my true passion. I have a gang of great players in my cohort on *WoW*, all my best friends that I never met are waiting on me.

They can't move out and conquer without me. Unless . . .

Oh shit. I have to get there and find out what's gone down since the last time I connected, did they even notice that I'm gone?

I will get a connection if it fucking kills me. I don't care what Mr. Sargent says.

See, Sarge claims we are cut off for our protection. He says not being connected to the outside world is a Good Thing. We are, um, safe within the Academy network— safe from viruses and kiddie porn and sex-crazed old geezers creaming all over their keyboards when they talk to us, plus he is protecting the system from evil worms and Trojan horses and all the other bad things out there in the world.

Like we are so ignorant that we would actually go to porn sites and download a worm or click on the wrong attachment and turn some virus loose and send it raging through the system, thus wiping out every computer in the school.

Sarge says there is no Internet left out there, there's only the Academy network, but that's a load of shit.

At these Assemblies he says trust him, if anything huge happens out there in the world we'll know it, and meanwhile we are safe. He says if any of our families try to get in touch he'll definitely pass on the word.

Like any of them do. Try to get in touch, I mean. They don't even want to, only poor Teddy doesn't know that. They hopped away like scalded bunnies before the staff had us processed and lined up for shots on Departure Day.

As for the news, I have my suspicions. Sure, Sarge shows the Nightly News at dinner, school nights and weekends too, but hey. If those are real newscasts of stuff that's really happening, where's it coming from? If we aren't connected, where is Sarge getting this shit, really? Think.

Does anybody besides me care?

I only stuck it to Teddy to stop him pissing about his rotten family. Even he has to admit that on the giant plasma screen, the wars and explosions are starting to look like things that happened before. It comes to us neatly time-stamped, but how are we supposed to know? Sure Sarge posts the latest every morning. Gory vid and links to podcasts of the world outside come up on the Academy page, which, and this is weird, is the only Web page we can reach, no matter how much we dink with our machines. And that's another thing.

Get it?

Sarge is connecting. It's gotta be where he gets this stuff.

If he can do it, we can.

Fuck it. We will. Ted and I are together in this one. He may be a prince, but he's just as committed as me.

He's got his reasons.

In addition to this thing about the coup and the royal family, my friend Teddy depends on this, like, online support group for kids like him? Not royals. Seizure disorder kids. In real life he would be getting, like, a hundred e-mails from kids a lot like him, posting about how they handle living with their condition, and Teddy would be sending gazillion, everybody mailing everybody else, bucking each other up, mailing like crazy to keep from getting bummed. Now he gets zero e-mail, so he is pretty much cut off.

Plus, I find out, at home he was deep in this MMORPG that is like, specific to royals? *Regalia.* Sounds like something you wear but he says it's this amazing virtual kingdom that makes Second Life look like something a chimpanzee threw at a wall.

Go figure, how many players could a royals-only kingdom have? Teddy says it's beautiful, he says when I see it I'll want to move in and forget about *WoW* and the flaming mess the grownups have made of the outside world. Teddy says if I want in, he'll see to it, never mind that I don't have royal blood. He says if I can get him and me connected, he'll get me a character in *Regalia* so I can be part of his wonderful world and online or off, we will always be friends. He'll convince them that I'm his long-lost cousin the prince of Bavaria or some damn thing, and we'll be free. Well, not FREE free, but free in cyberspace, even though we're locked up here.

He also says he hardly ever seizes when he's playing regularly, and if he accidentally does he sends a shout out and hears right back from a hundred friends.

If he can't play it might kill him. I mean, the last one was really bad. He says it's these, like, electrical storms in his brain? He says he can feel another big one gathering up in there; they start with this crackling which I guess is the forewarning, and it's about to blow in like a monster thunderstorm.

Without *Regalia* to help him chill, Teddy is twitching, and me? I'm in the worst stages of withdrawal.

So fuck Sarge. Fuck the parents. We have to hurry. That's clear.

This is why we are loose in the Academy tonight, even though

Lights Out was hours ago and we're supposed to be back in our room like the other kids who are all in their bunk beds tucked in for the night and zonked out on Whatever, sleeping like toads.

We are, in fact, risking capture and detention or something worse at this very minute, running down the cold stone hallway, keeping low as we pass the monitor's box across from the Assembly Hall. We're heading for the superintendent's office at the end of the Administration wing. We want to sneak into the office where, I happen to know, the Academy server is stashed in the closet behind Sarge's desk which is, naturally, off-limits to us. Don't ask. My secret is safe with me.

Now Sarge, Sarge is proud of saying, "If anything comes up, my door is always open," but I don't think he means it. He sure as hell doesn't mean in the middle of the night. The light's still on, so we belly up to the door and listen. I ask Ted if he hears anything and he shakes his head. He asks me. Nope.

Thanks to Teddy's Platinum Card, which he got to keep because it's useless here, we have no trouble getting in. It's a hop, skip and a jump past Sarge's desk and into the closet, given the lock-picking tool I made in Shop, which— this is weird— which it turns out we don't even need. The door is open a crack and all we have to do is slide it the rest of the way.

God this is exciting. We have figured out what to do.

I am carrying my laptop and the cable I made with the stuff I stole from Shop. Although Sarge had Mr. Joannides pull the Wi-Fi cards out of a hundred regulation laptops, he forgot to make him remove the Ethernet cards. Like either they thought we were too stupid to know or Mr. Joannides forgot. I am carrying a pair of blue Ethernet cables. Plus I have stolen a yoke. We are going to jack into Sarge's server and use the Academy's connection to download all the stuff we need to keep current with our games, and when we get back to the room I'll do CPR on Teddy's laptop and bring it back to life.

Then we can play offline until our eyes cross and tomorrow night we'll sneak back in and upload. If there's time, sure we'll also check out bbc.com (Ted because he really does care about that lame-ass royal family) and cnn.com (me), just to make sure we're getting a straight story here. With a guy as uptight about discipline as Mr. Sargent, you never know.

The motherfucker has been accessing the Internet, no problem. It's obvious as soon as we jack in. I use the yoke to connect the server, my laptop and the PC on Sarge's desk.

Never mind the big red WARNING box that flashes on my screen. I am connected!

"Whoooo-eeee!"

Teddy goes, "Woo-hooooo!"

I go, "The world is ours."

"HOOYAAAAAA." His voice is maybe a little too shrill. He pushes me aside. "Get out of my way."

"Dude, it's my laptop."

"You can use the PC in his office. I want this."

"No way. You might hurt something."

"Please, I can feel one coming." He is zapping and crackling like if I don't let him, he'll pitch that fit, and it convinces me when he rasps, "I need this."

"OK, OK!"

"Oh man." Teddy is sort of gargling. "Ooooh, maaaaaan! Wait'll you see *Regalia,* I can hardly . . . I can hardly . . ."

I move around to look at the screen but he crouches over my laptop, cradling it so I can't see. This pisses me off but I feel sorry for the kid. I tell him, "Just download fast and get out, OK?"

"Oh shit," he says. "Oh, wow. Oooooh, shit!"

I suppose Teddy meant to say, "Wait." One of his circuits must have misfired. "Are you OK?"

Instead of downloading like we agreed, no stops for e-mail, he is distracted. Running ahead of this fucking electrical storm, the asshole has put that family first. He's mousing and clicking like a mad thing, watching a month's worth of communications download. His fingers are spidering up and down the keyboard and then up to his face and back. I can swear I see little electrical sparks, like something inside him is going *Zap!* He is way too excited. I ought to be checking out my own stuff, but he has preempted.

I run out to Sarge's PC to keep tabs on him.

Before I can sit down I hear him go, "Aaaahhhh!"

I rush back into the closet. "You're not, like, having that fit?"

"No." I can practically hear Teddy crackle. His eyeballs are whirling like those sparky-toys that spin when you turn the key. His breath comes out in a don't-bother-me gasp. "No way."

"Ted?"

He doesn't answer, he's too wrapped up in the real live images that are filling up his laptop screen. It seems like a good idea to load the hypo, just in case, which is why I'm not on deck to yell, DON'T CLICK ON THAT.

I am sticking the needle in through the seal on the serum bottle way, way carefully just like Nurse Cassie told me when Teddy goes, "Agggh. Oh, noooooo . . . !"

I practically knock him over, rushing to stick the needle in, but my friend Teddy isn't spazzing out. He is banging on my keyboard, hitting CONTROL/ALT/DELETE over and over and over again and mashing the ESCAPE key and going, "Shit, shit, oh, shitshitshit."

"What's the . . ." I don't have to ask him what's the matter. I know. I drop the hypo and look at my screen. Then OMG I look at the monitor attached to the server. What's happening is, while I wasn't looking, Teddy did something amazing-stupid and my laptop went out there into the wild blue and connected to some evil, evil place. It is downloading gangs of mean-looking code so fast that the characters are breaking up. Junk is piling in and piling up and up, scrolling way too fast to read. "Oh," I say. "Oh, shit."

"What are we going to do?"

"Hang on," I tell him. "Maybe it's just us."

I leave Teddy for a minute and back out of the closet and into Sarge's office. Then I freak because his desktop screen looks just as bad as ours, but bigger. It is swarming with lines of 0s and 1s and a mess of things that look a lot worse. Now every machine in the superintendent's office— server, his machine, ours— every one of them is overflowing with vile, twisted and malicious code, the crap is scrolling so thick and fast that there's no telling if it's piling in *on top* of the code in the server, or fucking erasing it.

Teddy's voice comes from deep in the closet. "Is it OK?"

The first thing I do is zoom in and yank our cable out of the server. "Not really."

Faster than *that* I pull it out of the yoke and detach Sarge's PC, but the crap on the boss's monster screen goes on scrolling up to make room for more crap, and it scares the living shit out of me.

"What are we going to do?"

Why do I have to say, when it's fucking obvious? "Get the fuck out. We were never here."

You know how sometimes when you do something really terrible you think you can go home to bed and put your head under the pillow and when you wake up in the morning, it'll be all gone? Like it never happened at all?

I mean, like freaking hit-and-run drivers do, pretending they didn't really hit that old lady plastered to their windshield crying and bleeding in their garage, and she isn't really going to die?

That was Teddy and me.

We collected our shit and ran like hell back to the dorm wing and holed up in our room. We shoved all our crap under Teddy's bunk and brushed our teeth like normal and pulled the covers up so high under our noses that when mewling Miss Earhard, who was standing in for Mr. Bogardus, stuck her head in, going, "Are you all right?" she couldn't see us, which meant that when we didn't answer, she figured we were both sound asleep, so she said, "Night-night," and left.

I don't know if we thought faking would work for us and the trouble would go away, or if we were so stupid that we thought even if there was real trouble in the morning, nobody would ever know it was me and Teddy that let the virus in.

EIGHTEEN

CASSIE RAN; SARGE RAN, TEARING DOWN THE HALL IN A STATE of emergency. They could have crawled and still made it in time to catch up with the old man and the intruder.

They find frail old Benny propped against the stone arch just outside the Assembly Hall, weighed down by responsibility. He is fixed in place by the weight of the fugitive, whose arms are locked around his neck in a death grip. Crisp in pristine scrubs, the stranger could be anything— hospital orderly, escapee from an institution, she doesn't know.

"Oh please," Benny cries out of love and grief. "Oh, *please,*" he says, and he is sobbing.

The man's pale arms are knotted around Benny as though he'd died hanging there and Benny alone is left to support his earthly remains.

Only a pulse in the neck tells Cassie he is still living.

Sarge was a Marine MP for too long. He orders: "Don't make a move!"

Cassie loves the man but she does not love what too many years at war have made of him. In a way she hopes life here will bring him back to what he used to be. "Don't you see he can't?"

Benny's burden shifts unexpectedly as he staggers under the weight. The fugitive's head rolls back, exposing his face. Cassie is struck by his beauty. Unkempt as he is, inert and febrile, the stranger has the unearthly, chiseled features of an angel. In spite of days cramped in that confessional, he is beardless and unnaturally clean, as though he sneaked out after Benny left and plunged into cold mountain water. Straight black hair falls away from a dead-white face. It's like looking at a fallen statue. She resists the urge to reach out and touch him.

As the body slips in Benny's grasp, Sarge's hand moves to his hip so fast that she's glad it's just habit. "Don't move!"

There are no firearms here, at least none that Cassie knows about. She touches his arm. "He can't, Sarge. He's out cold."

Damn you Sarge, you don't want to see. The man wants a confrontation. "Step away from the monk."

"He can't hear you." Cassie doesn't have to look to know Benny's mouthing the words, *I'm not a monk,* a distinction that has always escaped her. "He's unconscious."

Meanwhile Benny is begging, "Don't shoot."

"I'm not armed."

Sarge shows open hands as if to reassure them but Benny is not convinced. Burden and all, he backs away. "Please, Mr. Sargent, please don't hurt him."

"Who is this, Benny? What are you doing here?"

"I'm only trying to help him!"

Seeing how close the old man is to breaking, Cassie offers, "It's OK, Benny. Let go and I'll take care of him."

"I can't let go. I won't!"

"Step away and I'll take over," Sarge says. "Benny, that's an order."

"I have to hold him up." Benny backs away with his eyes blazing. "It's my duty!"

Sarge could overpower the old man, no problem, but Cassie fixes him with her glare and instead, he starts over. "Benedictus, who is this man?"

Either Benny won't answer or he can't. He is overloaded and trembling. Even his voice shakes with the effort he puts into coming up with the only answer he will give. His hands shake and his lips quiver but finally he manages, "He's sick."

It's as if Sarge just hit a wall at tremendous speeds. His head jerks back so fast that his neck snaps. "Sick!"

"Sick bad," Benny says, as if that explains everything.

"And you kept this a secret?"

"I was only trying to help him!"

The silence that follows is terrible. When Sarge can speak again his voice comes from somewhere new. It is cold and terrifying. "Do you know what this means?"

A chill rattles the stranger's long bones just then and Cassie watches poor old Benny's body shake in a sympathetic shudder that stirs the skirts of his frayed habit. "I know he needs help."

"Disease, in a place like this? I'll tell you what it means," Sarge says so sternly that tears start in Benny's eyes. "He's a danger to the community."

"Is not," Benny says stubbornly.

"Danger? Sarge, the man is unconscious."

Benny cries, "He isn't hurting anybody!"

Cassie can guess at the nightmare scenarios passing through Sarge's mind: LTCOL Sargent Whitemore, formerly of the U.S. Marines, an officer with a hundred-some souls to protect and defend; her Sarge, Sarge the precisionist, who is dedicated to making lives march in order, is face-to-face with the unnameable and unexpected. Outraged, the man Cassie has loved since she was four-teen years old bunches his shoulders and raises his fists so abruptly that she is afraid for all of them. And lowers them. She thinks she hears him counting to ten.

In spite of which, he explodes. "You don't know what he's hurt-ing!"

Benny reels as if battered by a strong wind. "I'm sorry."

"Sorry isn't enough. Now who the fuck is he?"

"I don't know. I don't know!" One more minute supporting the unconscious fugitive and Brother Benedictus will collapse under the weight of his responsibility. His voice is thin and his eyes film over with tears of regret. "I'm so sorry!"

Benny is so near tears that Cassie tells him, "It's nothing you did, Benny. Really."

"Who knows what kind of trouble you let in here, old man . . ."

"I'm just so sorry."

Stalled in the dim hallway with the two men— deeply tanned Sarge with his white-blond hair, and the pallid, black-haired fugitive— she thinks, *Dark and light. Dark and light,* as though they are the two sides of a coin, and the hell of it is, she doesn't know which is which; she says, "We need to get him into bed."

". . . what kind of pestilence." Sarge looks ready to hit him.

"He's just sick," Benny sobs. "He's not dangerous."

"And you invited this in?"

"He already *was* in!"

"He got in and you didn't report it?"

"Bless me Father." Close to collapsing under his burden, the old man fingers the wooden rosary hanging from his belt. "I'm try-ing."

"You kept it a secret?"

Benny may not know what he means but he repeats, "I'm *trying.*"

"Stand down, old man. I'm trying to help you."

"Not me," Benny cries. "Help him. Help him!"

By this time even Sarge sees that the old man is broken. He measures out his next words like cough medicine. "Do you know what a danger he is to the rest of us?"

"He can't hurt anybody." The old man blinks in a pageant of misunderstanding. "He's too sick to hurt anything."

Old Benny is so exhausted that even Sarge softens. "That's the point, Benny. He's sick, and we don't want anybody to catch it. Now, stand down. If you won't let me do it, let Cassie take him."

"Benny, please. He's terribly sick."

Confused, he smiles at her. "So . . . you'll cure him?"

"I'll try."

"Isolate him, Cass. Find out what we've got here. OK, Benny." Sarge extends his hands. "Now." Still Benny makes a dogged half-turn, evading him. "I said, *now.*"

"We don't have an isolation . . ."

"Dratch's room. Evict the drunken bastard, if I had my way I'd throw him off the mountain. OK, Ben. It's time to let go."

"I can't."

"But you will."

"No." But Brother Benedictus is at the end of his strength, spent and too weak to do anything but raise bony fists in a pathetic gesture that topples him, burden and all. He goes down wailing, "No!"

"It's OK, Benny, it's OK." Sarge lifts the stranger's locked arms from around Benny's neck like a farmer removing a yoke from a draft horse. He picks Benny up and dusts him off. "Go hit the sack. You need it."

"Please . . ."

"This is an order. Go to bed!" He points Benny in the direction of his quarters and gives him a shove. Inertia sends the old man lurching toward the stairs that lead down to his resolutely monkish cell. Like it or not, Benny is weak where Sarge is strong. Old. Bony and so unsteady on his feet that the slightest breeze will blow him the rest of the way. Whether or not he intended it, Benny arrives at the stairs. Cassie watches until she's sure he's gone down and let himself into his room.

Then she watches until she's sure he'll stay. She turns in time to see Sarge lift the stranger so easily that she wonders if the fever leached this man's bones and left him weightless.

"OK, let's move him out before some other fool runs into him and gets infected."

"Wait." She has to run to keep up with him. "We're not sure what he has is . . ."

"Isolate him," Sarge says over his shoulder. "Treat him. Figure out what we need for prophylaxis. Cipro. Gamma globulin. Whatever you've got. God knows what pestilence he's carrying."

". . . infectious. What if it's just exhaustion?"

"He's burning up."

She knows. Odd, she thinks, since the stranger is so pale. "Could be sepsis. Given the stuff he stole, I think Benny was treating some kind of injury."

"Take cultures. Whatever else you people do. Until you find out what he's got, he stays in isolation."

"Dratch will be pissed."

"Fuck Dratch. God knows what's hatching inside this guy."

"Don't." The Jews have a phrase for this circumstance; Cassie thinks it's spelled *kaina hora*. There are some things, she knows, that are better left unsaid. This is when some people throw salt over their shoulders or mutter whatever charms they know to keep trouble from coming down on them, but one of the reasons she has always loved Sargent Whitemore is that he walks through fire without blinking. He isn't afraid to call the shots. She tries to make this sound like a rational request. "Don't speculate."

"Do what?"

"Name it and you may bring it."

It is as if she hasn't spoken. At the door to the Infirmary Sarge turns. He spells out what they most fear. "In a closed situation, disease spreads like wildfire."

Frightened, she answers. "I know."

NINETEEN

SYLVIE HAS A SECRET BOYFRIEND THAT NOBODY KNOWS
about and she goes around all day excited. That's one reason she
has to be so loud about not giving a fuck about sex when they're
snorting chocolates in the fat girl's room. When you're doing
something you're not supposed to be doing, that's when you most
need to keep the good news to yourself.

He is so cute! Greek, she thinks, with this curly black hair like a
god, although he is somewhat skinny. No beard because Mr. Sargent made him shave it off which is not so bad because beards are
soooo over, as far as Sylvie's concerned.

She ran into her secret boyfriend in the AV room her first week
here, and you would have to say they hit it off right away.

Actually, she went in to Google herself to find out what's going
on out there. It's not like *her* coke bust shows up on Mr. Sargent's
Nightly News that he dishes up like ketchup with dinner. I mean,
his news is all these miserable wars and the gazillion ways in which

the world is going to hell which makes Sylvie wonder, where's the beautiful people news, which she is generally featured in? Has anybody out there noticed she is missing? Like, on other shows they aren't getting, are they covering what the beautiful people are doing in the face of Whatever. The hardship. Coping parties. Crisis wardrobes, there's so much she doesn't know! Is the right stuff showing up on *Access Hollywood* or *Hollywood Extra,* and why doesn't Mr. Sargent ever show them *E.T.*?

It's not so bad, being in this jail, except for the no real news about things that are really important, like, who misses her. In fact it takes the pressure off of her thrice-daily What to Wear sessions, and at home three changes is a bare minimum, given the reputation she has to maintain. Plus it keeps her from having to make any of her famous bad decisions, like, every two minutes; face it, when you're Sylvie D'Estart in the real world, the pressure is intense. In fact, the worst thing about the Academy is not the loss of freedom, which is kind of a relief.

It's not knowing what the major media plus bloggers and podcasters have to say about Sylvie D'Estart getting sent up the river by her unfeeling parents and Hard-Hearted Hector, her life coach, who is no better than he should be but very good at what he does.

Shit, she didn't even get the Bronco overhead coverage like every other two-bit studio slut that she can think of, when she left, there wasn't a helicopter in sight. Damn her folks to nether hell for doing it on the quiet. I mean, a thing like this has got to be bigger than any of those skanks, her showbiz rivals, going to jail for five minutes, or slashing guys' initials into their bald scalps or popping in and out of rehab, and as far as Sylvie knows, there has been zero coverage, but in a place like this, how will she ever know who cares about her?

All she wanted to do in the AV room was spend five minutes Googling, like, counting the references, I mean, even in the face of radio silence a personality as big as Sylvie D'Estart has reason to hope, and that's what Sylvie is. Until last month her every little fart got picked up on the news. So, hey! Maybe the fans are carrying the ball, maybe one of them captured a screen shot of her going away, sold it to the highest bidder, all that, in which case she knows the news is out there and *somebody* is planning a rescue, which is why she sneaked into the AV room after study hall and this gorgeous guy sprang out and caught her. He went, like, *eeek!* "What are you doing here?"

She did what Sylvie does, she did the patented D'Estart Thing, eyebrows arched, nose-holes flared, the look designed to strike pity and terror, and she thundered as loud as a ninety-five-pound girl can thunder out of a chest that isn't very deep. She stuck it to him in the usual way and waited for him to fall down and worship. "Do you know who I am?"

Then he said the most amazing thing. "Not any more." Then he flashed this beautiful grin at her. "But I won't tell anybody."

"You . . . won't tell anybody that I'm her?"

It was awful. He almost laughed. "Not any more."

"Of course I'm still me." OK, she'd put on a little weight and her hair was, maybe, inexcusable? She tried the voice designed to kill and maim. "Sylvia Cathcart D'Estart."

That didn't stop him. He didn't even stop grinning. "No-no, you're her, all right."

Outrageous, she thought, but she was also noticing that inside the black T-shirt, this guy that she couldn't tell how old or how young he was, was significantly pumped. Resolutely, she kept the tone. Hector, her life coach, called it *frigidarium*. "And you aren't going to tell them . . . what?" But why should she believe Hard-Hearted Hector, after what he did? He drove all the way to Crete with her and Marla without once telling them why they couldn't bring luggage or what the hovercraft was for. "I said, you're not going to tell them *what*?" She went all *frigidarium* PLUS and waited for him to fall back a step at least, if he didn't flat-out fall down and worship her.

But it was not like this had any effect on the cute guy in the AV room. He could care less about celebrity and whether or not she was one but oh, he had the most beautiful grin. "That it positively doesn't matter who you are."

"What?" It took a minute. Then the silver dollar dropped. When the machine stopped, it came up three lemons.

She couldn't decide whether to kill herself or cry, but he was so cute that she decided on the latter, which is how she ended up in this sweet guy's arms with him tousling her hair even though it had not been washed, rocking her nicely and going, "There there."

Sex, she thought, even though she hadn't thought about it for days, and then she wondered why it used to be such a big deal. She couldn't think of anything else to say so she said, "What are you doing here?"

Then her new secret boyfriend said the funniest thing, and she still doesn't know whether it was or wasn't a joke; he said, "If I told you, I'd have to kill myself," but he was grinning when he said it so they both laughed.

She thought she saw her chance to wheedle so she folded her hand backward on his collarbone in the patented D'Estart way and said, "I just, like, wanted to Google myself? One little click, one question, I promise."

"It'll never happen," he told her.

"Just for a minute?"

"It can't be done," he told her. "Trust me."

"How do you know?"

He gave her an astonished look, like, he practically said, *Do you know who I am?* "If it could be done, I'm the one who could do it. Believe me, there's no connection."

She slid the back of her hand along his collarbone and right

straight down between his pecs. "But if you ever, um, get a connection?"

And he kind of leaned into her hand, and didn't they get friends
then, and didn't it happen fast? By the time he left her at the end of
the dormitory wing he was saying, "If I connect, I promise. You'll
be the first to know."

They've been sneaking out to meet in different places every
night since. They haven't had sex yet, but almost as good as, which,
given all the different kinds of sex Sylvie had in public and private
places, the real thing is, frankly, no big.

They do **everything but,** which at this stage in her life Sylvie is
beginning to think is better than all the stuff she started doing with
all those guys the year she turned twelve. There's a lot to be said
for "almost." A lot and a lot.

Plus, she and her secret boyfriend that not even Marla knows
about? They both have reasons.

His reason for holding back on sex is, he's all, "I love you but I'd
lose my job if I got down with you," which she thinks is a humongous laugh since, if Sarge decides to fire him, where's he gonna go?
Over that cliff in a wooden bucket? She knows about the cliff because he took her out there last night.

Mostly because it's embarrassing, her reason for holding back is
a lot more private.

The thing is, Sylvie is not rightly what you would call herself
right now. Everything is still there but it's all sort of a dull gray, like
back when they had her on Prozac, which makes her wonder what
Chef Pete is putting in the food that keeps them all so not-caring,
like, everybody is zonked out. As in, nothing's interesting. Not
talking and not music and sure as hell not reading and certainly
not hanging out with Academy boys, who totally aren't interested
in them either. Sex isn't interesting, so she's scared of . . .

Like! What if she and her secret boyfriend decided to Do It and this experience has, like, turned her to stone and it turned him off her forever?

So she's happy to keep this thing between her and her secret boyfriend at: Almost.

See, the last thing Sylvie gives a fuck about in these hard times is not clothes or shoes and it isn't gulping, shooting or snorting the drugs she can't get right now, or being able to buy out the bar at one of the clubs on Sunset or taking a fifth up on Mulholland and getting loaded whenever she feels like it. It sure as hell isn't her Barbie bedroom at home or her trailer at the studio and it isn't Hard-Hearted Hector her life coach who turned her in and got her sent to rehab all six times.

It isn't even her dog.

What turns her on is that in a place where absolutely nothing happens, something just might happen to her after all, something that will never happen to Marla or any of the other dreary bitches here and certainly not to those gaudy skanks her showbiz rivals who are running free out there in the world and falling down with all kinds of guys, sometimes in the back of the car on their way out to that first date.

For the first time in her life *ever,* Sylvie D'Estart has something they don't have.

It's romance.

Yep. Romance, which is what she gets with this secret boyfriend that she can hug and kiss as much as she wants but doesn't fuck. This is why she likes romance so much. It's not like when it's your birthday and you get your big present and you open it and after all that wanting and getting exactly what you want, you're, like, *is that all?*

With romance, it's always just about to be your birthday, and you can spend forever and ever being excited, like, you can hardly wait for the day. Your big present is always on the way, it just hasn't come yet. In fact, the great thing about it is, it won't. So you're never disappointed. It's so cool!

Before is always better than after. Everybody knows that.

That's why she hit it off with her secret boyfriend. They've been meeting in the, like, *garden dome* thingy late at night after the monk guy goes home. Tonight he sneaked her *outside* and they sat on the cliff, which was the most romantic thing yet, unless you count that she doesn't know what happened after they said good night. "Wow," she said when a lightning flash outlined that Greek profile and the curly black hair— too bad he's so short— OK, the sky was weird, but in spite of what Mr. Sargent and Mr. Bogardus tell them in those health lectures, there's absolutely nothing the matter with the mountain air outside the Academy except maybe that slight burny smell that's been around Los Angeles for, face it, years.

Her secret boyfriend had this, like, weird *apparatus* thing with him? First of course they kissed and then he gave her brandied chocolates and she fed him one. They were holding hands and looking out at the weird night sky when he said, "I have a surprise for you."

At which point Sylvie thought, *Oh shit. I don't want to know what's in your pocket. I don't want to know what's in your pants.* The surprise turned out to be that it wasn't anything like she thought. He reached into his messenger bag and pulled out this contraption. "What's that?"

"Signal booster. I made it out of stuff I had."

"What does it do?"

He was like, *this is a question that you already know the answer, right?* "I did it for you."

"Cool." She wasn't about to let him know she didn't have a clue.

Then she did. He took her by both hands and he got all serious. "I know how much you need to make contact and I might go to jail for it . . ."

"Jail!" Oh, they are soooo bonded.

"But I love you *so much,* and I know. It's not like I'm what you would call Internet addicted, but when you've been connected all your life and then you're not . . . Plus, I have to find out what the Feds are . . . Never mind. Look," he said and Sylvie thought, *I'm in love,* "I need you to go back inside now. Can you find your way back to where I brought you out? Can you sneak back to your room without getting caught?"

As if. Her, Sylvie D'Estart, queen of the prison break. She said, "No problem," and kissed him on the lips. At the moment she's wishing they'd kissed a little longer given that she hasn't seen him since, but he was already fooling with the instrument or whatever it was he had spent the past few days making. "What about you?"

"This won't take long, I promise."

Sylvie got up. "I love you," she said irresponsibly.

"I love you too," he said.

"Be careful. If they catch you they might . . ." So this is what's keeping Sylvie awake right now. She doesn't know what they might do. She reached for him but he slipped away.

"Don't worry. I'll be in as soon as I get this thing planted." He was eyeing a crag just above them. It didn't look too-too high. "If this works I'll get us both connected. Just don't tell anybody."

"I won't. Oh, honey, take care." It was so lame, calling him honey, but hey, personal security. They never use his name. Then lightning flashed the way it does in bad movies and she said, "No. It's too high."

"Don't worry about me," he said, sticking the contraption inside his shirt and oh, the way he grinned at her when he said, "I'm at home in high places."

And for a minute there, she almost believed him. But it was so *high.* "Are you sure?"

"No problem." Dark curls and a gloss on him, like he really might be waterproof. "My dad grew up around here. He used to dive off cliffs into this very same ocean."

But still . . . She stood there on the mountaintop going "but-but-but" until he kissed her and sent her inside.

This is why Sylvie is lying in her bed in the middle of the night with her eyes wide open while Marla snuffles and curses in her sleep. She's wondering whether he can do what he said and when she gets up in the morning and turns on her computer she'll find it right there at the bottom of the Academy Web page, an instant message from her true love, which in this place where nobody texts and nobody can IM or any of that shit, means that she will be in private, secret, eternal contact with her better than actual, her almost-lover, a situation which Sylvie is convinced is the absolutely, positively, eternally best kind.

What a rush.

If I had my druthers, she thinks in the cadences of the Hollywood nanny who raised her, who just happened to be an actress from Charleston, *I wish it could be **almost** with him forever.*

TWENTY

IT'S MORNING. DRATCH IS SLEEPING IT OFF IN CASSIE'S ROOM where Sarge dragged him last night, stumbling and complaining. She'll have to fumigate the place. In Dratch's room, the sick man sleeps on fresh sheets.

Last night she did what PAs do more often than they'd like. She washed the patient as if for burial. That beautiful body was unnaturally clean, so still and so perfect that it was like washing the body of an athlete who'd died in his sleep. *Strange,* she thought, trying to stay cool and professional. *This is extremely strange.* It was particularly strange when she went to work on the gash in his thigh. The edges of the wound were red and puffy; the thing was festering. She touched it experimentally. He didn't even twitch. It was as though he was beyond pain. Using a surface anesthetic, she cleaned out the necrotic tissue and closed it with stitches, looking for a change in the breathing, fluttering eyelashes, anything to signal that he was aware. She set a shunt for the IV and added antibiotics to the drip and she did all this while her patient lay without stirring. Not sleeping, not comatose, she thought. Then, what?

It was as though he had drifted down through layers of painful awareness to a meditative state deeper than any sleep.

She left a bell on the bedside table with instructions to ring if he needed anything. He showed no signs of waking. She left it in case. She thought about adding a note of explanation but she had no idea what to write.

"This is for your protection," she said when she was finished, and locked the sleeping stranger into Dratch's room.

It seems to be morning. She is roused by Sarge's regulation trumpet call. On weekdays it comes at six. Fucking Reveille. Damn this narrow bunk. And Dratch, that useless lush, is sleeping in her quarters, which means she'll start the day in the same clothes she wore yesterday and the same underwear she wore all day and fell down in early this morning, unless it was late last night. She's lost track of what day it is.

By the time she unlocks the door to Dratch's room she is angry. She's even angrier when she sees that the patient is awake. In spite of the wound in his thigh he sits in lotus position. He looks fixed, as if he's been sitting that way for a long, long time.

She says crossly, "Why didn't you ring for me?"

Instead of answering, he shrugs. He is composed, at peace. Now that he's awake she sees that he is younger than she thought. What is he, twenty? Twenty-one?

His sweet half-smile angers Cassie because she can't figure out quite why she is so angry. Instead of asking any of the logical questions she says, "OK, where did you get the scrubs?" Then she challenges: "And don't even think about not answering."

After a night of no sleep Cassie is so tired and confused she's ready to fly off at the slightest provocation but the young stranger sitting on Dratch's bed smiles nicely and says, "Father Benny brought them."

"Not father."

"Yes."

"He's not a priest."

He dips his head. "He only thinks he's not."

Cassie can't be sure how she let the stranger lead her down this byway when they should be getting down to hard facts about him and this case but she finds herself asking, "What do you mean?"

Whoever he is, wherever he came from, the sick man sitting on Dratch's bed says in an odd, visionary way, "We never know who we are or why we're here until the time comes."

Dear God, she thinks, *tell me this isn't one of those things.* Briskly, she pats the pillow. "Lie down. I need to check on this wound."

"You stitched me up."

"I did. And you didn't feel it?"

"No."

"And you don't feel it now?"

"No."

"No soreness? No burning?" At this point in crap movies Cassie has seen, the mysterious angel/whatever pulls aside the fabric to reveal flesh so clean and smooth that it's as if there never was an injury. No belly button, at least half the time, at least in the movies. Bumps on the back suggesting vestigial wings. The people rejoice and mend their ways and the angel/whatever moves on, presumably to perform more miracles. She peels away the dressing with no clear idea what to expect, but she can't bring herself to look. Instead, she looks into his face. "How about now?"

His gray eyes are fixed on her. The question he asks is human enough but an unnatural pale light surrounds the pupils, diffusing the gray. "Am I OK?"

"Hang on." She looks. She is more relieved to see that the gash looks no better than she is to note that at least it isn't any worse than it was last night when she closed it. Whether or not he complains of heat or tightness, it looks ugly. No need to alarm him. She puts on her best professional tone, "No change."

"I know it's worse." Could he not sound so serene?

"Why did you let it get so bad?" Could she not let this upset her?

"I had to wait for someone I could trust."

"It could have killed you!"

Those odd eyes. "Would that have been so bad?"

"Yes it would!" Exasperated, she says, "Do you trust me?"

"I don't know."

"You know I could have put you under forever, and I didn't."

"I do."

"You know that until I cleaned this thing up, it was poisoning you."

"Yes."

"Then you can damn well trust me." She tapes a fresh dressing in place. "OK. What happened? How did you get hurt?"

"I fell."

"Where?" *Oh shit,* she thinks, *don't tell me you fell to earth.*

"I can't tell you."

"It would help if I knew what you fell on. What ripped your leg like that? Rock? Rusty metal, a nail or a broken hinge? A stick of wood?" *Could it have been skeletal: long bone or a femur,* she wonders, but does not say because she doesn't know where it came from or why it gives her the creeps.

He says again, "I can't tell you."

"Can't tell me, or won't?"

Then in that infuriating, cryptic way of his, Benny's mystery guest answers with a question, "What does it matter whether it's can't or won't when the outcome is the same?"

"Enough. Take these." She waits while he swallows his meds. Sticks a digital reader into his ear. "Your fever's through the roof."

Working fast, she palps the lymph nodes: enlarged. Listens to his heart. It's OK. She's been putting off the worst-case scenario for last. "Now cough for me. Cough again." The lungs are bad. Shit yes there is something going on.

Out of nowhere he says, "I'm sorry," and passes out, leaving her to re-set the IV and turn out the light before she leaves the room. The man is sick, no question. The only question is why it isn't any worse which, given her limited resources, is just as well. What she needs to know first is whether all this is directly related to the injury and if not, and this is where her throat dries up and her belly tightens, what communicable disease he's brought into the Academy.

The issue that troubles her most is how much to tell Sarge.

Nothing, she thinks, until I know more. Once she gets coffee she'll research this thing, trying to augment what little she knows.

Just the smell of coffee brewing makes her feel better. *I can do this,* she tells herself. *I have to, OK? So I can.* She pours the first cup and sits down at the clinic computer. In the next second Dratch comes lunging out of her quarters in a dudgeon, ranting and sputtering complaints. Groaning, Cassie gets up to apologize when she most wants to smack him because, shit, she was brought up a lady and in theory, at least, the old drunk is her boss.

As it turns out, she is spared the scene.

Outside somebody calls, "Ms. Cassie!" and she whirls.

The Infirmary doors swing open and trouble comes in. That plain, fat girl— what's her name, Sheela— that fat girl Sheela comes into the clinic at what, for her, passes for a dead run.

"Ms. Cassie, Ms. Cassie!" For a kid who makes it her business to look impassive, the child is pretty upset. "There's something the matter with Marla Parsons, she's been in the shower forever, like, yacking up her guts. Come quick, I don't think it's the truffles."

TWENTY-ONE

SARGE

For the first time since the day I started this, I have zero idea what today will be like. Me, the prophet of the Order of the Day. Who can predict what will come down when nothing you set in place so carefully is still working?

In an establishment like mine things have to come down by the numbers. What everybody does and where. What time. Everything SOP with a standard operating procedure for every contingency. The Order of the Day. This place runs like a finely tuned machine. When all about you are losing theirs, in the crunch, routine holds you up and carries you. I know, trust me, I've been there and I made it back. Joannides and I had all my systems in place and in working order before the first carload of staff set foot inside the Academy. I briefed them on procedures. It was more than orientation. They trained.

How else would I protect and maintain the sealed environment I have created here? If life is a disease, and it pretty much is right now, my people are in quarantine. Safe, for now, from the horrors and confusion of the outside world. There are no wild cards in play in my ideal community. No end runs allowed. No outside events. The key element is control.

Now everything is totally fucked.

How could something so good go bad overnight?

It's that guy.

This weird, sick bastard, whoever he is, breached our defenses, and he did it in the night and nobody but old Benny knew and he hid him for days, during which God knows what went down. I'll kill him if I have to, to find out how he breached the perimeter.

Pestilence came in with him.

Just when everything was going so well. All systems go, all the necessaries loaded, food and supplies for as long as it takes stowed. Proof against the world.

Organized.

My high level of organization keeps your talented, wild kids safe under this roof. Contained and controlled, ergo safe. When they go back into the world these unformed victims of free will go back improved. I'm turning brats into responsible human beings, and the method? It's how the Naval Academy makes officers. Through attention to detail. Everything comes down by the numbers, SOP. My long life in the Corps taught me the virtue of routine. Protocols. The chain of command.

Here on Clothos, the top of the chain of command is me. I call the shots. My staff is well aware. No outsiders, no communications from outside, at the first hint of an incursion, notify me. Bonded personnel locked in place for the duration, down to Chris Tackett and his squad, who carry on unseen. For what I'm paying, nobody complained. By the time the last carload came up on Departure Day and I secured Clothos, they all knew.

Nobody goes, I told my staff before they signed their contracts. And nobody comes. Clothos is a sealed environment. For our

mutual health and safety, keep it that way. Be wary of the unexpected and even more wary of things you can't explain. Repel all
boarders, and that's an order.

You come bearing gifts and I turn you away, no problem, but by
the time I found him, this weird, sick bastard was already inside.

Everything's at risk: the discipline, the Order of the Day. Once
you open the door to the weird and irregular, anything can get in.
The ranks of hell could be forming, set to rise up and come down
on us, crazed fugitives running ahead of the end of the world.

Some fool— Benny? Cassandra, you would *not*— then who?
Somebody let trouble into the installation. In a secured situation
like this one, any outside event is a threat. The unknown. Correction. Not knowing how much you don't know.

I should pitch the inexplicable bastard off the mountain. It
would eliminate the problem, but there are questions. Minus the
symptoms, I could take him topside and throw him off the cliff,
but we're holding the ultimate wild card. No telling what foul disease the man is carrying or who he infected.

Whether it's already too late for us.

We won't know shit until I wake him up. There's nothing on
his body to indicate where he came from— no scars, no studs or
tattoos, no gang symbols or bar codes or numbers on his arm to
inform us, no visible clues, just the fever and the gash to tell us
how he was, which is: sick as a bastard. No ID on him, no jewelry, no papers, nothing to indicate how the fucker got in, and
this is bad.

Last night he was too trashed to interrogate; I had Cass go
through the pockets of the scrubs she took off him after we laid
him out in Dratch's room, prior to the cavity search which, as she's
a medical professional, I left to her.

The pockets weren't even his pockets.

What I should have done after we locked him in and I headed
back to my quarters was start a global search, typing in every detail

I could number. I should have done it first thing, but by the time I hit the door I was too messed up to start.

Correction. I didn't know where to start.

I wasted the long walk from the Infirmary at the foot of the cross back to my quarters considering. What search string do you give an Internet search engine when you don't know what you're looking for? Should I enter: **recent shipwreck** + **survivors** + what? **Plane crash** + **mountain**? We'd have heard it come down, shield or no shield. Right, the shield. About the shield. Don't ask. So maybe I should enter **Clothos** + **prison break**? + **enemies specific to Whitemore**? +**incursion**? Long day, tough night, my head was disappearing up its own asshole at tremendous speeds.

I could put Cass to work searching diseases, have her enter the symptoms and triangulate. If the plague was specific to a location we might know where he came from, but security comes at a cost. In the morning I'd turn her loose on the medical DVDs I bought for Dratch, who never cracked the shrink wrap on the first one.

That left me. Crossing the *T* and heading down the long hall to my office I thought: **disruption** +**contamination**? No. **Pestilence** + **infiltration**? I was so fried that my guesses were getting wilder and wilder. **Unknown** + **bastard** + **disease**? By the time I got back to quarters I was too pissed off to do shit.

OK, I thought. This was the last thing I thought before sleep poleaxed me. *You're too trashed to do anything. 0600, when you're fresh.*

Life in the military taught me one thing, maybe too well. There is virtue in routine. When you're running on empty, systems kick in and carry you through. *One. Two.* I learned that **in country**. *Three.* Go through the motions and you get what you expected. Systems pick you up on the count of three and put you down at . . . Wait for it . . . Four. I always secure the server and lock the secret compartment at midwatch before I quit my quarters to walk the perimeter. SOP.

But Cass pulled me out to catch this guy and I lost track. When I got back to quarters it was after 0400, which meant ergo, certain things had been done. I always did them, QED. Get it? The numbers. That's how you know. It was done. So was I.

I hit the rack and like a helpless asshole, I dreamed.

Brain poison, brain candy, dreams sucked me in. Last night's dreams were murky, strange. Wet dreams. No. Not wet like you think. Wet like this: I was submerged, with water at knee level and rising fast. We were all in the belly of a submarine with death raining down on us through split seams in the hull. Not depth charges. Water pressure, we were that deep. My tin can made a crash dive and hit bottom ten fathoms lower than the Mindanao deep. I was in the main compartment with a hundred others— my crew, I think, or survivors from my unit **in country** or, shit. The people from here. I know we were bonded and I was responsible; we were packed so close that I could smell their fear. Unless it was my fear— that I couldn't save them no matter what I tried. I could hear them screaming but it was so steamy inside my drowned ship that I couldn't see who they were or where they were, only that they were trapped.

It was so wet in the sub that mushroom gardens and weird jungle shit twined up and around us as I watched; the vegetation was rank and so thick that I couldn't see my people. They were howling like the damned and I couldn't get through. I shouted but nobody heard.

If I didn't get there in time the vines would swallow their bodies and squeeze the living blood out of them. The water level was rising so fast that they could scream and no sound would come, only bubbles shaped like screams. If I didn't make it they would all drown, but the air in the compartment where we were trapped was so thick that no matter what I tried or how hard I struggled through the swampy mess I'd fail and they would all die. My people!

I had to warn them or it would get them, and the fuck of it was that I didn't know what *it* was. I had to get through or the *it* would get them all.

No, I didn't wake up screaming. Marines don't scream.

When the *it* is about to get you, you get busy. By the numbers, right? I rushed into the compartment where my server lives and it did not occur to me until I sat down at the keyboard that I hadn't unlocked the door.

Then it did, but by that time the detail was just that. Duly noted. Too late. Pestilence entered the compound some time in the night, but not the kind you think.

It was crawling up my screen.

First I tried to reboot. It's what you do. Like medics hitting a flatliner with the paddles, charging and re-charging when the only life in the corpse is the shudder of a dead thing being shocked, I re-booted, shocking the thing over and over beyond the point where it has any point because in the presence of death, it's what you do because you aren't strong enough to face the truth.

You keep on doing it because nobody wants to admit that another person is functionally dead. I kept trying to reboot. Again. Again because I couldn't believe it and again because I didn't want to believe it and I kept on doing it until I realized how totally, absolutely fucked we really are.

Whatever I thought I was going to do on the machine: research Marburg and Ebola, diagnose blood fever, study disease prevention or research all the weird, sick bastards who drop out of nowhere and violate the security of the last safe place; whether I thought I was going to research operating procedures, research ways of re-booting, research the contamination that whacked my computer or for God's sake send for help, I was totally fucked.

Where it ought to be showing me the usual, the display my server dished up had gone to black, but the screen was by no means empty.

Empty, now, empty would have been good, but this!

The black screen was rapidly turning white. It was teeming with white bugs; they were not exactly letters or numbers and they were coming faster than bullets of ice in a hailstorm, until scraps of code I recognized and symbols I didn't turned the screen from black to gray to arctic white. Instead of showing me the user-friendly expected, my server, OK, the beating heart of my Academy was yorking up endless white 1s and white 0s mixed in with outrageous characters that made cuneiform look like your ABC's and the whole mess was scrolling up the screen so fast that I couldn't follow; the code was getting thicker and thicker and nothing I could do would make it stop.

But for every eventuality, there is a protocol, right? It's the premise on which this place is built. In case of mysterious computer disasters, your IT guy is the man. On cyber matters, Joannides is my fallback, my point man. A good commander never initiates an operation without a fallback, it's SOP. So if my guts were shaking it was no problem, and I knew it.

But they were.

Pull yourself together, shithole. Give him five minutes with this thing and your problem is no problem.

I punched Steve Joannides's room number on the intercom and waited for him to come.

TWENTY-TWO

MISERABLE AS HE WAS WHEN THEY CAUGHT HIM LAST NIGHT, beaten down by his failure to protect and defend his beautiful, enigmatic friend, Brother Benedictus fell on the bed, so spent that he forgot to cross himself. He overslept in a desperate attempt to stay in the old dream that still comes unexpectedly and only when he is in a weakened condition. It's another of those odd, sweet dreams that sometimes surprise him in spite of his age, sudden, mystifying hints dropped into a lifetime of celibacy. They are so vivid that sometimes it's hard to tell which are events remembered and which are just Benny, dreaming.

There's the chance that it wasn't a dream that once, at least he thinks it wasn't, but that was so long ago that he is no longer certain. When it comes, the dream makes poor Brother Benedictus yearn for things he doesn't know about, and it always brings him back sobbing.

Resolutely, Benny clenches his eyelids, clutching at shreds of the shattered dream, but there's a terrible racket coming between them. It takes him a minute to realize it is the sound of his own voice, shouting.

"Lost!"

What did I lose?

Confused, he opens his eyes. He snaps to a sitting position so fast that all his old bones crack. The light on the ceiling tells him it's too late for certain things.

Dear God, I slept through Lauds!

What if Matins floats by without him? What if he loses Terce and Compline too? What's left to anchor him if he lets the Hours escape him completely? Grounded for all these years by the monastic rule, held up by the discipline, Benny feels as if he's been cut loose from everything he knows. Unmoored, he's adrift in thin air, flailing in a void filled with flying objects.

He lost Lauds.

What else has he lost?

Last night he lost his only friend, a like soul trapped and quivering like an exotic wild bird in this raw, brutal place Mr. Sargent calls the Academy. He and that nice Ms. Cassandra swarmed down on Benny and took his stranger away as if he, Benedictus, had no right to him.

"It's for his own good," Mr. Sargent said. They're going to make him well. They said so!

"He's burning up," Nurse Cassie told him, and she said exactly what Benny had cried in vain. "I'm only trying to help him."

Mr. Sargent said, "You'll thank me later." He sounded so *certain.*

He was mine, Benny thinks or prays without knowing what this means. He knows only that his heart is breaking. *He was mine and they took him without asking what he is to me or why this is so important.*

Worse yet, Benny doesn't know the answers to either of these questions. What he does know is that without the stranger to watch over and take care of, he is bereft. Hurt and confused and jealous. What right do they have, he wonders. What right do they have?

They, and not Benny, will get to the truth of this strange new person.

The nurse, or whatever she is, has him all to herself now. The young stranger is locked away in the Infirmary, where she will have the honor of feeding him and bringing his medicine, but that is by no means the worst part.

He particularly envies Mr. Sargent.

When the time comes, it will be Mr. Sargent and not Benny who questions the beautiful boy, and he won't quit until he gets answers. The stranger asked Benny as if he ought to know: *Do you know who I am?* Benny doesn't. He doesn't know! So this is what troubles his heart right now. *He was mine and they took him!*

Oh God, he thinks, praying or thinking or some sad combination of both these things. It is a cry of guilt and regret, the result of pressure on the heart that includes grieving, *Oh, God!* He should be down on his knees confessing, but he sits on the thin straw pallet with his worn, aching knees drawn up, not knowing what he did that was so terrible.

Now, Benny was brought up here in the abbey, educated by the Benedictines, who staked their souls on the Rule. On virtue, on the inevitability of sin and the grace that comes with forgiveness. It's all he knows. Troubled and unaccountably guilty, the old lay brother goes down his laundry list of sins he might have committed and can't produce anything that makes sense of the way he feels. Why does he feel so bad, when he can't number any sins of *commission*?

But Benny knows better than most that in addition to sins committed, of which he has a very short list over a long lifetime, there are sins of omission.

Things he should have done but left undone.

Don't you know me?

He should have known the answer! He should have cried aloud, "Tell me," but he was confused and embarrassed because he had no idea who this person was. He should have stayed in that confessional until the tall, gaunt youth who was not from here took pity on him and told him who he was and why he was here and how he got that hideous gash in his leg. With the source locked away in the Infirmary where he is not allowed to go, Benny will never find out. It's tearing his heart to pieces.

For the sake of love he needs to know who he is, and why this is so important.

For the only surviving member of an ancient religious community, the arrival was a marvel— a lovely gift for a man who has passed eighty-some Christmases on Clothos and never once gotten a present. Poor Benny should have homed in on the question while he had his treasure safe inside the confessional. He could have begged. Pleaded. Withheld food or traded medicine for answers. He should have found out while he had the outsider close, so he can count this as a sin of *omission*.

"Mea culpa."

Letting his treasured friend go without more of a struggle is another.

"Mea culpa."

But that isn't why he feels soiled right now. Guilty.

Over what? It is confusing.

If he had Sixtus here and tried to confess these things, the last abbot would be mystified. "Go," Sixtus would tell him. "Rest your heart. Come back when you know what's bothering you."

The trouble is, he doesn't. After a lifetime in the abbey, Brother Benedictus can certainly tell the difference between sins of commission and omission and this is neither.

He's doing his best. He is!

Then what about the events of the last week makes him grab his big toes right now, rocking and fretting over sins of *emission*? He doesn't even know what that *is*.

"Mea maxima culpa," he cries although in all honesty, he doesn't understand it.

This is what sticks in Benny's hide like a penitent's spiked cilice. What if the Director has his friend in one of the crypts torturing him to extract answers? What if Sarge, and not Benny, is there when his charge, *his responsibility*, finally reveals his secret? They took him away before Benny could ask, leaving him to ponder the question posed by his secret friend.

Weeping, he murmurs, "Do you know who I am?"

Dear God, he can't figure out why or how in such a short time, the mystery became the center of his life, and he prays to God to enlighten him. *Please.* There are prayers to be said, prayers specific to this hour, but this is the only one Benny can find right now.

If he could only get back into the dream he might recover the event, the sin— no, the *memory* that floats in his past like a scrap of driftwood in a black ocean. Something happened back then, in the early days before he got so old, before he became who he is, before it became so hard to remember, but— *Please*— no matter how hard he prays, the truth eludes him.

ZANDER BIRCH IS dreaming too, or he was until the morning trumpet sounded and he woke up cursing. Life in this hard place sucks. No wonder he sticks his head back under the pillow, trying hard to avoid it. He'd much rather be running through the parks and dance clubs of his dream, garbed in purple, which he always is when in these dreams about graceful Alexandra; he'd rather die than get up right now. He'd rather retreat into his glamorous secret self than face another day as Zander Birch, inmate of the Academy. He'd like to lose the sad fat boy he sees in the mirror and come out as his true self, but that's many steps away. The gorgeous

Alix is his future, a lovely girl who wears high heels and runs, trailing brilliantly colored designer gowns with gauzy trains and flying panels, through grand hotels in exotic foreign places.

See, in dreams Zander usually turns into Alix, but last night she eluded him and— this is not so bad— he dreamed a completely different person.

In last night's dream, the one he just lost, Zander was naked and happy, running barefoot through soft grass in a genderless world where there were no boys or girls, just human beings, and every one of them was pink and lovable. They all had soft, round bodies and lovely long hair that floated as they ran. They spoke in ambiguously gender-free voices and in this ideal landscape for the first time in sad little Zander Birch's complicated life it positively, absolutely didn't matter *what* he was.

No. It didn't matter what *ze* was, ze being the transgender-approved gender-free pronoun. Appropriate to a preoperative tranny, which is what Zander is because the dread dad is such a brutal, unforgiving asshole.

If only Dad loved me.

It is all so confusing. All ze ever wanted was to be accepted. As ze is. Well, look where that got us. Now ze is here.

Now, about here. Academy, sure. Put on the uniform and march through the days. Hup. Two. Reep. Fo. Do this. Do that. Do the same things at the same time every day and whatever you do, be the same and don't let anyone know you are different.

Refuge from the end of the world? Not so much. As in, as a kid who knows from experience that there is no real refuge anywhere, Alexandra knows better.

And this is strange. Reveille sounded a while ago, but the silence in the hallway indicates that in fact, today is different. On a weekday morning in a strictly organized institution where everything is on the clock, nobody is up and running, so far as ze can tell. Nobody's up at all.

Woo, ze thinks. Classes canceled? Special holiday?

Luxuriant in satin, ze stretches, wondering what to do with the free day, if it really is free.

As if Sarge would let a day go by without a plan.

Still, ze can hope. Back home with a free day ahead and time on zer hands, ze would be going to the happy place on the Internet to complain about Dad and talk about hairdos and outfits and when ze will be old enough for the electrolysis. In Darla's Chat Room, ze can exchange stories with other kids in transition, who share everything from details on the necessary steps in the unveiling of the person within to horror stories, and everybody has one.

On the Internet Zander and zer best friends ze has never met can say everything, and never be embarrassed. The ones who have survived the change without heartbreak give hope to the others, listing necessary steps and side effects and numbering the many ways of breaking the news to the family. On some very special nights all the beautiful people, and they are all beautiful in Darla's Chat Room, even Zander, talk about what happened to them when they did come out to their parents, their wives, whoever.

And when it's late and the talk starts going deeper they will tell you what it feels like, and when they first knew.

In Zander's messy life back home, when things got bad, which was usually, ze could go to Darla's Chat Room. Where everybody was always glad to see zem. It was zer lifeline. Now it has been severed, so fuck Dad for sending him here although of course he said it was for Zander's own good right before ze socked him. Now look. Like a thumb-sucker with a screen wire cage tied on zer thumb to break the habit, Zander has been deprived of the Internet. Ze thinks it's a special punishment the dread dad dreamed up to get even with Zander for being the first person he told.

This is so hard, ze thinks. *This is so **hard.***

Then when ze's just about to break down and cry, ze hears:

"Dude, can I come in?"

Alexandra bridles. Nobody comes into zer room. Nobody. Nobody wants to. Ze is modulating zer voice, not exactly necessary since it hasn't cracked and gone deep yet and, actually, might never crack but, OK, in preparation. That girlish lilt. "Who is it?"

"It's Teddy?" Whisper from the hall, as if the speaker has put his mouth right on the keyhole, which means if ze wanted to, Zander could get out of bed and sneak over and whip it open so the doorknob knocked the kid's teeth out. "Teddy Regan?"

Oh shit. It's spazzboy. "Go away."

"Can I come in?"

Oh, shit. Because Killer Stade told him that this spazzboy is also some kind of prince guy and he, Killer, will beat the crap out of anybody that bothers the kid (like, Stade offed someone back on earth so you'd better believe it) Zander says cautiously, "You're not going to have a fit on me or anything."

"Oh fuck good grief no." Regan opens the door and comes in uninvited. "Everybody knows I have pills for that, and I take them. I need to see your computer."

"Say what?" Alix slithers out of bed in the black satin jammies the dread dad bought zer, his only wardrobe concession to the march of fate, maybe Dad thinks satin's OK because black makes his only child and ostensible heir look thinner plus more like a guy, although not necessarily the guy Dad wants him to be.

"Your laptop. Mine broke." Teddy does not say the rest. That in the throes of his worst seizure yet, he was bouncing off the walls and he accidentally trashed the thing, and the useless piece of junk is back in the room, underneath all the crap in the bottom of his and Killer's closet.

Alix sniffs. "What's the point? It's not like I get Internet."

"Because, OK?" Teddy has more than one reason for asking to use this kid's laptop, but he's not about to tell weird little Zander that. Like, if Zander Birch's official Academy computer's OK, as in not contaminated because he, Teddy, has never touched it, then maybe what happened in Sarge's office last night was only a bad dream or a fluke, which is the best-case scenario.

Like, what happened might just have been a temporary glitch in the system, instead of something stupid that he, Teddy Regan, did. Totally by accident! It happened so fast that it scared the crap out of him. Killer too, and Killer doesn't scare, which is the scariest thing about it. They ran out panting and raced for the room like a couple of warlocks fleeing the vile and terrifying Illidan_Stormrage and all his minions through the dungeons and caverns of *WoW,* but worse. They fell into bed and pulled the covers up over their heads to shut out the enemy, shivering like little kids.

But hey, it *could* be a dream, right? That he, Frederick IV of a country he is embarrassed to name, never broke into the Academy server and clicked on that stupid thing on the Internet and that the horrendous electronic train wreck never happened, like, that he only dreamed it?

As if.

Strange Zander is watching him warily. Now he asks in this weird, girly voice, "Because what?"

Of course Teddy is not about to tell him. Never mind that back in their room, Killer is cursing and screaming at this very moment. His friend the supergeek can't make his computer talk sense no matter what he tries, and he's been trying for, it's . . . like, been hours. "It's no big," Teddy says because in circumstances like this it is most urgent to appear casual. "It'll only take a minute, OK?"

"Why?"

Ewww. Black jammies. Still. "Seriously, I need it."

Blink. Blink. That voice. "Why?"

Is this kid wearing eyeliner? Is that glitter on his eyelids? Teddy says nicely, "Please?"

"Why do you need it?"

"I need to check a Thing."

"Fuck," says Alexandra, but in a voice that's more like normal. No. He's Zander, for now. Shrink says if you're in close quarters with boys who don't understand you, don't fight it; sometimes it's easier to blend in. He tries on that butch voice he picked up from his perfidious father, like, when he drops his voice like this Zander sounds pretty much all guy, almost as if he's spent the last eight years in guy school. "But dude," he says, "if you think I'm, like, hiding that I've got Internet, you can forget it. All I get on this rotten Dell is the Academy page. School song, Order of the Day, all the usual shit."

"Yeah, well," Teddy says. "That's kind of what I need to check."

SYLVIE IS SO totally bummed today because (*a*) Marla was tossing and turning all night like she's sick or something. The miserable skank was running back and forth to the bathroom disrupting Sylvie's sweet dreams about her secret best beloved, plus, the last time Marla went out to yack or whatever Marla does in the bathroom, she didn't come back, and (*b*), which is really *a*, capital *A*, Sylvie woke up this morning expecting something wonderful and it wasn't. When she turned on her standard-issue Academy laptop there was *no* secret message up there on the screen for her, which her best beloved new boyfriend practically promised, so what was the point of him crawling all over the mountaintop before the moon came up?

But Sylvie believed, so first thing this morning she turned it on, all excited. There wasn't shit on her black, black computer screen today except a lot of shit. Like, this garbled jumble of numbers and letters and other pieces of junk that kept swimming upstream like piranhas in a flood, boiling up the screen like a pack of wild tropical fish freaking out in the Long Beach Aquarium, you bet she's unhappy. She hoped for so much today and got so much nothing that she goes back to bed and pulls the quilt up and flops the pillow over her head so if the hall mother comes by on a room check, the bitch will think Sylvie's gone off to class or whatever's supposed to be happening right now and she'll get demerits for not making her bed, not for still being in it.

So what if her dearest secret lover— what if her beautiful Steve, whose name it's OK to say out loud only when she is alone in here and only into her pillow so if they've bugged the room nobody will hear— so what if her Steve didn't get his special signal booster rigged up on that awful cliff, is that so terrible?

Hey, Sylvie can handle it. So what if he was smart enough to turn around before he got to the top of that rock because it was so high and scary? What if he did come down without planting his antenna or whatever, is that such a big, bad deal, really? In fact, when he went crab-crawling out on the rocks like that last night Sylvie was a little worried. So what if they don't get Internet, she'll live, no problem. She'd rather have her Steve right now than bazillion new friends on her MySpace page, and she means it.

Who needs to IM or text or iChat or any other mechanical thing when she can sneak out and snuggle with the actual warm and wonderful, breathing person?

As long as they're stuck on Clothos, Sylvie can count on him, and she might want to hang on to the boy after the world ends or whatever, and they get out of this jail. She loves her brand-new boyfriend. He is the absolute best ever partly because they haven't had sex yet but mostly because it is their secret.

Well, that and he's an Older Man, he's gotta be at least twenty. She can count on sneaking out to meet Steve tonight and every other night that they stay stuck on this blasted rock, and it's not like he'll be stepping out with anybody cuter, everybody in her posse is looking greasy and disgusting. She and her Steve can keep on snogging and talking sweet in one of their secret places, which, for Sylvie, is a fuck of a lot better than having sex right now; she'll have her own dear Steve live and in person, and that's plenty enough for her.

So handsome, she thinks, with that Greek god profile and those glossy black curls, even though he is skinny and all slouched from spending his whole life bent over a computer. *Steve Joannides,* she writes in her head. *Mr. and Mrs. Stephen Joannides.* The very idea makes her stretch and wriggle. With him around, who cares about Internet? She absolutely, totally doesn't mind being here. With no club scene and no paparazzi trailing you and no media feeding off your every mistake, the Academy's got its own funky kind of freedom. She likes the place. In fact, she might almost love it.

FIRST I THOUGHT I could fix it, I really did.

Like, nothing stops Killer Stade, geek extraordinaire. Hey listen, I'm not really a murderer as you already know, plus, I could tell you a thing or two about computers. They are like home to me. Compound of Mom, Dad, the family dog.

The thing about machines is, they are loyal if you treat them right. They do what you say and when push comes to shove, a computer may go bananas but it will never stiff you and it will never, ever, get you in its car and try to hit on you.

I've been in tight with computers ever since I was little, it's like, so, sooo better than watching your parents fight, and hey. I could probably build you one if I had to, Mr. Joannides says I'm the best he's ever worked with. Nice guy, he never once asked me what I did to bring the law down on me so I never once asked what kind of hacking he did to bring the law down on himself, which, I gather what he did was pretty impressive.

He says that with a little of this and a little of that I could be a brilliant hardware hacker. I mean, look at the code I downloaded on my iPod just so I could play *Doom* on the fly, and look at the iPod case mod I did, which is how I got the fucking thing inside this jail. Nobody but me knows it isn't just another book, which, while all about them were losing theirs, is the only reason I got it in here. Electronics got scoped in the scanner and other kids lost everything they had, but me? They took my phone but my little Podbook or bookPod slipped through the turnbuckle along with this other kid's Bible, you bet I am a geek, I am a megageek, which is why first thing this morning I thought I could fix this.

I thought shit, maybe a reboot was all it would take to do it. I thought I could reboot my machine and fix the whole network before Sarge finds out it's broken.

No problem, right?

Fuck yes, problem.

I've been messing with this thing since before it got light enough to see and I am fucking nowhere. How are you going to run diagnostics when you can't speak to your machine because it forgot the language? I tried everything and no way is this cheapjack laptop sitting on the table in me and Teddy's room about to speak to me. I've tried everything and like a street person on speed the insanity just scrolls on up the screen, corrupted code scrolling on and on without stopping.

If this crap laptop they gave me won't stop scrolling long enough to listen, there's no way I can get it to talk to me.

Yes I tried everything.

Reboot. Disconnect. Turn on and see that jumble, and we aren't even fucking connected. It's like hearing a whole asylum full of lunatics screaming to heaven, and I can't make it stop, it is obscene. This machine is sicker than crap, and if this assaholic toxified code I see is coming up in our room on our one remaining Academy regulation-issue computer, it's probably coming up on every machine on the whole Academy network, thanks to whatever vile force of evil Teddy unleashed last night when he clicked on the wrong thing and brought the hounds of hell into Sarge's private, secret, sacred and totally Internet-connected server.

Fuck. We are so fucked, and we are even more fucked when Sarge finds out it's us that did it, which is why I so urgently need to fix this thing.

When Teddy woke up, I asked. "You know that time you fell out and trashed your laptop?"

He went all whites-of-the-eyes on me. "What about it?"

Oh, fuck. Don't spazz out on me. The kid has visions: weird, but maybe I could make it work for us. "When you were out that time, did you, um, like, *foresee* anything?"

"You mean, like this? Me crashing the server? No." I could almost hear Teddy thinking. He was still torn up about that, things he does that he can't help, like: guilty. "No. Not really. No. Do you think I would have . . . Oh, fuck."

So I guilted him into checking out the laptop of this kid Zander, that's scared of me.

If Teddy bombs out in this Zanderina starlet wannabe's room, like, if that weird, pretty guy's Academy laptop is as sick as ours, it's on to Plan B, which just might be OK although I'll have to let Mr. Joannides in on it. Fuck. I can't even text Teddy in Zander's room to find out how it's going.

So OK, I give him another ten minutes, during which I keep dinking, in hopes of hitting the magic keystroke combination. Then I'll sneak into the IT lab and without, like, giving too much away, I'll just tell Mr. J. we have this problem. Then I ask for a little tech support, I mean, that's what Sarge hired him for. I can tell him it's like, *entre nous,* which is how much French I learned from that suck-egg Mr. Berringer.

Everybody needs a fallback position and Mr. Joannides is mine. He's so good at what he does that he totally almost went to jail for it, so, hey. If I can't do this, like, fix this thing on my own, Mr. Joannides definitely can, him being an even bigger geek than me, for which I am eternally grateful.

And if we can't fix it? Shit knows what's going to happen, especially when Sarge finds out who did it, which he will, like, I heard Mr. Sargent was a guard at Guantanamo, you know, the kind that does all the interrogations.

Network's down, server's wack. Good thing I'm in good with Mr. Joannides.

TWENTY-THREE

SHEELA

I don't know what's going on with Marla Parsons, but it's awful.

It's awful to watch and it's awful because every time I look at the girl it makes me feel shitty, like guilty and scared, I mean *scared*, way down deeper inside than everyday end-of-the-world terrified.

The first time she came scratching at my door I thought she was faking it so I'd take pity and lay on more of my justly famed Godiva truffles, but that was early in the night. She snuffled and whined at my door like a big fat drama queen, and believe me, since I started with the candy orgies, the girl has gotten seriously bigger. She whinged until I opened it a crack; then she pleaded. By the time I let her in she was coughing like this wasn't the Academy on Clothos, which is *so* this century, she took on like she was dying of TB in Toulouse-Lautrec or somebody's loft at the end of some trashy movie.

I thought it was a trick, like, Sylvie and them were lurking out in the hall waiting to pounce because now that the truffles are well

and truly gone they were fixing to storm the room and tell me
what they really think of me.

How was I supposed to know Marla was sick for real, and it was
urgent?

It was like, hours and hours after I ran out of truffles and they
all went home. It was late and for personal reasons, I didn't want to
see anybody. Then Marla choked out this wrenching sob. I only
opened the door a sliver, just enough to hiss at her and the horse
she rode in on. "Go away."

"It's me?"

Are you asking or telling me? "Go away, I'm out of truffles."

She was trying to whisper, but it came out a strangled cough.
Blugh. Blugh. Blugh. "Aren't you going to say, 'Who is it?'"

"To tell the truth, Marla, I don't really give a shit."

"Please, I'm sick."

"No you're not. And in case you're worried about it, I am really,
truly out of truffles."

She didn't say anything but she didn't go away, either.

"Marla?" I thought she was doing the stony silence, like, to
shame me into helping her. I still can't say for certain whether she
was playing me. For a minute, all there was out there in the hall was
darkness and the sound of Marla gagging, and the noise? It was like
the girl got back her Manolos and was stomping on my Achilles'
heel with four-inch spikes. *Oh fuck,* I thought, *she's really sick. Is it
the truffles?*

"Please, I'm so scared."

"Of what?"

She was *whuf-whuff*ing the way you do when you're trying not
to cough. It wasn't exactly an answer.

"Whatever it is, let Sylvie take care of you. Now go away." I
tried to sound firm, but I had doubts.

"No she won't."

"She's your best friend."

At which point the notorious *Page Six* baby celeb featured on TV news *and* the entertainment channels goes, "As if we had friends in this business. Besides." She is coughing up her guts.

"Stop that."

"I can't. Sylvie . . . HUAGH!" When she could breathe she said, "Sylvie isn't anywhere."

"Now, where would that be?"

"Don't dick me around, Sheela. I'm really sick."

"You're not sick, you're probably just pregnant."

"As if! My mom had my tubes tied off just in case, OK? Now let me in, I'm sicker than shit."

Oh fuck, she was retching. I was, like, Hold the line, Sheela. Try to pretend she isn't expiring out there in the corridor, but I could be blamed and it made me timid. "What with?"

She gave back that pitiful cough.

OK, girl. Bull's-eye. I put my lips into the crack so nobody else would hear me whisper my deepest fear, that was practically killing me. "Was it the truffles?"

First she didn't answer. Then she tried to, but it came out in a whoosh of air that turned into that ghastly cough. When I peeked she was rolling on the floor, holding her belly because she couldn't stop it.

I yanked her inside. Maybe it was stupid because whatever Marla's got, by this time I too am probably infected, but in my secret heart I thought it might have been the hazelnut truffles I handed out last night that did it, which I remember Marla in particular kept jamming into her mouth faster than quarters into a slot machine, that girl was snorting truffles like the world really is self-destructing and there's no tomorrow.

I never would have let her into my room if I'd known she was going to yack on my rug. It would have been OK, I guess, but when she couldn't cough up whatever it was the whole thing escalated into dry heaving and OK, I'll admit that it was guilt that made

me drag her down the hall to the bathroom and hold her head so
that next time she threw up her hair wouldn't get in it. See, in my
secret heart I was convinced it was the truffles, of which she had
eaten a shitload. It was just her and me in the room after Lights
Out because there wasn't enough candy left to cover the whole
posse and I had only invited her and Sylvie.

Although we were never friends we all come from the same
neighborhood in Los Angeles, go west on Wilshire, take a right
five blocks after Rodeo Drive and you'll find us. Welcome to the
enclave where rich people live, although of course unless you're a
personal friend, plus you have to be on the family A-list, you will
never see the house. You won't make it past the gatehouse.

So given our social context I was, like, feathering the nest for
when we get out when I invited just Marla and Sylvie to empty the
last box of candy, but, crap. Only Marla showed up. Instead of
coming to me, that bitch Sylvie put on lipstick— lipstick! and went
off somewhere.

So when Marla got waaaay sick, and I mean drastic, I ended up
tending her even though we aren't exactly friends. She could have
gone looking for Sylvie but when they've taken away all the things
that used to make you pretty, throwing up makes you look even
worse, and she was so embarrassed.

If she didn't want Sylvie to see her like that, what does that
make of me? A person that you don't give a ratfuck what they
think of you, that's what.

And it's not like Marla is going to thank me. She just needed
somebody to hold her head, so it's her fault if I get it too. It got in
her hair. When we landed on Clothos, Sylvie's hair was just growing out from where she had shaved it, which was either a personal
meltdown or a fashion statement, who cares? Naturally her posse
cut theirs short to match, that is, everybody but Marla. She has
long blonde hair that some hairdresser had to iron daily, although
it's gotten manky since she gave up on washing it. She was too sick

or too stupid to put on a scrunchie, even though any fool knows serious coughing leads from gagging to puking. I should have cut off her damn hair while she was too weak to stop me. This didn't happen, like, just once. She woke me up, like, four times.

The last time I dragged her into the shower so the puke could pour out and go right straight down the drain, stupid me, I thought it would actually wash away, but it didn't. The yack noise was so fierce that it woke up Miss Earhard, who is our ostensible dorm mother and therefore responsible. She came running into the bathroom flapping like a helpful angel, but that's before she saw Marla was kneeling in a puddle of vomit.

I guess it scared her. She scared us too, the fool. I guess she sleeps naked. She confronted us in her Harvard hoodie which I guess she put on to keep from alarming us with her naked body, although I could have told her that it was too short to cover the really scary part, which is that pussy like a hairy Post-it tacked on the bottom of her humongous belly. Nice lady, I guess, at least when she's dressed. Marla was puking fit to yack her heart up in a rush of blood and we would have to see it flopping around on the floor in the shower, and I guess Mrs. Earhard couldn't handle it. You could hear the gears in our English teacher's gray head meshing. Clank. Clank. Clank.

Finally she said, "Girls! Bulimia is no substitute for diet and exercise," and then because she was afraid, she rushed off to bed like nothing happened. At the door she stuck her head back in to say, "Don't forget to clean up after yourselves."

The fifth time I thought: fuck, and took her to the Infirmary, for I dished up the truffles and therefore I am the cause of Marla's suffering.

I guess because it was a long time until the PA opened up for clinic hours, the doors were locked. I didn't care. I hammered and yelled until Ms. Cassie came out and let me in, and this is the scary part.

She already had somebody in the back room.

It was a guy; I didn't see him but I could hear him. It sounded like the exact same kind of coughing. Ms. Cassie came rushing out as soon as I yelled, and I'll say this for her. She got Marla cleaned up and tucked into one of the beds with an IV full of electrolytes prontino, plus a little sedative, thank God, but here's another scary part. When Marla konked out Ms. Cassie put up the side rails, like she thought Marla might implode or something worse and hurt herself. Then she took a couple of swabs and made slides of the gunk in Marla's throat and fuck, I saw her put on gloves and one of those surgical face masks when she did it. Then she gave me a bottle of Cipro pills and told me to go back to my room and take one right away and another one every four hours until they were gone and let her know the second I started feeling bad. Except for that, she went through the whole routine without talking and I respect her so I didn't say anything, just waited.

When she was done, I asked. After everything, I had to. It was pretty clear that we were into something awful that I didn't know about. I wanted Ms. Cassie to tell me what dread disease we were fighting, what did Marla have and would I get it. Like, was it psittacosis that brought her down or was it more like anthrax or bubonic plague or Ebola or what. Her face did a lot of things but she kept her voice in place. She said chill, it was probably nothing, but it's always smart to take precautions.

Just then that asshole doctor came out of Ms. Cassie's room scratching his nuts and smelling like hangover. He sidled up to her with a bunch of complaints, handing them out one by one like flowers, and I thought, *Are they having sex?* Then I thought, *ewwwww,* but one look told me different, she could hardly stand the sight of him and she sure as hell didn't want him to touch her. She was all *ewwww* just having him stand that close to her.

He thought he was in charge but boy, you should have seen her face when she waved him over to his desk. "Sit down." The last thing I heard her say before she rolled one of those white screens between the desk and me was, "Something's going on. I need your help. The computer's down and I can't get at my references."

I could have lurked and found out, I could have hung in there long enough to overhear everything Ms. Cassie told the assaholic, I might even have found out what disease Marla was carrying and whether or not it was catching, except the outside doors banged open WHAM, no knocking and no yelling, and that curly blond kid Teddy came lunging into the Infirmary dragging the tranny pretty much like I dragged Marla.

This Alexanderina/whatever they call themselves was making a sound that in one long night had become way, way too familiar. He was on the way from coughing to gagging while Teddy held him up by the armpits, calling, "Ms. Cassie, Ms. Cassie!" at which point Ms. Cassie lunged out from behind the doctor's white screen, took one look at the situation and rushed the kid onto a bed at the tippy far end of the room like it was important to, like, isolate him and Marla.

It's not like that doctor did anything while she was running around with IV bags and syringes, although I saw the fabric in the screen that hid him moving. Ms. Cassie did it all and I thought, *OK, in real life, I am going to be a doctor.*

Then she saw me there gaping and she glared me out of the Infirmary. I'm outside, but it's not like she got rid of me. I'm hunkered down waiting for the next person to come out, at which point I get in. This is my fault, and I have to be there for Marla.

TWENTY-FOUR

THERON IS DREAMING AGAIN. IT IS A LONG, DEEP DREAM IN which he sits down by candlelight among handsome, gracious people who are happy to have him there. No matter what goes on in his waking life, these best friends he's never met are always glad to see him. In this tremendous, gorgeously fitted house with many rooms, Theron is always welcome. No. He is more than just welcome.

He is recognized.

Probably because the infection that's been entrenched in his body for so long has taken over and he's sick as a bastard, he dreams all the time now. He dreams so deeply that waking, he can't decide whether that night in a sumptuously furnished dining room is the afterimage of some significant event in his life that he's forgotten and ought to recover or only Theron, dreaming.

It's late morning in the narrow cell where he is imprisoned but he slips in and out of that beautiful night, in which he sits down at

a long table with friends who are eternally glad to see them. They
are in the glowing dining room of the great house where these
dreams always take him. No matter how many days and nights of
dreaming bring Theron back to the table, it's always for the first
time.

Each dream is so fresh that he always comes in happy and excited. In dreams he is surrounded by lovely women in soft gowns
and men in black, except for their gleaming white shirt fronts,
everybody dressed for the banquet. The room is like nowhere
Theron has been in his waking life, with a high ceiling and crystal
chandeliers lighting the ends of the long table. There are deep red
walls and swaths of red velvet pulled across tall windows. Happy
as he is, there is one detail that breaks his heart. White fluted
columns flank the doorways like pillars holding up the Parthenon,
which Theron saw exactly once, on a day he has tried all his life to
put behind him.

Dreaming, he can forget.

It's always night in the room where he is happiest. The beautifully set table is flanked by crystal candelabra, so that his loving
friends' faces glow in the warm light. A small garden of silver trees
hung with crystal leaves and flowers runs down the center of the
white tablecloth, floating on a mirrored river. On these amazing
nights Theron spends far away from his hard, poorly furnished life,
food comes in on silver trays, platter after platter, but he doesn't remember them eating.

The people at the table are more interested in what Theron has
to say than in anything that's served to them. He and his wonderful friends are talking and laughing, and Theron? Dressed as he
was when he fell asleep, in clean white scrubs, he is the reason for
this party. To his surprise, men and women older and much more
important than Theron lean forward to catch his every word, and
he is eloquent. They listen with delighted smiles, murmuring and
nodding in agreement.

He can't bring back anything that's said at these dinners but he will never forget the glow of approval. When he comes back to himself Theron knows he's lost the dream for now, but no matter where he is in the daylight world, no matter how hard his life has become or what troubles him, he wakes up drenched and supremely happy.

These departures from real life are richer now that his thigh is neatly stitched up and covered with a dressing that masks the fact that deep inside, it's festering.

He knows there's trouble with his body. It's the same sick, *changed* feeling he had when he broke a bone as a small child. Something is profoundly wrong. Why can't he tell the doctor? Why didn't he tell her at dawn when she came in to dress the wound? He'd rather cultivate the fever. It makes the dreams come more often, and they're getting richer. Should Theron be glad that he's sick, is that why he nurses the infection growing inside him? Is he glad he got injured?

The injury is all mixed up in his mind with the cough that lodged in his throat after he blundered into the monks' old burial chamber after too many weeks inside the mountain. He ignored it at first. It wasn't much. Just an internal itch, as though something inside his chest had been bitten.

Then he got hurt, but when?

It was before he dragged himself up the rough stone stairs to the abbey's subcellar, starved and hurting, looking for a place to hide, before he entered the vaulted stone room at the heart of the abbey and long before he crawled into the box he recognized from deep childhood as a church confessional. Before all this, something went terribly wrong with his body. Before Brother Benedictus.

It was dark wherever he was in the mountain that night— how long ago?— when everything went bad. Theron has been here for so long that he's stopped counting. The only certainty he knows is that he's badly damaged. Odd. He can't tell whether it really was an accident or whether some unrecognized, greedy part of him invited it.

Safe inside the mountain, Theron temporized. He was here on a mission that he was avoiding. He'd been hiding for weeks—months?— when he blundered into the chamber of unburied dead and left it trembling. He reached out in the dark and dust flew up, filling his lungs. Something crumbled under his hand: a human skull swathed in rotting cloth. By the time he left the monks' last resting place, he was coughing.

Still, he thought he was doing all right living in the dark, but he was mistaken. He'd been inside the dark mountain for so long that he believed he was at home here, strong sure-footed, but he was wrong about that too. He was running out of food. He was coughing. It was time to go up into the abbey, find the right man and ask certain questions. The way was steep and the footing treacherous. Somewhere along the way an unseen object ripped his hide but at the time, Theron didn't know it.

He thought he was going along all right, he thought going up was no problem. After all, he'd been here before and the territory was familiar. He thought the timing was up to him.

As if anybody can choose his moment. Then he reached down and felt blood.

It was like finding armed robbers at his throat before he knew anybody was in the house. The insult was so harsh, so unexpected that it took him a while to catch up with the truth of his changed condition. He was hurt bad, and he still doesn't know how it happened.

Deep inside, the gash in Theron's leg is festering, and he knows it. But he dreams. He dreams!

In the dream he is always just about to fall in love, although he could not tell you who the woman is or where she's sitting at the table, only that the attraction is stunning. The outlines of Theron's life on Clothos have blurred so completely that he falls in and out of the dream whenever. Day or night, he is forever sorry to leave it, and when he wakes up this time at the sound of the door opening, he is aroused.

She is in the room! She says, "Good morning."

It's the lady doctor. Beautiful gray eyes on her, he notes because it is full daylight, he is awake for now and for the first time since she found him, he can see her clearly. Good-looking woman in spite of the paper mask she has put on for this encounter. His heartbeat spikes. *What's wrong? Am I contagious?* She has that soft, thick hair of no particular color pulled tight today, another disturbing sign. She's tied it back with a scarf— not to make her look pretty, but as if she had to clear the decks for action.

He does what he can. "Hello, Doctor."

Behind the mask she is wearing, the woman who keeps him here looks worried and distracted. "You're back." She sounds surprised.

"I'm what?"

"Back from wherever you were in your head."

There is no way to sum up what he feels. "I'm sorry."

"No, it's a good thing."

"If you say so, Doctor."

The mask puffs out with the force of the words. "I'm not a doctor."

Theron hears what he said to Benedictus when the old man knelt before him in the stuffy confessional, muttering, *Bless me father.* He thinks: *I'm not a priest,* and doesn't know whether to apologize for the many things he is not. Instead he apologizes for mistaking her. "Sorry. But you're more than a nurse."

"PA," she says, pulling on rubber gloves. "So, yeah. I'm glad you're back."

"What?"

"Back in your head, I mean. I'm relieved."

"I'm not." He'd rather dream forever.

"You were too far out for it to be healthy."

"Was I?" Theron blinks. There are too many things he can't re-member.

"Trust me." She pops the thermometer into his ear. Takes his pulse. Makes conversation while looking at her watch. "Where were you, in the zone?"

He squints because he does not understand her.

"I mean, meditating?"

"No." He does not say, *I only know it wasn't here.*

"You were pretty weird. Last night. This morning when I tried to help you. Where were you in your head?"

He blinks, grubbing for an answer. "Thinking."

"About . . ."

In fact, he was trying to remember. Why he came to the gutted and severely altered abbey on Clothos in the first place, what unar-ticulated need brought him here and why he imagined he'd learn anything useful at the top of this inaccessible mountain. After weeks lurking in the caverns below and days spent folded up in the priest hole, Theron has forgotten why he thought this pilgrimage was so important. Because the tense, raggedly lovely woman looks different this morning, shaken and tremulous, he asks a question instead of answering, "What's wrong?"

She glances at the thermometer. Her eyebrows shoot up. "You're not the only person with a fever."

"Right." He sighs. Whatever he thought he had going here is about to be broken. His circle of privacy? His connection to her? His comprehension? When she came into the room this time a racket followed her. People pounding on doors. Feet scuffling. Distressed adults shouting and children gagging and squawking. "What's going on out there?"

"Don't know. Something . . ."

She's about to tell him that she has to go, that it's . . . He sup-plies, "Urgent."

"Urgent. Look. I took samples last night, but I can't wait for them to culture out. I have to get on top of this before it gets on top of us."

He tries to smile helpfully, but the imagery is confusing.

"Now." She pulls down the mask to let him know that this is serious. "Tell me everything you can about your condition. When it started. How you hurt yourself."

He ought to help. He wants to help. Instead Theron says, because it's why he's here and it's eating him up, "Do you know who I am?"

"That's not important right now. I need details. When you first knew you were sick, who might have infected you . . ."

"Do you know who I am?"

". . . what was the first symptom."

How to explain it? He can't. He persists. "Do you?"

"No!" Frustrated, she turns to his chart. "Do you?"

"Not in any way that matters." He waits until she's busy with his IV drip because he doesn't want her watching when he admits, "Well, my name."

She is listening to his chest. She thumps. "Breathe in."

"Do you want my name?"

"Out."

"Do you, Doctor?"

She whirls in a sudden spray of rage, moving so fast that the IV shunt rips out of the back of his hand. "I don't care what your name is, I just want to know what's the matter with you!"

Then the woman who cares too much sees what she's just done to her patient and does something that scares the living grief out of him. She drops his bleeding hand and hurries to pick up the other, already feeling for a fresh vein. Tapping to bring it up so she can insert the bloody shunt. Then with a baffled look, she rips off the mask and starts crying.

It is not a logical thing to do but he is beyond logic. Theron's body takes over and in a serpent's nest of IV tubes he puts his arms around her. He ought to back away. He ought to apologize. He ought to say something useful but all he can manage is an illegible mixture of expressions as for seconds only, she rests her head on his chest.

The next thing he hears is the door slamming wide and an outraged roar. "Get your hands off her!"

"Sarge, don't!"

"Back off, kid, or I'll murder you."

"Don't, he's only trying to . . ."

"I don't care what he's trying to do!" The big man drops words into the room like baggy brutes, blind and ignorant. "What is this, Cassie? What in the name of prurient, corroding misery is this?"

Stricken, she puts herself between Sarge and her patient but whatever she has to say to the angry ex-Marine is wiped away by the explosive sweep of his arm as he brings his drawn pistol down on Theron's head like an angel sent to defend her.

TWENTY-FIVE

SARGE

Put yourself in my position.

It was one bitch of a night. It's been one son-of-a-bitching day so far, in which I rechecked the perimeter to find everything disrupted. None of my kids where they're supposed to be, no staff people in place except for Tackett in Security, good man. Doors snapped shut up and down every hallway as I passed, what are they hiding from? When the time comes I'll roust them but not before I know what we've got here, which is increasingly hard to diagnose.

Day two, and look at us. Obvious problems? Server down, communications network down and Joannides AWOL. Sickness on the premises, plague until proved otherwise.

This place was running like a clock and now my clean machine is busted.

Reveille sounded at 0600 just the way it always does but the Order of the Day has gone to hell, along with the academic schedule. Bells ring on a regular basis but the classrooms are mostly empty.

People scuttle around corners so fast that all I see are shadows. I can't be sure which ones are running away or why. I don't know whether in fact, instead of hiding from invaders or any of the real terrors out there, they're avoiding me.

And my key people? Joannides nowhere. Dratch, that useless rummy, laid out in Cassie's room, while she . . . Never mind. My checklist is a wipeout. Fedders and Agnes Earhard: feeding each other's fears while Wardwell cringes. Bogardus: panicky and sly, like he's hatching something I don't know about. God knows what's up with the others. They don't show themselves. Even Benny has gone below. He's running around somewhere deep, where I can't find him.

Only Chef Pete is on deck, mystified by a hundred untouched plates in an empty Refectory.

"What," he asked me; he grabbed my arm as I went by the deserted Refectory and pulled me inside to survey the uneaten breakfasts on neatly set tables. He was oozing hurt feelings. "What's going on?"

"Too soon to tell," I said on my way out; I have things to do, and this is his problem.

He shouted after me, "What's gotten into them?"

"I'll have to get back to you on that."

"Where are they?" He came thudding down the hall after me. "Where are they all?"

I said the only thing I could think of. "Hiatus."

Now this.

Server down, systems wack, slithering plague on the premises and I walk in on the only woman I ever trusted, locked in the arms of our destruction.

What was I supposed to think, seeing this silent interloper with his arms closed around Cass and my girl locked in tight, with her face mashed to his heart as though listening for whatever secrets he has hidden there?

Long, clean hands spread on her back.

Who knows where those hands have been? Who knows what contamination the man is harboring? Even if the bastard tests clean, who's to say that inside that pale, perfect body, behind that noble-looking face, he isn't a mess of evil intentions? Is he here to steal Cass and corrupt these kids, or did he break into the Academy to ruin me? Worse, is he out to destroy the world's last outpost of peace and order? Did he climb Clothos to dig up the monks' secrets or sink the Academy, or does he only want to take my Cassandra and fuck her brains out? There were no answers, nothing but this stranger, holding Cass but looking over her head with his face closed tight, regarding me.

There was no knowing what goes on behind those slate-colored eyes. What was I supposed to think, and what was I thinking?

All of the above or none of the above.

It was like a grenade went off inside me. WHAM!

What *was* that?

He's only a kid! Nineteen from the look of him, twenty, tops, and yet that blind brute part of me that I declared dead on a bad day when I was his age and based **in country,** my suppressed but still resident killer broke out and took over. It was like the kid and I were stud horses facing off and not what we are, which is Director of the Academy overloaded with responsibilities and a young and unformed, heedless, inconvenient and possibly diseased stranger who has no business being here.

Everything in me rose up in anger. I wasn't exactly thinking. Yes I am embarrassed. No I am not sorry.

It wasn't just obscene, seeing them. It was outrageous. Lab rat or no I should have murdered him, throat cultures pending and diagnosis notwithstanding. Given the exigencies, given everything I am and all I am trying to do for my people, it's embarrassing to remember that I drew my gun but did not shoot him. I wanted to

murder him but stupid jarhead that I am, some deeply encoded
sense of probity made me hold back.

I hit him instead, and even I was surprised by what I was
thinking.

It spelled itself out like skywriting inside my head, one letter at
a time: *This is my place and she is my woman.*

Never mind what Cass was screaming at me when I did it. I
palmed the gun and bashed him on top of the head with it. He let
go at once and turned a smooth, empty face to me, blinking. What
did he, shave for her before we caught him and make himself beautiful again today, before I got here? I should have shot the bastard on
the spot and claimed I did it for her protection, so our sweet girl
Cassandra Rivard, PA, who is more than just an employee, can
damn well thank me for standing down.

Instead she rose up off of Dratch's bed and backed me out of
that skinny, lust-propelled, febrile interloper's cushy private room
and on out past the scared kids whispering in the Infirmary, who
turned white when I looked at them, and outside into the long hall
as though I, and not the unwanted stranger and not the coughing
and stricken-looking children lined up in there waiting for clinic
hours, as if I, LTCOL Sargent Whitemore, USMC Reserve, was
the source and sole carrier of the infection.

She even gave me a shove to make sure I kept going.

"Priorities, Cass." Even I didn't know what I meant.

"Just go."

This is my place and she is my woman. Where did that come from?
I, who had the best of all possible intentions, was being rushed off
the premises, shunned before I could scrape together the right
words for an explanation. All that, and I haven't even told her how
I feel; with all this going on, how can I?

I watched her until the double doors shut for good and I
watched the doors for a long time after. She went back inside to

tend the dent my Colt made his head, I suppose. That pious, marauding, opportunistic bastard. After I hit him he blinked three times and like a church lady in the courtyard of St. Peter's in Rome, the son of a bitch crossed himself and kissed the thumb of the hand he did it with. Then he had the nerve to smile at me. I saw all this over Cassie's shoulder as she charged me like a fullback and pushed me backward out of Dratch's room whereupon she slammed the door between me and her treasured patient as though of the two of us, not I but her lanky, black-haired Spartan warrior was the one who mattered.

On another day I would have killed him for certain.

OK, we are all spread a little thin. Cassie doesn't know the half of it.

Mark this Day Two of a long, bad week in which unforeseeable events have put everything I tried so hard to build here in jeopardy.

I did what I could. I did what you do.

I started a log.

Then I made a list. Item one: find Joannides.

Two. Get him to jump-start the server.

Three. Whether or not server is running, restore systems. Get this place back on schedule.

Four: In the interest of same, establish in-house communications even if it means getting Maintenance to utilize number 10 cans and string up speakers.

Five: Produce hard copy on everything. Establish a big board at the Academy crossroads for posting of same until the network is viable.

Do everything by the numbers and maybe you can make all this add up. By the time I was done the list numbered thirty items. I went looking for Jerry from Maintenance to locate materials and construct a board. Centrex is still working but he wasn't answering his phone. The way things are going, you don't know whether the personnel you're looking for have jumped ship or if they are dodging responsibility or if you're going to find them collapsed in some corner, stricken by It.

I don't know what got into this place or what it's doing to my people, but at least I have a name for it. It.

Chef Pete caught me on my way back down to the crossroads. His big pink face looked like a ruined corsage, bruised by hurt feelings. "I just wanted you to know. It's nothing I cooked."

There were a lot of things more important than Pete's feelings, but I couldn't shake him off. "OK," I said. "What?"

"I tested everything."

"In the Science lab?"

"No. I ate it."

"Shit, Pete. You didn't have to."

"Yes I did. Everything they ate last week, chapter and verse. I deep-freeze all leftovers, in case we run short."

"We're never going to run out of . . ."

"I even drank the water." Proud. Oh, the man is proud. Look at him ticking off items on his fingers. "It takes salmonella eight hours to kick in. Botulism a little longer. If it's anything they ate, I'll be down by six tonight. I serve clean food, Sarge."

"I'm sure you do, Pete." Seeing a guy as big as him that close to tears is alarming. "Look. Everything the kids ate, I ate too and I'm still walking around, so don't sweat it, it might not be anything you served."

In seconds, he turned ugly. Bad sign, given his history. "What makes you think it's the food?"

"It's gotta be something. I'm just . . ."

"Don't go pinning this on me."

"I'm just looking for the source. Something's wrong."

By this time he was swelling up like a big black cloud. Glowering. "What do you mean, something's wrong?"

"Kids are stacked like cordwood in the Infirmary."

"Say one thing about my work and I will fucking kill you."

"Don't." I tapped the Colt.

The white rings around Pete's eyes told me that this wasn't a first for him.

"Now, back off." *Tap.* "Let's think."

"Right."

Only a very special kind of personnel signs on for a post so remote that no outsiders come and the only news they get is the news I give them. It takes a damaged or desperate person to accept the terms of the Academy contract, which is open-ended, with no home leave and no terminal date specified, just guaranteed employment, with commensurate pay for as long as it takes, which is by no means certain. Absolute authority demands absolute agreement.

I've staffed my Academy with people who need to be where whatever they did can't catch up with them. Personnel willing to work in enclosed situations like this one generally have things in their past that nobody needs to know about. Problems they think they are escaping. Everybody has something, and it's up to me to forgive them. Out here they can be who they want, with no baggage.

Listen, they're entitled, and you've got to admire them, soldiering on at the top of Mount Nowhere. It takes a lot of guts, financial security and assured protection from sudden death due to possible end of the world notwithstanding.

Look at Pete, checking off items on his clipboard, more anxious to please than I am ready to let him. Not counting that lapse, he's a good soldier, the kind of guy you'd want walking point if you were leading a platoon **in country.** And he's good with the kids. Trust me, if the murder and arson charges had stuck I never would have hired him.

"OK then. Sources." Pete starts a new list. "Rats in the food supply. That could cause it, but I've got rats covered."

"You're sure." I know better than to make that a question.

"I checked the pantry and the ground-level storeroom. No compromised entry, no damage, no feces."

"Good to know."

"No food damage, no vestigial hair in crevices."

"Good."

"Check. Second, no weevils in the flour or the cereal cartons. Any ova that came in with the stuff on the supply ship died off when you activated cold storage."

"Great." You've gotta admire a guy with a checklist.

"No grubs in the meat. I cross-section every cut that comes out of the freezer."

"Check." He almost smiled just now when I said it.

He makes a new entry. "Could be something off the fungus that old fart is growing down below."

"Where?"

Smug grin. "Off-limits."

"So you think it might be Benny." I am testing Pete, but he doesn't know it.

"Could be on his 'shrooms," he says.

Watching him carefully, I say, "Or on someone Benny knows."

Pete's face is blank. "Fuck that shit. He doesn't know anybody."

OK then. As far as unauthorized strangers on the mountain go, the Academy cook knows nothing. He makes a skull and crossbones on his pad. "Poisons. He's hatching them in that fucking *garden dome.*"

"I'd know."

"You don't know shit about Benny, it's not like you screened him or anything, like you did the rest of us."

The tone change is so sudden that I don't pick up on it. "I pay him a lot less too. He works for food."

This is when Pete goes sour. "You just took him at face value."

"He works hard too."

"You're saying I don't?"

"I'm saying he's harmless."

"This disease thing didn't come out of nowhere." Pete is coming to a boil.

"We don't know where it's coming from."

"We have to fucking find out!" It's like watching a helicopter settle and then rise, settle and then rise and then settle; if it ever gets off the ground it will tear me apart with its rotors. He chops off words like a teppanyaki chef. "We have to hunt this thing down . . ."

"It's not a thing," I tell him. "We don't know what it is." We don't know what it is but I know what Pete wants.

"And get this thing . . ."

He wants something to blame.

I try to head him off with, "When we know what it is."

"Or who it is." All Pete's knives are sharpened now.

Careful, I have to be careful. Grief in the Infirmary and all hell shaping up to blow but I manage to put my hand up like a scout in enemy territory, waving him off. "We don't even know whether it's a person."

Then he scares the crap out of me. In a community as tight as this one, a moment like this, a brief show of intentions, can tell you which way the wind is blowing before you know what kind of storm is coming but too late to batten down against it. When it blows in, you're done. Talented cook, eager to please, Chef Pete may not even hear what's coming out of his mouth.

I can smell its foul breath. "Don't," I say, but before I can stop him, the thought comes out and there's no putting it back.

"We have to get this thing before it kills us . . ." The immediate future yawns, ravenous as a Venus flytrap. Pete serves up the rest chunk by chunk, in case I didn't get it. ". . . and kill it."

Petersen is one big fucker; he's a killer who could take me in a second, but I can't let this go by.

Some asshole trained in physics developed a theory: in baseball, there is a moment in the game that changes everything that came before and affects everything that comes after. He must have been a Marine. Everything hangs on what I do next.

This is when I push Chef Pete up against the wall and make clear who's in charge here. It's what a CO does. I didn't push boots at PI for nothing. I know the drill: whip them into shape, use what you know to make them grovel. It's a matter of life and death. When shit comes down, they have to fall in and follow without question. I open my jaws like the gates to hell and let him see the fires waiting. My voice is low. My tone is controlled. No one but Pete will know that I am also roaring.

"You make one move on this, Petersen, you say one word about it and I will fucking rip your ears off."

TWENTY-SIX

KILLER STADE

"It's" "It's" "awful" "*awful.*"

This is the sound of two people using the exact same words for two entirely different reasons, which I do not know when Teddy comes in. It's like Frankenstein and the Wolfman running at each other across the arctic waste, meeting up at the North Pole. They are coming from completely different directions.

I have been pissing and sweating over this fucking keyboard since the crack of whatever and my machine still won't speak to me because it is fucking infected. Ted, on the other hand, was due back like, five minutes after he left, ten tops. Like, hopefully— which Mom says never, *ever* use like this— hopefully he would come back soonest, bringing the gladsome news that the tranny kid's laptop was up and running, which would mean that the Academy server was OK, we hadn't fucked up last night after all, thereby bringing down the whole mess on our heads, plus the wrath of Mr. Sargent.

It's been hours.

So I assume he's been hanging out in this kid Zander's room all this time, using the crash cart on the tranny's laptop and it's definitely a croaker. Therefore when Teddy goes, "It's awful" at the exact same time as me I think it's for the same reason, as it is obvious to all of us that this is where I'm coming from, and why I said it.

This puts the edge on my voice. "What took you?"

I don't know what it is with Ted. He can't get any words out. He just stands there.

"What!" Forgive me for yelling. We're both on edge.

Whatever went down, it's turned him the color of a person you should have dug up before it died. It's kind of awful, watching him try to tell me. He has to chew it over for a long, long time, like a piece of overcooked liver, before he can make it small enough to spit it out so we can be done with it. "It's Zander."

"What, did he flash you?"

He doesn't laugh, he doesn't answer, which kind of sucks since all we have here is each other, and we are both in this together.

This odd silence falls around him, like a glass over a lightning bug. He's so still that I go, "You're not going to fall out on me, are you," even though I promised never to say that. No it is not a question. With him it's a done deal. It's like: he has resolved never to do that to me again. Good thing. Him spazzing out scares me shit, which when he did it that time, I was way too polite to tell him.

"Um, is there a problem?"

He doesn't answer. He just drops on the edge of his bunk, like, *crump,* and his arms drop down like they got stretched an extra foot from him carrying something tremendously heavy, a rock from the Refectory wall or something he had been carrying for so long then it wouldn't let him let go of the damn thing and just drop it.

"Dude, did you take your pill?"

That look that you have to be royalty to engineer: one eyebrow up, borderline sneerish.

"Right. Um. Like, maybe you need another?"

He sighs. It comes out *sheesh,* as in, *How could you be so stupid?*

"OK, you're fine, it's fine, so what the fuck kept you?"

Then when I am about to fall on him prince or no and punch some words out of him, Teddy tells me this basically funny thing like it is no laughing matter. "Zander fell on me."

I do like you do when you're laughing so hard that your milk comes out of your nose; I can't help it.

But he is shaking his head and shaking it, and this is how my friend Teddy Regan, HRH Prince Frederick, heir apparent of some lame country that's ashamed to have him around because he's different, makes me forget the devil in the machine and the trouble we're in at least, for now.

He says, "It was the vomit. He could die. There was blood in it."

TWENTY-SEVEN

AT FIRST CASSIE IS TOO TIRED TO TAKE IN WHAT'S GOING ON IN the Academy dayroom, where Sarge's academic misfits sit huddled around the communal ashtray, smoking weed. Where she heard shouting before she opened the door on them, the conversation has damped down to a buzz.

"Medicinal purposes," Herb Wardwell tells her with that smarmy smile.

Dave Bogardus looks up. "It's a potent antianxiety drug and don't go running to the Director, he knows."

He either does or he doesn't. She shrugs.

Wardwell says, "Toke?"

"On duty. Can't."

She escapes the group without much caring what they were yelling about before she came through the door or why they're muttering now. She flops on the far sofa and turns her face to the wall.

Another night she might have let the French teacher roll her a joint, but she's never liked pretentious Wardwell with the waxy complexion of the undead and the cold sweat of anxiety glistening on his slick, pale face. In fact, with the exception of Joannides, who never comes to the lounge, and the sly, mink-faced girls' gym teacher whose name eludes her every time Cassie runs into her, she doesn't like any of these people very much. Still, she'd rather be in the same space with Sarge's collection of grumbling academic misfits than back in the Infirmary, coping with Dratch.

She used not to like the man. After this morning, she despises him.

When he tried to examine her first patient she saw that he was too shaky to handle a syringe, draw blood, listen, for Pete's sake to a kid's heart with a stethoscope. With that bobbing head and his hands flapping uselessly, the old drunk wasn't fit to take care of the sick. He would not consider changing soiled beds or dealing with the bodily waste problem for he was, after all, a *doctor,* and she a mere PA; she even couldn't trust him with the pills. With the Infirmary computer down, she sent him to the *Merck Manual*— which turns out to be the only medical reference he bothered to bring— to get him out of the way. The tactic worked, but only until he found some new and ghastly item that set him off. Just as she finally had one or another of her frantic patients reassured and settled down, Dratch would come lurching out from behind that infernal prophylactic screen he insisted would protect him from the infected, waving some page he'd ripped out of the book. He came out ranting: "Cholera, set up evacuation protocols," or, "Lockdown imperative. It's typhoid/Ebola/bubonic plague, quarantine!"

The fool upset her kids with his escalating medical-disaster scenarios, squawking and flapping until finally she shot him full of the strongest thing she had and locked him into her room. By the time he came to, she had found and dumped every bottle of liquor

Dratch had stashed, including the ones hidden in his— Theron's room. Her patient has a name now; it's the last thing he told her before he lapsed into a state somewhere between lucent dreaming and fevered sleep. She's not sure where Theron is when he phases out, any more than she knows what he came here looking for. As for the liquor, she got to Dratch's stash too late, she realized when he started hammering and she let him out. He came out of her private quarters with her purple silk tap pants knotted on the side of his head like a pirate's do-rag.

The doctor is hung over, but at least he's alert. Given the beaker of coffee and the vitamin B_1 shot she gave him, he should be good for the few minutes she needs to lie here with her face to the wall, remembering who she is. Bad night, long, confusing day, too many sick, needy kids that she can make comfortable, but can't figure out how to cure. She'd never leave Dratch unsupervised. She has Sheela Mortimer, the fat girl who brought in the Parsons girl, watching the creepy bastard, the kid hung around until Cassie took pity and gave her something to do. Where she used to be a little bitch just like the others, now cranky, opinionated Sheela is eager to please and she's tough.

The Parsons case was the first sign that whatever had hold of Theron was not a random stroke of nature. Sheela dumped Marla Parsons on the examining table with a look of panic that Cassie still hasn't sorted out. It isn't fear of contagion; she'd have dropped her burden and fled. Instead Sheela hung in at the Infirmary in spite of Cassie's kind attempts to send her away. If the girl was afraid of catching it she wouldn't be sitting at Marla's bedside right now, monitoring her condition like a charge nurse in Intensive Care. There must have been classes or something else going on today, mealtimes at the very least, but Sheela won't leave. She hangs in with that tense, conflicted look on her face as though the fate of the world hangs on Marla's condition.

Strange days in the Academy, Cassie thinks. Strange configurations of people. In a place set up to run like clockwork, the tempo has changed.

Until tonight she hasn't been free for long enough to find out what's going on. Everything was different today, and it wasn't just the crisis in the Infirmary. She could hear kids laughing for once, running loose in the halls, as though everything Sarge tried to do for them was a waste. It's odd. With everybody else running around out there, Sheela *would not leave* the Infirmary. She did all the things Dratch wasn't fit to do for the ten who are sick, bringing fresh linens, emptying the kidney-shaped bowls on bedside tables when they filled, stolid and dutiful as the ambulance girl at the front in some old war movie, the only difference being that those girls were pretty, unlike this determined adolescent who refuses to let go.

Once Cass and her new assistant had everybody settled, Sheela stationed herself at Marla's bedside as though she and the pretty, arrogant, entitled snot from Bel Air are best friends, adjusting bedclothes, laying cool compresses on her head, alert to every little thing Marla Parsons needs. It's clear all this exposure to serious illness is hard on her but every time Cassie tried to move her out the girl begged her to let her stay. For some reason she needs to be with Marla— standing guard, in case.

Intelligent, responsible girl, Cassie thinks, but weird.

Still, it's not a bad thing. With Sheela on duty, it's safe to leave the Infirmary, at least for now. She promised to watch Dratch and come for Cassie immediately if anything comes up. In case of emergency, she tells herself, at a dead run it takes less than five minutes to get from here to there.

OK, she needed the space.

For the moment all her patients are comfortable. Theron in Dratch's bed, stable and serene; turning to go, she saw the bright, deep eyes change back to slate as he went back to doing whatever Theron does inside his head. Most of her Academy patients are sleeping and the rest are drifting in some quiet, safe place where none of this is happening. Ten sick children settled, for now.

She's done everything she can for the ten who stumbled into the Infirmary, beginning with Parsons, the walking eating disorder. Mysteriously, the girl has gained thirty pounds; she's almost as big as Sheela now. Since dawn the Academy PA has been dealing with her little psychological train wrecks on a case-by-case basis, saying whatever it takes to ease their fears. Zander Birch needed to be told that whatever he's caught won't mess up his hormone therapy, although at this point she is by no means sure; she told Marla to cheer up she'd come out at the other end of this thing five pounds lighter at the very least. The smalls, of whom there are several, needed to know that Cassie's green plush dinosaur, which sits on a table in the middle of the ward, will keep monsters away until their mommies come back for them.

With no idea what's attacked them, she is treating them symptomatically: sedatives where indicated, although by this time they're too debilitated to worry. Something to rehydrate them, something to bring down the fever, something else to ease their breathing, something stronger for the cough. Where necessary, she's introduced anti-nausea drugs.

Thank God there are only ten. It's late night and there have been no new cases since noon.

It's the only reason she's OK with stealing a minute here in a room where the conversation of Sarge's paid misfits plays on and on, like white noise.

Until her personal instant replay quits rolling and she can stop rehearsing the day, she is more or less hermetically sealed inside her skull. She can't be sure how long she stays insulated from the rest of the world, only that to keep on going the way she must if they're going to get through this, she needs to lie here for as long as circumstance will let her, zoning out.

Lying with her back to the room, Cassie is so still that flaky

Wardwell, love-starved Agnes Earhard and the others assume she's asleep. Unless they've forgotten that she's there. Or have stopped caring.

It's OK, really, that the buzz around the coffee table amplifies from background noise to room-quality transmission. It begins as the unwilling exiles' unvarying litany of complaint. Sameold this. Sameold that. Sameold bla bla bla. They bitch about Sarge and his obsessive schedules and his military regime; they bitch about those who are not present and about people sitting right here with them, about the students, the decor, the cold stone walls and the resulting chill that never goes away and the crappy sameness of institutional food. In a way, lying here listening to them natter is a comforting exercise, like being inside an MRI where there's so much ambient noise that no thoughts can intrude.

Then, as though they don't care who overhears him or what comes of it, they go back to talking about whatever they'd been talking about when she first came in.

"Monkey Zero," Wardwell says.

Shit, Cassie thinks. *Ooooh, shit.*

For a teacher, Agnes Earhard is pretty slow. "Is that, like, um. Typhoid Mary?"

No.

Bluff, bulked-up Dirk Fedders says, "Like, *they* don't get sick but everybody else gets the disease?"

"Pretty much."

"Like, a carrier that isn't even sneezing, so you don't know they've got the bug."

Her belly convulses. *Wrong.*

Somebody says, "If you ask me, it's Chef Pete."

"Yeah, he has that *look,* like he'd step on you if he could."

"The man has issues."

"He's the cook, he has the power."

"What if he's spitting in our food?"

It takes them a few minutes to chew that over, during which her least favorite person on the mountain, the tweedy, self-important guidance teacher Dave Bogardus, says, like a born motivational speaker, "If it was Pete, we'd all be sick."

"Or worse."

"We'd probably be dead by now."

"OK then." The mink-faced girl pulls up her hoodie. "If there's a carrier, who's the carrier?"

The speculation begins. "Maybe it's . . ."

"No, it's more likely to be . . ."

"It's gotta be some kid," one of them says, "you know how filthy children are . . ."

"Or one of us."

Wrong.

Now they have come down to it. "But which one?"

Like tigers circling a tree with their quarry trapped in its branches, they worry the question, going faster and faster until, like the tigers in the old story, every piece of speculation blends into every other, the whole mess fusing at tremendous speeds until it turns to butter.

Cassie stirs uneasily, wondering when would be the best time to get up and go.

Oblivious, Sarge's hand-picked personnel try to triangulate, hissing over who saw which children cough on which others and who's sick now and who isn't— a problem, since few of them know the students by name and nobody seems to know any of them well enough to say who they are. They may not care.

When Wardwell presses Earhard about Marla Parsons, whom he thinks of only as "that skinny, *skinny* girl," Agnes says airily, "Oh, Herb, I don't bother to learn their names unless I have to give one of the bitches an A or send somebody to detention."

Ignorance compounded by indifference fuels the conversation, hyped by anxiety. "No problem," Wardwell says finally, because he

is the most anxious to be reassured. "By this time, Sarge has probably posted a sick list."

"To say nothing of an interim schedule."

"Plus instructions."

Almost as a by-the-way, Fedders adds, "Last time I checked, my
computer was down."

"That's weird. So's mine."

"Mine too. Probably a virus."

"Good to know. I thought it was something I did."

"Nope, it looks like the whole network."

"Virus for sure."

If they keep fretting over electronics, Cass thinks, *I can say something friendly and get out fast.*

But that blowhard Bogardus won't let them stray for long. He is
intent on Topic A. Rolling over when she hears him clear his
throat, Cassie watches through meshed eyelashes. He stands to get
their attention. "Believe me, that's the least of our problems."

"No network, no directives."

Somebody laughs. "No more orders from Sarge."

"Not such a bad thing." Fedders laughs, but nobody else does.
They are all squirming, scratching parts of themselves that don't
itch. Something is wrong inside Sarge's citadel. People are getting
sick. Set down next to the problem in the infirmary, the computer
crash is nothing. Computers, after all, are only computers, they
soberly tell each other; Joannides can take care of that, let's take
these things one at a time. As for the other thing, the doctor has it
under control, after all, he is a doctor, but they are whistling in the
dark, howling at the moon, whatever people do to ward off that
which they are most afraid of. "So all we have to do is wait," Fedders says, but his voice is thin.

Bogardus is still on his feet. Like an inflatable rat at a strikers'
rally, he sways back and forth over the table. He adds in a sports
announcer's BOOM, "Until one of us gets sick."

"We can't."

"We won't get it. We got all our shots."

"What if there is no shot for this?"

Now they are at the heart of the matter. Fretful, sweating Herb Wardwell is the first to say, "What if we get it?"

And like tigers who can't let go of each other's tails, they go back to circling the tree. Disease is resident in the Academy. Until it's stopped, everybody is suspect and every one of them is at risk. The question floating on the stream of words is what to do about it.

It is Bogardus who brings Cassie to her feet and sends her out of the room with the terror hard on her heels. "We have to identify the source, and fast."

He doesn't know, she tells herself. *He couldn't possibly know,* but his last words follow her down the hall and back to the Infirmary where he is safe, at least for now.

Bogardus shouts in a tone designed to send packs of howling villagers out with torches, "And when we do, we drag him out and throw him off the cliff."

TWENTY-EIGHT

BENEDICTUS IS IN THE SECRET SUBCRYPT KNOWN ONLY TO those who truly belong in the abbey, so for the moment he is safe from intrusions. Sited two levels below the undercroft of the forlorn, deconsecrated chapel, this particular crypt is specific to the monks. Nobody else on the mountain knows that it exists. Even Mr. Sargent doesn't know.

As for who truly belongs here, Benny is the last. This is his quiet place. Now that the chapel has been transformed into Mr. Sargent's ranting platform, now that the beautiful young stranger has contaminated the confessional with his bundle of pain and doubt, Benny has only the crypt. It is the last place in the world where he can invite his soul.

He is visiting the ranks of the abbey's unburied, an orderly row of dried, enshrouded corpses— the last generation of monks to inhabit the mountaintop. The Benedictines Benny knew are all dead now— everybody he cared about, including Sixtus. Gone from this earth. Only their shells are present. In a way, their mummified bodies are good company, and he visits them often. Remembering what they used to say. How they walked. It's like looking for re- minders of people you loved in empty houses long after the occu- pants have packed up and moved away. It's all he has left.

Being the last surviving member of a community is terrible. When the community is the only home you know, it's worse. There's nobody in the world outside for Benny to turn to because he's never been outside, noplace to go. It isn't just the responsibil- ity to keep things going that weighs on him, although the pressure to praise God and keep the Hours is intense because he's the only one left who remembers how. It's the solitude. In a community bent on heaven, Benny is lonely as hell. Here in the crypt, at least, he has company, even though everybody he cares about is dead.

Mysteriously, the monks got sick one after another and died in spite of all his prayers. When Sixtus died, Benny prayed to God to let him die too, but if you've lived with God all your life you know that not all prayers are answered. Take it from Benny; he knows. He'd has outlived the others for close to twenty years. He supposes God has other plans for him.

It would have been merciful, he thinks, as it's been hard. The monks were friends, family, everything. In the absence of known parents, Sixtus was his earthly father. The abbey was his home. When they all died his world ended. How could he do this alone? Without the others working alongside him, keeping the Hours, kneeling next to him in the vaulted chapel, propping him up, would he go mad and curse God?

End up disconnected and raving?

Run frothing off the highest peak?

He hasn't. Yet.

Never mind that he begged to die. He lives on.

No matter what God has in mind for him, which is by no means clear, Benny thinks dying would have been better, but God seemed to want him to carry on. He did what was expected. He laid Sixtus in the crypt next to the others and moved his things into his mentor's cell. It gave him a certain peace, occupying the same space where the last abbot lived and died. He kept the Hours. He maintained the vegetable garden. He combed his hair. He worked. He prayed. He persevered.

When the helicopter set down on the little butte the monks called St. Benedict's Peak, he ran outside, shouting, "At last!" It was like a message from God. He was happy and excited, running over the rocks with his arms wide open to the future. He greeted Mr. Sargent grinning; it was his first smile in twenty years. God sent the visitor. He just knew. Look at the man! Sun-bronzed, strong and forceful. Self-assured. He talked so loud! It was thrilling, hearing the sound of other human voices, as the Director led his team of surveyors here, there.

Benny showed them the premises and walked Mr. Sargent through the cloister, jabbering uncontrollably: "And this is the Refectory, where we take our meals. The abbot reads Scripture to us during dinner . . . and this is where we sleep . . . and this . . ." Proudly, he showed Mr. Sargent the chapel. "This is where we pray." When a stranger smiles while you are talking, you assume you both want the same things. Proud of having kept the abbey going, Benny talked on and on while Mr. Sargent tapped notes into an odd machine smaller than Benny's hand. It made him feel stronger, pacing off the cloister with this confident stranger who took big steps and smelled of the outside world.

Where there was nothing on Clothos but the abbey, Benny thought, there was money out there in the world. Mr. Sargent had it, and he would have more. His soft leather jacket, his amazing boots spoke of prosperity. Helicopters! Success. Where Benny knew only the mountaintop abbey, this man had mastered the world. When he came back to Clothos he would bring money, men and materials to restore the crumbling stone and set the abbey to rights. Architects. Powerful machines. Exalted, Benny assumed that God had sent Mr. Sargent to Clothos to rebuild everything he'd thought was lost.

Together, they would get it back.

This, he told himself. *This is what the Father had in mind.*

With his blueprints, his work crews and his world of money, Mr. Sargent would restore the abbey and bring in new postulants. A persuasive man like the one the old man is much too shy to call Sarge would have no trouble convincing Benedictines from other abbeys to come to Clothos to teach the candidates, and soon there would be many monks praying here. There would be music in the bare, ruined choirs. Chanting at the proper times. Together, Benny and wonderful Mr. Sargent and the others would work and pray. Good men would come begging to be monks, pilgrims would come; the bishop would send a priest and he could confess! The abbey bells would ring again and— some day!— some day the Holy Ghost would come as promised, to renew the face of the earth.

In those early days Benny went about the business of the Academy in a state of what passes for joy. He did his best. Now everything is out of control.

He did all this in hopes, and look how that turned out.

Worse. Benny, who reads— the Scriptures, Revelation, the Venerable Bede— Benny knows that he has brought pestilence down on this house, which was so close to being restored. It came into the Academy with the lean, intense stranger he found, weak and feverish, hiding in his next-to-last private place.

How old and cracked am I, he wonders, *that I mistook him for a priest?*

He let pestilence into the abbey, and with it, a breathtaking torrent of guilt. *How old am I,* he wonders, *that the plague on my house comes here thinking that I know him, and I think I do not? Is he lying?*

Trapped in a circle that that he can't escape, he considers the question. **Do you know who I am?** No, he thinks, stricken, and his heart founders. *Do I? Did I forget?*

Does God want him to follow this thread to the end and get an answer? Or did He send the gravely ill stranger as a reproach for some long-forgotten sin?

Do you know who I am?

He doesn't; he almost does. Memories roll in like surf that breaks up on the rocks before Benny can read them. He does know that he sheltered this man and fed him and kept his presence a secret in spite of the illness, and long after he should have told Sarge. Now he has to wonder whether he did it out of hope for the future of the community or whether he kept his secret out of naked selfishness.

Dear God, he thinks, or prays— the two are all mixed up in his head— *Who is he?* Why can't he remember? Guilty and excited, he bites his knuckles until they bleed. *What have I done?*

He falls to his knees at the foot of the stone oblong where Sixtus lies, praying for enlightenment. He kneels on the dirt floor for so long that when he's done, it takes him several minutes to come to his feet. By the time he straightens and totters a few steps, regaining his balance, it's late. The watch Sixtus gave him for his eighteenth birthday tells him that above stairs, it is deep night. This makes him think that he ought to recover some shred of the Liturgy of the Hours, the outward and physical sign of the discipline he's let go to hell starting today, when he overslept and woke up grieving and confused. If he can just manage Compline . . . No, if he can only remember the opening prayers, maybe the rest will follow and he'll be all right.

Everything hurts. He can't bring himself to kneel again. Standing here among the dead, with the chapel desecrated, the abbey transformed and everything slipping away, he tries to remember the words.

He would say them all if he could, but he can't.

A lifetime spun out here in peace and order, supported by the discipline, and now everything— even his concentration— has gone to hell. Benny tries to pray; he tries and tries, but the only words that come to him are the ones that drove him down scores of stone steps to the deepest cavern in the first place.

They fill the room. *Do you know who I am?*

Groaning, Benedictus toils up the stairs. *No, but I have to find out.* He has to find out tonight.

"Do you know who I am," he mutters resentfully. Every joint in his body produces a twinge or an ache but he is bent on the answer. "No, but I will know. I will."

It takes him too long to struggle up the eighty stone steps to the subcrypt where the last of the monks' dwindling stores are kept and to go on to mount the scores of steps up to the vast chamber that has become Mr. Sargent's storage area, stacked high with provisions, and it takes even longer to climb up from there to the undercroft, numbering the last flight of stone stairs with every breath he takes. Emerging, he tries to run. He is racing against creeping daylight. He needs to make it down the long corridor without being seen and sneak into the Infirmary before they can stop him. The journey takes Benny what seems like forever, but he hasn't slept much and he can't remember when he last ate.

Everything about him is getting thin.

By the time he reaches the swinging doors— the last barrier between him and the truth, the Gothic windows glimmer with morning light. Then he looks up.

This is bad, he realizes. *It's all changed.*

There's a big red sign posted on the closed doors. It's bright red, with sinister black letters rushing across the top. At the center of the red sign is a black circle of tangled, barbed crescents that look too much like linked devils' horns, and what the lettering says confirms what Benny already knows. *I have brought pestilence on the house.*

The letters race across the poster on the door like murderers in a hurry:

QUARANTINE

"God," he murmurs, distressed but determined. He opens the doors a few inches and, crossing himself, he slips inside. Benny stands there for a moment, murmuring under his breath, "God, dear God, dear God."

Then he sees what's going on.

What have I done?

His friend— *they took him away from me!!!*— is not the only patient here. The room is filled with a double row of cots. Benny's too upset to count, but there are people tossing and fretting in more than half of them. Children, he realizes, looking at the shapes they make under tightly tucked coverlets. None of the sleeping patients' bodies are long enough to be the person he brought under this roof and kept safe without telling anyone. He kept him for as long as he could. Now all these children are sick. *What have I done?*

He tiptoes through the ward, down the aisle between the cots and ducks into the infirmarian's ell, the area the monks partitioned off to make two private cells. This is where Brother Francis, the infirmarian, lived until the plague took him. Across the narrow hall is a smaller cell where Brother Aloysius, his assistant, slept whenever a stricken monk needed a night nurse. Or did until the plague took Francis and Aloysius too. Trembling, Benny wonders. *Do these babies have what my brothers had? Is this what my stranger brought in with him?* A great weight falls on Benny's soul. Gasping, he leans against an archway, considering. *What have I done?*

It will be morning soon. He looks at the two closed doors. Which one, he wonders. Which one?

He chooses the larger room. Putting his lips to the door, Benny whispers, "It's me."

Why did he imagine his new friend would answer after everything Benny did and everything he failed to do?

Still he tries, "Are you in there?"

When you have been betrayed by someone you trusted, when he has let you fall into the hands of your enemy, will you answer if you hear him at your door?

Benny can feel himself shrinking. Soon he won't be anybody at all. But. He sighs. He will live on.

Then he thinks: *What if he needs me? What if he died in there?*

He opens the door.

His sick friend is alive, he sees; at least he's moving. It's clear he is beyond speech. Swaddled tightly to keep him from hurling himself off the bed, the young man Benny thinks of as the Unknown Friend lies raving in the mechanical hospital bed that has replaced Brother Francis's straw pallet. A deep groan rises from somewhere inside his helpless friend. It's a harsh, metallic sound. The agonized rasp that comes out of the man speaks to him of last things. It's a sound Benny knows. *Oh God,* he thinks, praying because it's the last means of communication left to him, *oh God oh God oh God.* He touches his charge's forehead and springs back, scorched. "Oh don't," he cries, in the same words he used to make Sixtus to stay inside his body just a little longer. "Please wait!"

The woman must have heard. She flies into the room like an angry spirit, shouting, "What are you doing in here?"

There are no words for what Benny has to say.

"You," she says to Benny. "What did you do to him?"

He shows her empty hands.

She doesn't care that Benny sneaked in without a plan, or that if she asked, he couldn't explain what brought him here. Roughly, she pushes him out of the way, not noticing and probably not caring that he staggers and almost falls. "Don't you know this thing is highly contagious?"

Hurt and confused, Benny lies. "I'm trying to help!"

"Well, you can't." Tears fly as she whips her head around and for the first time looks into Benny's face. Her voice draws a thin line between them. "I don't know if anybody can."

"Please," Benny says. "If you can't help him, let me take him."

"No!"

Desperation drives him to forge on in a frantic attempt to shoulder her out of the way but Benny is old, too frail. "At least let me talk to him."

"He isn't talking, Benny. The patient is not responding." She has him by the shoulders now and before he can pretend to struggle she's turned him so that there's noplace to go but out.

Oh God, make me strong. Prayer is prayer, Benny knows, and sometimes God listens. Sometimes He does not. He leans back with his full weight, digging in his heels with all his strength, but she is young and he's too old. "I have to know something," he cries.

"Shhh, you'll wake them." Her angry hiss stops him.

"But I have to know!"

"You have to go."

"Please!"

Thanks to the discipline, Benny has never cried before. He's more surprised than the woman doctor when he does. He just can't help it. As she pushes him through the Infirmary doors, cutting Benny off from his last friend in the world, some part of his heart breaks. Without knowing whether he intends to pray for a lifesaving miracle or bury the boy, he sobs, "Let me take him. I'll take care of him!"

"Like you did when you hid him in the priest hole? Benny, there are *children* here. How could you be so careless with so many lives?"

"I tried, Miss Cassie. I tried!"

"You." Her rage is terrible. "Why didn't you tell me? Why didn't you tell before it was too late? Look at you, Benedictus whatever-the-fuck your last name is. Look what you've done!"

"Bless me Father . . ." The rest of the words won't come.

"He was febrile and raving and you knew it, and you just let the fever rage on." She is sobbing too. "Now Theron is sick and the children are sick, and I can't help them and God only knows what it is."

Theron. He has a name! "I didn't mean to hurt anybody."

"Look at them," she whispers, pushing the doors wide so he has to look back into the darkened ward, where the young toss and whimper in their sleep.

He is blubbering now, sad old man who seldom smiled after the others died and who never, ever cried, being rushed away from the last person in the world that he cares about. She is cutting him off from his lost friend Theron. He grabs the name like a prize: *Theron,* the only one in this Godless place who knows . . .

Knows what? Like *that* it slips away. Everything slips away. He sobs, "I was only trying to help."

"Look what you did to them!"

Benny's guilt is feeding on itself now. Helplessly, he begins, "Oh my God, I am heartily sorry . . ."

"Now go." She gives him a shove to start him down the hall, away from the Infirmary with its dozen sickbeds and the long row of empty cots awaiting more. They won't be empty for long. "Get out of here before you do something worse."

Desperate now, old, helpless and weeping, Brother Benedictus, the last surviving member of the Benedictine community at Clothos, prayerful and faithful keeper of the Rule, cuts and runs.

He runs without knowing where he's heading, only that with Theron, *Theron* unconscious, perhaps dying, with children sick and the lady doctor, *his friend,* turning against him, he can't bear any more.

A different person would have scrambled up the ladder into the kitchen garden and hurried across it just as Benny did, not caring which beds of seedlings he stirred up with his flying sandals or which root vegetables he trampled in his flight. Another man, feeling what Benny felt just then, would have run headlong to the lip of the dome and thrown himself against the roll bar and let himself out, which Benny did.

The difference is that anyone else in Benny's desperate state would have run too, but he wouldn't have stopped at the edge. He would have gone tearing across the plateau with a different end in mind. Anybody else driven by this measure of grief and guilt would have run on, just like Benny, but when he reached the crag where Benny was heading now, when he came to the edge where the surface of the earth gave way to a stupendous drop he would have run on. Unlike Benny, who stopped at the brink, a weaker man would have kept on running, thrashing in midair until he lost momentum and plunged, screaming, thousands of feet to his death.

Not Benedictus. He is, after all, who he is.

No matter how hard Benny runs today or how fast he runs, he can't or won't outrun the belief that there must be a reason why God scooped him up like a minnow out of a pond and spilled him out here.

Therefore he stops. He knows there is a ladder; it is firmly fixed to the ledge. Tediously, painfully, he turns and puts his foot on the first rusting rung. Then step by step he descends backward. He is going to the ledge where the Benedictine community's old basket relay begins and ends. If he can only bend his old legs well enough to get into the basket, God will help him to find a way down.

If he makes it to the bottom, he will find a way to go for help.

At the bottom of the ladder, he turns and looks. Nothing is right. The pulley the monks fixed in the rock centuries ago dangles from a broken hook. The basket is gone. It's as though some heavy object fell on it. There's nothing left of the first stage of the monks' basket relay but a length of frayed rope.

Praying to God for the strength to climb down to the rock shelf that supports the second staging area, which he prays he will find intact, he crawls out on the crag and looks.

Here, there is no ladder. He sees a broken body sprawled on the rocks far below. It's a man.

There is the brief, mad second in which Benny imagines that God has sent another stranger for him to help and take care of, so he will have a fresh chance to redeem himself. He will do better with this one, he thinks. He will!

Then he sees the angle of the neck, the shard of iron sticking through the body— a broken winch— and understands that whoever he is, the man he wanted so much to help has died in the fall. So Brother Benedictus knows that he will have to go back inside alone and that whatever he does next, he will have to do alone.

He does what he can. No. He does what Benny does best. Uprooting a turnip from the kitchen garden, he gnaws on it to restore his strength. Then he goes back down the scores of stone steps to kneel at Brother Sixtus's feet. He prays.

TWENTY-NINE

DIRECTOR'S LOG
Crisis, the Academy at Clothos
Cause: Unknown
<u>LTCOL Sargent Whitemore, USMC (RETD)</u>
Status report
Week One, Day Three:
- Infirmary: 13 patients, one critical
- Breakdown of affected personnel currently in sick bay
    total, 9
        students from upper school: 4
        students from grades 1–8: 5
    staff, 3
    unidentified patients, 1
- Active medical personnel, 2
- Volunteer aides, 1: Sheela Mortimer, age 14
- Deaths: none

- Situation: under control
- Academy schedule: Same
- Classes: proceeding as usual. Substitute teachers where needed
- Attendance: full complement in each instance minus personnel reassigned to sick bay
- Food service: on schedule
- Food supplies, AOK
- Attendance at meals: normal
- Academy IT officer: AWOL
- Academy server: down. Attempts to reboot to date: 600
- Reconfiguration possibilities in this situation: .05 percent
- Assessment: Situation severe but not critical
- Plan of the Day: SOP

IN HIS PA'S tight little bedroom in the Academy's Infirmary, Mel Dratch, MD, PC, surgical residency at Johns Hopkins University Hospital, who did his postdoc program in Virology and Gene Therapy at the Mayo Clinic in Rochester, Minnesota, and practiced in metropolitan hospitals up and down the East Coast, struggles to get his own attention.

Given the way things are with him right now, it's a stretch.

Ten years of boozing and three days in stir with nothing to drink but coffee and bottled water have left Mel shaky and unsure of himself, which could be cured for certain if he could only get his hands on a Scotch. Shot glass, pint, fifth, it doesn't matter. He only needs one. After she caught him trying to make a little something for himself out of isopropyl alcohol and terpenhydrate with codeine, Miss Cassandra Rivard, PA, shoved him in here and locked the door.

Basically, he's been in detox.

The bad news is that it's working.

His brain went out to lunch and stayed there when the bad thing came down in the ER. Now it's coming back.

Like she cares.

No matter what he tells her, steely Ms. Rivard only opens the door to take out the bedpan and shove in the next dinner tray, pointedly removing fruit, juices, raisins, anything that he might set aside to ferment. Anything he could cook up. As though he thought for a minute that he'd find enough junk in this austere room to make a functional still. The suspicious bitch is so harsh that yesterday at the last minute, she took the mini-pack of raisins off his plate before she shut him in with the tray.

"Let me out. I want to help."

"Fine," she said in a voice that would debride necrotic flesh. She threw in the *Merck Manual.* "Research the symptoms, and tell me which are the right meds."

"You bitch!" After the door closed he managed to say what he had been trying to tell her. "It isn't in the book. It's all in my head."

Still, it's interesting. Why did the girl sign up for Clothos in the first place? With a whole world out there, why would a lovely woman with nothing to hide settle for a narrow bed in this mean little room, tucking herself away like a nun? Mel knows why he's here— the malpractice suits, the prison term— but why would an intelligent girl like Rivard come here? She didn't buy that end-of-the-world shit. Neither does he. Even before what looks like the first wave of a burgeoning epidemic rolled into the Infirmary, this was a very bad deal.

The situation in the ward outside is terrible. The beds are filled and new patients are drooped over chairs dragged in from the dining hall, waiting for beds while the coach and his assistant, who come in fully sealed inside their HAZMAT suits, drag mattresses in from the dormitory wing.

With his ear to the door Mel listens to the coughing, the retching, adults moaning and children complaining in the dark.

Marburg? he wonders. *How does it communicate? What can we do?* More: *What can I do?*

He doesn't have to see around corners to know that the PA has been working alone for too long, treating new patients, fixing IV shunts and administering antibiotics in conjunction with decongestants, muscle relaxants, anti-nausea drugs, trying everything in the cabinet with no positive results and doing all this on very little sleep. They are engaged in a desperate holding action, or she is.

If only I could help!

In the absence of anything to do, Mel Dratch does what he can. He thinks. As his mind clears, his medical training kicks in. He doesn't know what to do but there's at least one protocol they can try. It depends on his taking a couple of the slides his PA has cultured out and getting into a workable lab.

"Let me out," he shouts. "I can help."

She sticks her head in. "If you want to help, stop wasting my time."

"It's not what you think. I want to help!"

"You just want to get drunk."

"I just want to get out." He is useless in here, and now that he's back, it's killing him.

Clever Mel. She won't see the chink in the door where the seltzer pop top he folded so carefully does its work. When things are quiet, when he thinks he can pop the lock and slip away without being noticed. He'll take a couple of smears and escape before she knows. Then he can make a run on the science lab where, with any luck, he get the right equipment to identify this thing and deal with the problem at hand.

DIRECTOR'S LOG
Crisis, the Academy at Clothos
<u>LTCOL Sargent Whitemore, USMC (RETD)</u>
Status report
Week Two, Day Five:
- Infirmary: 18 patients, four critical.

- Breakdown of affected personnel currently in sick bay
  - students from upper school: 9
  - students from grades 1–8: 5
  - staff, 3
  - unidentified patients, 1
- Active medical personnel, 1
- Volunteer aides, 1: Sheela Mortimer, age 14
- Deaths: none
- Situation: under control
- Academy schedule: Same
- Classes: as scheduled. Substitute teachers where needed.
- Student attendance: ¼ capacity
- Food service: On schedule
- Attendance at meals: below average
- Food supplies: Surplus. Possible food-based sources of con-tamination destroyed
- Academy IT officer: Missing in action
- Academy server: Down. Attempts to reboot and reconnect, SNAFU
- Assessment: situation critical
- Plan: under review

ALEXANDRINA BIRCH IS beyond dreaming; ze is delirious. Every time ze feels hands on zer changing body, ze turns in zer fevered sleep and murmurs, "Father, is that you?"

It never is.

Ze is awfully sick. Hands wipe zer face. Drowning in an ocean of dreams, ze goes fishing for the last person who cares what becomes of zem, but these waters are so deep that ze calls like a baby, "Daddums?"

A rocky girl-voice answers, definitely not Dad's. "It's me, dude. Sheela. You know, Sheela from school?"

"Mummy?"

"I'm here to take care of you? They won't let me get near Marla any more."

Ze feels hands clutching the blanket that covers him. Him! Something important is slipping away. One more sick day and terrible night and it will be gone forever. The illusion that ze is changing . . .

"Like it's something I did. Dude?"

A great sigh rips out of him. *Gone.*

"Oh Zander, what if she dies?"

Oh shit, I'm only ever going to be a boy.

"Dude, can you hear me?"

Gone forever. Noises come out of Zander but none of them make words.

"It's me, Sheela Mortimer, remember? I'm another reject, like you?"

He gurgles, but he can't make words.

"I know why you're in here little dude, and I'm sorry, and I don't only mean about the getting sick. It sucks that they wanted to get rid of you. My mom did too, and believe me, she can afford it. It sucks, having the richest mother in the world."

He wants to tell this Sheela that he probably has the richest father, and Harold packed him off for the same reason, just like her. He'd like to tell her about the itch under the fat pads on his chest, but it's too hard. Everything is too hard, even opening his eyes.

"Oh please, little dude. Don't just lie there. Say something."

He rolls his head on the pillow the way he did when he was small and Mummy was alive.

This girl with an ugly voice leans closer, washing Zander's face with her sour breath. "Is there, like, anything I can get for you?"

Candy. Daddy. Hormones. My mom.

"Dude, are you in there?" She has a sigh like a fish exploding. "Just tell me what you want!"

Zander could name bazillion things he wants now and afterward but his throat closes. All that comes out is a wheeze.

"Um, tell me that's not a death rattle, OK?"

There are things he would like to ask right now and things he
wants to tell this girl, but he's too sick to unstick his lips and let it
out. Sick as he is, he knows the sound of a person losing patience.

Harold the harsh taught him that.

"Just let me the fuck do *something*," she rasps, "you're all sick as
bastards and I think it's my fault. See, I gave something to my
friend Marla, like Marla was ever my friend. It didn't even have any
stuff in it? But next thing I knew she started yacking up her guts,
and what was I supposed to do? I brought her here."

He hears the nice woman who wipes the puke away and gives
shots and puts new stuff in his IV talking, but he can't make out
what she says.

"Yes ma'am," Sheela says, "I'll keep it down." She whispers,
"So, except for weird guy in the back room that they don't talk
about? I think Marla was the first. I know she was the first of the
kids, and why Marla got sick instead of that bitch Sylvie . . . It was
in the truffles, see; I only gave them to the girls to make them fat,
which, excuse me, I think you understand . . . Anyway, she got sick
and then you got sick and now . . ." She breaks off. "No ma'am,
I'm not bothering him, I'm trying to *help* him." She waits for Miss
Cassie to go away.

"Anyway, I gave these truffles to my friend Marla— well, she
isn't really my friend, and she ate the whole box. OK, I did it because I hate those girls, they are all shitty to me, and it made her
sick and now everybody's getting sick . . ." Through the haze Zander hears her trying hard to finish even though she is sobbing.
". . . and I have to stay here and take care of everybody until *somebody* gets cured because it's all . . ."

The letters— H O P E L E S S— drift across Zander's brain like great big balloons floating past behind his eyes. He hears the nurse lady; he hears the girl.

"All right, I'm *going*."

But she doesn't. Zander can smell her sour breath.

"I told you, I am!"

He hears footsteps.

"Ms. Cassie, please . . ."

There is a flap and a scuffle.

Then he hears Sheela-girl whining, "I was only trying to help!"

Right before he sinks back into the fluffy cloud where he was floating when she came up and breathed on him, Zander Birch hears her saying, "Ms. Cassie, I have to help them. This is all my fault!"

"DON'T YOU THINK it's weird?" Dave Bogardus is going where most men on Clothos are afraid to go. He has tracked Chef Pete to the heart of the forbidden territory. He is about to confront the most dangerous man in the Academy in his spotless kitchen.

He is that intent on saving his hide.

People are getting sick all around him, even people he knows. If they keep carting his contacts on the staff off to the Infirmary at this rate, he'll run out of allies before he can stage his coup.

Whatever foul plague felled teachers he knows and students he doesn't care about is on the loose, and it's spreading. The source of the contamination is out there, slouching toward him, Bogardus knows. He just knows.

Sometimes he thinks he sees its shadow going around corners just ahead of him; at others, he sees it looming in his sleep but he can't make out its face. It gets closer with every teacher felled— his girlfriend Ms. Earhard!— and it is huge.

She collapsed yesterday, right in the middle of class. His biggest ally in his battle for health and safety, flattened like a fly as the dark angel struck her down and without looking back, moved on. His office was right next to her classroom and he heard her scream right before she fell. One of the few kids who was still coming to class these days ran for help and two men Bogardus had never seen before came and took her away.

He followed the gurney at a safe distance, stopping only when Sarge's Security men bashed open the Infirmary doors with the steel foot of Earhard's gurney and rolled her inside. Everything about it spoke of danger: HAZMAT suits on the amateur EMTs to begin with, although they'd come out so fast that they forgot their protective hoods. *Poor bastards, they're probably already infected.* Big red QUARANTINE sign on the door. Part of Bogardus wanted to follow; the prurient part of him wanted see the carnage inside.

In addition to which, he had to get in good with poor Ms. Earhard before it was too late, tell her to take care of herself, tell her he'd love to hook up with her when she gets out, propose if he had to, anything to secure her loyalty.

Don't die, I was counting on you.

But the place reeked of disease. Instead, he ducked behind a Gothic arch because he was terrified of getting caught and even more afraid of getting sick. The amateur EMTs backed out of the Infirmary on the run, followed by the Director, who pulled the headpiece off his HAZMAT suit and stood there in the hallway, raging.

"Off-limits, assholes." Distractedly, Sarge pulled off his HAZMAT gauntlet and ran his fingers through his short, white-blond hair, shouting, "Don't you know how dangerous it is?" Then his voice dropped and Bogardus couldn't hear what he said next. Whatever it was, body language told him that it was important. He was tempted to creep closer. He shrank. He was too afraid.

He isn't just pissed about them not wearing the helmets, he thought, watching. What was the Director telling them?

There are secrets inside the Infirmary that bluff Mr. friendly-friendly Sargent Whitemore with his military carriage and that no-nonsense glare will go to any lengths to protect.

The Infirmary isn't just for sick people, Bogardus thought, creeping back the way he came.

It's in there. He shuddered. *The source.*

Whatever it is, he decided, *it has to be destroyed.*

Bogardus has lost so much sleep over this that in his sleep and in all his waking nightmares, Typhoid Mary has fused at tremendous speeds with Monkey Zero. To do what he has to do to save himself, Bogardus knows, he needs to hunt down and slay the carrier. With a little help.

Unfortunately, the only strong-arm man left in the institution is Chef Pete, and nobody really knows who he is. Grapevine says the man's an escaped serial killer. Circus strong man who ran amuck and killed the manager, he's heard. Deranged cuckold who . . . They say he learned to cook in the kitchen at Ossining.

Gulp. He taps on the kitchen door.

The man is huge. Shaved head, scar bisecting one eyebrow, God only knows what he did. Pete looms over Bogardus like an Easter Island head. "'Fuck are you here about?"

"Um." Sound casual. "This thing that's going around."

Pete straight-arms him out of the kitchen. "It isn't in the food."

Trained to read body language, Bogardus grins disarmingly and talks the talk. "Fuck no."

"So get the fuck out of here."

"Wait. There's something you should know."

By the time he's done he has Chef Pete and Bradley, his bulky second in command, at the faculty table in the Refectory, listening. Obediently, Bradley sits opposite him. The problem is, Pete won't sit down. He looms with his arms folded. At least he's listening. Allies in the battle to come, Bogardus thinks, although only one of them is nodding.

Partly because of his training, Bogardus talks in bullet points. He has a very orderly mind. Probably why Sarge took him on. Like a motivational speaker, he lays it out for them.

First: identify the source.

Second: find HAZMAT suits for the people he lines up to do the job.

Bradley says, "I already have one."

Secret bullet point: find out where Bradley got it. Five big guys in HAZMAT suits and he'll have the muscle to do this. He thinks he's lined up Coach and his assistant. If he can convince these two and come up with one more, he'll have five pawns to do the job.

Bradley is still talking, but Bogardus is too preoccupied to hear. Too bad.

He has them now. Motivating, he adds, "Together we can beat this thing," but his mind is running ahead. Most of the faculty still standing are on the fence about this thing, but when they find out he knows how to stop the plague they'll fall in, no question. All he has to do is get Chef Pete and his assistant here signed and sealed. If only Pete would sit down! *Leader of men. I can do this. I can.* Five more minutes and he'll have them. "Say you're in and I'll tell you how."

Pete smashes the business end of his cleaver on the table so hard that the plank splits. "Fuck that shit."

"Wait." Damn that plaintive tone. "I have a plan!"

Pete stomps back to the kitchen.

Oh fuck.

"Sir . . ." Nobody knows what bad past Bradley was outrunning when he signed on as waitperson; it couldn't have been much. The stocky kid has a mashed-looking head straight out of a picture by one of the Dutch Masters, pasted on top of an overpumped weight lifter's body. Broken teeth show when he grins, which he is doing now. "I'm in, Mr. Bogardus."

"Oh, Bradley." His voice sags. "Good man."

"Sir . . ." Bradley has his own HAZMAT suit, a major plus, but Bogardus is talking too fast to want to hear any more from him. He found it in his locker the day the Quarantine sign went up. He puts it on after Taps, which is when he makes the food runs to the Infirmary, which he does while the Academy sleeps.

"Not now, Bradley. Let me finish." Having lit the fire, Bogardus asks Bradley who else he knows. "I need big guys. Men strong enough to kill the monster that this plague rode in on."

As soon as he figures out who the carrier is, the unidentified Typhoid-Mary-Monkey-Zero, Bogardus will lead them to the Infirmary like villagers with torches. His HAZMAT team will storm the place and rout out the monster who brought all this down on them and then . . . *back, Davey,* he tells himself. *Don't let him think you are hysterical. Down boy. Down.*

They'll eliminate the source.

Then— and this is the part he will not tell anybody, not even his recruits— then . . .

To prevent further contamination, they'll seal the sick and everybody who ever touched them inside the Infirmary and torch the place.

SYLVIE IS OUT where nobody is supposed to go, wandering in the rooftop garden, grieving for her secret lover. She's been sobbing so hard for so many hours, the noise she makes is so loud and it's been going on for so long that echoes have filled up the dome that covers the place like the plastic shell over a take-out salad. The noise is so sad and so terrible that she can't stand it another minute. Moaning, she crunches through the raspberry thicket, looking for the spot. *Here,* she thinks. *Here. No, here.* She burrows until she finds it. *This is where he kissed me and we went out.* Then she digs until she uncovers the hatch where she and Steve went outside to walk free on the mountaintop on their sad and mysterious last night.

She misses him so much!

I will go out there and climb up that place where Steve went and if I can't find him I will fucking jump off it.

It takes her a long time to open the hatch.

Never mind what Sarge says, never mind what everybody on the mountain thinks. It isn't poison out here, the air is positively fine, in spite of the fact that the night sky is an awful color. The other kids could all be, like, out here running around free like her and . . . She sobs. Like her and Steve, if they weren't all sick now.

They could have been running around out here since Day One if they hadn't all been such credulous assholes. They might have been fucking escaped the Château d'If here and gone back to real life, her and Marla and them, and her secret, perfect lover that she hasn't even had sex with, that's been gone since . . .

She cries to heaven, "Baby, where are you?"

Alone out here with her grief, Sylvie yells to the sky and is astonished as surrounding rocks magnify her voice. She can hear it all around her, getting bigger and bigger. "Honey, please answer me!"

Before long it's ginormous, big enough to fill the Astrodome, "Steve! Stephen Aegisthus Joannides, where the fuck have you gone?"

Then on the deserted plateau somebody or something rises up out of nowhere, a thin shadow. It answers. "You called?"

Her heart leaps up. "Steve?"

"I'm sorry," the shadow-man says, and her heart falls.

"Who is it?" Sylvie cries. "Who's there?"

Whoever the fuck he is, invading her personal grief in her private space, not-Steve says sadly, "It's only me."

"Then go away."

"Please don't be mad."

Surprise, it's the old guy that they used to see with the fertilizer and the garden hose and the wheelbarrow and the shovels, the one she and Steve had to hit the dirt when they heard him coming. "Oh, right. The gardener."

"Not any more." The old man's voice is almost as thin as he is.

"What are you doing here?"

Flat answer: "Grieving."

He's such a nothing person that Sylvie answers, "Me too."

"And atoning. I live out here now."

"People can live out here?"

"I do." Poor old man, he sighs. "I lost a dear friend."

Sylvie's belly goes soft. "Me too."

"And now you're out here and I'm out here . . ."

"Grieving."

"Yes," Benny says.

It took Sylvie too long to reach the end point— all the days since Marla got sick and other kids started falling like redwoods— but here she is. Her Steve is gone, lying dead somewhere at the bottom of this terrible, Godawful mountain. "Oh shit, Mr. Benny, I'm so sorry." Sylvie D'Estart got to be who she was in the tabloids by never letting the people see her cry, but she's beyond it now.

"You poor thing." Benny spreads his arms, weeping for both of them. The old man is scrawny and he smells bad but for Sylvie, it's a relief to have somebody holding her while she sobs her heart out.

When she can speak, which is not right away, once arrogant Sylvie D'Estart, media bad girl and scourge of every club owner in Manhattan, London and Paris and territories surrounding Beverly Hills, says timidly, "Would it be all right if I hung out with you?"

DIRECTOR'S LOG
Crisis, the Academy at Clothos
LTCOL Sargent Whitemore, USMC (RETD)
Status report
Week Three, Day Four:

- Infirmary: 27 patients, seven critical
- Breakdown of affected personnel currently in sick bay
    total, 27
        students from upper school: 13
        students from grades 1–8: 8
    staff, 5
    unidentified patients, 1
- Active medical personnel, 1
- Volunteer aides, 1: Sheela Mortimer, age 14
- Deaths: none
- Situation: critical
- Academy schedule: SNAFU
- Classes: suspended
- Attendance: N.A.
- Food service: On schedule
- Attendance at meals: uncertain
- Food supplies: surplus. Possible food-based sources of contamination destroyed
- Academy IT officer: Missing in action, presumed dead
- Academy server: down for good
- Assessment: Situation desperate
- Plan: FUBAR

HERE ENDS DIRECTOR'S LOG

Crisis, the Academy at Clothos

LTCOL Sargent Whitemore, USMC (RETD)

ADDENDUM: eyes only

DIRECTOR'S NOTE: Server down, ergo external communications kaput. No distress signal transmitted and none transmittable at this time.

Probability of bringing fresh medical personnel, further medical supplies, zero.

Possibility of importing fresh staff, zilch.

Return of hovercraft and removal of uninfected students and staff impossible until signal is restored.

Morale: less than zero

Outside event: trouble in the ranks

Note to self: watch Bogardus

THIRTY

THE FIRST TO DIE IS POOR LITTLE ALEXANDER BIRCH WHO
wanted so desperately to be a girl, although he was so sick that his
body gave up on the project long before he did. No. His body gave
up on life, but the poor, sad baby lingered for days. Cassie blames
the hormone treatment, a year of illegal estrogen supplements before his father condemned him to hard time at the Academy, God
knows what else the child was taking to hurry things along. It
weakened his resistance, that she knows. Killed off antibodies,
friendly bacterial flora, God knows what else it did to him. She
tried to taper him off with the estrogen patch— too late. Poor re-
jected child. Metabolically, he was a wreck. His immune system
was seriously compromised long before he reached Clothos, and
when infection struck, it hit hard and rolled right over him; he had
nothing left to fight with.

Late yesterday the boy slid from delirium into a coma. At least
the flood of fever dreams washed him away smiling, so whatever

powers look after troubled children must have supplied this one with dreams of a happy life. As a woman? She doesn't know. It's no longer an issue for him. Once Zander lapsed, all expression slid off his face; he could be anybody now.

No, Mr. Birch, he didn't ask for you. There were no last words Alexander said that she can tell that son of a bitch, his domineering father, but she has a few. She has a lot more to say to the opportunistic doctors who let the child start on so much so fast, when he was much too young.

Standing by the bed, she holds the boy's hand until his soul leaves his body. Not that he knows. Just so he'll have somebody there in case that part of him that's leaving the building happens to look back from the ceiling or wherever it's going to see whether he had to die alone.

Then she hears a man cry out.

Theron.

She doesn't need to close Zander's eyes. That part of him left for good when he became comatose. No need to fold his hands; the body lies there on the bed with the hands clasped, proprietor absent, remainder carefully composed. *Better wait to pull the sheet over his face,* she thinks, *can't let my other patients know; remove him before you unhook the IV and pull the shunts.* She'll prepare the body when she can figure out where to do it without alarming the other patients or upsetting pathetic, lumpy Sheela Mortimer, who can't be convinced that she'd be better off back in her room. The girl has hung in since the beginning, carrying trays that Bradley brings every night, schlepping bedpans, reassuring patients whether or not they hear her, or care, overwrought but generally more useful than not. Sheela's off duty at the moment, currently napping under Dratch's desk.

Don't wake her, Cass. Let her sleep. When she finds out somebody's died, it will kill her.

Instead she hurries to Dratch's room, where Theron lies. It's odd. He's no better, no worse, lying there with open eyes as dark and opaque as slate. Absent, but not dead. She says, because she thought she heard him shout:

"You called?"

She already knows that he won't answer. Still: "Somebody called, Theron. You?"

He doesn't speak. He hasn't spoken for days. It's as if his operating system has crashed.

Frustrated and exhausted, emotionally ripped from top to bottom, she says, "Don't worry, I'm here."

To give herself some reason for standing here, studying the beautiful, fallen stranger, she looks at his chart. Nothing on it makes sense. Not the spikes and drops in fever, not the fact that the wound in his thigh is no worse, but refuses to close. Outside in the ward every bed is filled and like Theron, her patients refuse to get better. She can only be grateful that they aren't getting worse. *Except for poor Zander,* she thinks, mourning. She'd like to let it all out here, where none of the sick and vulnerable children and the panicky adults can see her tears, but she's too far beyond tired to cry. She covers her face with her hands.

It's too much. It's just too much.

Then as if moved by an outside agency she finds herself kneeling— kneeling! by the bed. She takes the sleeping stranger's hand. "Oh Theron, Theron, what's the matter with you? Where did you get it, Theron, how did you get here and what happened to you on the way? What made you so sick and what can I do to make it go away? Please. Theron, they're all sick, they may be dying and I don't know what to do."

Theron won't answer. He never does.

"Oh Theron." She buries her face in her hands, saying through splayed fingers, "One died."

There is no pressure on her arm, there's nothing to alert her. After a long time praying for poor Zander, for all the sick patients and for all the others who are not yet sick, she lifts her head and looks at him.

Theron's eyes have come to life. Without moving, without speaking, he regards her.

Shaken, Cassie stands. "If you know how to pray, start praying. It's Zander."

She can stand here waiting forever, she realizes, and not see any change in him, not even a flicker. Is this a sign of improvement? That he's awake and . . . She thumbs through the stages of cognition and upgrades Theron, not to *alert,* not yet. She will not insult him by asking him to count fingers. A true clinician, she sweeps her hand through empty air in front of his face, interrupting that strong, intelligent glare. He doesn't move; he doesn't blink. She scribbles on the chart: *aware.*

"All right then," Cassie says, but she can't seem to leave.

Fixed in place, she tries to figure out why, when she has poor Zander's body to deal with, as well as the twenty-some living patients swaddled and strapped to every flat surface in the place, she can't get out the door. Sheela will be awake soon. Bradley will be rolling in with his trolley filled with the next day's trays; she doesn't have long.

In the end she tells her first patient what she came here to say. Cass didn't come into Theron's room because she thought she heard him shout; she isn't here to check on his condition. She came in here to cry and is stricken because she can't; not with Theron *aware.* She's here because she has to tell somebody, and when Zander died Theron was the first person she wanted to tell. At least she can manage this part. The telling. She has to get it out, so she can leave. "He was only a kid."

Theron watches, but does not speak. *Alert,* she understands too late; she's done with the chart. She's close to done altogether. After too long, she tells him:

"If one dies . . ." Her voice shakes. *They can all die.* Don't say that, Cassie. Not out loud. Instead she says, ". . . any one of them can die."

He gives back silence. Right now it's all he has to give. For the first time she realizes that she is standing here with her surgical mask pulled down, revealing raw grief. With a shrug, she turns and goes.

The PA shuts the door too soon to see her first patient sit up. He raises his right hand. In a form of blessing that comes back to him from deep memory, Theron makes the sign of the cross in the empty room.

Of course Sheela Mortimer, who *will not leave* the Infirmary, helps Cassie wheel Zander's bed into the ell between the private rooms. Instead of being freaked by the dead body, the girl is anxious to help. When certain things are done she pushes Cassie aside, saying, "It's right."

Then without turning a hair, Sheela washes Zander and helps Cassie sew him into the canvas shroud she found in the cell she occupied before the troubles. A *memento mori* for whatever monk slept there, she supposes, that Sarge's renovation team failed to remove.

Her old room is empty now. The good doctor is gone. Dratch has been here in the past few days, she's seen signs, but not when she's around. Like the Phantom of the Opera, he saw his chance and slipped away. Now he comes and goes as he wishes, unseen. The first time she caught him sneaking back in she tried to herd him back into his cell, but he shook her off. "Not now."

"Then make yourself useful instead of running away."

"I am." All fire and purpose, he headed for Marla Parsons's bed. "I came to take a couple more smears."

"I did that."

"Blood, maybe. Sputum, of course." He looked at her sharply. "Vaginal smears? Stool samples?"

Sententious bastard. "No." She was too beaten down to explain that with a roomful of patients, all in serious condition, there was no time.

For the first time since they landed on Clothos, the doctor was focuses and professional. Sober for once. "Trust me, I'm working on it. You'll see." He took what he needed and headed for the door. "If there's an emergency you can't handle, send somebody down to the lab."

As if she had anybody to send. There are exactly one PA and one overeager ninth-grader on the job here, barely making it. Coping. She grabbed his arm. "I could use a little help."

He tried to shake her off. "I'm helping!"

"What," she cried. "*What?*"

"I do what I'm good at. Now, let go."

He said it with such confidence that she let go. There is the outside possibility that the man is on to something. She stood back as he left, feeling like an early explorer: *Very well. Alone.*

The solitude is awful. When Bradley comes with the morning trays, she sends him back to the administrative wing with a message for Sarge.

Within minutes her only friend in this awful place pushes through the double doors in the HAZMAT suit, with the faceplate shut. Glad as she is to see him, Cassie is relieved to see he's taking precautions. Last time Sarge came in here he got pissed off and removed the hood. Cassie did what she had to: she drew herself tall enough to look him in the eye and bared her teeth at him like a drill sergeant, chewing him out.

She does not say, *Thank God you've come,* but she is thinking it. "We have a problem."

She pulls him into the ell, where Sheela's tucking the canvas shroud under Zander's feet; the boy was small, the shroud is long, she seems anxious to make it fit nicely. "I'll take care of him, Sheela. Now go. NOW, Sheela. They'll be wanting their breakfasts. At least, the ones who still try to eat."

Sarge says in a low voice, "Who died?"

"The Birch boy, poor little guy." Grieving— she spends all her time grieving— grieving, she tries to sound professional. Detached. "We can't leave him here, and I thought you probably had a contingency plan. So what I guess the question is . . ." Her voice shreds like gauze under a scalpel. When she can go on she says, "Is it burial or burning, and where?"

The man who always has a plan doesn't answer.

Without looking at Sarge, she goes on, trying hard to keep it cool. "Or do you want to keep the body on ice for pathology?"

"He's so small."

When Cassie turns, Sarge has ripped off the HAZMAT hood, baring his face. *Bare naked.* To her, the naked face looks impassive, like the bronze mask of a demigod, but there is something not right about the composition. It takes her a second to understand that where she is beyond tears, Sarge is doing whatever he has to, straining in every fiber just to keep his expression in one piece.

Oh fuck, she thinks. *Please don't.*

It costs him, but he won't. Then Sarge, whom she has loved since high school, Sargent Whitemore of Beaufort, South Carolina, speaks and she wishes to God that he hadn't. Instead of ticking off orders, Standard Operating Procedure in cases like this, he says in a new, strange voice, "What did I think I was doing?"

The tone is controlled, but the tremor is terrible.

The uncertainty is terrible.

"What have I been doing all this time?"

This is not a question begging for an answer. It's not a question Cass is feeling strong enough to hear, let alone field. She can't tell him to brace up; she can't pull him into her arms and tell him everything's going to be OK because it isn't; she can't do anything but wait for him to finish.

Sarge, brooding:

"Did I really think I could bring them here and protect them and make them better people? A bunch of rich misfits in times like these?"

With that bleak, fixed face and eyes like the desert after a nuclear blast, her long-term love has gone somewhere that she can't follow.

"Did I really think I could change their habits?" He is dredging up words from rock bottom. They land one at a time, like stones. "Did I really think I could change their lives?"

Cassie does what she can. She touches his arm.

"I wanted to protect them. Now, fuck. Just, fuck."

She touches his face.

With a jerk, he comes back to himself. Nerves, synapses all rebooted, connected and clicking. The process is not visible to the naked eye but Cassie can hear the *snap*. "Right. We have to move the body out without any of them seeing. One of the crypts, I think, at least for now. Get Dratch sober enough to do an autopsy, and do it fast, before the burn. Precautions. This is the thing: no distress signals going, Cass, ergo no help on the way. Server's fucked." His eyes were leached of color. "We're going to have to tough it out."

They are moving out with what's left of Zander Birch thrown over Sarge's shoulder, rolled in her Kilim rug like Cleopatra, to keep from alarming the sick. As they push through the Infirmary doors, Dratch intercepts them. "You've had a death."

Cassie bristles. "Who told you?"

With a curette in one hand Dratch lifts the corner of the carpet with the other, no apology, no explanation. "I need a tissue sample," the doctor says.

THIRTY-ONE

TEDDY REGAN WON'T KNOW WHEN HE SEIZES THIS TIME AND falls out— BANG! that at this exact same moment, Zander Birch is exiting his body. Where Zander is gone for good, Teddy will be back, and he knows it. It's awful, but he always comes back.

A minute or two before he is taken, HRH Frederick Regan wakes up alone in the dark, although he does not know he's alone. He assumes his feisty roommate is in the top bunk. Stretching, Teddy wonders why he's awake so early— warm and drowsy in his nest of blankets, but he doesn't wonder for long. He should know by now that storms usually come on when he's most comfortable, about to go to sleep or just waking up, but he lies there, enjoying the moment.

In the next, returning consciousness picks him up and drops him in a place he knows. Within the aura. He knows it too well, although he's never been able to explain it to the king's neurologists: the aura that precedes onset.

He should be afraid but he welcomes the powerful, irreversible, seductive and oddly pleasant prelude to what comes next. *The shot will take care of it,* he tells himself. *Killer will give me the shot and I'll come right back.* Stupid, like a farmer shouting into the wind, as if yelling ever holds off the storm that will destroy his crops. As if anything can slow down roiling black thunderclouds speeding over the prairie or the rushing wind coming down on him. As if anybody can stop an electrical storm, which is what this is, hissing and crackling in Teddy's brain.

It's coming in fast.

In another minute it will be upon him. It's far too late to find the syringe and jab it into himself and in the strange, separate part of Teddy that knows what's ahead and what the storm may bring with it, he understands that whatever comes down right now, whatever happens to him in the weird vacuum where the seizures take him, he needs to let it play.

These seizures are a lot less terrible for Teddy than they are for whoever happens to be standing by when one comes on. He scared the crap out of poor Killer that first time; Bogardus didn't want to touch him even though it was his job. Oddly, they aren't a problem for Teddy, although he hates what comes after: the shocked looks, the way he feels, drained and exhausted. In a way, the physical manifestations don't touch him. After all, he's somewhere else the whole time. Far from the flailing and the frothing, the distress and cleaning up after. People who care about him and people who don't are the innocent bystanders who get hurt. Horrified and helpless, they watch Teddy coming apart. In the last second before his back arches and his head jerks on his neck and his body flies out of control— before his arms fly wide and the storm picks him up carries him off with it, the captive prince cries out in a thin voice. "Dude. Storm warning!"

Wasted effort. He's alone in the room.

Even if Killer heard and hopped out of his bunk and filled the syringe and got down here and stuck it in him, it was too late. Thunder and brilliant, jagged streaks of lightning are crisscrossing Teddy's brain, flashing trails of sparks that leave an afterglow, mounting in color and intensity until the inside of his head becomes a blinding light show that dazzles and confuses him until it ends in the burst of fireworks that sometimes jolts him into a new place.

Altered, riven by the ecstasy and the terror, the young prince does not dream because he is not sleeping and his brain is by no means peaceful.

He sees.

Trapped, suspended in the vestibule of the unforeseeable, HRH Frederick Regan, prince of a country much too small to be found on world maps without a magnifying glass, Teddy Regan goes out looking for the near future.

If only he can seize it, if only he remembers enough to *tell*, then the bruises, the bloody tongue and the exhaustion he always wakes up to after these things, the bystanders' looks of horror and surrounding damage will be worth it. If only he can hang on to what he sees long enough to bring it back! Something weird is going on that makes this physical event tremendously important.

When he does come back to himself, which won't be for a while, Teddy will remember that since the troubles, he's been very bad about taking his meds, which he hates because although they may keep him stable, they definitely make him stupid. With the Infirmary off-limits and Ms. Cassie stretched thinner than a spiderweb, he let himself run out of pills and forgot or neglected to replace them. So, was he inviting this thing or was he just being considerate by staying out of her way?

This is a call Teddy won't be prepared to make.

He will remember that before he left for Clothos, the palace doctor came into his room with a bag of oranges and a case full of syringes and showed him how to give himself the shot, although he mauled several oranges under the doctor's indifferent scrutiny and refused to jab the needle into himself. Truth? He'd rather rot in hell, and it isn't fear of the needle. It's what he sees when he isn't here.

He isn't afraid of the mysterious flash-forward this time. He is inviting it.

Therefore, in the seconds before he lost control of his body just now, Teddy may have had time to prevent the storm that has him in its jaws now, rushing him away. Maybe it was his choice. He never told Killer because he didn't want to scare him. He didn't tell anybody, and he has reasons. In his first seizure on Clothos, he did in fact see ahead, but he was homesick and confused and too upset to talk about what he saw.

He thinks he saw Zander Birch lying dead on a table.

And this time?

Shuddering and twitching, he comes back to himself in stages. And what he saw just now? What he saw in the place where this fresh seizure took him?

Teddy thinks he was looking at a gorgeous, sprawling biological nightmare. He thinks he saw a vivid tangle of cells and neurons, bacilli and DNA, visible through a badly focused microscope. It was alive and pulsing, and it was huge, as if he, Teddy, had shrunk to fit into this smear on a slide made by a cosmic pathologist, but when he tried to identify the confusion of light and color, moving shapes and cryptic symbols, it defied examination. Nothing held still long enough for him to make it out; it wouldn't hold still! He thinks he fell into the middle of a gaudy parade of the mucus, tissue and blood and cells gone mad, swept along in a pageant of the corruption that attacked the Academy the night the server crashed.

In that brilliant, terrifying moment Teddy saw it all: pestilence and cause linked in a graceful dance that would not end until and unless he figured out where it was coming from and how to stop it.

Lost in the intense burst of light and color spreading in his brain, Teddy Regan saw the tangled, writhing agents of hell itself mixed with corrupted code, all of it scrolling unchecked up the cosmic screen of the unimagined.

THIRTY-TWO

KILLER STADE

There is a mad doctor loose in the science lab, which is where I am huddled in my despair.

Days and days dinking on my laptop, trying add-ons from the IT lab, ten days trying to teach the sucker everything I know, which is plenty, and it isn't showing me dick, I can't even make out half the code it keeps yorking up on a loop like gallons of toxic vomit. I couldn't reboot an alarm clock with the fucking thing. The server's still down, Teddy and me did it, and everything I care about is out of reach.

Except my iPod.

It and me are hiding out in the science lab. We've been sneaking in here together ever since I found out about the no Internet, so where every other kid who had a keyboard to drum on and a joystick for a rattle is in withdrawal, I've been getting my fix.

I have a cover story for Teddy, in case he wakes up. It used to be I was going someplace else to scream my guts out and Bogardus wouldn't wake up. Lame, right? No matter. Except for the night he spazzed out, the kid sleeps like a toad. When the server crashed, my cover story morphed. If Teddy wakes up I can say I was out hunting the magic microchip, or some heretofore undiscovered boot disk that Mr. Joannides either hid or took with him or duplicated before he ran away. I could tell him I was out hunting for an orphan, un-networked, ergo-therefore uncorrupted hard drive that will solve all our problems, but with the anti-spazz pills Ted sleeps like a dead guy, so it hasn't come up.

As it turns out, I'm not doing any of those things.

I should be out there hardware-hacking or back in the room dinking, dinking, dinking, making magic that will jump-start the server, but I am maxed out. Plus yesterday three more kids got carted off coughing and yacking so everybody's freaking, even adults that for crap's sake are being paid to keep calm. Ms. Cassie is running on empty and yesterday Mr. Wardwell ran out of class sobbing, which sucks. Everything sucks. Things are so bad that I can't do shit except hide out here in the lab, blowing monsters away.

So I am in the science lab with my iPod case mod, the only functional technology on Clothos since the troubles, as far as I know. To the naked eye it looks like a boring leather-bound book, the kind your mom gives you to write your thoughts in. Like she wouldn't flop over dead if she knew my thoughts!

What I'm doing in the lab, and because not even Teddy knows about the notebook aka iPod, I have to sneak in here to do it, is playing *Doom*. Everybody knows *Doom*; everybody's played. *Doom* is the great-granddaddy of all um, practically 3-D RPGs— that's role-playing games to you— the only drawback being that where in *World of Warcraft,* and that second *M* stands for Multiplayer, you are surrounded by allies and enemies, in this one, and I'm thinking maybe this is more like life . . .

In this one you have to play alone.

Sure it's great, blowing stuff away and going one level higher because this time you just might defeat the game, but personally I'd rather hang out online with other players. In *World of Warcraft* I have friends. Although we don't meet F2F I know them better than most people, and I know I can count on them. In *WoW* you judge people by how they play and what they're carrying and— this is important: by what they say and what they do. It cuts through the crap, like whether people are handsome or ugly, fat or thin, because you know what's inside their heads. And *Doom*? When you're as deep into an MMORPG like *WoW* as me, *Doom* is a fallback position, even *Doom 4*, which I downloaded practically before it came out. It's the game you play between things. The one you learned on and keep coming back to because in *Doom*, the only wild cards are the ones dealt by the game.

Here's the thing.

When you play with people, no matter how good you are and no matter how good you think they are, there are accidents and surprises, people being what they are. Being alone in a game is, like, *soothing*, you know? Predictable. Just me against the game. When *Doom* loads and I hear the rumble, it's like home. Sameoldsameold, ominous and familiar. Weird, where especially when the game gets scarier and gnarlier and all you're doing is killing, killing, you feel so secure.

So the day the mother bashed my door open and started throwing my stuff in boxes without explanation, I thought: *Wherever you're going, Stade, you'd better be prepared,* so I got busy. When she finally noticed she was like, "Why aren't you packing?" and I was all, "Don't bother me."

I had better things to do. I was loading my new iPod with stuff it didn't have. Dink a little and you can get an iPod to do anything, sort of. Mine already did more than they taught it in the factory. Like any geek I get off on taking a new machine, even one this size, and making it my own, i.e. making factory hardware loaded with somebody else's applications sit up and beg for me. I loaded all my faves. My images. Linux, which I loaded because I thought I was going to jail for killing Mr. Berringer and I wanted to play *Doom* and guys don't get their own computers on Death Row. I loaded *Doom,* even though the iPod screen is teeny compared to the twenty-three-inch plasma display in my room at home and I couldn't go to jail empty-handed. I love the way you can tell that the thunder is on a loop and the same images keep coming up, like, *luring,* in case you weren't already twitching, and you let the buzz build up until you can't stand it and you enter the game. The monsters in *Doom* are gnarly at any size; the ship is cool and Mars is a blast, the only drawback being that unlike *WoW,* where I have my online friends and I was rising in status before Clothos, *Doom* is what it is. Still.

Yes, I am in withdrawal. Sit in front of any computer long enough and your body needs it, like it's a necessary part of you. This isn't only about the game. The shrink the court unleashed on me told me it was a physical addiction, in this Eureka voice. Like, sur-*prise.* You'd think it wouldn't be such a big thing, but when you can't connect, you start getting weird and from there on, it's downhill all the way. When you can't connect and you can't play and you can't even keyboard, you get really weird. You get weird and you'll stay that way until you get your hands on a machine, even a small one because in a life that totally sucks it's the one place where you can take control.

Where everybody else in this place is fucked, I still have *Doom.* And playing in secret? Yeah!

Some things are best done alone.

So I'm down here gaming in the dark which makes me feel dirty but I love it, like, there's nothing but me and the world inside my iPod. I am hunkered down under a lab table, so nobody going by in the hall will see the little screen glowing and take my precious or blow the whistle on me. I have just killed everybody and done everything on Level Four and slaughtered Five and am advancing to the brand-new highest level when all the overhead lights go on, scaring the crap out of me. I jump like a scorched hoptoad out of pure shock and my head bonks the steel underside of the lab table. *Fuck.*

This creaky, old-guy voice goes: "What's that?"

Like I am about to answer.

"Who's there?"

I mute the iPod because the ear-buds leak sound. I am already holding my breath. Could I just not be here? No.

"I know you're in here. Come out."

Sure, fuckhead. It reams me out but I shut down the iPod, thus ending the game. Just when I was doing so well.

I can hear his footsteps— well, his shuffle. A guy is circling the lab tables, *tap, tap, tap.* Then his face pops into the space under the table, extra-creepy because it turns out old people's skin runs down to all the wrong places when you see them hanging upside down. There is a clank as his glasses fall off and hit the stone floor.

"What are you doing here?"

It's that old drunk, which as far as I am concerned, makes him worse than useless. Negative quantity, like my ex-dad. It's fucking Dr. Dratch. *Asshole, where were you the last time Teddy needed you?* At least I hope it was the last time. I look out for the kid. He claims he's taking his pills; you don't want to be where Teddy has to go. While I'm mulling this, fucking Dratch gets back his glasses somehow, and puts them on.

He is still bent double looking, and upside down like that, he is a dreadful sight: huge nose holes, long nose hairs. "Well?"

I have to say something to make him go away. "Nothing."

He stands up like a corroded Tin Woodman. Creak. Creak. "I know who you are. You might as well come out."

Fuck that shit. It's not like he can make me. I'll hang in here and wait for him to go away.

"Or else."

The thing I hate most about grownups is that meaningful pause after they say "Or else," in the long minute before they let you have it. Just so you know they've got you whipped. Like the winner's *tell* at a blackjack table, when you've put in all your chips and he's fixing to lay down his ace and his ten. I count: forty-nine, fifty . . .

Dratch goes, "Unless you want me to call Sarge."

"OK, OK!" You bet I take my time. I pocket the last mortal remains of my brain, which are safe inside my bogus notebook, and slide out from under. What is he, after all? He'll be so drunk that he forgets me before he passes out. So, right, it makes sense to take the advantage while he's still on his feet. I get a little taller by sucking in my gut and raising my chin to where I feel tall enough to stick it to him. "And you're in here . . . why?"

Significant pause number Two, but this one means nothing.

I start in on him, larding on the scorn. "You here to stew up some vodka in a test tube, or do you hide your backup stash in here, or are you, like, messing in something I don't know about?" By the end I'm panting. This is the most I've said to any grownup since the boat dumped us here.

"No," he says. Then he says in this truly dignified way, "And yes." There is something different about the doctor; even I can see. To start with, you can stand this close to him without getting scorched by dragon breath.

I say, "You're not drunk."

He says, "Not any more."

"You're not even hung over." And that's the last thing either of us says about that.

He asks the obvious question. "Now, what are you doing here?"

I dish up the fallback story. "Scoping. I have to cure the server."

"Cure what?"

Wow, the man is *old*. Before he can focus on what I just said and tell me that the science lab is hardly the place to do it, before he can go, what am I *really* doing here, I ask him right back. "What are you really doing here?"

"Trying to cure the plague."

"Plague!" It's the first time anybody's said the word out loud, at least where a kid would hear.

He doesn't bother with explanations. He doesn't try to tell me anything calming. It seems he doesn't have time. "I think I've identified the bacillus."

"What's that?"

"Don't be stupid. The thing that's making people sick."

"Cool."

"Now I'm trying to build something that will stop it."

"Oh."

"Is that all you're going to say?"

"Um, like, a shot that cures everybody?"

"In a way. I'm . . ." He gives me a what's-the-use look, for I am just a kid who won't get it because I'm only in seventh grade. Then he decides to tell me anyway. "I'm isolating a bacteriophage," he says, and I do not know if he is crazy.

"Right." If he thinks telling me all this is useless, he's probably right. It's, like, Greek to me. Either that or he's older than I thought and this is senile dementia. Plus, it's getting light. In a minute, Teddy will wake up and find out I'm not in the room. If he comes out looking for me Bogardus will catch him and the shit will come down on both of us. "Thanks, and I've gotta go."

Then Dratch puts a claw on my shoulder with this intense look, like what he's saying is very, very important. "If I can isolate it, if I can grow it and introduce it into the system," he tells me and I know in my gut that he is on the level, "it should kill every single one of them."

"The germs?"

"Malignant strain of bacteria."

"So, great." I shake him off. I'm halfway out the door, about to launch into a dead run but I have to deliver a farewell speech so he won't chase me. "So good luck with that. Now I've really gotta go."

On my way out I hear him screeching, "Watch out, don't *touch anything.* I've got stuff growing in dishes all over the place!"

When I get back to the room Teddy is awake, so, fuck. He's sitting up in bed looking trashed and completely wasted. Weak. "Where were you?"

Oh, shit. "Oh, shit. You had another fit."

"Seizure. Where were you, anyway?"

"Seizure. OK, I was over in the science lab."

"Trying to fix the server?" There is an edge on Teddy this morning, even wasted as he is. His face is practically transparent, but the eyes are on fire. "That's horseshit. Their terminals are down, just like everyone's. The screens are fucked all over the school."

"Dude, I'm sorry I wasn't here to shoot you up. Are you OK?"

"No. Yes. No matter." He gives me a look that it will take me from here to 2050 to figure out. "It was no big."

Oh God. "Bad?"

Teddy knows I am relieved as fuck to have missed it. He shrugs. "Not that bad."

I'm waiting for more so I can try to make up for what happened to him, but his face shuts up tight. Teddy is a good guy in spite of the fits. Excuse me, in spite of the seizures. In fact, he is my best friend, which I only realized just now when he forgave me without saying anything about me crapping out on him. I have to give my friend *something,* but as he is sitting there on the bed looking wiped, it has to come out of me. So I rummage around in my head and I give him everything I have, which isn't much. "So, down in the lab? Guess who caught me, but he'll forget it before breakfast so it probably doesn't matter?"

He doesn't guess.

I give up waiting and tell him, "It was Dr. Dratch."

He doesn't even say, *Oh.*

I tell him, "He isn't drunk any more."

He has stopped looking at me.

"I think he detoxed."

It's not like Teddy cares.

He could care less and I know it, so I get my shit together and give my best friend that I abandoned in the night the best thing I have. I give him everything I've got. "But get this.

"He might not be crazy. He thinks he's, like, finding this. Um. Bacteriophage? Or creating it or *something.* Fuck. If he gets one, dude! When it gets into your veins it chases all the bad guys that got into everybody and made them sick."

The silence changes.

I throw in another question mark, hoping he'll bite and ask me what, which means he will stop not speaking to me. I go, "And when it catches them?"

At least Teddy is watching now.

"It, like, murders them or something." I am sweating and desperate, trying to sort out exactly what the doctor told me, which wasn't much. I go, "Unless it eats them all up."

This is how Teddy Regan makes me grin. He gets over not speaking to me. "Holy shit."

So, cool, at least we are still friends. But I was up all night and I'm trashed and wrung out, completely over with. "Night, dude."

"Wait. Bacteriophage."

"Later, OK? I'm wiped." I start climbing up to my bunk so I can crash, at least for an hour. But Teddy grabs my ankle and yanks. I try to kick him off. "Cut that out!"

He digs in. "Wait!" His fingernails are cutting through my sock.

"Ow, stop that! OK, OK!"

Teddy hangs on until he has me back on the floor, standing on his zebra-skin rug from the family room in their old palace. While

I wasn't looking, his face came back to life. It's all excited and getting pinker, like he's fixing to explode. When he has us standing close enough so he can whisper in case our room is bugged, when he has us nose to nose, my best friend Teddy says, "Bacteriophage. Don't you get it?"

"Not really."

"In the system. See?"

I am too tired to see anything. "No."

"Gack! Get a grip, Stade. This is important." He is trying to be patient, but whatever got into him, it's driving him nuts. He says in that spooky whisper, "When I fall out, I see things, right?"

"Right."

"Get it?"

"Got it." Not really, but if I go along, maybe he'll let go.

"Great. Now, the doctor. Listen. He said bacteriophage, right? He said, in the system?"

"I think that's what he said."

"Asshole, don't you get it?" He's so excited that I'm a little bit afraid of him. That voice: "When I fell out just now, I saw something."

"I still don't . . . ." I would like to back off and up the ladder. I would like to be unconscious right now but Teddy is on a roll.

The pale, skinny guy I felt sorry for because he throws fits morphs right in front of me. He's all prince now, giving orders like he's entitled, moving me across the room with a wave and a glare. Teddy Regan, my best friend, points to the Mr. Coffee like he's used to giving orders and having people obey, and that *leader* look is enough to make even me fall in and follow, no question. "Shut up and make coffee. We've gotta talk."

THIRTY-THREE

PROBABLY SYLVIE OUGHT TO GO DOWN TO THAT CREEPY hospital place and see how Marla is, they're so-called friends and roommates after all. Truth is, although they share clothes and certain shoes to say nothing of the mauve lip gloss, and they snorted stuff from the same dealer back in the day, although they hung out together in all the same places, that's *so* over that she isn't even sad. They can't wear each other's clothes any more since Marla got fat— which she guesses Marla never figured out because toward the end there, Sylvie would reach in her closet for her fave nightie and she'd come away all, *eeeewww* because it was greasy and ripped. Plus, Marla is a bad influence. If it wasn't for Marla, Sylvie definitely would have been in all the papers, but in a *good* way, instead of getting busted for running down that pissy talent agent with her Hummer and ending up here.

Plus, she has to stay up here in the garden dome, where she can watch the sky until Steve comes back for her. He will come back, he *will*. She has to watch the sky, so what's the point of Marla, anyway? Plus. The truth is, this crazy old monk guy is a way nicer person than Marla even on a good day, and he's a lot more, like, *simpatico*. When she totally lost it and went running outside that night weeping and yelling for Steve, she found skinny old Benny tottering around on the rocks. It's so barren out there that she was glad to see *anybody*. She smiled and then he smiled and they got talking.

It didn't take long to figure out that she and this shaky monk guy were out there at the peak of Mount Nowhere, singing the same sad song. Like, they've both been in love in their lives, and they lost the person? So they both know exactly how each other feel.

Nobody else here does, and Sylvie knows it; the other girls are lame and superficial except for that smart, smug bitch Sheela Mortimer, who's just mean. Not even Marla knows what it's like to break your heart over your lover that you lost, and this is in spite of that Marla and her had sex with all the same guys. Like that careless, reprehensible skank has ever known true love. No wonder she got sick. When Marla leaves a guy or comes out of the bathroom and sits down for a Frappuccino, she doesn't even bother to wash her hands.

Unlike old Benny, who takes care. He follows her around in the garden dome, patting down every plant she accidentally steps on, like, fluffing up every little leaf. He's lived on the mountain forever, and he knows all the ins and outs. He's shown her hidden paths, and told her which things you can pick and eat without being discovered, although now that the candy bitch has run out of truffles, Sylvie has reverted to her old habits, as in, she doesn't eat much. It was good she ran into Benny when she did. She could still be lunging around out there in that windy, dark place, yelling for Steve and freaking when he didn't yell back. Nice old Benny talked her down, and what do you know?

They were both crazy miserable on the mountaintop for the sake of love.

Of course whoever sweet old Benny loved, it was a hundred years ago, like, the old lady would be shriveled down to a white raisin by now, unless she's dead, whereas her Steve . . .

Never mind.

This is the thing. Although Benny had been wandering around outside the dome for, like, *days* when she found him, he wasn't even coughing and he certainly wasn't toxified. So, like, in spite of what Sarge says, the air is *not* bad for you. What it is, is, it's cold as a bitch. In fact, by the time they quit talking even Benny was shivering, and in spite of her lifetime habit of scarfing and barfing for aesthetic purposes, i.e. her figure, he has a lot less body fat on him than her.

Sylvie had to coax him inside before the night winds came in and froze them to death or blew them off the cliff like . . . *Careful, Sylvie, don't go there.*

She will *not* go there. She can't.

Her man Steve isn't lost, or dead, he's perfectly fine. He can't talk to her right now because he has reasons. Steve has escaped, is what it is. He loves her like she loves him, he will come back for her, he totally will. Her man Steven Joannides made it down the mountain, she's certain. He's out there on the ocean in a raft right now, braving riptides and killer waves, going to get help. The signal booster thing was just a story he told her to get her safe inside before he escaped. Every hero knows it's easier to run away when you don't have to worry about the girl you love breaking her ankle on the rocks in her Manolos and getting you both caught because of having to carry her. Some day soon she'll look up and the sky will be black with a swarm of helicopters. It will be, like, the massed armed forces of eight countries coming and up front will be her new man Steve, riding in to lift her out. Her secret lover will slide down a rope or float in under a Mylar parachute and carry her off, and it won't be a secret any more. When she gets off this rock she can sell their story to MTV, or E!

Waiting is hard, but when he comes back they'll be together forever so she can handle this, she can.

This is how Sylvie D'Estart gets through the days: the only guy she ever cared about isn't hurt or dead. He's coming back for her. All she has to do is watch the skies.

Meanwhile she has Benny to look after. The old man is distracted and mumbling, twice he called her Callidora, which she totally doesn't understand, and then he went, "You are so beautiful," which she did.

"Oh thank you," she said, as softly as she could.

He gave her the sweetest smile and went on, "the only woman I've ever loved," which is confusing because for a minute there, Sylvie thought he meant her.

So she went, "What!" in the voice you use with the valet parking kid when he hits on you and whatever was going on in his head, good old Benny came back into his right mind.

He shook his head, blinking. "Where was I?"

She could have blown him off. She could have said something mean; what she said was, "I'm glad you're back." And she meant it. She really did. Sur-*prise.*

"Oh," he went, covering his poor old face with his knotty hands. "Oh!" Then he started up with that creepy "Bless me Father, for I have sinned—"

Sylvie was, like, "Dude, what the hell is *sin?*"

So it turns out that this stringy old geezer who's lived at the top of this Godforsaken mountain with a bunch of dried-up monks since forever . . .

It turns out that in spite of the, um, *restrictions,* Benny did fall in love at least once in his life— and a hundred years later, as in, just now, in an off-the-wall and disconnected fugue state or whatever, for a minute there he thought Sylvie was the girl. "Dear God, forgive me."

She ended up patting him on the shoulder. "Shh-shhh, Benny, no problem."

Thank God he cried himself to sleep.

Leaving Sylvie D'Estart, who in Bel Air, Brentwood, Beverly Hills, plus Nice, France, and both glammer and scuzzier environs, leaving Sylvie, who until now ran through life at high speeds with no room in her life for reflection, time to think. It is a weird feeling, but not all bad.

Thinking about Steve: not good.

Thinking about Marla: counterproductive. Shallow airhead, self-absorbed plus a bad influence on you. Fat and therefore over as a worthy person. She used to look classy and she was a great dancer but she wasn't very smart, so her getting well is no big issue. Girl, turn that page.

Thinking about the plague: why? I don't have the plague.

That leaves Sylvie's sudden, unwelcome incarceration on this wretched mountain which, now that she thinks about it, could definitely be a scam.

World is ending, Sarge warned Mother and P, and they bought it. Last safe place, he swore, and they believed.

At least that's what they told her. "This is for your own good," they said when they cut up her plastic and disconnected her services and railroaded her into the closed car and the locks clicked. "End of the world," they said. "We're doing it for you!"

Was Sarge lying? Were they?

"Shit," she says out loud and then covers her mouth when she sees Benny is still sleeping.

Sylvie D'Estart, who is in fact an extremely bright person in spite of the fact that she designed her life to hide this and ran fast so she'd never have time to think, begins to think.

Thinking seems to be easier now that she's walked out on the Refectory meals and is eating fruits and vegetables pulled out of Benny's garden. So that's another thing. The stuff that made them stupid. Is it in the bottled water or were they putting it in the food?

Trankies/saltpeter/whatever is not, however, the biggest thing that keeps her and the others inside the monastery buildings and the hermetically sealed garden dome. It's Sarge's warnings. Fear of going outside.

But Sylvie went outside and lived, and it's all because of Steve. Her breath catches. *Steve.* Where she was digging in her heels and maybe holding her breath a little as they left the dome that night, her lover was not scared. Wuoww, they didn't drop dead. Wow. She thinks now that it wasn't Steve's first time. One proof.

Then she totally lost it and ran outside to find Steve and she still isn't dead. There's another proof.

Truth is, Benny is all the proof she needs. When they found each other, he'd been outside for days, with nothing between him and the outside air but that raggedy monk's dress, no hidden astronaut gear, no secret stash of oxygen, no pills to cure him if it got hard to breathe. In spite of which, with that bony rack for shoulders and his brittle birdcage ribs and only a layer of thin skin to cover the mess, Benny survived outside, no problem. Except for the fretting and the bemoaning, he was fine.

So the air is no threat. Could be nothing else is, either. And yes. She can tell from the way her parents waved goodbye laughing that they knew.

Which means this whole Academy operation, with its shit and secrecy and isolation, is founded on a lie. When Sylvie gets out of this place she will hunt them down and destroy them, Mother and P. For a few minutes here, she indulges herself. Writing her speeches. Writing theirs when she breaks into Casa D'Estart in her camo outfit with her assault weapon cocked, looking cool in her boots and the olive drab tankini top. And, she thinks, a brace of ammo belts for effect. She will crash into their boudoir, roaring to wake the dead, "What did you think you were doing, locking me up?"

The 'rents, of course, will be scowling and blustering. Then Sylvie will wave her rifle and her combined armed forces will come down on them . . .

But wait. How does a not-yet-fifteen-year-old girl whip up a revolution? With kids getting sick right and left and no IM and no texting to rally the ones who are still standing, she doesn't know. If things are good and Steve gets back in time, Sylvie won't have to do this. And if he doesn't come . . .

She sits in the dirt chewing on her knuckles, thinking. In her own way, she's always been a leader. The first in her clique to get the cheek stud, diamond nose ring, the first to get her pussy tattooed, first in her grade to go out dancing in clubs where dress code is two sequins and a thong. The cool thing is, the posse fell in and followed. Her clique did whatever Sylvie did. A rich, pretty girl growing up free and privileged doesn't know how much she can do or how good she is at it until somebody forces her up against the wall.

Like now.

It will take her a while to figure out the safest and best way to reach the necessary people, i.e. how to rally the troops. Who and what she needs to overthrow the screws and bring this off, and where they'll meet . . . And once she gathers them, what to do next. Ug. How to do it. To get off this mountain, they need to bring down the adults, take Sarge prisoner, deliver the ultimatum, the whole nine yards.

Benny could be a major asset. He's lived here forever, and Sylvie would bet everything she has that he knows places that Mr. Sargent do-everything-by-the-numbers-control-freak Whitemore has never seen. He's been places Sarge has never been, like, there must be gazillion secret passages that only Benny knows about. As soon as he wakes up she'll ask. So that's one.

Plus, this plague thing is working to her advantage. It's already taken out several teachers and one coach, so pretty soon the kids will have the staff outnumbered for sure, although she thinks Sarge has guards that they don't see.

Now that she's totally detoxed for the first time in forever, it turns out that Sylvie has a very orderly mind. Better not wait passively while Steve risks his life trying to bring help, she decides.

Now is always better than never, particularly when you have to do something awful.

When push comes to shove, Sylvie D'Estart, whose feet are only a teeny bit warped from a lifetime of stalking around in spiky Manolos and Jimmy Choos, Sylvie D'Estart, formerly beautiful and stronger than she thinks, will do what she has to. Get out and find him, right? With Internet, she and the only man in the world she's ever been in love with although she has fucked several will find each other, no problem.

Right now, she has to plan.

At some point she sleeps, but only for a little bit. When she wakes up Benny has prepared breakfast— fresh fruit and tea made from the leaves of some green plant she doesn't know about, except that it tastes good and it's strong. She used to snort, shoot and drink stuff to stay stupid. Something Chef Pete serves kept her that way, and for a while there, she truly didn't care. Whatever Benny gave her to drink just now actually makes her smarter. Well, sharper. She's sitting up straight, alert and ready to break the news to Benny so they can get started. She'll get into it with him as soon as he finishes . . .

Shit, he's crying!

She says what you say when you know somebody isn't what you are about to ask them. "Are you OK?"

When Benny answers he looks like the sad clown, with his open mouth shining, all glazed over with tears. His poor voice is shaking. "It was only the once."

"Once what?"

Benny shrugs helplessly. It has cost him about a million tears to get this far. "With her."

One time and this old guy is, how old is he? "Oh, Benny. That's *sooo sad.*"

"And I never saw her again."

This whizzes by like a bullet, too close. *Not me,* Sylvie *Not me.* "You couldn't, like, find her?"

"She left the mountain."

"And you couldn't go down and find her?"

Now shame overcomes him. "I didn't look."

Oh, that explains it, Sylvie thinks, relieved. "So, you didn't love her."

Stuff builds up inside Benny until he looks like he's about to fly into eight thousand tiny little pieces, but in the end only three words come out in little puffs. "I loved her."

"I know what that's like." Sylvie is thinking, thinking, anxious to get to the difference between them because he lost his and she can't bear to lose hers. "But she didn't love you."

"I think she did, but I don't know." His face twists in a tight knot. "We didn't talk."

"Why not?"

"She didn't speak English. I never learned Greek."

"Greek . . ." *Steve.* "She was Greek?"

"A pilgrim from the mainland. Oh, Callidora . . ."

"Sylvie."

"Oh, Miss Sylvie, I loved her *so much.*"

"I know what that's like."

Then Benny cries, "I'm supposed to be a *holy man.*"

A little bit embarrassed, Sylvie says, "Really," in a tone that makes clear that it's not a question, although she has no idea what that's like. Probably she's hoping he won't explain.

Which he doesn't; maybe he can't. He cuts to the chase. "I had to tell her."

"Really?"

"Sixtus spoke to her. And then she went away. I loved her so much."

Sylvie picks up the lament. "I love him so much."

"But she went away."

"But he went away." *Shit, this is bad. Really bad.*

"And now Theron . . ."

"What?"

"I don't know," Benny groans, troubled and suffering, sorely bemused. "I don't *know.*"

His lament does not tear Sylvie apart; she won't let it. Instead it makes her impatient. She stands up to get his attention. Then she says briskly, "OK then. Life's too short to sit around grieving, right?"

Blinking, Benny nods. Right now, it's the best he can do.

"OK then. I need your help."

THIRTY-FOUR

SARGE

OK, computer code is Greek to me. That's why I hired Joannides. He hacked into the Feds' computers and got famous for some jokes he played, which was after he waltzed in and rearranged the brains of Wal-Mart and Citicorp. The laughing mad doctor was deep in the innards of Bechtel when they caught up with him. During the trial I thought, *I want that,* and while he was still under house arrest I went in and extracted him. I recruited the kid because he knows the language and I don't, although I do get this part: in the brain of the computer, although there are many forking paths, i.e. options, and new ones open up every time you make a choice, no matter which path you take, it unfolds logically. Everything marches in line.

I love the code. It is so clean.

Absolute. Give a machine X plus Y in the right order and you'll always get Z. If you happen to know what X is. Ergo Steve.

At computer logic, he is the master.

I saved the fool kid from serving four consecutive life sentences because I needed his beautiful mind, and now the ungrateful bastard is nowhere. Not in his quarters, not in the IT lab, noplace inside the installation, and he knows better than anybody why we don't go outside the perimeter, ever. In spite of which, bingo-bango. Gone. It's like he walked off the mountain, the thoughtless son of a bitch. When he gets back I'll rip his scalp off and shove it up his rectals for crapping out on me. He just takes off, right when I need the hell out of him, no contact info, no forwarding address and me with no means of getting in touch if he had left one. In spite of the microchips my staff wear in their left earlobes, I can't even track the guy: GPS is blown. With the system down I can't get off an international distress signal or put out an APB on the little shit. OK, the Feds would scarf him up if I did, or Interpol would and I'd never see him again, so forget it.

So what if I can't restore communications? Everything else is in working order, so, look. It's all in the planning. No matter what comes down, my Academy is a triumph of containment. In spite of the server crash, the place is running like a clock. Not counting the human element, all other systems are Go. The building's in sweet working order: heat and generators, office phone system, air and water purifiers all up and running. Thanks to technology they'll be running into the next millennium, long after the last of us has caught the Creeping Death, or whatever the fuck is going around, and died at the top of the world's safest mountain. Library's in order, empty except for Miss Rafferty, who's taking the opportunity to print book details on catalog cards to file in case I can't fix this. Chef Pete serves meals on schedule as always, just fewer plates at each sitting. I continue to stand the midwatch and post the Order of the Day. In the face of adversity I do what I do at 0600 every day, SOP.

Holding the line.

Look. In spite of what I told the clients to get their children here, the sun will keep on coming up, no matter what. Old Benny will go on praying his Lauds or Matins or whatever by the numbers, although I never see him. Those old monks knew the power of the Rule and as their last living practitioner, Benny is a master.

I used to get off on the similarity: the Corps, systems and discipline. The absoluteness of the Rule. Do things by the numbers and you'll always know what to do. My life in the Corps taught me that. It kept me going **in country** and in worse places. The predictability of systems held me up, and I counted on it here. I thought: *Benny has his marching orders. His absolute God has absolute laws that he's supposed to obey absolutely.*

Now I have to wonder, *How does he know what God wants?* You go through your life counting on certain things and then you come to a day when you can't count on anything. Fuck! *What if you don't know what Rule, or which rules?*

Base your life on honor, on order and valor and you can still end up compromised. My personal life, the integrity of the operation, my server: everything's at risk. A hundred kids in danger, thanks to me. All I wanted to do was protect and save them; I thought once I got them here that I could save them from themselves. Now look. Plague on the premises with panic and disorder snuffling at the door, disaster pending and Cass won't let me interrogate the source and carrier of the contamination; I love her and she shut me out, our systems are shot to hell and what I see on the screen in front of me looks like a great sprawling colony of bacteria gone mad.

Like the outward and physical manifestation of something I did.

Stow it, Whitemore, brace up. When everything is going to shit and perdition, you do what Marines do. You carry on.

In the absence of Joannides, I have to fix this thing. What would he do? Like a jarhead under fire, the boy knows how to keep calm and hang tough. Or he did until he went AWOL. OK, if I had him standing here in the compartment with me and the corrupted server, Joannides would tap the box like a professor tapping the lid on his brainpan and tell me, *Think. The answer's in here.*

When I hired the little dude he was a magician, installing, downloading, inputting data, doing miracles at light-speeds, morphing a blind, ignorant machine into a thousand-pound gorilla that can scale towers and sit down wherever it wants.

He was like a neurosurgeon putting his fingers into a patient's skull and rearranging the living brain; I could see the joy in him when he did it. With a machine in front of him, the nerdy kid you knew would wash out in his first week of boot camp was all power and control, and he talked along while he worked. A little speed rap came pouring out of him, like song. *"In the beginning was the Word. Language. Math came. They were the world's two great systems of logic— of course nobody foresaw the analog computer but God. But we caught up."* He started laughing. *"Then somebody created it. There were two great systems of logic and now . . ."* When all systems on my server were GO and he had it uplinked to the satellite he flashed me a blazing, if-only-you-knew-what-I-know grin. *"This is the third."*

Yeah, asshole. Sure it is. I give the cabinet a kick. Like that's going to help. Five more minutes messing with this thing and I'll take a sledge to my berserk monster and bash the crap out of it. No. My long life in the Corps taught me discipline. Rule one: in the face of fire and death, no matter what kind of hell is raining down, stay cool. Whether or not you are **in country,** keep your head down. I didn't bring my people this far to crap out on them. Back off until you can cool down and think.

At the moment, the network is the least of my problems. There's trouble in the ranks. That white-collar felon Bogardus is mounting some half-assed insurrection. I rescued the corrupt little shit from federal prison in Danbury— embezzlement— and now he's out raising an army, well, good luck with that. Pete told me. Chef Pete knows which side his life is buttered on. Our cook is safe here. As long as I'm in charge they'll never extradite him, but everything depends on me standing fast in spite of plague and setbacks, personal misery and potential mutiny, posting the Order of the Day at 0600 and following it by the numbers, insofar as I can.

Which is how I end up in front of the Big Board outside the Assembly Hall with Dirk Fedders standing too close. Not a good hour for staff to be out of the sack anyway, not to mention outside their quarters and loose in the halls, and I know from the way the stupid chunk is leaning into me that he's not the only one off-limits at this hour. He's so big that he breathes the words down my neck, and I am not a short man. "Are you with us or against us?"

"Not now, Fedders." When you've been a Marine as long as I have, you know how to kill a man with a glare. "Stand down."

Slouching like a bad child, he goes. I double back on the faculty lounge when I see where he is heading. There's something going on. Clearly Bogardus and Askew— and Fedders, apparently— are colluding in the lounge along with whoever else they've dragooned, but I've discovered that until you're ready to call a summary court-martial, you don't level charges. It's better to lay back until you have enough. So I follow. Not going in, just walking past. Not skulking, not trying to overhear. I don't look in to see which ones are talking against me, or how many there are. I walk with my head up and my palms aligned with the seams in my khakis like a Marine in formation. Hup-two. From double-time I gear down and march half-time past the frosted glass door. I want them to see a nice big clean shadow profile of the Director: *semper vigilans*. The conversation damps down to a hiss when they become aware of the military presence. Force as a deterrent to violence, right?

Whatever works.

But the Marines also taught me to cover my ass. This means a detour to the Security barracks on the lower level. I have twelve on staff, one on duty at all times. Chris Tackett is on duty; he served with me on my last tour **in country.** Good man. He comes to attention with a salute. "Sir."

Some of us never leave the Corps. Good man. Except for Tackett, the barracks is empty. The others are gone. I don't ask. He doesn't volunteer. We both know. Underneath that military layer of composure, the man is frustrated and pissed off at what he sees as failure to control his troops. I return the salute. "As you were."

This is a man I can count on. Even though we're both civilians now, which makes us equals, he responds smartly, like a good Marine. "Yes sir."

He is awaiting orders. There's nothing in the book to cover this situation. I will issue orders as soon as I can figure out what they are. I do what I can. I salute and before I make my about-face I tell him, "Semper fi."

THIRTY-FIVE

"THERON?" EVERY MORNING IS THE SAME. CASSIE COMES IN and speaks to the patient by name, as though that will rouse him.

Every morning his eyes follow her. That's all.

He's so still that coming in, she always wonders if he died. He hasn't spoken for days. She always finds him composed with his hands at his sides and that handsome head centered on the pillow, exactly as it was when she left him. Only the eyes move. They follow. It's what keeps her coming back. She wants to break him out, if the man is in fact trapped in there, waiting to be freed. If instead Theron chose to go inside and shut the doors behind him, she needs to break down the door or go over the walls like a cat burglar and haul him out into the fresh air. There are lives at risk in the Academy and like Sarge, who comes on too strong, with his big fists up and his blunt jaw set as though force settles everything, she wants to crack him open too. She's just better at it.

"Theron." She always calls twice.

As she works she will talk to the patient, whether or not he responds.

"There are lives at risk, Theron. I need to know everything you know, so we can get past this thing." Soft. Keep your voice soft, although it is an effort. "We need your help."

Every morning she speaks to him in hopes. Even though she gets nothing back she will go on talking because in a life circumscribed by the desperately sick, the hardest thing is the silence.

She tries, "You don't want to be like this for the rest of your life, do you? You can't want to go on the way you are." She groans. "I don't. It takes guts to change."

She gives him everything she has. He gives back silence.

Setting up his meds, she studies him in detail. Theron's hands are strong, a workman's hands, but the head . . . the head looks more like a scholar's. Agh, Cassie. Try.

"You can't hide in here forever."

What if he's decided that he will?

Zero. OK, keep trying. With interrogation finished for the day she proceeds just as she has done every morning. She talks. Sometimes she reports briskly on the weather, other times, she tells him about deteriorating conditions in the Infirmary. She's got to tell somebody, and she and Sarge aren't speaking right now. She goes down the case roster, listing each patient's condition as she names the names because unlike the others, this patient is alert. Sometimes she tries to slip a fresh question into the recital but every time she does she has the sense of Theron receding, the spirit trapped behind the eyes going one layer deeper, eluding her.

She knows he's in there, compressed intelligence pacing its cage.

Because she never gives up Cassie will talk until she runs out of things to say. She'd tell him what's happening elsewhere in the building if she knew, but she hasn't left the Infirmary in days. Except for sleek, obsequious Bradley with the food trays and Sarge, who thinks he can grill her patient and squeeze answers out of him if she'll just step aside, no one comes. She tells Theron what little she can. She talks until her voice thins out into a sigh.

He lies on the bed, no better, no worse, a seriously ill stranger locked inside his secret.

What Theron does when she's not in the room remains a mystery. Sometimes she thinks she hears him moving around in here. Sometimes when she comes back into the room she thinks the position of small objects has changed. She can never be sure. Trays come and go untouched but she can't shake the suspicion that he's found a way to eat a dish without disturbing the surface, or to hollow the day's apple out from the inside. On a hunch, she left her Seattle diary on a chair by his bed last week but as far as she can tell, it's exactly as it was. Thoughtless bastard, he knows it's in here; he could reach it without getting out of bed but he chose to leave the best gift she has to give him untouched, the best and most painful words she has to offer him, unread.

If after she leaves the room Cassie stands in the ell for a minute, looking through the crack in the closed door, nothing changes that she can see. She's too busy to stand there for long. She's too pressed to dwell on what Theron does once she's returned to the ward and what happens in the empty room after she goes away. She has too many the others to treat. They are no better, but they don't seem to be getting any worse, although there are new patients every day. At least no more have died. Stable, her patients seem to be stable, even Marla Parsons, who came to the Infirmary in the worst condition, maybe because she was the first. Marla is no better, no worse. Everybody stable. Fingers crossed. Cassie wonders. Does she dare hope this thing is wearing itself out?

There's too much Cassie doesn't know. Some protocols work better than others so she's settled on which drugs, which liquids, determined what Chef should put on the trays that mouth-breathing lout Bradley brings every night, in hopes. It's the best she can do single-handed, which is what she is.

After days of faithful service, her only helper vaporized. She hasn't seen angry, agonized Sheela Mortimer since the Birch child died. Just as well, she thinks, the poor girl was a wreck. Bad for the patients sometimes, she knows. Once she found Sheela with her head down on one of the white cotton spreads, sobbing into a fifth-grader's chest. *Back in gen pop,* Cassie thinks with a little twist of the heart. *Doing kid things with the other girls her age. I know she wanted to atone for **whatever**, but she's a lot better off.* And Cassie? If this is redemption, she'd rather shovel coal in some suburb of hell.

One health professional. Thirty-some patients. It's too much. She just wonders how much longer she can work this hard and stay standing if she has to do it alone.

Until they get better, she supposes, *or until they all die.*

Or I do. In a way, it would be a relief. She envies Theron, peaceful as a plaster saint, still and serene in his clean bed.

At least Dratch has stopped badgering her with wild theories. In fact, right now she could use a few ideas. Some magic bullet that will stop the plague in its tracks and turn her patients around. They won't be stable forever. If they don't improve, their organs will begin to deteriorate. Their chests will fill up and they'll die.

Their cases may not be hopeless, but after days and days of this, Cassie is.

And Dratch? The doctor ducks in and out of the ward when he thinks she's occupied elsewhere, taking pipettes, samples, tubes, slides from the medical supplies on the sly, and on this last run, a carton of disposable syringes. What's the man up to? What does he think he's doing out there in the high school science lab? Why is he wasting time when he could be useful here? If she tries to stop him the doctor grows an inch in front of her, his head swells up and he turns ugly. He won't answer questions, even though he seems to be sober and in his right mind these days. If she asks for his help he barks, "I'm *helping.*"

She caught him this morning before sunup, slipping through

the double doors on the far side of Bradley's service cart. She stuck it to him.

"I'm *helping*," he snapped.

She poked a finger in his chest. If she'd had a scalpel, she'd have stuck it in deeper and finished with a twist. "How?"

He pulled his glasses down and looked at her over the rims. "Let go. I have to get back to the lab." That officious, superior tone came from somewhere just above the bridge of his nose. It was an old debate-club trick, but she saw the sweat of anxiety greasing his eggshell face. Yes, she despises him.

"An epidemiologist, and he's useless," she tells Theron.

The silent outsider's eyes follow as she takes his temp, his pulse, listens to his chest, makes notes in the usual places on the chart. She changes his dressing with a sigh. Clean. The young man's long body is disturbingly clean. He doesn't eat. With the IV, he doesn't have to drink, but. She's never taken a bedpan out of this room. Is his body in stasis too? Does he take care of all that in the sink? If he can get up and walk to the sink, why doesn't he . . .

"I'm just so tired." Frustration makes her cry, "Do you know what it's like to be this tired?"

Not Theron, peaceful as the carved figure on a Greek sarcophagus, composed on the bed.

As always she takes her time hanging a new bag of dextrose solution, starting the fresh antibiotic drip, adjusting the flow on the IV. "And Dratch . . . 'Don't bother me for I am the *doctor*,' the conceited little shit. You want to know where he is in this? He's nowhere."

Theron is nowhere too.

"I hate him," she says angrily, pulling up the sheet with a jerk. She tucks in the white cotton spread a whisker too tight. *You want to be the corpse under the canopy? Fine.* And he is only the first of the patients on her rounds, this is only the first of the beds. Beds. The beds all need changing today but there are too many meds to administer, too many vitals to check, too many trays to vet and too much laundry piling up, and Dratch . . .

Words hit the wall like splashes in a paintball war. "He doesn't care whether you live or die!"

God she hates these silences.

Pressed, she says crossly, "Do you?"

It's like talking to one of the saints in the bas relief outside the Assembly Hall.

She prods him. "Care?"

Theron is maddeningly serene.

"Do you care if you live or die?" She already knows he won't answer but Cassandra Rivard, PA, is too far gone to know that she's spread too thin and about to snap.

The devil doesn't make her do it. Exhaustion does. Bending, she leans over Theron and pulls off her surgical mask. Their faces are too close. They are so close now that there will be no mistaking what she is saying to him, or that this time, she expects an answer. No retreat, because her drained, troubled face fills his world. Like a moon obscured by an angry sun, the rest of the room disappears. Her face is the only thing he sees. She repeats. "Do you?

Maybe he's exhausted too. The shutters come down over those slate-gray eyes.

"Come back, dammit. I want answers." She takes him by the shoulders. "Well, do you?"

When he doesn't answer she shakes her patient harder. "Do you?"

Screen shot of Cassandra Rivard, losing it. By the time the door opens and Dratch comes in, she is shouting. "Do you?"

Oblivious, Cassie rages on as though they are alone, shaking Theron so hard that she forgets who she is and where they are. She knows only that she's desperate and he is not responding. She doesn't hear the sobs that come rattling out of both of them, or feel the pathetic sheet of tears rolling down her face. She's too distraught to hear Dratch hurrying into the room with quick, authoritative steps. She is not aware that the recovered alcoholic has put strong hands on her arms, setting her aside, or that he has moved in on her patient as though he, and not the PA, has always been in charge here.

She doesn't know it's Dratch.

What she does know is that the hands that remove hers from Theron's shoulders are steady and surprisingly firm. "Don't, Cassie," Dratch says. "Just don't."

She looks into her hands, horrified.

For a minute they are both silent. All clinician now, the doctor surveys the room. Studies the patient's chart. Sidelined like a bad schoolchild on a time-out, Cass notes wildly that underneath the lab coat, the man is wearing cream-and-brown plaid pants. This defies logic. He defies logic. Her worthless, reprehensible, lazy alcoholic asshole of a chief infirmarian is all doctor now.

Transformed, Dr. Dratch asks no questions. He gives orders. "It took too long to formulate, but I isolated it. Then I started some cultures. I had to wait for the little suckers to colonize. Now I've got enough serum to do what I want." He is filling a syringe. Tapping it to release any trapped air. Looking through the liquid to make sure. "If there's no adverse reaction with this patient we'll move on to the next. Now, uncover him and turn him over, please. This one goes into the buttocks." As if to forestall protests, he says, "Subcutaneous injection. Think of this as a clinical trial."

Humiliated by her own failure, Cassie does as told. She doesn't hesitate and she doesn't ask. Once she prepares Theron, she backs away and waits.

The doctor is too absorbed to notice that where every exchange between them has been a struggle, his resident gadfly hasn't opened her mouth.

Beaten down by the siege and defeated by her own folly, Cassie doesn't challenge the doctor, she doesn't object. She just waits.

The needle goes in. He rolls Theron over so once again, he's on his back. He checks the pulse, listens to the heart, rolls back the lids to the closed eyes, shining his light into the pupils, the irises, checking the color and quality of the tissue inside the lids. Then he gives Cassie's constant companion for the past weeks an indifferent pat and steps away. "That's it then." He covers a silly, inadvertent laugh. "Would it be a cliché to say, 'Ms. Rivard, now we wait'?"

She can't speak.

"Ms. Rivard?"

Cassie nods. She's been through so much in the past few days that she is beggared. Fresh out of words.

"All right then."

They are both watching Theron now. Worried, frightened, strangely relieved by the sudden absence of responsibility, Cassie stands by the bed with her neck rigid and her knees locked, rapt. Waiting, just as the doctor said.

After a long time, Dratch looks at his watch. "This is good. Ten minutes and no adverse reaction. Yet." He fills a second syringe and puts it on the table. He says giddily, "Ten more minutes and I'm outta here. Use this if you see signs of anaphylactic shock."

In the zone. That's what trauma and exhaustion do to you. Dratch might as well be at the top of the bell tower, speaking into the wind. *Am I in the zone? Is this where Theron is?* She tries to get back in time to respond. She tries.

A weird little flag flaps in front of her: Dratch passing his hand too close to her face. "Ms. Rivard! How many fingers?"

Cassie snaps to. "Stop that."

"Need vitamin B_1 to get you up to speed?"

"I'm fine."

"Or are you used to something stronger?"

She shuts him down with her harshest voice. "I'm fine!"

Dratch may be sober, but he's spiteful. "Well, you don't *look* fine."

They are both exhausted. This is enough. Silent for now, they watch the patient. Nothing changes. But nothing goes wrong.

"Bacteriophage," Dratch offers, as though she has asked. "If this works, the good guys are in there chomping and destroying. If this works, we're going to ream all the bad guys out of his blood."

"And if it doesn't?"

"Best-case scenario, it doesn't hurt him. Worst-case . . ." Now that they are safely past some imagined crisis, Dratch is all business. "Worst-case scenario, follow adrenaline with epi. The paddles. Call me if he codes. Shit." He looks at his watch. "Things to do, flasks and syringes to line up, patients to stick. I need you to stand by and observe the patient. If he doesn't die, we move on to the rest."

THIRTY-SIX

DEPRIVED OF FREEDOM OF SPEECH, WHICH IN THIS CENTURY means forbidden access to cell phones and other handheld devices, loss of e-mail, iChat and every other known form of instant messaging along with all the other the amenities technology brings; silenced by the Director and threatened by pestilence in the house, the society sealed inside the abbey on Clothos reverts to primitive means of communication.

They resort to furtive drumming, tapping out code on every available surface, using body language, hand signals, whatever occurs to send the message: *Get me off this mountain.* Their citadel has become a trap. Others are sick, they hear somebody died— *Not me, Not me, Not me*— they've heard there are others— *Not me*— although the Director denies it. He keeps the Infirmary sealed tight, no apologies, no explanations, no intruders except those authorized, while in every way they can think of, people shudder— *Anybody but me.*

Anger ignites and starts rolling like an infernal machine fueled by panic. It roars through the halls, gathering momentum as news spreads, sped along by a swarm of rumors raised by everybody in the enclave. They have to know, they need to tell! Anxious, they get the word and pass it on in any and every way they can. Thrown back on the old modes, kids and Academy staff alike reinvent the language of rebellion. They devise codes, communicating through signals transmitted by the way they walk and what they put on their bodies. Girls flout dress regulations with makeup, which before the troubles, was forbidden; kids signify with hastily drawn tattoos, paper clips hanging from holes left when their studs were removed, fresh scars from cutting, which was one of those things they were sent here to correct. The young and adults alike send messages with belts buckled in back or worn slung over one shoulder, scarves knotted in significant places, unauthorized baseball caps tilted at aggressive angles, telegraphing solidarity.

Take away more sophisticated means of expression and people talk.

They whisper. They collude.

Guidance Counselor Dave Bogardus in the Faculty Lounge to Coach Askew, Coach Dirk Fedders and others:

"People, our friends are falling left and right. We could be next!"

"What is this thing?"

"Anthrax, I heard it's anthrax."

"Whatever it is, we've got to stop it!"

"I heard smallpox."

"People, we could be next. Do you see where I'm going with this?"

"Yes, Mr. Bogardus."

"All right! Now, let's rout it out before it gets us."

"How?"

"Symptoms, I say we look for the symptoms."

"People, all you need to know is that it kills you."

"I heard it starts with a terrible cough."

"Nausea and vomiting."

"No, blood in the urine."

"I heard you drown in your own drool."

"No way, your belly swells up and splits wide open."

"Unless it's Marburg."

"I heard your tongue bloats up and you choke to death."

"Shit no, Ebola."

"Everybody, *focus*."

"Cholera. My God, boil the water. Are we boiling the water?"

"People, shut up and listen! I got you here for a reason."

". . . typhus."

". . . typhoid."

". . . black fever."

"DON'T MAKE ME YELL. *It doesn't matter what gets you after it gets you. We have to stop this thing before it gets us.*"

"Yes, Mr. Bogardus."

"Goooooo, Dave."

"Thanks, Fedders. OK people, first we identify the carrier."

"I heard people cough on you."

"No no, you touch something they handled."

"It's carried by rats."

"There are no rats here."

"That you know of."

"In a place like this, you don't know *what* there is. If this thing spreads, we're all dead men."

"Mr. Bogardus!"

"And women, Melanie. No offense."

"None taken."

"How do you know if you've got it?"

"That's the problem. You don't."

"You mean . . ."

"When these people go, it's always a surprise."

"Like poor Agnes."

"Yes, Wardwell. This plague strikes without warning. We have to strike first."

"Sarge says stay calm, he'll handle it."

"Yeah, right. Askew, they're dying like flies."

"Who says?"

"Lockdown in the Infirmary, nobody gets in . . ."

"Except me. Sir . . ."

"Not now, Bradley. Doors sealed like the Great Pyramid, they're hiding something. HAZMAT suits for personnel so you won't know what they're doing in there."

"Who?"

"Not sure. Faceplates pulled down. Nobody sees who gets in."

"I do."

"Bradley, shut up!"

"Or what they're hiding, right, Dave? That's why we're having this meeting."

"My point, Fedders. It's the carrier."

"What?"

"The carrier is in there. The Monkey Zero, if you will. And those fools are protecting him. OK. Now. We need to identify the source of the infection."

"Sir . . ."

"Not now, Bradley. Pull him out like an abscessed tooth. Eliminate him . . ."

"When?"

". . . as soon as we have a plan of action."

"Lay out the plan, Bogardus. What's the plan?"

"I told you. Identify and extract the source—"

"How, Dave? How do we get in?"

". . . Annihilate the carrier . . ."

"Kill him."

"Boil him."

"Set him on fire."

". . . Then, if we have to, we'll . . ."

"What, Dave? What will we do?"

"I'll have to get back to you on that, OK, Dirk? Moving right along. Now, there's no point attacking . . ."

"Attacking! Bogardus, I can't do this . . ."

"Fine, Askew. Then go ahead and go."

". . . I won't. I'm done."

"*Now* . . . There's no point attacking if we come out infected. We have to extract the carrier and throw him off the mountain."

"We can't go out there. The air is toxic."

"Toxic. It'll kill us dead."

"That's why we need HAZMAT gear. So. First we break in and extract him."

"And we're going to do that how?"

"Trust me, Fedders. I have a plan."

"Sir—"

"The issue is, how many here have lined up HAZMAT suits?"

"Me."

"Me."

"I scored a dozen from the locker down in Security."

"You weren't stopped?"

"We're all here, Mr. Bogardus. Everybody but Tackett. He's on guard."

"You mean, to throw off suspicion."

"No. Ex-Marine. Him and the Director are tight."

"Good to know. Now, weapons."

"Covered. We cleaned out the Security locker."

"Good. Very good. Excellent! OK, about the source . . ."

"Sir!"

"Bradley, not now! Then the shit will fly. I'm going to need every man we have. Sorry, Melanie. Every man and woman."

"We know, we know, Dave. Now, hit the bottom line. The bottom line is: when?"

"I told you, Fedders. When we're ready."

"Which is . . ."

"When we're at critical mass."

"Which is when?"

"Don't make me repeat myself. I *said*, when we're ready."

"How many times have we been around this block, Dave? All fucking talk and no action."

"You do your job, Fedders, and I'll do mine."

"Dave, are you weaseling? When?"

"Yeah, Bogardus. When? If we wait too long, we'll all get sick. I saw Agnes go . . ."

"Wardwell, that's enough."

"Agnes turned into something else. Her head rolled back and her skin was all green and it was awful, she was . . ."

"I said, that's enough!"

". . . vomiting blood and it . . ."

"Listen to him, Dave, that could be us."

"Damn straight it could. We've gotta act fast."

"I told you, I have a plan!"

"What's the plan?"

"As stated, Dirk. Identify the carrier."

"Sir . . ."

"Bradley, not now! Extract and eliminate. Then if we have to, we . . ."

"We what?"

"Er. Ah. Closer to the time."

"Fuck that shit, Bogardus. Cut to the chase."

"Soon, Fedders. Just as soon as I . . ."

"Show us the money."

"How many times do I have to tell you? Soon!"

Killer Stade and Teddy Regan in their room:

"Dude, what's with the bike helmet?"

"Last time I fell out I cut my head."

"That sucks."

"What are you . . ."

"Screen capture. I'm trying to figure out this fucking virus."

"Like you've had any luck with that."

"Fuck you, Teddy. Why don't you go bang your head on the wall?"

"Fuck you too, Killer. So, what's with the book?"

"Case mod."

"You made a case mod?"

"You think I could make it in here without some kind of electronic fix? Video iPod."

"You have a video iPod?"

"Pretty much."

"And you didn't tell me?"

"Look, I'm sorry as fuck that I didn't tell you, but how did I know you were cool enough to keep your mouth shut?"

"How did I know you'd be farting around in the lab when I pitched my fit and needed you? You swore you'd stick me, right?"

"Sorry about that. I had stuff to do."

"But, wuoooowww. You sneaked in an iPod. Hey, Killer, you sneaked in an iPod! How cool is that?"

"Don't bother me, I'm coding."

"On your laptop?"

"In your dreams. On my fucking iPod."

"You are waaay geekier than me."

"I am the supergeek."

"What have you got on that thing?"

"The usuals. Linux. *Doom*."

"You've been playing *Doom* all this time?"

"Pretty much."

"You've been playing *Doom* and you didn't tell me?"

"Like I said, I didn't know if you were cool enough to . . ."

"Keep my mouth shut. Like, I didn't know if you would kill me in my sleep, fuckhead. All right?"

"Don't get pissy."

"Just getting serious. It's the truth, right? That you really killed that guy?"

"Never mind what I did. Leave me alone so I can do this."

"Do what?"

"Point. Click. That shit. Nothing but this teeny touch-wheel to work with. Do you know what a pain in the ass it is coding on this thing?"

"I'll go away if you tell me what you're building."

"Right. As *if*. Cross your heart?"

"Spit in your ear, whatever."

"Hope to die and all that crap?"

"Just tell me."

"You won't think I'm crazy? I take it back. Bike helmet indoors, visions and shit, you probably won't."

"I can't help it if I have visions."

"Right. OK, you know that bacterio-whatever and the mad doctor and all? Like, he's making a thing to kill the thing that's killing people? Well, I'm trying to make a thing that . . ."

"Wow! Like in my vision."

"Yeah, dude. Like in your vision."

"You believed me, man! You believed me and now you're trying to make a . . ."

"A thing that will eat up this fucking virus . . ."

"You're making a *virophage*!"

"Trying. But . . ."

"What, but?"

"But it's taking forever. Fuck this fucking touch-wheel . . ."

"Killer, shut up."

"Whaddiyou mean, shut up? Fuck this fucking virus, fuck this fucking, fucking . . ."

"Shut up and hide that thing. Somebody's coming."

"Done. Shit, it's Bogardus."

"Bogardus! What does he . . ."

"Teddy, when he comes in, you pretend-spazz out and start frothing. Quick, we have to get rid of him!"

Sylvie in the Refectory, to Chef Pete, the kids still standing:

"Guys, it's all a lie. Everything about this place is a lie. The air outside isn't poison. It's just like always out there."

"How do you know?"

"Because I've been out. I walked around outside and all? It's just like normal. Colder than shit, but perfectly OK to breathe."

"So, the air isn't really poison?"

"It never was. It's totally safe and I can prove it."

"So they're keeping us in here because . . . Because?"

"Nobody wants us walking around out there."

"Because it isn't safe?"

"Because we're us, get it?"

"Why us, why here?"

"Do I have to, like, write it in lipstick on this table? Because they're sick of us. They paid to get rid of us."

"Shit. They really want to get rid of us!"

"So what are we going to do about it?"

"Rebel."

"Break out of this hole!"

"Break out and do what?"

"We have to do *something*."

"Guys, listen. We get out and get even. *Any way we can.*"

"Goooo, Sylvie!"

"So, Syl. We're having, like, a war?"

"If that's what it takes. Face it, there's more of us than there are of them."

"Kids, you mean."

"People they lied to, just to get us off their plate."

"I get it. Out of sight, out of mind."

"Out of their face."

"Out of the papers. No more bail money, no rehab videos, no having to explain."

"Locked up, so they can forget they ever had us and party on."

"Right! So, Sylvie. We're really having, like, a real war?"

"Let's call it a show of force."

"Wuow, D'Estart, you are so smooth. Cool! Pep rally?"

"Parade."

"Mob scene."

"Demonstration."

"Mosh pit."

"Whatever it takes. In case you were too stupid to notice, we have them outnumbered. We always did, but they kept us scared and they made us stupid, I think they were giving us *something* to keep it that way. It's in the food."

"It's in the food?"

"It's in the food, it's . . ."

Crowd noises, *budda-budda-budda* mounting, *budda-budda* . . .

"It's not in the food."

CRACK!

"What was that?"

"It's a cleaver."

"Holy crap, it's a cleaver!"

"Watch out, Sylvie. It's the chef."

"Everybody watch out, he's got an axe!"

"No. You watch out what you say."

"Put that thing down!"

"Not until you apologize."

"Not until you stop yelling."

"Who do you think you are, coming in here bad-mouthing my food?"

"I am Sylvie D'Estart of the D'Estart family of Nice and Beverly Hills, you know, the D'Estart conglomerate? And I—"

"I don't care where you came from and I don't give a ratfuck who you are."

"If I tell you that I am the YouTube queen, four million hits and counting?"

"Really?"

"Really. So when I talk . . ."

"That was you on that laughing pussy video?"

"Yes. So! When I talk, people listen, OK, Mr. Pete? Now put that thing down and later, I'll give you a live demonstration, OK? Thanks, that's better. Much better."

"No problem. Talk now, live demo later."

"OK, Mr. Pete."

"That's Chef Pete. Now, start talking."

"Right. To begin with, I didn't say you did it, I said *they* did it. They grind it into the flour before you get it, at least that's what Benny says. While I was outside we got friends and he told me a lot of things."

"Those bastards! And?"

"They're lying to us."

"About what?"

"The air. The end of the world. Probably the 'no exit,' you know, the shield. The whole thing. Like, I've been going out and coming in all the time, no problem."

"And."

"Don't you get it? If it's safe to be outside then it's safe to leave this miserable mountain. We have to make them take us home."

"Home!"

"That is, if you want to go home. Like who would, after . . ."

"Sylvie, are you OK?"

"I'm fine! There are plenty of other places we can go. There's a whole world out there, and when we get out, we can go anywhere we want. Are you with me or against me?"

"Gooooo Sylvie. Go!"

Coach Dirk Fedders, in the faculty lounge:

"So, we're doing this today, with that asshole Bogardus or without him. Are you with me, or against me?"

Teddy and Killer in their room:

"If this thing wasn't just so fucking *slow*!"

"Use my computer."

"You wrecked your computer and threw it in the closet."

"Just the screen. Stupid laptop."

"You threw it away and you only broke the screen?"

"Princes don't use things that are broken, it looks bad. It's in the user's manual. Broken and worn-out stuff make the royal family look, you know, weak. Easy to overthrow. Like, if the king can't afford the best, he probably can't pay his army to fight insurgents, and the whole country is up for grabs."

"That's crazy."

"I'm sorry, that's the way it is. Plus, my screen looks like it got hit by an ink bomb."

"That's really all that broke?"

"I think so. That time I fell out, you know, right after we got here."

"Like, that time before the server crash?"

"Uh. Before it crashed."

"You mean, before you made it crash."

"Go ahead, Killer, cut my left hand off. Unless it's your nose, to spite your . . . Fuck you anyway. Fine."

"But you've got a, like, uncontaminated laptop in that closet?"

"With a crappy screen. What's with the evil laugh?"

"Let's see it."

"Cracks, black stains, it looks awful. OK, OK. Here. At least it loads like normal, but it's hard to read."

"Not when you're desperate. Wuow, that isn't so bad. If I had a way move the code off my iPod I could do this a lot faster."

"I have a flash drive."

"You sneaked in a flash drive?"

"Princes have to be prepared, in case they assassinate your father and overthrow the country? You know, for the exile government?"

"Not really."

"So the crown can raise support for the counterrevolution, stupid. They put one in my shoe in case somebody whacks Dad and my brother gets knocked off too."

"Dude, that's awesome!"

"Pretty much. How cool is this? They hid it in the heel. But how are you gonna get that onto this and back onto the iPod?"

"Like I am going to let you in on my secrets. Geekorama case mod, remember? I got this thing totally locked and loaded before I ever landed on this rock."

Brother Benedictus, in the secret passage:
"I know now! I know why you're here! Hold on, forgive me. Pray for me, I'm coming to help you!"

THIRTY-SEVEN

KILLER STADE

Think dead pig in the sunshine, I haven't been this happy since Mr. Berringer bit the big one, never mind what I was thinking at the time.

For the first time since the crash I have an uncorrupted machine in front of me. OK, the screen looks like cracked mud around a dried-up watering hole in the Arizona desert but unlike every other laptop in the Academy, which, they are all infected, this one is up and running. My 'Pod is great, but everybody knows you code a lot and a lot faster with a functional keyboard. If this works I can bring back the Academy server. The entire network. I can get us *all* online!

Teddy's dream or whatever it was that started this mighty quest must have been extreme; the kid is crashed out on the bottom bunk like a stoner. It sounds mean, but spazzboy turning into coma boy is good for both of us. I get to work without distractions and he gets to recover or invite more visions and see something useful, whatever.

You know. Either way, I am inspired. Here's what I did. I moved everything I had on the 'Pod to Teddy's damaged Dell klunker and messed with it and messed with it until my thumbs cramped and my eyes crossed. I kept messing until I made something extremely God-awful gashly and waaay dangerous.

At least I think I did.

It's a virophage. I want to thank the Academy and I want to thank you, Teddy Regan, with your spooky insane visions and your nagging, for hitting the hot link in my brain that enabled this prodigy of coding. And thank you, Mr. plaid pants mad doctor, for going first with your bowls of festering gobs, ergo showing me the way. I will go into *World of Warcraft* and reward you with all my treasures, as soon as I am connected. And thank you, creator of the multi-gigabyte video iPod I cannot live without, and in conclusion, I . . . Is this better than *WoW* or what?

They don't call me Killer for nothing.

Death to the plague that took down the network. Death to the virus, along with whatever worms and all other demon parasites that slipped into the server in that nanosecond when my back was turned. Death to you and the Trojan horses you rode in on. Death to the destroyers.

Killer rides!

Killer's scared.

Time to unleash the son of a bitch. *Go forth, you little fuckers. Go forth and slay, all right?*

You bet I am strung out. I kinda, kinda think that what I have here will do the trick, but the evil spawn that swarmed into the Academy server and corrupted every machine on the premises is so humongous and powerful that the fucker could take me down before my critters can get in there and go to work. It could take me down and take me out, game over, you're dead.

I only have one shot at this.

I ought to test-drive my sweet little Engine of Death on my

corrupted Academy laptop. I could probably do death's magic on
the sick machine right here in our room, but what if it doesn't
work? If the little fuckers don't do their job the evil virus could rise
up and take out my iPod, live-boot and virophage notwithstanding. It could take out Teddy's laptop if I connect it to the network,
like, how fast would I have to be with the this, and the that? Plus, I
don't have time to mess with any klunky turtle-paced laptop that
Sarge dealt out.

There's weirdness out in the hall outside our room which, after
Mr. Bogardus backed out, I locked the door, thank you. Good thing,
it's bad out there. Now that I'm done coding I pick up the vibe: running and yelling, which I guess has been going on for a while— no
words I can make out, just pissed-off roaring and snarling. It's like,
after weeks of routine and discipline and pretty much silence, our
stone jailhouse is talking out loud, and even the dopiest kids are in
a hurry.

Me too, OK?

Gotta get the fuck out of here with my little Engine of Death,
gotta take it to the source and jack in, gotta give it a chance to get
into the guts of the server and get cracking.

If this works and I can clear out the crap it won't matter if the
virus wiped the entire Academy hard drive, I, Killer Stade, have
enough stuff on my iPod to live-reboot the server and unleash
the virophage, thus curing the disease that took us down. If it
works, I can save the network and this time, trust me, we will all be
connected. After I load Linux, any fool can download the rest, I
personally am starting with Firefox and mass-mailing Whoever to
come down on this mountain and get me the fuck out of here.

That means sneaking into the Director's office without asshole
Bogardus or Security or Sarge himself catching me. Alone, sorry
Teddy. So I slip my nerdy leather notebook, aka case mod under
my shirt, God bless you, Mr. Joannides, for giving me the extras
that made all this possible. I take a deep breath and plunge out in

the hall and start running, the surprise being that I'm going with the flow, i.e. there are kids I know out here and kids I never bothered to meet all spilling out of their rooms and running the same way. Everybody's heading for the crossroads in front of the Assembly Hall, like someone I don't know about called a big meeting and I didn't get the memo.

The weird thing is, grownups are running too, Coach and the lady coach, fucking Mr. Bogardus; teachers I know and teachers I don't know are clogging the hallway, along with a bunch of Security droogs that you don't usually see unless you are somewhere you shouldn't be. It looks like everybody in the place is out here, milling around, but the crowd is split. There are two gangs, kids and Others. There are so many kids frapping and stomping that Bogardus won't notice one more, not even a kid on a mission.

It's weird, they're all together in this, like, *uprising,* but they aren't.

The grownups are all yelling, "Kill him" and the kids are all chanting, "Freedom now." Well, all except one of them, that I am about to bump into.

I snake my way through the factions, but when I clear the insurrection or whatever my best friend Teddy's subjects call those things— when I head down the hall toward Sarge's office I get hit by another wave of kids boiling out of the Refectory and heading for the crossroads yelling, "Freedom now!"

It's like spawning upstream in the rapids, getting bumped left and right by big and little kids. Everybody in the place but me is loaded for bear and running to join the mob. I have to do a lot of elbowing and broken-field running to get through, keeping up the nonstop, "Excuse me, pardon me, excuse me, get out of my way, excuse me." They part and flow past me right up to the end.

Then this great big chunk of moving humanity smacks into me and stops me dead. Unlike the other kids with their "Freedom now," she's howling, "Kill him!"

Me? I go, "Ow!"

She sure as hell could have. Fat Sheela is mad enough to trash me. *"Get out of my way!"*

Give her an inch and I'll end up flat on my back with great big fat footprints marching up my belly and a great big fat heel mark on my nose, which she would totally mash. I have to lean into her and lean hard, until she stops pushing. You bet I am pissed. "You get out of *my* way, fat girl."

"Move!"

"No, *you* move."

"It's . . ." She's so frustrated and crazy that words start piling up inside and she blows up like a Burger King balloon until she finally spits one out. "Wrong!"

"Wrong what?"

"Wrong!"

"Wrong way?"

She's pissed and so hysterical that she gives me this mean, wild push, where her hands slide off without hurting me. "Wrong everything!"

"Yeah, fine. Move."

"All wrong. This is awful. Gotta get it!"

"What?"

"Hit Marla. Killed Zander."

Shit, she is sobbing. "What did?"

"Get it before it gets us."

Incoherent much? "What?"

"Carrier! Down there." She kind of points, but she's so weepy and strange right now that there's no telling which way she's pointing. "Him!" She gargles, "Kill!"

Kill who? Tick. Tick. I see time running out of her mouth and I have to get past sick Sheela and her sick problems. I give her a push. "Fine. You kill him. Now, move! I've gotta go."

Naturally she shoves back. We do this little bump and ricochet thing that gets her off to one side and lunging after the rest of the mob so I can get free. She goes thumping down the hall like a crazed rhinoceros, yelling louder than the upper school put together, "Out of my way, you stupid fucks."

So, whew. I am alone in the hall. Breathing again. Walking, like normal.

Things have gone to shit in here. Junk in the halls, starting with trash outside the Faculty Lounge, smashed coffee cups and crumpled lists of things. There are torn clothes and broken plastic crunching underfoot outside the Refectory, bloody napkins, like there was a fight in there and kids got hurt. It's pretty clear that the usual guys haven't been out sweeping up shit since forever, where are they all, anyway?

Turns out getting into the Director's office is a piece of cake. Sarge left it wide open. Whatever is coming down is so heavy that he left without locking up. Better yet, he was in such a rush that he left his sacred server exposed. Either that or when his baby crashed he went, like, *futile*, and gave it up for dead. Heh, asshole. Stand aside.

To Killer Stade, supergeek and genius hardware hacker, nothing is futile. Bring it on. Carrying cable to jack in, iPod loaded for bear. Everything I need. What could go wrong? But now that this monster virus and me are facing off, now that I'm setting up to do the live-reboot, I can't quite do the thing. The evil spawn I'm attacking is, after all, the biggest of them all, badder than anything you'll meet in a lifetime in *World of Warcraft*, and me one warrior alone against the cohort of hell.

Fuck, I freeze up like a PC that crashes for no reason.

I am fucking scared.

Ack, a voice! Going, "So, what?"

"Yow!" Hearing that when you think you're alone in the one place nobody ever comes but Sarge can make you lose it and freak. I crash backwards into the DVD case. "What the fuck?"

"Chill, asshole. It's me."

"Ted!"

"Yep."

I would like to store the grin lighting up my friend Teddy on a digicam and keep it forever. It's bright enough to light our way out of here. "You made it through that mob without getting trampled?"

"You were going to do this without me?"

I don't mean it to come out sounding all defensive, but it does. "I had to hurry."

"You were. You were going to do it without me." He sounds all pissed and hurt, like my mom.

"I was going to do it however I could do it, OK?"

"Alone."

"I'm sorry, OK?"

"Dude, what were you thinking?" Unlike my mom, Teddy doesn't play games. He is holding the flash drive. "You came out without backup."

"Shit." I am eight colors of embarrassed, like, dying. "OK, I was in a hurry."

"Don't shit me. You wanted the rewards," Teddy says, like we are back in the game. "Big gold medal that says Hero, Supergeek, top man at the top level. But you're not exactly doing it alone. That's my vision you're working with."

"Sorry."

He's pissed, but he's grinning. "Fuck sorry, you know what? I wanted to beat you to it."

I love this; I confess. "Me too, OK?"

He nods, like: *there*. "OK then."

We don't shake hands on it, this is better. I go, "OK. I take the server . . ."

"And I jack into Sarge's PC . . ."

"Right. I get into setup and live-reboot . . ."

"And I do the same." It is Teddy's turn to be embarrassed. "But, gack. You've gotta tell me how."

Don't ask which one of us gets into the system first or how we unleashed my Engine of Death that I created. OK, that I coded on Teddy's laptop because Ted gets these visions and the last one gave me the idea.

We both climb up on the tightrope, high board, whatever at the exact same time.

We hold our noses and jump in and on the count of three, we start. Setup. Reboot, Teddy from the flash drive, me from the 'Pod. Unleash the virophage. Attack. Again and again, until, and I don't know which machine the right version of my killer app was running on, until one version of my sweet little Engine of Death cuts through the crap and starts gobbling up evil code.

I hear "Awesome" from the other room.

"Shut up, they'll catch us."

"I don't give a shit," Teddy yells, "this is *awesome!*"

No, we do not stop for the victory dance, we restore the Academy connection. We download browsers and open our mail simultaneous, Teddy and me, and no side trips to see who we heard from, which was thousands. We hit SEND.

In addition to my *WoW* offline friends, I mail Mom. I mean, what the fuck, she got me into this.

Teddy mails Interpol.

THIRTY-EIGHT

SARGE

Disorder in the halls. Disease in the air and destruction pending.
This place is sicker than the world I thought I could save you from.
They're heading this way with blood in their eyes.
I will make this thing right if it kills me.

THIRTY-NINE

THERON'S EYES SNAP OPEN.

"You're awake!" Cassie ought to call Dratch, but she sits without moving. Waits.

It isn't for long.

Theron speaks. "I made a mistake."

His voice is strong. Whatever jungle juice Dratch injected on a hunch seems to have done its work. Bacteriophage, really? Could Dratch actually isolate such a thing and distill it and put it to work? She doesn't know. Color rises in her patient's face. He is coming back to life. All she has to do to summon the doctor is press the buzzer but she sits, preserving the silence. *Not yet.* They are both so quiet that Cassie can hear herself thinking. *Not yet.*

"It was a big one." Theron sits up.

Whatever he was when he came here, the injured stranger who when he came in was so sick, febrile and mysterious and disturbing, has returned to his natural self.

He is who he was, not who she thought he was.

For the first time, Cassie sees that person shining. Young. Masculine. Alert. Bristling with confidence. Handsome, in a disorganized way— flawed profile, irregular mouth. Unquestionably human.

Saying, "This is my fault."

Why is she disappointed?

He starts to get out of bed.

"Careful." She reaches for his wrist, where blue veins stand out. She turns his hand, as if looking for figures in the palm. She checks her watch and takes his pulse to cover the fact that she's trying to keep him in bed where she can for the moment, *dear God,* take care of him. For the first time, the pulse is steady. The flesh is cool under her hands. So is his forehead. This is the hour when she usually washes him and slips on a clean gown. It's her job to do these things. She needs to assess the situation, figure out what's going on. So she can tell Dratch, she supposes. But Cassie's patient is restless. "Wait. Take it slow."

"Why?"

"You were sick for a long time."

"I'm fine."

"You need to sit a while."

Her patient stands. Strong, even for a well man. Decisive. "I never should have come, but I had to." Coherent. Changed.

"Very sick. Wait!" Can she help it if she misses the visionary stranger who was silent and so still under her hands?

"Look what I've done to them."

"Who?"

"All these sick people. You."

"Oh Theron, please." Why is her voice so thin? Why is she shaking? Words won't keep this man in place now that he's come back to who and what he was before she found him. Nothing will. Still.

"Look what I've done to you."

She reaches out. "Please let me do this."

He disengages her hand, saying in a voice ragged with regret, "Look what I've done to them all."

"Just hold still and let me do this." She wants to look into the wound, listen to his chest and mark all the right places on his chart just the way she does every day; she wants more than anything to complete the daily routine that so excited and frustrated her. Unconscious, Theron was all potential, a mystical strongbox with secrets locked inside. Now he is here.

Asking. "How many have died?"

"Don't." She needs to keep this clinical, figure out what's going on with him. She needs . . . Everything comes out on a high note. "I need to evaluate you."

"It's because of me." Brisk and self-assured, he backs away. "Because I came looking for my father. Don't. I'm fine!"

"At least take it slow. You were sicker than you think."

As though he hadn't spent weeks immobilized and days unconscious, Theron wheels. He crosses the room to stand by the slit in the stone that passes for a window, looking out at the bleak, stony surface of Clothos. He is silent for too long.

Cassie groans.

"She warned me not to come."

She is about to capitulate and go for Dratch when her patient's story pours out of him like song out of a dying bird.

ALL MY LIFE I wanted a father. I knew I had one somewhere, but she wouldn't tell me who he was. I went around empty. It was like a black hole in my heart.

My mother made me promise not to look for him. She made me promise when I was small and she made me promise all over again every time I asked. She said, *He has his life. He has his own love now,* but she never told me what that meant.

Until I found out, I was a stranger's bastard.

Everybody knew. Try growing up in a town where every other boy in the schoolyard has a father and you get the idea. Even the widows in our village had a man in the house, but not my mother. She was still in love with him. I told her I had the right; I said, Everybody needs some story to tell, and she cried. He loved her, she told me, but she wouldn't tell me who. She didn't tell me until she was dying, but that was later. I needed information right then, when I was small. I used to come home crying. At first I couldn't help it. Then I saw what it did to her. So I cried that day and every day after I came home crying until she finally told me something I could use.

On my last day in the village school I came home bleeding, it was the usual boys. I caught her in a weak moment. While she cleaned up the cuts and bruises, I cried. I cried until she started crying too. I was so crafty, she thought I was so innocent. My father was English, she told me finally, and that's all she'd say. I guess I was too hard to handle. Or she couldn't have me grieving, at least not at home, where she had to see.

She sent me to the American School in Athens, that's why my English is so good. There was money. It came from her family, although they were estranged. She thought she'd given me everything she had.

On the bus to Athens I asked her, *If I went to England would I find him?*

She would do anything to make me feel better. She told me, *No. Think of your father as near, but far away.*

She was a very religious woman. It was time to play on this. I asked, *In heaven?*

My mother said, *No. In the world.*

If he's nearby, can I see him?

No.

Mother. Why can't I see him, Mother?

Because it's our secret, she said. *Now leave it alone.*

Theron Gregorides, going off to Athens with a hole in his heart. It was bad.

She knew who he was and she wouldn't tell me. The more you know a thing without knowing all of it, the bigger it gets. I needed to see him. I needed to know!

She kept his secret until she found out she was going to die. Then she called me home. I left university to take care of her. Maybe she felt guilty. I think she wanted me to forgive her, I don't know. At the end she told me who he was and what he was, as if that would make me forgive her. She told me everything but his name.

My mother fell in love with a man who was in love with God. She met him on a mountain where monks live and only pilgrims go. She had trouble in her life so she went there as a pilgrim, to pray. Her family gave her the money but they never understood why she chose to pray with the monks from England, not the Patriarch, another reason they weren't speaking to us. She and my father fell in love. He was older, she told me. Much older. She said it was beautiful. So was he. Untouched. Perfect. She was untouched too. First love. She thought he was on the mountain because he was an orphan. She thought they'd leave together and be together forever on the mainland. She went to the abbot. He was her spiritual advisor. She asked for his blessing. She was in love with my father and she thought he was in love with her, but when she left the mountain my father stayed behind. He said he loved her, but he was in love with God.

At least that's what the abbot told her when he blessed her and sent her home.

She went down in a basket, just the way she'd come. There were no letters, no promises. Just me.

On my mother's last day in the world she told me which abbey and where. I had to promise not to go there, but need makes you do what you have to do. As though knowing what kind of man

I came from and why she couldn't have him would be enough to keep me rooted in her world.

I kept the promise until the cancer took over and she died. I meant to keep it to the death in her name, but death cancels imperatives.

Need makes you do what you have to do. It changed my mind faster than her soul could exit her body. I had to confront him. I needed to look into the heart of this man who changed my mother's life and made mine. I had to know whether our two skulls were alike, his and mine. I needed to take his skull between my hands. I wanted to see what came out when I squeezed. I wanted to see myself reflected in his eyes and I needed to know what makes a man love a woman and send her away.

Bastard, bastard. I wanted him to *know*.

That poor woman. She cried for him on so many nights. She refused all those other men who wanted to love her, men who were *there* for her to love. If she'd let one in we could have walked down the street like an ordinary family: man. Woman. Only child. Instead she cried. I grew up with a hole in my heart and I cried.

I wanted to tell him what he had done.

So strange, being tied down by a promise all your life and then your mother dies and, like that! You're free. I left the university. After I confronted him, I could go back, knowing who I am.

I heard there was a big construction project starting on Mount Clothos, so I got a job with a crew. Masons, working with mortar and stone. In real life I'm a student so I had to train. Weights. Running. The hands. On the day, I stood tall and talked dumb and they hired me. My team worked in the undercroft and the caverns, shoring up archways. Adding supports under the chapel floor. We came in by helicopter from the mainland and at the end of the day we went home. As though our employer didn't want us set loose on the mountain to explore. With carpenters and painters and electricians, we changed the face of the abbey.

Cloister, chapel, statues and icons all gone.

The monks were long dead. That's what the foreman told us. Why did I think my father was still here?

I did.

When the last crew left the mountain I stayed behind. Remember, I worked in the undercroft and in the upper crypts for weeks. I knew where to hide.

HE TURNS TO see whether she is still listening.

Why can't she ask him to go on? She can't. She is trapped in the recital. She has to wait.

Waiting, Cassie is sharply conscious of noise outside the cell. Escalating conversation. The ward is coming back to life. She hears sick children jabbering. Strong adult voices ordering them to keep it down. She hears Dratch. *Not yet.* In her bones she hears Sarge approaching. *Not yet.* She hears, or thinks she hears heavy equipment rumbling toward them from a distance. She thinks she hears yammering as something huge approaches. She shudders. A mob? She thinks she will die if Theron doesn't finish his story. She wonders if he will die.

Woman, get a grip.

She manages. She does. All trained professional now, she says, "Tell me how you got the wound."

"Below. In the crypt nobody knows about." Turning his back on the window, he goes on. His face is bleaker than the mountain now.

IT WAS WEEKS before we finished and the crews cleared out. I couldn't show myself because the employer had left guards on the mountain. To protect the facility, which is what the abbey had become. If they saw me, I'd be apprehended and rushed off Clothos before I had a chance to look. It would be weeks before you and the others came and there were enough people around that nobody would notice one more, so I hid. I had to stay hidden until it was safe to show myself. If you saw me the day everybody landed, you'd think I was just another person. With people around, I could hunt for my father and nobody would know.

But by that time there was trouble. I couldn't show myself.

Remember, I lived in the dark, so nobody would know. I ate what I found and slept when I could. By the time you came and it was safe to come out, my leg was torn. You saw the gash. I hit something sharp in the lower crypt. I was running away from the sub-sub crypt. If you wondered how plague got in, it's in the bodies of dead monks lying hundreds of feet below, in a place so deep that nobody goes. Remember, I lived in the dark for weeks. Pencil flashlight, batteries I had to conserve. To keep from dying of boredom, I explored.

I blundered into the place where the dead monks lie. I didn't know until I put my hand on something. I thought it was a log until the shroud split under my hand and my thumb went into a dead eye. Skull, I suppose. So stupid! I screamed and ran. I covered my mouth to stop the noise but I couldn't stop running, and in the dark I hit some jagged object and tore this hole in my leg. I'd been down there in the dark for too long. Maybe I went crazy. Maybe whatever killed all those old men was working on me. I got dizzy. I had a fever. I was delirious. I came up at night, looking for help. The last night, I found the chapel.

My father came. It was nothing like I thought.

AMAZING. THERON SMILES.

How simple it is, Cassie thinks. *And what grief it has brought down on all of them.* She corrects herself. *On us.*

FORTY

MEL DRATCH IS HIGH AS A KITE, AND HE ISN'T EVEN RUNNING on fumes. For the first time since his life went downhill, the doctor has done something to be proud of.

What a rush! It's better than any high he got on any mixture of booze and controlled substances. Look at them! In beds and on cots all over the crowded Infirmary his patients are sitting up, startled and blinking. Stretching. Talking. Alive. Puzzled as to why, when they're perfectly well, they're stuck in bed, barricaded inside the Infirmary. In fact, the security man Whitemore posted has begun moving heavy furniture in front of the padded double doors. *Smart,* Mel thinks, because he only thinks about himself. *He knows I have to keep them here.*

The doctor has reasons.

The first, of course, is data. Without it, he can't write up his experiment. If he can document this, he'll land the cover of the *Journal of the American Medical Association,* to be followed by a name chair at Hopkins or Yale. Worst-case scenario: it will pull his medical career out of the toilet. He'll follow with a trade book about how a medical breakthrough redeemed him. He has the first line: "My name is Mel Dratch, and I'm an alcoholic." Part of him is thinking, *Nobel Prize?*

First he has to back up his findings. He can't let these people go until he has everything he needs. Great this guard has barred the doors.

He'll get Rivard to collect data, starting with his patients' vitals, the first step in preparing his article, where is she anyway? Oh, right. Observing the alpha patient. He calls.

"Nurse!"

Damn. Why don't beepers work here? He needs the woman to palp three dozen bellies and listen to three dozen chests, take smears and prepare slides and petri dishes for cultures. They need to get urine specimens and stool samples from each victim for the lab so he can measure the **Before** statistics against the **After.** He has to draw blood for a dozen different tests the lab needs to run before he can confirm what he believes. Never mind that there *is* no lab. He'll wing it. Mel has notes on this phase of the experiment starting way before he injected the alpha patient. Now he will note individual recovery rates as related to age of patient, onset of symptoms, day and time each was admitted, quality of muscle tone and level of alertness, but he needs more. Where is that girl?

"Nurse!"

Oh, right. She isn't a nurse. "Rivard!"

They have to fine-tooth-comb data. He needs thorough case studies, patient exit interviews, exact details to substantiate his groundbreaking discovery. He has, after all, produced the first successful bacteriophage to be created in a substandard lab in primitive conditions. And he did it under the gun!

An hour ago these people were dying. Now look. He's done miracles.

If he'd been clean and sober when he signed up, he'd have brought his digital camera.

That piece in *JAMA* puts him squarely in the front ranks of internationally famed epidemiologists. It will restore his reputation. It may even resuscitate his marriage. With only a high school science classroom and a PA to assist, he's turned this thing around. Diagnosis, research, bacteriophage, all pursued under pressure. Spot-on. Nobody needs to know that he had to sneak out of Rivard's rehab lockdown situation to do it. His radical new protocol saved these people, assuming there are no relapses.

All he needs to do is keep them long enough to prove it.

He should have a battery of interns collecting the necessary samples right now. Where is Rivard, anyway? Right. In the private room, observing the alpha patient. Maybe they should have moved the man to the open ward so she could work while she kept an eye on him. It's been more than an hour. Ninety minutes, counting the time he spent observing his test case, standing by with the crash cart in case of an adverse reaction. At the end of the critical period the patient was stable, so Mel moved on to the others. Three dozen syringes in thirty minutes. Ka-*ching*. The rest are recovering at exponential rates.

Has his alpha patient died in there?

Recovered? He doesn't know. Why hasn't Rivard reported? What are they doing in there? He needs help here! He needs to collect his data before any of this bunch can be discharged, and they are getting restless.

"Please, it isn't just me," he says to them, although nobody's listening. Don't they know they have to stay until the quarantine is lifted? They can't go out the way they are.

Better let Rivard break that news. He's done his part. Enforcing rules is her problem. It's what PAs are for. The scut work. Let her take the flak.

Let her tell these people why they can't leave. She can say she's waiting for clothes to be delivered. The restless patients are ambulatory now, milling around in unbleached cotton johnny coats that expose sagging adult buttocks and bony ones, parts of children and adolescents that the less stable adults on Sargent Whitemore's staff probably shouldn't see. Mel happens to know that Rivard destroyed everything they were wearing when they came in to avoid further contamination. Disease can travel in blobs of mucous, blood spots, specks of dried vomit, right? In addition to the decency factor, she can cite the warmth factor. In spite of central heating the stone building is cold. They can't go out the way they are.

They are also giddy and irrational. After being helpless for so long, these people seem determined to take control of their lives. Teenagers take up their beds and totter. The first patient logged in— Marla somebody, he thinks— collects her followers and sets up camp in a corner, where they giggle and hiss and comb their hair with their fingers.

Elsewhere young scavengers fight with adults over food left on trays by people too sick to eat— was it only last night? Why haven't the trays been removed? For that matter, where is the orderly with the breakfast trays? After days of not knowing or caring whether they ever ate again, these patients are ravenous.

A bunch have congregated around the useless Infirmary computer, at least he thought it was useless until a postpubescent hulk so big that he frightens Mel shouted, "Wow!" Now hulking boys are fighting with girls for control of the keyboard, over which porn site to bring up and who gets to check e-mail.

The adults are grumbling. Some of the women and a couple of men have begun to cry. Let the PA deal with them. He shouts. "Rivard!"

Scuffles break out as some of the adults make for the heavy double doors, which the Director's security chief has closed and bolted, either for their safety or for the protection of the healthy segment of the community. Good grief, the man is armed.

Louder. "Rivard, I need you out here!"

Irresponsible girl. Meanwhile Tackett— if that's his name—
Sarge's man Tackett stands guard with an assault weapon at the
ready and again, Mel doesn't know whether it's to keep patients in
until Whitemore lifts the quarantine or whether he's stationed
here for more sinister reasons. *Are they in real danger? Am I?*

"Ms. Rivard!"

She won't answer. God knows what's going on in there. What if
the alpha patient crashed? What if he's in cardiac arrest? She'd better keep damn good notes on his test case. Where is the woman,
anyway? Doesn't she know that it's like *The Night of the Living Dead*
out here? Damn patients won't stay where he puts them. They
keep milling around.

He calls, "Cassandra, please!"

Elsewhere in the Academy, people who have been undecided
until now coalesce, marking a shift in the subtle equilibrium of the
place and changing the nature of the air in the long hallway outside. Mel Dratch won't know why at this exact moment his head
comes up and his mouth fills. Startled, he gulps, tasting bile.

Until now, he's been too jazzed to notice the atmospheric shift,
how long has it been coming on? Cold as the old stone abbey on
Clothos is, he's stifling. Where the doctor was humming along,
high on accomplishment and working fast, he crashes.

The world outside the Infirmary is changing.

As it turns out, his recovering patients have more than the obvious
reasons to stay inside a sealed ward, *hors de combat,* as it were. There's
big trouble outside. It may not be a combat situation, but things are
not good out there. As he goes about his rounds Mel thinks he hears
drumming. No, he feels the vibration shaking the ancient stones. The
padded double doors are heavy enough to muffle all but the loudest
sounds but he thinks he can hear voices rising.

Something's wrong.

He doesn't know who or what it is or what's coming.

Apparently his nurse— dammit, his PA— has sharper hearing.

Before Dratch is aware of shouting at the door, before metal clacks on metal in some kind of urgent code, before Tackett and the man tapping on the brass hinges outside can exchange sign and counter-sign, Ms. Rivard is in the ward. She comes racing out of the ell with her arms open wide.

"I'm coming!"

"Rivard, your patient!" He moves to intercept her.

"Not now."

"I need his stats!"

"Not *now*!" Frantic, she tries to dodge him, shouting to Tackett, "Let him in, Chris."

"Where were you?" Mel grabs her arm, yanking her around so that they are facing.

Rivard's face is bleached, like the rough cotton of those skimpy hospital gowns. She is shaking. "Tackett, let him in!"

"Where were you all this time?"

"Let go."

Then over her head Dratch sees his alpha patient standing tall in the ell with his handsome head lifted and his shoulders high, watching from the shadows. *Recovered! Notes. I must assess him and take notes.* He gives her a shake. "Why did you not tell me he was up?"

"Let me go or I will murder you." She is looking at Dratch but when she calls, it is to someone else. "I'm coming, hang on. Hang on!"

"Woman, do you understand what's at stake?"

"Do you?" She tears away his clamped fingers, one at a time. Her voice is something more, or different than it was. Deeper. Forceful. Charged with urgency. "Let him in, Mr. Tackett. It's Sarge."

ALL OVER THE Academy, laptops and desktop computers come to life in empty rooms. All over the Academy, terminals blink and turn vermilion. All over the Academy, a cheeky chartreuse banner streams across bright screens in racing block letters:

FUCK YOU ALL. COMPLIMENTS OF THE MANAGEMENT.

It's a brilliant display. Too bad there is no audience.

Killer and Teddy could still be inside the Director's office or holed up in their room, with Killer playing *World of Warcraft* and Teddy checking the royal web site for bulletins on the uprising or playing whatever Teddy plays, but there's too much racket. It's too loud even for two game-aholics with an Internet connection for the first time in forever. They hear kids yowling and adults shouting as the gnarly clump of people in front of the Assembly Hall overflows the space. The commotion brings them out into the hall.

As they approach, the milling crowd at the crossroads coalesces, morphing into something hideous as they watch. Changing so fast that their ears pop, the mass turns into a mob with a purpose.

Now Teddy and Killer are close enough to hear the words Coach Fedders brings out like vomit. They see him take off at a dead run, with creepy Bogardus scrambling to catch up so he can pretend to be in the lead. In minutes everybody is charging off down the hall, rushing somewhere which, now that the boys have the server up and running, is shaping up to be more interesting than any online game they could possibly play.

"Games later," Killer says, kicking the door shut behind them. "Play now."

"I don't think they're playing." Teddy Regan, who has seen mobs like this one shaping up in his own country, says, "This doesn't look good."

The shouting morphs into a wet, guttural snarl. It is the sound of a mob turning savage. Killer's head comes up. "Uh-oh. Something bad is coming down."

"Really bad." Teddy grins.

"Damn straight." This is bad but Killer can't help it. He's grinning too. "Let's go!"

They trot out to join the mob. As they round the corner at the crossroads and enter the long hallway, Teddy says, "Killer, they have silver suits. Astronaut suits."

"Naw. HAZMAT. Dumb! Whatever they're fighting, it ain't toxic fumes."

"Good thing. They don't have nearly enough of them."

"Like I said, no big." Then Killer's voice goes soft in the oddest way. "Dude, they've got guns."

"Oh. Like when we almost had the revolution," Teddy says in that tired, sad, pretty-much-been-there tone. "This is really bad."

"How cool is this?"

Teddy laughs.

Killer starts running. "Hurry or we'll miss the action!"

"Go, Killer." Teddy starts running. "We're in it now!"

As they go thumping down the hall to join the others one of the two friends says— and when they talk about it again years later when they're grown, and they will talk about it again and again and again decades later, when they are both old, old men— neither of the boyhood friends who are friends for life will remember which one of them said it, "Forget *WoW*. This is Warcraft for real."

GRIM AND ASHEN behind the warlike scowl, Chris Tackett unbolts the double doors while Sarge slips inside and just as quickly, re-bolts them. In the slice of hallway Cassie can see from the contagious ward, the first of the swarm of mismatched, hysterical marchers come running up her man's heels, some in HAZMAT gear, others with raw, ugly faces opening jaws like garbage chutes, with their sharp teeth exposed. That's all she sees before Sarge slams the door shut and shoots the bolt.

The Marines exchange salutes as if the war Colonel Whitemore and Gunnery Sergeant Tackett came back from is still going on.

"Gunny."

"Colonel."

"As you were. Good man, Tackett." Sarge turns to Cassie.

Running to the man she loves— Wait. She loves? Running, Cassie sees the man she loves now and has loved since the first day she saw him as a kid; she sees her Sarge transforming. She has to rush in before his face shuts tighter than the visor on an iron mask and he becomes Sargent Whitemore, **in country:** war machine. It isn't just a metaphor.

They are facing something big and dangerous. The mob outside is like a carcinoma. A deadly organism, metastasizing, out of control.

"Sarge!"

His arms fly out. "Cass. Sorry about this."

She walks into the hug. Says into his chest, "Oh, Sarge. Take care."

"I always do."

The thud of bodies, flesh on warm flesh, reminds them both of who they are inside the clothes, behind the attitudes that get them through their days, before backstory and beyond the terrible exigencies of the moment.

Woman. Man. Cassie and Sarge colliding. It shakes her out of the long dream that settled in her head like ground fog the day she found the alpha patient. *Theron.* When Sarge lets go in another minute and Cassie steps back she will see Theron Gregorides watching. She perceives him as a tall, receding shape, backing into the shadows of the ell as though the stranger she felt so close to for so long knows before she does that whatever connection they had broke just now, when she wasn't looking.

It's all Sarge now.

It always was.

Outside, someone hammers on the bolted doors. Closed in her arms, Sarge snaps to attention.

She ought to release him but at the moment, she can't bring herself to let go.

Sarge's tone says *I love you* but the words he uses to tell her so before he takes her by the shoulders and gently sets her aside are, "I have to do this."

"I know." *I love you.*

"And fast. They're coming after your patient."

Turning to the ell, she sees Theron blend with the shadows. In the next second, he is gone.

NOW THE INCOHERENT roar filling the hall outside resolves into words. The men in the lead are chanting loud enough to be heard even through the padded doors. "Stop the plague."

The chant gives way to threats. "Break down the doors."

"Find the source."

"Decontaminate."

"Exterminate."

A man shouts in a voice clotted with hate, "HAZMAT team, get ready!"

"Destroy him to save ourselves."

"Kill the carrier."

Others take it up. "Kill him, kill him!"

"Kill!"

It gets worse. Before the babble devolves into a roar, Dave Bogardus, so-called guidance counselor and motivational speaker loses it, crying in a high, hysterical voice, "Kill them all."

SYLVIE IS TOO pissed for words. She had all her people yelling, "Freedom now," until stupid Mr. Bogardus and Coach Fedders and the adults outshouted them. Now they're all about this "Kill" thing, which she thinks is a shitty idea, although Sheela Mortimer with her greasy hair and sweat rolling down her angry red face totally got into it. She climbed up on top of the battering ram thing they are rolling along to break down the doors with and, yuck. By the time Sheela was done shouting "Kill him," she had Sylvie's whole posse and a gang of boys and half the lower school shouting "Kill" along with the rest of the mob.

Wuow. Sylvie shudders. This is a far cry from quiet days with vegetables in the garden dome, getting all silent and broody with sweet old Brother Benedictus, who is worth all the rest of them.

Benny. Where is Benny, anyway? She hasn't seen him since she came down from the dome to find out what the excitement was, back before this thing started, at which point she got the kids psyched up to break out of here. She hates the way this is going and wishes to God she was back outside, hanging out with that sweet, peaceful old man.

"QUIET, PEOPLE!" EDGY because he's afraid some fool will ask why he isn't in HAZMAT gear, Dave Bogardus is standing on Coach Fedders's shoulders, trying to mobilize his core group. A good motivational speaker knows that it's hard to bring a mob to order. He has to do this thing right and do it now or he'll never get his extract-and-destroy operation off the ground. If asked, Dave would say he gave up his HAZMAT suit to protect one of the others, and he would be lying. He knows where to be when push comes to shove, and it's not on the front lines.

He shouts, "People, focus!"

Craven Bogardus is using all his special people skills to bring this messy mob to heel. Once he has them, he can send in his cadre to do the dirty work. When it's safe, which means after his men have gutted the place and burned out the disease along with *everybody who's been exposed,* then it'll be safe for him to go in and inspect.

Then watch him declare the installation clean. Won't everybody praise and thank and look up to him then? If things come down the way he wants, he'll be the one running the school, with all that this implies. Power. The money. What could go wrong?

"Now, let's get in there and do this."

First he has to get the job done.

"You," he says to his cadre. "You are my elite force."

Armed and secure in HAZMAT gear, the members of his cadre push back faceplates and stand with their backs to the crowd, surrounding him like a protective fence, straining to hear him. Fedders. Bradley, he thinks, although he isn't sure. Eight security guards. There are ten in all and for the moment, their broad silver backs form an effective barrier between Dave and the rest of his loud and insistent followers.

"At the signal, I want you to get in there and break these doors down."

At which point stupid Bradley, the burly kitchen kid, says from the back— wait, why isn't he in the line?— Bradley bellows, "Why, when you don't know what the fuck you're doing?"

Idiot, just when I was on a roll. Not so *loud!* "That's enough, Bradley. Now put your backs into it . . ."

But someone yells, "And do what?"

"Break in, fool. First things first. Now . . ."

But Bradley has pushed through the ranks. His bellow is so loud and close that something inside Dave's ear rips. "And do what?"

Bastard. Did he split an eardrum? "Don't make me spell it out for you. Get in and extract the carrier."

Hulking Bradley, who was always so quiet at meetings, swells up to twice his size when pissed off. So does that awful voice. "Like you know who that is, asshole. Treating me like shit when I . . ."

Mutter to him, Dave. Keep this *entre nous.* "Will you say no offense if I say none intended? Now Bradley, if you're done . . ."

Instead of stepping back like a good boy, Bradley jumps up on the metal food cart he used like a snowplow to push through the crowd and yells. He is all raw anger, "Shut up yourself, you stupid son of a bitch."

Somebody in the front ranks gasps. Then somebody— Fedders!— grabs Bogardus from behind, holding him firmly while Bradley speaks.

The bulky kitchen helper stamps so hard on the stainless cart that it bongs like a steel drum in a calypso band. It's enough to silence the others. Then Bradley amps up the volume until even the kids in the back can hear. **"Do you see what I'm standing on here? It's a food cart, asshole. I make the food run. I make it twice a night. I know about everything and everybody they've got in there."**

Now that he has their attention Bradley goes on in a voice so big that behind the padded doors, even Sarge and his security chief, the doctor and the exhausted PA and their milling, distressed patients can make out every word.

"It's this tall, weird guy that nobody but me knows about, they keep him hidden in a back room. I could have told you last week, but you wouldn't listen." He is his own PA system, broadcasting, **"That's your Monkey Zero."**

Bogardus knows a good thing when he sees it. As a professional guidance counselor he's been trained to turn objections to his advantage and therefore as his cadre stands back and Bradley charges the door with the food cart, Dave raises the shout: "Send him out. Send him out. Send him out."

Soon they are all chanting, "Send him out."

By the time Fedders lets Bogardus go, he has united the factions in the hall.

They part to make way for the team with the battering ram. Dave's men shove Bradley aside and take his position, poised to break down the doors. Every man, woman and child in the clogged hallway is stamping and shouting, "Send him out!"

AS THE NOISE outside the Infirmary mounts to a terrifying level, creaky and cautious, anxious old Brother Benedictus emerges from the abbey's secret stairway by turning a stone. The wall in the little corridor where the private rooms are opens silently and Benny slips into the ell. One of the doors stands wide and light makes a slice in the shadows on the stone. His heart leaps up. *He's here!* He can hardly wait to tell him. *I know who you are!*

Alone in his single room, Theron sits on the bed. He doesn't seem to know there are people outside intent on breaking in and yanking him out like the shard of iron out of his unhealable wound. If he did know, would he care? The beautiful young man he felt so close to, the stranger, who has *changed* somehow, is silent and still.

He is looking into his hands, considering.

Benny has no idea what he is thinking.

No matter. Benny is here because he has something important to say. He has no idea where to start. With the only world he has ever known collapsing around him and no idea how to begin doing what he came here to do, he depends on the grace of ritual. He starts the way he always does. "Bless me Father, for I have sinned."

Theron turns. "I'm not your father."

In Benny's split-second of hesitation, everything changes. He draws himself up.

"No," he says and a lifetime of sadness pours out of him. "I am yours."

Where he was silent and reflective, sad because of the failure of so many of those efforts he is aware of making but can't name right now, *Cassandra,* Theron stands, transformed.

"You know who I am!" His face opens wide.

"Yes. Theron." He cannot quite bring himself to say it, but Theron knows. The old man cries, "Forgive me."

"Of course."

Staggered by what he sees, Benny thinks: *What a beautiful smile!* He says, "Come." They are both smiling now.

Father leads son *I am his son* out of the room and to the blind alley in the little ell where *I am his father* Benny turns the great stone one last time and the wall swings open. Together, they head down the secret stairway to the passage that leads back to the garden dome which is silent and empty now, although it won't be silent for long.

"SEND HIM OUT," Dave Bogardus shouts so bravely that when the time comes he hopes nobody will notice that he stands way, way back, far from the captive Monkey Zero. Not going to catch what that thing has! Not going near it.

The battering ram keeps cadence. "Send him out." HAZMAT hoods come off as Dave's people charge the door again and again, roaring, "Send him out."

"Send. Him. Out." At each word, Bradley bashes the stone archway with the steel cart, although that's not what he's really mad about.

"Send him out," Sheela shrieks and she could not tell you why she is so angry.

"Send him out."

"Send him out." Sylvie prays in her heart that this mystery person they are all yelling for will come out and it will turn out to be Steve. She is too overwrought to wonder what these people want with him or what they'll do to the man she loves; she's too disturbed and disrupted to think past this point to wonder how, if she had to, she could save him.

"Send him out." The mob shouts as one; it is tremendous.

"Send him out," everybody with a different reason, "Send him out," they cry in mounting rage and frustration, "Send him out," they shout, with no clear idea why they are so angry. The escalating chant is so loud and clear that there's no mistaking it. No matter what the individual kids and adults in the throng think they want, this is something everybody can get behind.

"Send him out," Chef Pete bellows, surprised to discover that although he says the exact words, which have become an incantation, he is thinking in pre-Columbian terms. Given the cadencing, the savage mass chant sounds more like SACRIFICE.

SACRIFICE.
Something to feed the hunger.

IN THE INFIRMARY, Sargent Whitemore clicks into combat mode. With Cassie standing by, with Mel Dratch flailing and a room full of people glowing with health but agitating in their skimpy johnny coats, he has only Gunnery Sergeant Tackett to help him fight off the enemy forces. Sarge left the Director's office packing his service revolver, nothing more. Bad move.

He can't use weapons against this mob anyway. Not given who they are. His staff. His children, that he built all this and did so much to protect and defend!

All chanting louder. "Send him out." "SEND HIM OUT." Louder.

If those were terrorists or trained militia in the hall, hostiles from any of the countries Sarge has served in, this would be simpler. There are oxygen tanks in here, big, dangerous suckers he could dink with and roll into the hall, triggered to blow the assault force all to hell. He's sure Cass could give him ingredients for smoke bombs, poison gas, whatever he needs, but the mindless mass howling at the Infirmary doors are his people, the kids he is pledged to protect and save, and the adults he hired to serve, teach and take care of them.

The obsessed mob, shouting. "Send him out."

BOOM. Something heavy hits the doors.

He knows what they want.

"Send him out."

It is his duty to defend everyone in here and everyone in the hall outside.

"Send him out."

Battering. BOOM.

They are the civilians.

"Send. Him. Out."

He is the Marine.

Inside the Infirmary and in the vaulted corridor, the people of the enclave are too caught up in the moment to hear anything but the urgent thumping and hypnotic chanting that overflows the hall, too distraught and obsessively focused to know that elsewhere— outside, on the top of the high mountain, something major is going on.

BOOM.

At every thump, Sarge's teeth crash shut. *End times. Here. Now.* It is nothing he expected, but here they are. *End times.* Regret rolls into him like an M1 Abrams tank, all sixty tons. *And I brought this on.*

While outside . . . The poor bastards don't know what they're doing. They're only civilians, blind and helpless, shouting, "Send him out!"

Civilians. He'd rather deal with armed hostiles. That, he knows how to do. But he brought these people into his Academy, and now. Now. This is not the place for grandstanding or fire and explosions. It's not the time for end runs. He has to protect them somehow, repel all boarders and keep them safe all at the same time, and he has to do it without hurting anyone.

BOOM.

The racket obscures the background noise an alert commander would be listening for, that he is too pressed and distracted to recognize.

His man Tackett stands by the shuddering wooden doors with his assault weapon raised, ready to take the head off the first ones through the opening and blow away as many others as he can before he falls. "Sir?"

"No." Sarge shakes his head. "Stand down, Gunny."

"Sir!"

"Gunny, stand down."

Good man, Tackett. By the numbers. SOP. "Yes sir."

Like Theron, LTCOL Sargent Whitemore, USMC(RETD), who distinguished himself in combat on three continents and the isthmus of Panama, is thinking.

When he does what he does, Sarge won't know that as he does so, there are helicopters landing on the plateau outside the garden dome, disgorging rescuers, medical teams, UN inspectors who will be astounded by conditions they find on Mount Clothos: the orderly design of the installation, the chaos inside.

In due course they will make their way into the dome and down the staircase into the hallway outside the monastery's former chapel, where they will follow the racket made by incessant pounding, the sound of shots being fired, the savage cries. When the rescue forces finally reach the demonstration outside the Infirmary, the mob will fall back, thunderstruck. Ashamed, as though confronted by angels, or people from some civilized future, who will look on the destruction and judge. Nobody inside the Academy will know how these strangers got to Clothos or what brought them here.

They may arrive too late.

Abrupt, visceral, irreversible decisions are being made.

Whether it's because Steve Joannides actually lived, and crawled down the mountain and made it back to the mainland and brought help, or because Killer Stade's mom picked up his frantic e-mail and immediately called the White House, or because, as Teddy is now ruler of a small country, Interpol is responding to Teddy's SOS or whether all three of these things happened at the same time and brought news of the situation in the Academy to the outside world, is not important.

They are here.

The people outside the Infirmary screaming for a sacrifice just don't know it yet.

When he does what he does, Sarge won't know whether the mob will buy it and assume he is in fact their Monkey Zero and torch him and call it done before they find out otherwise, but he has to try.

Even with help on the way, he'd have to act. There are things men want. *Cass.* Then there are things Marines have to do.

Before anything, Sargent Whitemore is a man of honor. Although it's nothing like he intended, his own failed hopes brought these people here. Now it's all gone to hell. He shored up so many systems against disorder and built so many walls to protect his people from chaos that the rebellion comes as a surprise. Outside, they are clamoring for a sacrifice. He let it come to this. He may not have *made* it happen, but he saw it coming and in spite of all his efforts, it happened anyway.

End times. We are in end times. He is up against it now. End times demand desperate measures. Nothing he can do, nothing else he can think of will stop this thing without people getting hurt.

Help may be on the way, but nobody here can guess whether it will come in time. Stripping, he throws on Dratch's lab coat. Like a plague victim or a leper trying to hide his disfigured face, he throws a towel over his head and unbolts the door.

Then he marches out, into the face of whatever is coming.

The Marines made him. Overwhelmed by the sound of their own voices, the crowd may or may not hear their Director sing out, although at some level they'll hear it all their lives. Everything that went before and everything that comes after will be scored by Sargent Whitemore rushing at them shouting:

"Semper fi."

FORTY-ONE

CODA

They are sitting together in the most beautiful room in the city, a paneled library rich with books in morocco bindings, oil sketches by famous painters and maquettes of work by sculptors only billionaires can afford, all gleaming in the golden light. The pale leather chairs that sit on the Persian rug are deep and seductive; the two friends slouched in the down cushions are so comfortable together that nobody needs to sit taller to make a point or get up and start pacing to command attention. Why should they, when in their own widely different worlds, they are both men of power?

They're perfectly happy sitting on their spines in chairs so deep that they never want to get up, delighted to be together after so long. In this room, in this company, they can say what they think and never have to explain. It's been years since the two last saw each other but they're such good friends that they pick up the conversation as though they'd never left off.

"A Brancusi. This is extremely cool!" The new bronze stands on a low table.

"It's no big, but I thought of your library as soon as I saw it."

"Perfect with the Van Gogh, and you know it." Although they both live well, it is Killer's library, at the top of his town house. Beautifully appointed, comfortable room, no ugly objects allowed, nothing ostentatious. Although his collections are amazing, he reserves a lighted shelf for gold-framed snapshots of the family. The room is the heart of Killer's house. It is the outward and physical manifestation of the best things inside his head. Although his work online made him a billionaire and he goes to work online every day, he spends his happiest times offline. Like this one, sitting down with his best friend in this or any other world.

"I'm glad," his friend says, "I knew it would be perfect for this room."

"Where did you find it?"

"Private owner in Rome. I was there that week last summer."

"Right. You were running the G-Nine summit."

Nice, self-deprecating grin. "Pretty much."

"That went well. Who knew your dumb little country would get so big?"

"A lot happens when you turn a kingdom into a republic. Who knew they'd decide to elect me?"

"Yeah, right. Spazzboy." Where as a kid he was a bullet-headed little monster, Killer has grown up to be something better. He turns now to look at his old friend: still handsome, but stronger than he was. Steady. There is color in his face now. He is no longer tensed and ashen, forever waiting for the next bad thing. It's OK to tell him, "God that was awful."

"Tell me about it!" Ted Regan, the former Prince Frederick of a minor principality and now premier of the growing republic, taps his brainpan, where the implant is embedded. "That thing you invented kicks ass."

Killer grins. "Lightning rod, to diffuse those rotten electrical storms."

"Useful at the UN." Teddy's bright smile flickers. He says reflectively, "I still miss the visions."

"I know."

"How's Michiko?"

"Great. She and the kids are in Yokohama this week, seeing ancestral types. And Syl?"

"Waiting for me at the Waldorf. It's sweet, but . . ." Ted swallows a sigh. "We love each other but she knows and I know . . ." He will only say this to Killer, and only in private. "She never got over Mr. Joannides."

"I'm glad I married somebody from the game."

"Man, Clothos was its own kind of game." Beneath the urbane surface the two friends will be kids all their lives, but they've matured. They are men of substance now. They flow with the times and their language has flowed. Killer doesn't use *fuck*. They don't call each other *dude*.

"Mountain Death Trap. Too bad I moved on from game design."

"Even though it made you a bundle. Clothos." Teddy says, "It was weird, you know? All that intense stuff coming down in such a short time."

"Like, minutes."

"Seconds. Then WHAM. We get airlifted out before we see what went down." Teddy grimaces. "Interpol."

"Unless it was CIA." Secure in the home he's made for himself and his family, Killer says, "And then global silence. Like, no trace of the whole business on the air and nothing on the Web, like the whole thing had been erased. And I scoured every database on the planet. It's like they threw a big fur blanket over the entire thing."

"And we don't know who *they* are."

"I looked for a long time, you know."

"We both did." Teddy sits up straighter.

The most powerful geek in the world tells him, "It wasn't just me. I had my best people on it for years."

Teddy's voice is soft. "All our resources, and we still don't know what happened back there."

"Like where Ms. Cassie went afterward." Killer's fingers move on his thighs as they have on thousands of keyboards. "Or what really happened to Sarge."

"He was nuts but he was kind of noble, you know?"

"He was."

"I liked him."

"We all did. He didn't know what he was doing, but he tried like hell."

Teddy can't bring this story to resolution but he supplies the coda. "He did try, and it was sad."

But Killer can't let it go. He has that kind of mind. "What was it all about? What was it really about?"

The two men are beyond conjecture. This leaves them silent for perhaps too long. The light in the room is changing. They both have things to do, appointments to keep but they can't quite leave. It's not that they're still looking for answers. They aren't. Gamers both, but in real life now, they would tell you that incomplete actions keep them here. Stories unfinished and unresolved.

After a time Teddy offers: "But that horrible fat girl!"

Killer laughs. "Sheela Abercrombie, Nobel laureate."

"Epidemiologist extraordinaire."

"No, that was me."

"Right. Killer Stade and his fabulous virophage. What do you suppose happened to Bogardus?"

"Maybe they killed him and ate him."

Teddy laughs. "Serve him right." He is getting to his feet. It's late; Sylvie and the kids will be waiting to go out to eat; in another minute he'll ask Killer to join them and Killer will accept, but he'll insist on giving them dinner at his club. It would be nice to give this story an ending, but the accomplished diplomat has only this to give. "Too bad she had to share the prize."

Killer lingers; like Teddy, he doesn't want to leave this moment just yet.

At last he says, "In a way it's kind of cool. I mean, Dratch booted her into med school and put her to work in his lab."

They are both on their feet now. It's time to go.

Acknowledgements

With special thanks to my friends the novelist Keith Brooke of the University of Essex, U.K., who pointed Killer and me to the bacteriophage; Stuart Compton and Brian Quinette of Idyllon, LLC, inveterate gamers, tireless coders and designers of the MMORPG *Idyllon*, who read for accuracy and helped me figure out how Killer's plan would work; Joseph Reed, my military advisor; and especially to my editor, Melissa Singer of Tom Doherty Associates, who saw the potential and made this project possible— and whose questions prompted the Coda.